I0595993

Songflight

THE DRAGON SINGER CHRONICLES | BOOK 1

MICHELLE M. BRUHN

SONGWEAVER
MEDIA

Cover by Kirk DouPonce, www.DogEaredDesign.com
Map by Soraya Corcoran, www.SorayaCorcoran.com
Edited by Katie Phillips, www.KatiePhillipsCreative.com

ISBN 978-1-7349925-0-2 (paperback)
ISBN 978-1-7349925-1-9 (e-book)

*For the voiceless
and those who would hear them.*

TABLE OF CONTENTS

ARRAN
F'renn's Mnt
Rorenth's Mnt
KADDIN
PARRIN
Serpent's Fangs
AZRON
L'RANG
Western Hill Country
Southlands
@SorayaCorcoran

Belin
Sea
Eastern Forests
Nissen River
Twi-Peak
Me'ran
Soren
Cherrin
N. Russig
E. Russig
Russig Lake
S. Russig
Fool's Landing
Tsamen & Paili's Mnt

PRONUNCIATIONS & DEFINITIONS

A'dem (ah-DEHM) — *the planet*

Alísa (ah-LEE-suh) — *slayer, wayfarer, daughter of Karn & Hanah*

Allara (ah-LA-ruh) — *slayer, the second known Dragon Singer*

Anam (AH-nahm) — *soul*

Anatoss (ANN-uh-toss) — *dragoness, flight-trainer in Bria's time*

Aree (ah-REE) — *dragoness, hunter, mate of Saynan*

Arran (eh-RAN) — *the continent on which this tale takes place*

Azron (AZ-ron) — *Alísa's home village*

Bodhrán (BOW-rahn) — *a wide, flat drum played by mallet or hand*

Branni (BRAH-nee) — *the Eldra of warriors and slayers*

Bria (BREE-uh) — *slayer, warrior, the first known Dragon Singer*

Céilí (KAY-lee) — *a dance for two or more partners where steps are called; also shorthand for a social gathering with music, dancing, and story-telling*

Chrí (chree) — *drek, name gives the impression of lavender*

Crakil (KRA-kul) — *dragon, beta commander in F'renn's clan*

D'lann (dih-LAHN) — *dragon, scout, mate of Koriana, father of Graydonn*

D'tala (dih-TAH-luh) — *the first Eldra of wind and spirit*

D'tohm (dih-TOHM) — *the Eldra of wind and spirit, new name of Tohmra*

Drek (drehk) — *small, dragon-shaped creature that lives in the forests; social; strong telepaths; plural form: dreki (DREH-kee)*

E'sall (eh-SAHL) — *the Eldra of those whose work concerns nature*

Elani (eh-LAH-nee) — *slayer, wayfarer, Alísa's aunt, wife of L'non, mother of Levan & Taer*

Eldra (EL-druh) — *an angelic being given stewardship over specific aspects of A'dem; plural form: Eldír (EL-deer)*

F'renn (fuh-REHN) — *dragon, alpha in the center of the Western Hill Country*

Faern (fayrn) — *dragon, scout, father of Komi*

Falier (fah-LEER) — *holder, percussionist, son of Parsen & Kat, brother of Selene*

Farren (FEHR-en) — *songweaver, wayfarer with Karn's clan*

Graydonn (GRAY-don) — *dragon, son of D'lann & Koriana*

Hanah (HAH-nuh) — *weaver, slayer by marriage, wife of Karn, mother of Alísa*

Harenn (HEHR-en) — *dragon, scout, son of Tsamen & Paili*

Iompróir Anam (YOHM-proh-ihr AH-nahm)—*soul-bearer*

Kallar (kuh-LAR)—*slayer, wayfarer, apprentice of Karn*

Karn (kahrn) — *slayer, wayfarer, chief, husband of Hanah, father of Alísa*

Katessara (ka-teh-SAR-uh) — *holder, wife of Parsen, mother of Selene & Falier*

Kerrik (KEHR-ihk) — *slayer, wayfarer, training master, deceased*

Komi (KOH-mee) — *dragoness, scout, daughter of Faern*

Koriana (kor-ee-ANN-uh) — *dragoness, scout, mother of Graydonn*

Korin (KOHR-in) — *dragon, warrior, mate of Rayna*

L'non (luh-NON) — *slayer, wayfarer, brother of Karn, husband of Elani, father of Levan &* *Taer*

Laen (layn) — *drek, name gives impression of rain dripping off leaves*

Levan (LEH-vehn) — *slayer, wayfarer, trainee, son of L'non & Elani, twin brother of Taer*

Me'ran (meh-RAN) — Falier's home village

Nahne (NAH-neh) — *the Eldra of those whose work concerns people*

Namor (NAY-mor) — *slayer, retired, elder of Me'ran, husband of Tenza*

Nissen (NEE-sihn) — *the river dividing the Hill Country from the Forests*

P'laenn (puh-LAY-ehn) — *dragoness, warrior in Bria's time*

Paili (PAY-lee) — *dragoness, alpha in the Prilunes, mate of Tsamen*

Parsen (PAR-sehn) — *holder, husband of Kat, father of Selene & Falier*

Prilunes (PRIH-loons) — *mountains dividing Arran's North and Southlands*

Q'rill (kuh-RIHL) — *dragon, nurse, son of Rorenth & Tora*

Rayna (RAY-nuh) — *dragoness, warrior, mate of Korin*

Rorenth (ROHR-enth) — *dragon, alpha west of the Nissen river*

Sareth (SEHR-eth) — *dragon, scout in Rorenth's clan*

Saynan (SAY-nen) — *ice dragon, combat trainer, mate of Aree*

Selene (suh-LEEN) — *holder, flautist, daughter of Parsen & Kat, sister of Falier*

Sesína (suh-SEE-nuh) — *dragoness, human-illuminated*

Soren (SOHR-ehn) — *a village just south of Me'ran*

Taer (tayr) — *slayer, wayfarer, trainee, son of L'non & Elani, twin brother of Levan*

Taz — *slayer, wayfarer, from Me'ran, best friend of Falier & Selene*

Tenza (TEN-zuh) — *slayer, retired, elder of Me'ran, wife of Namor*

Tora (TOHR-uh) — *dragoness, warrior, mother of Q'rill*

Toronn (TOHR-ahn) — *slayer, chief, village-bound to Azron*

Trísse (trees) — *slayer, wayfarer, best friend of Alísa*

Tsamen (TSAH-men) — *dragon, alpha in the Prilunes, mate of Paili*

Twi-Peak (TWIE-peek) — *double-peaked mountain just north of Me'ran*

Yarlan (YAR-lun) — *slayer, village-bound to Me'ran*

PROLOGUE

A rattling inhalation was all the warning Karn received before fire rained from the skies. He raised his bronze shield with a warning to his men, his shout swiftly drowned out by the rushing of flames. His arm ached as he pressed against the blaze. Sweat poured from his body, sticking ash and dirt to his tanned features and plastering his fiery red warrior's braids to his neck.

His men were tired. *He* was tired. After nearly six hours hiking and climbing this mountain, they now faced hours of battle ahead. But one glance into any of his warriors' eyes would confirm their resolve. They fought for their families and for the physical and spiritual good of the country of Arran. They would return victorious, or not at all.

Against the evil of the dragons, there was no other option.

As soon as the flames ceased, Karn lowered his shield and watched his attacker fly high into the sky. He leaned on the shaft of his spear as he took quick stock of his slayers—thirty-one able men hiking the rocky incline, each cloaked in armor of dragon scales and bronze. Each wore war-paint in the color and symbol of his station, though status meant nothing in the heat of battle. All that mattered was who bore the responsibility of bringing them home, and the red across Karn's own brow declared it his.

Five scaly beasts flew over them, each taller than a man at its withers— two of them twice that. Their flames could incinerate a man in seconds; a slap of a tail could break him; each tooth, talon, and spine could tear him to pieces; yet his slayers pressed forward.

Karn locked his eyes on the largest of the beasts, its scales the dull green of cloud-shaded hills. He reached out with his mind and prodded against the dragon's psychic defenses.

Hard as the mountain. This one would have to be killed by spear or sword.

At the rush of flight behind him, Karn raised his shield and ducked low. The flames lasted only a moment, yet his heart pounded into his throat. An overwhelming terror sank deep into his stomach and sent his thoughts into a jumble.

That was too close!

This mission would be his last.

He would never see his wife and daughter again.

The dragons would destroy the village they were protecting.

Burn his wayfarers' tents to the ground!

Take——

Karn shook his head hard, gritting his teeth against the fear forced upon him. He focused on rebuilding his telepathic shield. He had let it down while prodding the green dragon, and this second dragon had taken advantage of it, sending a cloud of terror over him. The fear lifted as his psychic energies sealed over his mind.

This shield was the only reason he and his men had a fighting chance on this dragon-infested mountain. Without it, the beasts would either drive him mad with forced emotions or take his mind in full possession. Normals couldn't do this job, nor could the women left behind at camp. Though slayer women, too, held a psychic gift, they were merely empaths. They could sense and project emotions, but were unable to focus their powers into blasts or shields. Those without such protection could only last so long in a battle against dragons.

Karn glared after his empathic attacker as he rose back to his feet, a new hatred coursing through his veins. The dragon would pay for this violation of his mind. It would suffer for all the times its kind had infiltrated his daughter's mind. She couldn't stop it, couldn't protect herself, couldn't help but feel the emotions of even the weakest of dragons. He would snuff out every dragon in the world to make sure their evil couldn't affect her anymore.

His rage became a psychic spear—emotion focused to a point, then launched from his mind to the dragon's. The beast screamed as Karn's mind tore past its defenses, and its flight faltered, dipping closer to his men. The slayers had been waiting for such an opening, and three of them launched their spears into the air, one finding a lethal hold in the dragon's soft underbelly.

The creature's brethren roared in outrage and dove at Karn's men. Another spear found its mark in a dragon's heart. Warriors dove to escape flames. Karn kept moving, his boots gripping the dirt and gravel. He changed his grip on the spear in his right hand as a dragon dove for him, thrusting up as the creature flew overhead and drawing a pained roar from its throat. Not a fatal wound, but it would slow the monster down.

Six dragons flew above them now, new beasts replacing the slain. They were drawing the monsters from their caves. If Toronn's information was correct, this dragon clan had twenty-some adults. His slayers would have to take them down quickly before the dragons overwhelmed them.

"Group up!"

His men followed the command, gathering together in predetermined groups of three and four. A seventeen-year-old slayer on only his third battlefield ran to Karn, carrying a long, broad shield. Of Karn's group of three, this young man was the weakest psychic and so would defend his elders as they attempted to choke dragons out of the sky.

Karn opened his mind once more and prodded another dragon, a black one. Its defense was weaker than the last, giving way under Karn's telepathy. Karn pointed out the dragon to L'non—his brother and third partner—and they attacked, focusing their powers into bolts of energy that speared through the dragon's psychic shield.

The creature roared in pain as the slayers' combined energies spread over its mind like oil. They squeezed the dragon's mind, cutting it off from its body and making it impossible for the dragon to control itself. It fell, its mind squirming against their hold as it neared the mountainside.

"Down!"

Karn and L'non dropped low at the call of their young defender, making it under the shield just as flames splashed over it, spewed from the maw of another dragon.

Karn cursed as the fire and shield cut off his sightline to the black dragon, ending his psychic hold. As the flames ended, a black shape climbed back into the sky, confirming their target had regained control before crashing to the rocks.

"Seems we'll have to try again," L'non said, the epitome of calm as always. Karn tried hard not to check him over for wounds or study whether the red tint in his brown hair was blood or merely the sun catching in it. Though Karn was the older of them, L'non was a more than capable warrior.

A scream of agony came from down the mountain, sending a bolt of lightning to Karn's heart. The cry lasted only a moment—one of his slayers claimed by dragon-fire.

Another cry drew Karn's eyes just in time to see one of his men hit the ground hard, his shield slapped by a red dragon's tail. The dragon trumpeted its victory. Karn gritted his teeth and pointed to it.

"Again, L'non!"

Together, he and his brother wrestled with the dragon's mind until they brought it crashing to the ground. But now there were eight dragons in the sky, all of them staying far out of reach of their spears except to dive-bomb the men. There were too many to take psychically, and they just kept coming.

A shout of rage echoed from further up the mountain, ripping from the mouth of Karn's apprentice, Kallar. His blue eyes shone in bright contrast to his black hair, and as soon as those eyes locked with Karn's, a firm prodding pressed against Karn's mental shield.

Kallar had always been more at-ease than other slayers when it came to using telepathy to communicate. The rest of humankind, slayer and normal alike, balked at such an invasion of privacy; but Kallar knew that, and he wouldn't address his chief in this way unless it was urgent. Karn relaxed his shield.

"We need to take the cave, Karn. Cover us."

Kallar pulled away before Karn could respond, shouted something to the men nearby, and bolted up the mountain. Six slayers followed in his wake, holding their shields over their heads and charging after him without hesitation.

It was foolishly brave—the dragons would see their direction and know their intent. But if they didn't stop the flow of dragons into the sky, they might not make it home.

A sapphire dragon dove at Kallar's troop, its eyes brightening as the fire within it brewed. Karn speared it telepathically and L'non followed suit, choking its mind just in time to stop the flames. The fall was too short for the dragon to die on impact, but another group of his men were nearby. They would end the brute.

"Forward!" Karn barked as he ran. The closer they got to Kallar, the better they would be able to defend him and his men.

"Left!"

Karn raised his shield and ducked as intense heat surrounded him. The fire lasted only a moment before it was cut off by a screech of pain and an earth-rattling thud. Karn stood to see the dull-green dragon on its side, L'non's spear protruding from its underbelly.

The dragon shook its head hard and stood with a moaning growl. Not a fatal wound. Karn raised his own spear and ran at the beast. The dragon coughed smoke, apparently out of firepower, then struck with teeth.

Karn dodged, then hit the dragon in the side of the head with his shield. The dragon curled its neck back like a serpent and struck again. Karn dove to the ground and pushed his spear up, aiming for the dragon's eye and just missing it.

A roar of pain ripped from the creature's throat and it stumbled. At its belly were Karn's partners, the young man's sword in the dragon's soft flesh. L'non jerked his spear out of the dragon and jammed it into the beast's heart, silencing it forever.

Beyond them, a cheer rose from the slayers. Karn pushed off the ground and rounded the dead dragon to see Kallar and his men at the cave entrance. The men stood side-by-side, their shields locked against each other like interlocking scales, and their heads low, ducking under a flash of fire. As soon as the flames ended, Kallar charged with a battle cry, his men echoing him as they followed.

Pride swelled in Karn's heart. Cave-storming was the most dangerous part of dragon-slaying, a job typically reserved for the more experienced slayers—those used to the danger, who could keep a cool head under pressure.

Kallar was anything but cool-headed, but what he lacked in calm he made up for in passion. He had soaked up Karn's teachings ever since his first day of apprenticeship, learning all he could about a dragon's strengths and weaknesses, studying battle-tactics, practicing telepathic shields and attacks. Even when Kallar's first cave-storming ended in disaster, leaving him with a burn scar that covered his left arm, he hadn't slowed in his training.

He would make a fine chief one day, a righter of wrongs and protector of Karn's daughter. If anyone could save her from the evil of the dragons, it was him.

A pained trumpet brought Karn out of his thoughts and back to the battle. There were only five dragons left in the sky, and so far no more had made it past Kallar and his men. Karn pointed to the dragon highest in the sky and combined his attack with L'non, choking it down to its death against the mountainside.

Victory was theirs.

1

DEADLY CEREMONY

Alísa lifted her eyes toward the mournful trumpeting. It settled in her heart like mountain stone, weighing down each step around the ceremony circle with its harsh reality. She forced a pleasant smile to her face, as she had for every ceremony since she was thirteen and her problem first manifested.

Tonight, she would suffer alongside the evil her clan fought, and she would do so in silence.

She ran her fingers over the ends of her frizzy mahogany curls, her fingers stopping at the sapphire dragon-scale necklace from her father. She fingered the scale's tiny ridges, her heart trembling. A wistful hope cast her eyes out over the verdant grasses. Just beyond that hill lay camp—empty, quiet, and devoid of anyone's emotions except her own. If only she could hide there in her family's tent for the evening. Surely after seventeen years she could miss one ceremony.

But no—tonight would honor her clan of wayfaring slayers, especially her father. His former chief and trainers dwelt in this village, and now that Karn was a chief in his own right, his clan and family must prove him worthy of his position.

Honor and duty came before comfort. The pleasant smile stayed.

Alísa glanced out over the crowd gathered in the circle. Most were slayers, all either of her father's clan or bound to protect this single village of Azron. Many of the wayfarers wore their dragon-scale armor, freshly cleaned of the blood and grime of battle. They gleamed in the sunlight in jewel-tones dulled with use. Some of the village men wore similar garb, but most wore the gold-and-green colors of Azron on kilts and sashes over their clean white shirts.

It would be hard for Kallar to hold back his derision tonight. *'No true dragon-slayer would own something so clean,'* or some nonsense like that.

The women, wayfaring and village-bound alike, wore their best dresses, some with tight corsets over their tops, others allowing the light fabric to flow more freely in the wind. Alísa herself had chosen a deep green dress with a gold-and-white sash over her sword-belt. She always chose the dress for ceremonies. The shade matched the astral color of peace and calm—hopefully it would stir some of the same feelings inside of her.

Only a few normals walked among the slayers today. The village chief made his rounds, clasping the arms of each of the wayfaring warriors, his wizened face creased with laugh lines. Songweaver Farren was somewhere in the throng, or perhaps was taking a moment of quiet before singing in honor of Garrett, a slayer who had fallen this last battle. Three or four holders walked among them, carrying trays of food and jugs of mead with their exaggerated smiles.

Holders were the darlings of every village, held in high esteem and honor for their generosity and hospitality. They manned the Hold, a community hall as well as a place for travelers to spend a night or two before heading on their way.

Holders also tended to be chatty and nosy, drawing people into long conversations. Alísa did her best to avoid them.

Everyone, slayer and normal alike, laughed and chatted like they didn't have a care in the world. For them, it was true. The dragon clan festering in the nearby mountain was ended at the wayfarers' hands—all but two hatchlings saved for tonight's festivities—and now Azron could rest easy. Tomorrow the village-bound could still rest easy, but the wayfarers would be on their way to the next mountain, always moving, never stopping until death took them or the war ended.

Another cry from the hatchlings brought her back to the present, and she shivered under the weight of her secrets. Each ceremony held the potential for their discovery, but to stay away would also raise questions. She had become quite good at hiding her shame these last few years; good enough that her parents didn't know just how bad it had become. As long as she was able, she would keep that secret. Her father had enough to worry about without adding her mounting problems to the list. She could handle it.

Would handle it.

Alísa loosened the reins on her empathy, allowing her powers to flow out from her and catch some of the positive emotions wafting from the clan. She rejected excitement's pounding and joy's tickling flight for the steady flow of relief. That emotion was one she could match to her own, one that could overcome the dread settling in her heart. Her father had returned safely, the clan was whole again, and this beautiful village where she had grown up was at peace.

This was reality, the deepest truth she had to cling to in the face of the coming onslaught. But it would only last for so long.

"Alísa?"

She twisted to meet a silvery-blue gaze that nearly matched her own. Her mother Hanah's twisting laurel of auburn braids caught the evening sunlight, its gentle waves settling over the shoulders of a finely-embroidered blue dress. A petite woman, only an inch taller than Alísa, but one others noticed when she stood before a crowd. She had an air of authority about her that showed through even in her softest moments—a necessary quality for the lady of a wayfaring clan.

Will I ever have even that?

"You look lost, love," she said, worry creasing her brow. "Will you be all right tonight?"

Alísa nodded once as she found an acceptable lie. "I was j—just thinking about you and P-P-P-Papá—"

She fought not to wince at her stammer. *'Confidence covers weakness,'* her father had told her countless times. But confidence and the mask she now wore were two completely different things. She knew what she was—the peoples' reactions told her every day. The eyes of pity, the impatient toe-tapping, the interruptions and guessing of the words she couldn't spit out. She was an annoyance in conversation and a hindrance on the battlefield.

Her mother gave a prodding nod, and Alísa breathed low and deep, allowing her throat muscles to loosen.

"—about how well you lead the c-c-clan. That's all."

Hanah gave a knowing half-smile. "Don't worry. Maker-willing, it won't be your turn for a long time, and you won't be alone."

Alísa followed Hanah's eyes to the chief's table, where Kallar and the village-bound slayers' chief, Toronn, spoke together. As always, Kallar stood tall, confident in his position as Karn's apprentice and the future chief of the wayfaring clan.

His raven-black hair flowed free of his warrior's braids, reaching to his shoulder on one side and shaved within an inch of his scalp on the other. His weathered blue scale armor accentuated steely blue eyes that gave her chills when he stared at her—not of fear or desire, but uncertainty. He unsettled her, trying to woo her with charm one moment, then turning into something cold and distant the next.

He and Alísa weren't betrothed, but the official declaration wasn't needed. Marriage was expected of them, and though she didn't love Kallar, she had mostly come to grips with that reality. He could command armies, slay dragons, and make the world a safer place. She couldn't even say her father's name without stammering or sit through a dragon-killing without choking back sobs. Many warriors had given their lives in this war—surely she could give her love-life.

Her mother took her hand and led her to the table next to Toronn's. They slid into their seats of honor, and Alísa inhaled the warm, savory smells of the roasted beef and sliced potatoes. Her stomach ached with both hunger and anxiety, twisting her up inside.

Soon. Soon they would eat, the younger teens would train against the hatchlings, and it would be over.

A burst of laughter came from her right, and she glanced at Chief Toronn and Kallar. The great chief's auburn beard had gained some gray in the two years since Alísa last saw him, but he seemed as sharp and strong as ever.

Toronn caught Alísa staring at him, and she looked away quickly. His cold black eyes made her feel weak and small—a mere sparrow in the presence of a war-hawk. She couldn't remember a time he had ever smiled at her. She was a disappointment to him—the only child of his apprentice, a stammerer, and a slayer who balked at killing hatchlings.

She fingered her necklace. *At least he doesn't know why I hate it. If he did, I could be ostracized, or worse.* Toronn was known and respected enough in the area to have that kind of influence, despite her position as a chief's daughter.

A hand found her shoulder, and she twisted to see her father's soft brown eyes smiling down at her. His copper curls were a couple shades brighter than hers, the top pulled back and bound away from his face. His hair and beard clashed beautifully with the dulled rubies of his dragon-scale armor, his deep brown fur-lined cloak acting as a barrier between the two warring colors.

Her heart swelled. Shame never clouded her father's eyes when he looked at her. In the light of his love, what did it matter what Toronn thought?

He bent low and whispered. "I know you don't like being here. Thank you for facing it."

He kissed her forehead and his beard tickled her nose.

"I love you, my Lísa."

She smiled back at him, trying to convey the strength she wanted so desperately to have. Everything she faced tonight would be for him, just as he faced the monsters for her. It was the least she could do.

Karn took his place next to Toronn, and Kallar slid into his seat beside Alísa. He took her hand and lifted it to the tabletop, holding it there as if to claim her in the eyes of all. He leaned in and whispered.

"Anyone give you trouble while I was away?"

She shook her head without meeting his gaze. He didn't mean trouble like looking down their nose at her or talking behind her back. He meant the young men of the village—did anyone make moves on her? He should know by now that wasn't going to happen.

Songweaver Farren, a tall, older man with deep inner strength, strode into the center of the ceremony circle. He had left Azron alongside Alísa's family nearly nine years ago. He was always kind, soft-spoken, and generous with his time, especially with young people who loved music, and his songweaving had inspired her own.

Farren raised his arms above his graying head, and Alísa stood with everyone else, village-bound and wayfarer alike. He lifted his baritone voice in prayer to the Maker—an honoring of the fallen and comfort to the living:

Why must the good die before their time,
And flames devour their prey?
When will our mourning be made right,
And smoke break for the day?

But in this world of suffering
The Maker holds us all.
His blessings follow those who stand,
Though some to home he calls.

Alísa joined quietly, hiding her voice under the others' as the people repeated the last lines.

His blessings follow those who stand,
Though some to home he calls.

All fell silent in a final honoring of those killed by the dragons, and she noted that Kallar had once again stayed silent. He had never forgiven the Maker for the loss of his mother at the flames of the dragons. He had only been a boy, nine or ten, but he carried the scars as he did the one covering his left arm—a mixture of pride and hatred.

Still, none of that should keep him from blessing Garrett's sacrifice.

She sighed softly. How many more of these songs would she have to hear in her lifetime? While the *anam*—the soul—lived on forever in the Maker's halls, why should his people be killed by the soulless? Why did the Maker allow dragons to live on when they obeyed the bidding of the Nameless, those Eldír who had turned away from him and now sought to destroy his humans?

His *iompróir anam*. His soul-bearers.

Chief Toronn broke the silence with his deep, booming voice. "Now we must honor these brave men by living the lives they died to grant us. Please, be seated, enjoy your food, and live!"

Kallar released her hand, and Alísa sat slowly, staring at the food in front of her. She had to eat something, and it would be easier now, before the dragon-training began. She chewed a bite of the savory beef slowly, praying she wouldn't lose it later.

"Karn, my friend." Toronn leaned over to her father, a wineskin in hand. "Pour out your water and try some of this—the finest mead this side of the Prilunes!"

Her father shook his head. "One never knows when a dragon attack will come. Best to be unhindered, though I thank you for your offer."

Toronn looked to Hanah. "I see you've failed to loosen him up, dear lady. Do try harder."

Hanah looped her arm through her husband's with a smile. "I wouldn't change him for anything."

Toronn huffed, shaking his head. "*Couldn't* change him is more likely." He looked to Kallar next. "I don't suppose he's gotten to you too?"

Kallar stole a glance at Alísa. "I'm afraid it makes my lady uncomfortable—but thank you."

Alísa looked down as Toronn raised an eyebrow at her, her cheeks warming under his scrutiny. Even when Kallar attempted to be considerate, he ended up making things worse.

Shadows against the setting sun drew Alísa's eyes from her half-finished supper. Seven silhouettes approached the circle—a man and four boys striding purposefully, dragging two hatchlings in their midst. Conversation faded to silence as the trainees approached. The boys, each between twelve and sixteen years, worked together to hold the hatchlings in a light mind-choke, keeping them weak, but still allowing movement.

Alísa's heart clenched. If only one of the boys would draw their sword now and end the hatchlings' suffering quickly. End *her* suffering before it began.

A young child called out one of the trainee's names in recognition, breaking the boy's concentration. The larger of the two dragons jolted up and trumpeted, pulling against the ropes around its neck. Alísa winced as its emotions broke through the trainees' psychic hold.

Fear and anger. A small taste of what was to come.

The trainer at the back of the group placed a hand to his temple and sealed the gap in the mind-choke. The hatchling slumped again as it lost control, and the young slayers forced it to march into the circle once more.

Alísa closed her eyes and breathed, their emotions contained once more by the mind-choke. *That was fine. I can do this.*

Her heart and stomach ignored her self-talk. The next wave would be worse.

She opened her eyes again, staring at the sagging creatures as they entered the circle. Though evil, they were fascinating—caught somewhere between animal and *iompróir anam*. The race had given up their souls to the Nameless centuries ago in exchange for greater psychic power. The few slayers she knew who had heard a dragon's voice told of demonic jumbles of words and images that threatened to steal a person's sanity.

Would a young dragon's be the same? What might it say?

She shook her head hard. *No. Don't go there. It's thoughts like this that add to your empathy.*

The dragons' gem-like scales shimmered in the sunlight, one like the sapphire ripples of a lake, the other like gleaming bronze shields. The only spots their natural armor didn't cover were their muzzles and underbellies, which displayed tough skin a shade lighter than their scales.

They were beautiful creatures in their own way, though Alísa could never admit that thought to her clansmen.

She shuddered at the razor-sharp talons curving on the end of each toe, the pointed spines protruding along their necks and backs, the horns growing just above their ears, the sharp teeth peeking out from their lips.

Beautiful, but fearsome.

In sharp contrast to the armor, the wings were large, graceful, and smooth but for the slashes that kept the hatchlings from escaping.

What I wouldn't give to have the freedom of flight, to become the wind and leave fear and doubt anchored to the ground.

The larger of the two, a blue hatchling about three-and-a-half feet at the withers, was built lean and strong like one of the clan's horses. The bronze hatchling was stockier than the blue—it would have grown to be a muscular brute, perhaps ten or eleven feet at the withers.

Both were far too young to breathe fire or take someone's mind.

Far too young to die like this.

Every muscle in Alísa's body tensed as the boys and hatchlings faced each other in the center of the circle. Kallar leaned forward at her elbow, his eyes fixed on the spectacle. He enjoyed the sport of it all, something she would never understand.

The young slayers drew their swords, while their enemies could only slouch low to the ground. In a moment, all of the boys would end the mind-choke and allow the dragons to move freely. The trainer would only intervene if the hatchlings threatened the onlookers.

Once the dragons' minds were freed, the suffering would begin.

FEAR!

Sweat covered Alísa's palms, and her heartbeat sped as terror gripped her, fear overtaking all other emotions. It was worse than the last ceremony; it had been a year since she had to fight emotions from two dragons. She would have to work much harder now to keep people from noticing.

She focused on the grooves in the stone table, grounding herself. *This isn't really happening. You're fine. This is all in your head. Keep it together.*

RAGE!

She clenched her teeth and fisted her skirt in clammy palms, fighting to suppress the fear and rage hitting her in alternating waves. Her mother placed a hand over hers and squeezed, trying to convey some comfort, but it couldn't help her fight the barrage.

She grunted as she pressed her empathy against the feelings, trying to crowd them out with her own.

It's been a while since I've felt rage at a hatchling-slaughter!

She shook her head. *No. Ceremony. Don't give in to the anger.*

The blue hatchling flared its wings at the boys and hissed, shuffling in front of the smaller bronze hatchling. Protecting it.

Nobility in the face of death.

Honor. In an animal.

The blue's stare lifted from the trainees until its gaze met Alísa's. Its deep brown eyes communicated an emotion nearly drowned by the flood of fear and rage—sorrow.

Tears welled behind Alísa's eyes. There was nothing she could do.

The blue broke eye-contact, fixated back on the boys, and charged, teeth bared and tail swinging. The oldest of the trainees raised his sword to strike.

PAIN!

Alísa's stomach churned as the sword glanced off scales and cut deep into a wing. She bit the inside of her lips and shut her eyes tightly, fighting back a whimper.

Keep it together. Make Papá proud. He doesn't have to know you feel their pain now too. No one can know.

Each cry barraged her with more pain and rage and fear. She hid her moans under the people's cheers. Why didn't anyone else feel it?

Because no one else is broken like I am. Defective. Weak.

A draconic cry crashed through her like it might crush her very soul. She whimpered, swallowing a scream. Two hatchlings were too much.

This isn't your pain. This isn't your pain! Eldra Branni, help me!

But no help came from the Eldra, no extra measure of strength, no passing of the pain. Alísa slapped a hand to her mouth just before a cry broke through her defenses—a trainee had just sliced through one of the hatchling's limbs.

She couldn't take it, not from two of them. She had to get away before she disgraced herself and her father.

Alísa stood on wobbly legs and staggered from the table. Eyes followed her retreat and shame mixed with her churning emotions. They couldn't know the torment she felt—they would probably think she fled because she couldn't stomach the violence. Either way, she had shown her weakness to her former village. To Toronn.

A hand took hers. "Sweetheart?"

Tears welled, and Alísa gritted her teeth against the cry threatening to breach her lips. She leaned into her mother's strength, grateful that the person taking her hand wasn't another slayer. Skin-contact with another psychic would transfer a part of the feelings. Though her mind begged for relief, she would never wish this pain on anyone.

They walked together to the Hold, slipping behind its walls. Alísa leaned back against the cool stone surface. Emotion still wafted to her like mists, unfazed by the physical barrier, but the distance dulled the feelings enough to keep her from screaming.

But the pain still throbbed in her skull, and the shrieking hatchlings battered her heart.

"What's going on, Alísa? It's never been this bad before—talk to me."

Alísa shook her head, pressing her lips together. She slid down the wall until she reached the ground, breathing deeply and counting—in for three, out for five—trying to focus on something other than the pain.

Hanah sat next to her, wrapping an arm over her shoulders and pulling her close. "It's okay. It'll be over soon."

Alísa's blood boiled. "It's *not* okay—I've brought Papá shame!" She winced at the tone her words took, influenced by the rage of the hatchlings.

"No, he's not ashamed of you. He's worried—he has been since this all started. He would have come too, but I told him to stay."

A death cry came from the circle, and Alísa cried out in tandem. She ground her teeth against the final spear to the heart before the feelings dimmed. One of the dragons' emotions could no longer affect her.

One to go. It should make the rest easier.

Another slice proved her wrong, the new pain still white-hot inside her skull. She leaned into her mother's shoulder, pressing for whatever tiny piece of comfort she could find. A final draconic scream pierced her heart, and she cried out as the death-pangs took her.

Her world faded to black.

2

SHAME

Alísa fixed her eyes on the ground and tried to bring the dirt and rocks into focus. Remnants of the hatchlings' terror and pain held her fast.

They're dead. They're dead, and a piece of me with them. How many more before I'm just an empty shell?

Her mother spoke to her, but the words were indiscernible, hiding behind the ringing in her ears and the pounding of her heart.

Is this what a mind-choke feels like? No control, no focus, no life?

Her mother wrapped a second arm around her. Alísa leaned into it as she tried to remember how to breathe normally, sucking air through open lips.

Hanah pulled back and placed a hand under Alísa's chin, lifting until their eyes met. Silvery-blue eyes of love grounded her.

I'm not dead. I didn't die with the hatchlings. I'm safe.

I'm safe.

Hanah whispered to her tenderly. "It wasn't just their emotions this time, was it? You were in pain."

Alísa stared at the ground. There was no way her mother would keep that information from her father. The secret was out.

"Do you want me to take you home?"

Alísa shook her head and whispered, a technique that eliminated her stammer. "Give me a minute."

She breathed shakily as Hanah tightened her embrace. She flexed her toes inside her boots, then wiggled her fingers, working through her whole body to see if she could control it. Once she could breathe without trembling,

Alísa pulled away and met her mother's eyes.

It was time to be strong again. *Branni, help me.*

"I'm ready."

Hanah searched her eyes a moment, then stood, offering her hand. Alísa took it and rose, shakily at first, but strengthening as they made their way back to the table. Toronn stood in the center of the circle, acknowledging the bravery of Karn and his warriors, but many eyes turned to her on their approach.

She straightened under their scrutiny. The people of Azron had known her to be squeamish at the killings since she was young—they couldn't guess the truth. Her father had tried to comfort her before by telling her there had been other women who felt dragons like this, but Alísa had never heard of such women from anyone but him. Azron couldn't know.

Karn turned and caught her eyes, his own filled with concern rather than judgement. Relief and embarrassment flooded her simultaneously, and she gave him a firm nod, trying to convey a confidence she didn't have.

She slipped into her seat, avoiding Kallar's questioning eyes. Now wasn't the time. She tensed and relaxed every muscle in her body one after the other, starting at her toes and working up to her neck.

This is reality. My own body. My control over it.

Movement pulled Alísa's attention as Songweaver Farren switched places with Toronn. The chief's eyes settled on her as he approached, suspicion flowing from them.

'Confidence covers weakness,' her father would say. 'Lift your eyes.'

She straightened and met the chief's gaze. She could only hold there for a second, but it was enough for her. If her father didn't look on her in shame, even in this moment, Toronn had no right.

Now if only her racing heart would believe that were true.

A respectful silence came over the circle as Farren raised his lute to his chest. This was the only part of ceremonies Alísa could enjoy—the songweaver's tale. Something new to focus on—music to help heal her torment.

She closed her eyes as Farren strummed the tale's introduction. The notes flew up and down the scale in her mind until the words painted pictures of a place far from her sorrows.

    O'er a hundred years ago, a slayer loved a maid.
    Garin vowed to win her heart, their love ne'er to fade.
    Bria's heart was fierce and strong—none would ever tame her.
    Sword and shield firm in hand, in her own right a slayer.

    But dragons are a crafty beast and hearts make easy prey.
    So, in the midst of battle fierce, they stole Bria away.
    Garin's strength was nearly gone, but hope still filled his eyes.
    And bolstered by courageous men, he sounded forth his cry:

    By scaled wing, by tooth and claw
    The dragons stole my maid away.
    But they won't have her soul tonight;
    I'll give my life to save her.

    To the mountain, toward the caves, up rocky crag and slope.
    Dragons charged them one by one, but none could end their hope.
    Fire blasts from beastly jaws met with battle cries,
    And as the day drew to an end, their song still pierced the night:

    By scaled wing, by tooth and claw
    The dragons stole our maid away.
    But they won't have her soul tonight;
    We'll give our lives to save her.

    From the cave the maiden cried, and Garin ran to meet her.
    Bria begged him for the life of the monstrous creature.
    Garin saw right through the guise—the dragon gained her mind.
    Our hero knew to save her soul the dragon had to die!

By scaled wing, by tooth and claw
The dragons stole my maid away.
But they won't have her soul tonight;
I'll give my life to save her.

I'll give my life to save her.
I'll give up all to save her!

Sword and shield to claw and scale, and slayer mind to beast,
Outside the cave, the slayers fought that Bria be released.
And Garin, strong of heart and mind, he tore the dragon out.
Monster dead and Bria free, he lifted up his shout:

By scaled wing, by tooth and claw
The dragons stole my maid away.
But they won't have her soul tonight;
I'll give up all to save her!

The final notes rang out into the evening air, and after a moment of reverent silence the audience applauded the songweaver.

Darkness now covered the ceremony circle, and a holder hurried to light the bonfire. With the end of the tale came a time of conversation and drinks that would eventually turn to dancing and go late into the night.

The rest of her table stood to mingle, but Alísa stayed to merely watch. After pushing through an overload of dragon emotions, wading into a pounding sea of excitement and dancing was the last thing she wanted to do. Only her mother gave her a questioning glance.

"I'm fine, Mamá," Alísa said, smiling through the remnants of pain.

A new female voice came from behind. "I've got her, Lady Hanah."

Alísa twisted to smile at Trísse, her close friend and only confidante in her secret of the dragons' pain. She stood tall and graceful in her deep blue dress overlaid with a sword-maiden's leather vest. Her glossy black braid and nearly-black eyes shone in the firelight.

Hanah gave Trísse a grateful smile, then followed after Karn. It was their last night in Azron and her mother had friends and family to attend to.

Technically, Alísa did too, but she had apparently scared her mother so badly that she didn't even try to get Alísa to come.

Trísse sat backward on the bench, her sword slipping under the table while she leaned back against it. She arched an eyebrow and said nothing, leaving Alísa to speak first. Alísa contemplated not speaking at all, but the intensity of Trísse's gaze brought the words out.

"How bad was it?"

"Bad. Really bad."

Alísa cringed. "B—Bad like, 'Oh that p-p-poor girl, unable t-to stomach the violence'? Or bad like they could f—f—f—f—"

"Figure it out?" Trísse finished, unafraid to step on Alísa's toes. She was perhaps the only one who could do it without making Alísa want to slap her.

Trísse sighed. "I don't know. Not all of them have the brainpower for it, and some of the others probably don't care enough to think it through. But if your parents and Kallar and your uncle haven't figured out you feel pain, I'd be highly surprised. And disappointed. I'd probably leave to find a clan with more intelligent leadership."

Alísa swallowed, unable to give Trísse even a chuckle. She lifted a hand to her dragon-scale necklace, but Trísse stopped her.

"Come on. Staying here like there's a problem will only make it more obvious. Let them see you smile and dance, then call it a night and let your mind heal."

"Easy for you to say," Alísa whispered, keeping her stammer at bay. "You aren't crushed by the crowds, physically or empathically."

Trísse smirked at the slight jab. She was an empath too, but her powers were far weaker than Alísa's. She picked up the emotions of those closest to her, both in proximity and relationally, while Alísa picked up the entire crowd.

"At least you can slip between people." Trísse helped Alísa to her feet, standing nearly a foot taller than her. "Making my way out of a crowd leaves me battle-scarred."

"B—Better lead, then, else I leave you behind."

Trísse stayed beside her the entire time, whether dancing to the holders' music, crowd-watching, or anything in-between. When the women enquired after Alísa, she simply smiled and claimed an upset stomach—half-truth, but truth nonetheless. While some still eyed her suspiciously, none pressed the issue.

Perhaps an hour in, Alísa could barely focus on anything. Though free of the dragons' pain, all the emotions of the crowd battered her mental defenses. They mixed and itched like the scents in the holders' spice boxes. Excitement, fatigue, joy, sadness, suspicion—she couldn't hold them back anymore.

She was just about to tap Trísse on the shoulder and excuse herself, when Tern, Trísse's pursuer, asked Trísse to dance with him. Trísse's hard eyes softened as longing rose in her, but then she looked to Alísa.

"I'm sorry, Tern, but I'm rather worn——"

Alísa placed a hand on Trísse's arm. "I'm okay, T—T—T-T-Trísse. I'm ready to g——go back to the t-t-tent." She pointed to her temple. "T—too many p-p-people up here."

A grateful smile lit up Trísse's face, while Tern grabbed her hand quickly, as though afraid Alísa would change her mind. He led her away to the bonfire, and Alísa watched them go. What would it be like to be in love? Could such a thing ever grow between her and Kallar?

She shook the thoughts from her head and began weaving through the crowd. Laughter, exaggerated movements, and spilling drinks abounded. Alísa dodged through the people, occasionally catching an elbow or bumping shoulders.

And Trísse says I don't get bruises in a crowd.

A particularly enthusiastic woman flung her arms wide, sending splashes of mead flying. Alísa jumped back to avoid the drink, only to collide with a young man. She turned to give an apologetic smile before making her exit.

"Hey, I know you," he grinned, his eyes and teeth gleaming in the firelight. Though she couldn't place his name or family, a familiar mirth spilled from him—one that made her want to run.

"Still sensitive to dragon-killing, eh, Alísa? Delicate flower of a slayer."

She forced a smile through the sickening stench of alcohol on his breath. "Excuse me."

She slipped away in the crowd, but he followed.

"I thought becoming a wayfarer would've toughened you up, but it seems the beasts have only gotten a tighter grip on you."

"You should have seen your face," another voice came. She turned to see two young men following the first, both familiar enough to place. These had set off tears more than once in her younger life.

She kept her eyes ahead of her and quickened her pace, crossing the road and heading for the Hold. These man-children wouldn't dare slander her before their holders, assuming there were any still inside and not at the celebration.

"White as a sheet."

"Tell me, dragon-lover, how does it feel to know you're going to die? To have a spear thrust through your heart?"

She swallowed. Did they know, or were these just drunken ramblings?

"How can you expect to be chief if you have a dragon inside you, little Lísa?"

"I heard Karn's giving the job to Kallar so she won't have to."

Alísa clenched her fists. Their words were daggers, reopening wounds from long ago.

"Just as well—no one can hear her whispering."

"Or sit through her st-st-stammering!"

A chorus of laughter. Shame threatened to rise into her eyes, but she forced it down. She wouldn't give them the satisfaction.

"Poor Kallar, having to put up with your crying and sniveling in the face of the enemy."

"Not to mention all the clans."

"Did you see Karn's face when she limped away? He was so embarrassed."

Alísa halted, her arms trembling.

"Shut up." The words came more quietly than she wanted.

"I would be too if my daughter was a dragon-loving wench."

"I'd have stepped down long ago before she revealed my shame!"

Alísa whirled on them, rage rising in her chest. "How d—d—d-d-d-d—" *Damn it! Why now?*

"There it is." The first boy laughed. "I was worried you'd grown out of it."

"Perhaps she's had too much to drink."

"Or a dragon's got her tongue!"

A burst of commotion, and the boys stumbled backward.

"Get away from her!"

Alísa started, relief and fear colliding within her. *Kallar!*

"Now!" He roared, grabbing one of the young men's arms and yanking him back. He moved between her and them, rage pouring from him. "Any of you so much as look at her again, you're dead."

One of the aggressors scoffed. "You've had too much. Three slayers against one is no match."

Another peeked at her around Kallar, a laugh in his eyes. "As I said, someone else fights her battles n—"

He stumbled against one of his companions, then slumped to the ground unconscious.

Alísa trembled, her eyes widening. *Did Kallar just mind-choke him?*

The others must have had the same thought, their lips curling into snarls.

"You dare use telepathy against your own?!"

The second fell.

The third didn't waste any more time, swinging at Kallar's face. Kallar caught the blow with a loud crack and punched him in the stomach, letting him fall to his knees with a moan.

Kallar's voice evened, but fury still rippled from him. "Your friends will wake with the worst headaches of their lives. Next time, you won't be so lucky."

Alísa jumped as he pivoted to face her, his eyes still hard. She dropped her eyes to his boots.

"What were you doing?"

She tensed. "I'm t—t-tired. I was just going back to my tent."

"By yourself?" He shook his head and grabbed her hand, walking her toward camp. Protectiveness poured through their skin-contact, soured by possessiveness. "I know this was your home once, but that doesn't mean it's safe. You should've asked me to take you back."

She looked away. There hadn't truly been any danger—she would have sensed if the man-children had intentions beyond mockery—but arguing that point with Kallar would not help matters. Best to stay quiet and let him take her home.

"Why didn't you tell me?"

"C—camp isn't far—"

"Not that. The pain."

Her shoulders slumped and her voice came in a whisper. "I've been able to keep it together if there's only one. I'd expected to handle two."

"I could have shielded you. I know Karn didn't want to at first—he said you'd grow stronger against the emotions given time—but if he had known about this, he would surely have changed his mind." His tone turned bitter. "Instead, your precious secret's been revealed to everyone."

She looked away. "I hoped they'd just think I c—c-c-couldn't stomach the violence."

He stopped, looking at her with incredulity.

"You moaned and whimpered every time a blow landed! I heard them talking, and not just the mockers like these. They're saying you have a dragon inside you."

His words were a knife in her soul. Normals used the idiom to shame those who disrespected tradition or authority figures. Used by slayers, though, it spoke of people possessed by dragons or else used by the Nameless to work evil in the world.

She shivered with the chill of night. Why? Why did everything have to turn against her? First her voice, then her empathy, now her people? She wasn't possessed! She hadn't been turned to evil, hadn't done anything except feel feelings she didn't want.

"Empathy doesn't mean I'm p—p-p-possessed."

"No, but it means you can't fight them."

She gave a bitter laugh. "Isn't that why you're here? Why my f-father chose you to lead the c-clan?"

"Why *you* chose me," he reminded with a point of a finger. "The clan needs a leader. You need a protector."

Kallar's eyes softened, and he threaded his fingers through her hair, stopping just behind her jaw. There was affection in his eyes, but entitlement clung to his every action.

"Why didn't you tell me? I would have shielded you, my love."

His presence fingered at her mind, his psychic touch gentle, yet unwelcome. She recoiled, pushing his hand away.

"I don't n—need you anywhere near my mind."

His eyes hardened again, indignation flaring. "You'd rather the dragons have access?"

"No." She walked past him. *But I don't want you slithering around in there either.*

"Then stop acting like it." He grabbed her arm, pulling her to a stop. "I know there was no love in this choice of yours, but I've done everything I can to win your affections. And you—"

He ended with a growl of exasperation, his frustration flowing into her mind. She didn't push it back, instead using it to speak the words she normally wouldn't.

"It's not like you've m—made it any easier for me! Your arrogance, your entitlement to me—"

"Alísa..." he warned, his eyes flaring.

"—t-t-taking pleasure in the k-k-killings not because they m—make the world safer, but b-because it satiates your bloodlust!"

As soon as the words left her mouth, she knew she had gone too far. Kallar snarled at her, pulling her within inches of his face.

"You know *nothing* of my motivations. Nothing!" His fierce eyes bored into hers, anger now dripping from his every pore, sending her heart racing. "I'm trying to help you—to save you. But all I get in return is your loathing!"

"Let me go."

"Well, I don't care. They won't have you, not on my watch!"

"Let me g—"

"I won't let you end up like Bria!"

She blinked. "B—Bria?"

His rage melted into stunned realization, as though he had gone too far or said too much. He relaxed his grip, and she immediately pulled away, covering her arms with her hands. He stared at her, his chest heaving with deep breaths.

"You can make your way from here," he whispered, nodding toward the hill separating them from camp. He turned around without another word and returned to the celebration.

She stared after him, her breaths short and shallow. In the absence of his anger, fear consumed her.

They know. Everyone knows.

She turned toward camp and broke into a sprint, running as though she could leave the thoughts behind in the village. Instead they chased her, nipping at her soul like wolves, crushing her heart like serpents.

Kallar's connection between her and Bria suddenly made sense. Bria hadn't chosen to be taken by the dragons, but still she was stolen. If the strong, courageous warrior woman couldn't stand against the dragons, what hope did Alísa have of shaking this psychic hold?

What if it became worse? What if she ended up always being affected by dragons, even outside the ceremonies? What if her mind turned against her and she ran to them of her own accord?

If she couldn't trust herself, how could her clan trust her?

She jogged to a stop at the edge of camp and placed her hands on her knees. The campfire crackled in the midst of thirty dusty leather tents etched with swirling designs of protection from the Nameless and their servants. A lilting baritone voice flowed from near the flames into the night.

Farren. If it were anyone else, she would have snuck to her tent to be alone, but the kindly songweaver could give her what she truly needed—wisdom and a sympathetic ear.

Farren sat alone on a fallen log beside the fire, singing and staring into the flames. He barely noticed as she sat beside him and closed her eyes, breathing in the final chorus and willing her heart to settle.

His song was a favorite of hers—the beautiful tragedy of Eldra D'tala and how she had fallen in love with Tohmra, a mortal man. D'tala was the first steward of wind and soul, and she loved Tohmra's passion for the sea, where he used her winds and his ship to bring blessings to his people.

A dragon told D'tala of a potion she could create to give Tohmra immortality so they could be together, and she had done so with great joy. But the dragon was a follower of the Nameless, and the potion D'tala created instead transferred her immortality to Tohmra, sucking away her life.

Tohmra's first act as an immortal was to shepherd her soul back to the Maker's halls. There, the Maker changed his name and gave him D'tala's former stewardship. Now D'tohm gathers the Maker's fallen *iompróir anam* and escorts them to the Maker's halls, each time catching a glimpse of his love.

Now he waits for the day when the physical world falls and he can be with her once more.

Farren's last note faded into the night, and Alísa opened her eyes to his grandfatherly smile. He truly wasn't much older than her father, but he had the wisdom of the songweavers and all of her clan treated him with the utmost respect.

"I'm sorry, Alísa, I didn't know you were here too. Did I wake you?"

She shook her head, fingering her necklace. "I just got here. I needed to get away from p—people."

"I understand." His eyes softened. "I suspect you've been through more today than most know."

No. Everyone knows, and that's the problem. She looked down. "Why didn't the Maker just fix things? Give D—D'tala back her immortality instead of letting her die?"

Farren's voice quieted. "I don't know, dear one."

"He could have! He has the p-power! He can fix everything, s—so why d-d-d-doesn't he?! D—d-did I do something wrong? Am I g—g—g—g—" Her throat closed up and she stared into the fire. *Am I going to do something wrong?*

"Sing it," he whispered. "No one else is here."

She swallowed. It wasn't an unexpected request—she never stammered when she sang, and Farren always claimed it was one of the best ways to let out emotion. He was the only one she had ever felt comfortable enough to sing for, and her throat felt like it might explode from all the emotions stopped up inside.

Keeping her eyes on the flames, she breathed low and deep and allowed words to flow.

By Maker's call I breathed my first,
my purpose borne in father's hands.
By Maker's plan I'm left in thirst,
my calling bound in verbal bands.

By Maker's hand the slayers' gift
pulsed anew inside my mind.
By Maker's will I'm left adrift
as dragon feelings intertwined.

By Maker's breath I did my best,
but by His work I am betrayed.
By Maker's light I am oppressed;
why does he hate the one he made?

She allowed her final, heretical note to fade into the night until the only sound left was the crackling of flames. Tears slid down Farren's cheeks. He reacted more viscerally to music than she had ever seen a man react to anything. But then, warriors weren't exactly known for overflowing feelings—they left that to songweavers. She leaned against him and allowed her own tears to flow quietly.

"He doesn't hate you, dear one," he said softly. "Sometimes we must be stripped of all we know in order to become our true selves. It is his way."

She shook with a sob and Farren pulled her close, allowing her to cry on his shoulder. The Maker had stripped her today, exposed her for all to see. Farren said she would find her true self now, but if the Alísa now broken and sobbing on his shoulder was the true Alísa—if the woman with a dragon inside her was the true Alísa—she didn't want it.

If only all her people were like Farren, compassionate and non-judgmental, she would make it through. But they weren't, and tomorrow would bring her nightmares to life as she faced a clan that had seen her shame.

3

SECRETS

"Alísa, wake up."

Alísa forced her eyes open to see her father. In the dim light filtering through the tent walls, she could see he was already dressed for the road, a dark green cloak over plain brown tunic and pants.

"You've overslept."

She pushed the comfortably heavy furs off and sat up.

"I'm sorry. I slept so hard." She grimaced as she stretched her arms and back, as stiff from yesterday's sorrows as if she had carried all her family's travel bags the day before.

Karn studied her, eyes full of concern. She looked away. It wouldn't do any good to talk about what had happened. She wanted to help pack up camp and move out, like it was any other traveling day.

"I g—guess I should start p-packing."

"No." He placed a hand on her arm, his voice soft. "We need to talk first."

She pressed her lips together and said nothing.

"Why didn't you tell me about the pain? I would have found a way to let you stay home, while still saving face."

Alísa shook her head. "If I stopped c—coming the clan would still know something was wrong. The p-p-pain was bearable until yesterday. I d-didn't want to bring you shame." A tear rolled down her cheek. "But I still did. I'm sorry. I'm so sorry!"

He pulled her to his chest and kissed the top of her head. "My brave, foolish girl—always thinking of others to her own detriment."

"And yours," she whispered, pressing into him. "Did I cause you trouble?"

"The clan won't turn against me for this. Some will be angry at my secrecy, but all are loyal. Camaraderie is a powerful bond—things will go back to normal come the next battle."

"And T—Toronn?"

His chest deflated with a quiet sigh. "If he wants to protect Azron from the next dragons to inhabit the mountain, he'll come around. But when that day comes, you would do well to stay away."

He pulled back and looked her in the eyes, his hands firm on her arms.

"The clan will have a difficult time trusting you now. You must be brave and show them you are still one of us. Show them a woman whose powers have betrayed her, but not bent her to evil."

She swallowed. "But what if it gets worse?"

He smiled gently, belying the fear trickling from him.

"You don't need to worry about that. Kallar and I will watch out for you and deal with things as they come."

Right. Kallar.

She looked down, knowing his next answer, yet needing to hear it again. "Papá, are you sure you p-picked the right man? For the c—c-c-clan?"

Karn raised an eyebrow. "Did you two fight again yesterday?" When she didn't look up, he continued. "About what?"

"D—does it matter?"

He sighed and spoke softly. "He's not going to be chief for a long while, Lísa. He's only twenty and has plenty of time to grow out of his idiot phase." He cracked a smile, but she didn't return it. "He will be a great man when he matures, and he's already an exceptional tactical leader and the strongest slayer I've trained. If anyone can protect you from the dragons, he can. It's bad enough you're forced to share their feelings; I couldn't bear it if they took you."

Alísa jerked her head up. "T—took me? Why?"

He shook his head as if to clear it. "I was merely thinking of last night's tale."

Bria again. But she was a warrior, in constant contact with dragons, while I've rarely seen battle.

"Sweetheart, do you trust me?"

She nodded absentmindedly. *Why waste his energies on such an unrealistic fear?*

"Will you let me enter your mind?"

Alísa started. "What?"

"Now that I know the problem is still growing, I want to see if I can find a pattern besides the ceremonies themselves. If I can find the reason behind these connections, maybe I can help you fight it better. Will you let me look?"

He had never asked to see her memories before. Despite the ability, slayers rarely used their psychic powers on other people. Married men would connect to their wives for private communication sometimes, but even those connections were few and far-between. The mind was sacred, and telepathic connections opened private thoughts to perusal. Some even said if two minds connected too often, the stronger mind would shape the weaker after itself.

But she did trust him, and he wouldn't have asked if it weren't important.

"Okay."

He smiled softly, raising a hand to her temple and pushing her hair back. His voice was soothing.

"I need you to relax. Calm your thoughts. This will be uncomfortable, but I'll be as gentle as I can."

She nodded again, and he laid his other hand on her opposite temple.

"Look me in the eyes and relax."

She did as he said. His mind pressed against hers, and she breathed slowly and deeply. Soon the pressure moved from outside her head to inside, as though her mind were stretching out past her head and into the chamber.

Visions of her past swirled around her as he searched, memories rushing to the forefront of her mind and leaving just as quickly. It was dizzying, but she focused on her breathing until a memory came into focus.

Three young men led a black hatchling to the middle of the ceremony circle. Alísa's five-year-old self gasped; she had never seen a dragon before.

Her father leaned over and reminded her of a story of dragons attacking a village. He told her the dragons must be punished for what they did. Then Chief Toronn gave the order and one of the men drew his sword and swiftly severed the hatchling's neck.

Alísa whimpered and leaned against her mother as tears streamed from her eyes. It was just a little thing, like her. If something so small could deserve to die, what would happen if she did or said something Chief Toronn didn't like?

Her mother's arms pulled her close. "Karn, I don't think she was ready for this."

More visions flashed in front of her—all past encounters with dragons, all ending with a slaughtering. As the memories drew closer and closer to present day, her empathic powers in them grew.

FEAR!

RAGE!

PAIN!

Tears wet Alísa's cheeks as Karn pulled from her mind. A single tear ran down his own cheek, and he wrapped his arms around her. She trembled as his fear washed over her. He was a mighty warrior—he killed monsters three times his size for a living. How could anything make him feel this way?

"I'm sorry," he whispered. "This is my fault. I exposed you to the slayings while you were too young to understand, and you've carried the trauma and fear with you all these years. That's why the door to your mind was left open to them. I'm so sorry."

She squeezed him tightly. "It's okay, Papá. You didn't know. I'm okay. I'll be okay."

"Yes, you will be."

He pulled back to look her in the eyes, his own set with resolve, and despite the uncertainty and questions jostling inside of her, she had never felt more safe. Even if everyone else gave up on her, he wouldn't. And if the door to her mind was opened by his actions as he said, perhaps it could be closed by man as well.

There was hope.

"Now, get dressed." He gave a half-smile. "You must eat something— we have a long journey today."

She got up from her bed-mat as her father left the chamber. The morning's chill pressed her to choose a long brown dress and heavy green cloak. She tied her hair behind her as she pushed through the canvas and entered the living space. Her father stood by the outside flap, waiting for her with a smile. She took his arm and they stepped into the sun together.

Weathered brown tents dappled the valley, and Alísa let out a soft sigh at the simple peace of camp. To the north lay new mountains to take back from the dragons—villages to set free from the beasts' reign of terror. In between lay rolling hills of green, the grasses tossing in the wind and beckoning the travelers.

Soon the clan would answer that call.

Breakfast had already been served, a combination of leftovers and fresh pork. Many of the clan sat in small groups, some chatting lively, while others looked like death warmed over. A few sat apart and shot glares at their loud clansmen as they nursed splitting headaches from last night's festivities.

Eyes met hers and quickly turned away as she passed. Whispers abounded, cloaked with suspicion and fear. Alísa fought to keep her breathing steady and stand tall beside her father.

I am the daughter of Karn, the greatest chief the wayfarers have ever known. I am burdened, but not bent. I am a slayer, and there is no dragon inside of me.

They came to the large, sun-bleached kitchen tent. One of its leather sides was propped open like an awning, allowing the savory scents to waft through the camp. Pots clanged and scraped as four clanswomen worked, finishing up the last of breakfast and packing everything for the coming journey.

Two holders worked with them, delivering food and drink for the days of travel between this village and the next. Everyone did their part in this war—if one couldn't fight, they provided for those who could. Some did so begrudgingly, but if these holders were among those ranks they hid it well.

One of the women served up Alísa and Karn's plates silently, avoiding eye-contact with Alísa. If Karn noticed, he didn't show it. After a word of thanks, he turned and guided Alísa toward their family with a hand at her back. Again, the eyes of the clan averted from hers, bringing shame's hands to clamp around her heart.

"Lift your eyes, Alísa. Your fear will only validate theirs."

"Will you speak to them? T—t-tell them I'm not d-dangerous?"

He nodded once. "Before we move out. Let them see you now, acting as you normally do, then give them time to digest the truth on the road."

Finally, they joined the rest of their family, sitting on logs and rocks amidst trampled grasses. Kallar sat beside Hanah, while Alísa's twelve-year-old twin cousins sat between their parents. Kallar studied her with unblinking eyes, neither smiling nor displaying any ire from the night before. He often stared like this when deep in thought, and though it annoyed her, she had learned to ignore it.

Kallar broke off his gaze and stood before Karn sat. "Karn, I would like to speak to you privately."

Her father nodded and they walked away together.

Is it about last night? The thought made her stomach hurt. If it had to do with her mind, her future, she wanted to know.

Her cousin Taer's voice broke Alísa from her thoughts.

"So, Alísa, we've been wondering something." He spoke through a mouthful of bread and cheese, his light brown eyes sparking with curiosity. His sandy hair looked wind-tousled, as though he had burst from the tent this morning before passing his mother's inspection.

The morning light flashed in Aunt Elani's blond hair as she smacked her son on the arm, her dark eyes narrow and stern. "Don't speak with your mouth full."

Levan was a cleaner mirror-image of his brother, his hair neatly combed down and his traveling clothes less frumpy. He made a show of swallowing his ham, smirking at his brother before completing his twin's thought.

"What does it feel like to have a dragon in your head?"

Alísa closed her eyes and swallowed. The boys were asking innocently, but the words were far too close to those of the man-children from last night.

L'non's brown eyes narrowed and he spoke sharply. "What did I tell you about such questions this morning?"

"It's okay, Uncle," she whispered. Perhaps the more she explained it, the more it would help them understand it didn't make her dangerous. She could bear the clan's fear if her family wasn't afraid. She met each of the boys' eyes in turn.

"It's like there are t-two of me in my head, one saying everything is fine and I'm not in danger, the other p-p—panicking and hurting. They fight each other and I get a splitting headache."

She felt eyes on her from outside her family group, but forced herself to only look at her cousins.

"When they d-d-die, I feel for a moment like I've d-died. Then the extra feelings leave and it's only me. The headache s—stays for a while, but it eventually goes away too."

"Why do you feel it?" Taer spoke through another mouthful of ham, prompting his mother to smack him once more.

Alísa looked down. "I don't know."

"It's probably because your powers are super-strong," Levan offered. "I hope I'm as strong someday."

"Maker forbid," Elani whispered.

Alísa forced down another bite. Strength didn't have anything to do with it—if it did, there would be others among the clan with the same problem. There was no answer.

Then again, both Kallar and Karn seemed to know more than they let on. Were they talking about it right now?

She had to know.

"Boys, I'm d-d-done with my breakfast. Do you want the r—"

"YES!" they chorused.

She chuckled and scraped the remnants onto their plates.

Hanah raised an eyebrow. "Everything all right?"

Alísa nodded. "I'm going to start p-packing."

This seemed to satisfy her mother, and Alísa hurried toward the tent. As soon as she was out of sight, she changed direction and walked cautiously in the direction Kallar had gone with her father.

It didn't take long for her to find them—their voices came from inside Kallar's tent. The soft grasses muffled her footsteps as she knelt at the back of the tent, straining to catch their words.

"—can't blame yourself." *Kallar's voice.* "If I were a father, I would have done the same thing to train up my child. We can't operate in what-ifs and might-haves. What matters is how we help her now."

Her father scoffed. "And you think telling her what she *might be* would help her?"

Alísa's heart raced. *'What' I might be? So, they do know something!*

"You still have doubts after last night? How many empaths can feel a dragon's pain?"

"The only way to find out for sure is to test her with dragons, which would only bring her more pain, both psychically and emotionally. No. Alísa was not made for war—I won't see her crushed by it."

Kallar's voice raised. "Not knowing is crushing her right now! Her mind is tearing itself apart. If she knew she was—"

"*Might* be. And she'd want to help, despite the pain it would cause her."

"Then let her help; I would keep her safe!"

"You've seen what two hatchlings do to her. Full-grown dragons dying all around her would kill her! As long as I'm around, she will not step foot on the battlefield! And you will not tell her anything!"

Alísa raised a fist to her lips as the men sat in silence. *What have I walked into?*

Her father sighed. "I know what man and dragon would do to her if they found out. For her sake, we must keep silent. Then no man will place her in danger, and no dragon will want to take her. That is my word, and you will respect it and protect my daughter. Swear it, Kallar."

Kallar was silent.

"Swear it!"

"I swear."

"Swear what?"

Kallar growled. "I swear I will never tell her what she is."

"And you will never put her in a position where she might learn."

"And I will never put her…"

Alísa snuck away quickly and quietly until she was out of earshot of Kallar's tent, then ran the rest of the way to her family's tent, crawling directly into her chamber under the side.

Her heart raced and her mind swam. She could barely control her movements as she stuffed her belongings into her pack, covering for her absence in case her mother came looking.

Power? What I am? Danger? Father has never kept secrets from me about my dragon empathy.

Why now?

What exactly am I?

4

JOY & SORROW

"Ouch!" Alísa dropped the hammer and grasped her throbbing thumb, leaving her tent-peg only partially in the ground. Somehow years of wayfaring didn't keep her from making stupid mistakes.

"Is there a dragon nearby, Alísa?" Trísse's younger brother Rassi laughed from his corner of the kitchen tent. "Or are you really just that clumsy?"

Alísa didn't glance at him, though she tensed with shame and anger. *If my father were nearby, he wouldn't dare speak that way!*

An exclamation of pain brought Alísa's eyes up to see Trísse grabbing her brother by the ear. He flailed for her arm to relieve the pain.

"Some slayer you make—attacking one woman, incapacitated by another." She pushed him as she let go. "Father would be ashamed."

Alísa hammered her tent peg once more, securing her side of the tent before she stood and walked away.

Trísse came up beside her. "How am I related to that dolt?"

Alísa gave a small smile in return, but even knowing she had friends and family who would defend her didn't fully soothe the ache in her heart. She had kept her empathy reined in all through the journey of the last two days, doing her best to avoid the disdain and scrutiny of her clanmates, but the effort exhausted her.

Alísa fingered her necklace, barely hearing Trísse's mutterings about inheriting all the brains in her family.

Trísse hurried to get in front of Alísa and walked backwards.

"Where are you going?"

Alísa stopped and surveyed her surroundings. They were nearly out of camp and she hadn't even noticed, walking with no destination beyond away. Camp settled in a field just north of a grove of trees. Miles beyond the grove, a tall mountain pierced the horizon—the next target in her clan's mission. They would reach Kannin, the village closest to it, in two days.

Alísa's eyes flitted to the horses picketed at the outskirts of camp. A gallop in the sun would allow her a reprieve.

"Riding." She smiled at Trísse. "Coming?"

"You have to ask?"

They hurried to the horses, each grabbing a carrot from a crate on an equipment cart as they passed. A gentle breeze rustled the grasses in an enticing song as Alísa approached a black mare affectionately deemed Sassy. Despite the horses belonging equally to the entire clan, the fleet-footed and playful mare was her favorite.

The sleek horse grazed quietly, not even looking as Alísa untied her rope from the picket stake. Alísa clicked to her, but Sassy didn't raise her head until she held out the carrot.

"Come on, you," Alísa scolded playfully. "I know you want to fly just as much as I do."

Alísa smiled as the horse reached for the treat. Why couldn't she speak to humans as well as she could animals? She almost never stammered when talking to them, or even to herself, but add one person to the mix and everything went south.

"Sneaking off, are we?" Kallar's voice broke into her thoughts.

Alísa jumped and faced him, startling Sassy just before she could take the carrot. Alísa pulled gently on the lead and breathed low, willing her heart to settle.

"Only if r—riding across the meadow with Trísse c-c-counts as sneaking off." She offered the carrot to Sassy once more and smiled as the horse munched. "Are you here to s—stop me?"

"Not remotely. I'm here to join you."

Alísa fought not to sigh. *Of course he is.*

She glanced at Trísse, already mounted and waiting for her. Alísa hid a smirk. Kallar hadn't yet grabbed a horse for himself. He would have to catch her if he wanted to ride with them.

She grabbed Sassy's mane and jumped onto the horse, then, gathering the lead, she launched across the field after Trísse.

Alísa and Sassy flew, wind whipping through hair and mane. Releasing her empathy to the winds, Alísa let out a whoop. Horses were magnificent creatures—such power in their limbs and goodness in their hearts. Sassy's joy emanated so strongly that Alísa could feel it without even trying. The mare must have really wanted a run—it was typically harder to read animal emotions.

Except for dragons. They were far too easy to read.

She pushed dragons from her mind and focused on Sassy's emotions, allowing them to add to her own. The joy of freedom, of flying over the land!

"Alísa!"

Kallar's voice was faint behind her, and she ignored it, reveling in the joy. It was like the wonder she felt when working with her father on controlling her empathic powers—the pride and happiness that came with learning what she was made to be.

Now halfway across the field, Trísse pulled her horse to the left to avoid the grove. Alísa followed suit, but Sassy resisted. How the name suited her. Alísa pulled again. *'Never give in to a stubborn horse,'* her father would say. They had to learn that humans were their masters.

Sassy tossed her head with a squeal and danced sideways closer to the grove. The hair on Alísa's neck began to stand on end, another of her father's lessons coming to mind:

'Always listen to the horse.'

Kallar called to her again, this time with urgency. She glanced back over her shoulder just as dark shadows swept across the grass. Massive green shapes blocked the sun and sent a chill to Alísa's heart.

Dragons!

Terror strangled Alísa's voice as she tried to call to Trísse, but the shadows had already warned her. Trísse and her horse whirled toward cover and Alísa kicked Sassy forward, gripping her mane tightly in both hands as they bolted for the safety of the grove. Kallar rode far behind them, his sword already drawn.

They entered the shadow of the trees and Alísa pressed feelings of peace into the air to calm Sassy. If she couldn't get the horse under control, she would be pummeled and unseated by the many low branches. She pulled Sassy's mane and spoke gently to her, willing the animal to stop. The mare snorted, but obeyed.

Trísse entered just behind Alísa. She attempted to calm her horse, but the animal reared and pulled against her. Alísa pushed her empathy harder, further, until her power added to Trísse's and overcame the horse's natural fear.

Kallar rode closer, his horse's hooves throwing up chunks of sod. Nearly twice as high as the trees, the dragons banked lazily over the field.

"They aren't following us," Trísse observed quietly.

"They don't seem to notice Kallar, either."

Judging by their sizes, one of the dragons was an adult and the other an adolescent. The younger followed the older, copying its every move. Wonder still pressed into Alísa—the wonder of a child learning from its parent.

So, it was their *joy I felt.* She should have been repulsed by the invading emotions, but she had never felt positive emotions from a dragon before. It was beautiful and pure, not at all an emotion expected of a creature bent toward evil. Perhaps it would feel this way as it torched a village, but in the simple act of flying?

The thought piqued her curiosity. They stood four trees deep into the grove, so the dragons probably wouldn't notice them now. Alísa pulled Sassy's mane until the horse turned parallel with the edge of the grove, and leaned to watch the massive creatures fly.

The bigger dragon climbed high and spun blissfully, the smaller following behind with slightly less grace. The older craned its neck and breathed fire beneath it, and the younger let out its own stream. Then, trumpeting a call reminiscent of a wolf's bay, they dove toward the meadow, delight emanating so strongly it made Alísa feel like she, too, was flying.

Trísse studied her. "Do you feel them?"

Alísa nodded and Trísse's eyebrows knit together.

"Come on, then, let's get you away from their influence."

"There's no pain, no fear," Alísa whispered back. "Only joy, deep and true." She bit back the question she didn't dare ask aloud.

How can an animal ruled by evil feel such joy?

A roar brought Alísa's attention back to the field. The larger dragon fanned its wings out, its flame-colored eyes burning bright as they fixed on something below.

Alísa's heart skipped a beat. It had seen Kallar!

The smaller dragon fanned its wings and banked left, wobbling as it flew. Despite its youth, it hadn't faltered before. *Kallar must be attacking it psychically!*

Fear and wonder clashed within Alísa, and Trísse's emanating concern turned to curiosity. They'd never been this close to a true psychic battle, nor had they ever seen the power of a dragon's attacks. The creatures hadn't followed or paid them any heed—perhaps it would be safe to stay.

She glanced at Trísse. "I want to watch."

"It will hurt you."

"We'll leave if it's too much."

She didn't wait for Trísse's response, closing her eyes and focusing until the astral plane became visible.

Blackness surrounded her. Small lights dotted the landscape like stars, created by the tiny minds of ants, beetles, and other insects. Sassy's dim brown outline matched the color of her deep eyes, while Alísa's own hands in the horse's mane glowed a stormy blue. If she focused hard enough, she could also see a deep green mist surrounding them, the manifestation of the calming empathy she and Trísse pressed into the air.

Her astral eyes latched onto Kallar, his incredibly bright blue form astride another dark-brown one. A blast of blue energy flew from his head into the sky, and Alísa followed the energy until it reached a shining amber form—the adolescent. The amber dragon formed a shield of sorts with its own telepathic energies, but it was no match for Kallar's strength. The shield shattered on impact, drawing a pained trumpet from the dragon and a swallowed whimper from Alísa.

A thunderous roar nearly made Alísa open her eyes. The larger dragon's red-orange form flew at Kallar, its jaws opened wide. Kallar and his mount dodged to the left. The dragon had probably just breathed fire at them, but flames were invisible on the astral plane.

Sassy squealed and pawed at the ground. Alísa rubbed a hand over the horse's neck, straining now to continue using her empathy. Neither dragon came anywhere near them, so they either didn't know the women were near or they didn't care. It was still safe.

Kallar continued his assault on the smaller dragon as it tried to fly out of range, striking again and again with his telepathy even as his form evaded the adult dragon's physical attacks.

Trísse whistled low. "No wonder the chief's so set on you marrying Kallar."

Alísa nodded, allowing herself a sliver of pride in her betrothed. Only the greatest of slayers could split their attention between the two realms this well.

The larger dragon abandoned its attack on Kallar and followed its offspring, taking only five wing-strokes to catch up. It flew underneath, taking one of the hits from Kallar with its own shield of energy.

A deep-brown bolt hit the adult dragon from behind. *Papá!* She would recognize that astral color anywhere. The dragon roared in pain and Alísa gasped in tandem.

"You okay?"

Alísa ignored Trísse's question, watching as a lighter brown bolt followed her father's. This one spread over the dragon's astral form like oil. Another bolt from her father struck and spread as well, adding to the coverage by the light-brown energy. They were attempting a mind-choke!

She opened her eyes and recognized the second newcomer as L'non. The adult dragon wobbled in the air under the fierce attack, then seized up and fell from the sky. Karn and L'non rode toward it, a spear in her father's hand and a sword in her uncle's. The younger dragon trumpeted in alarm and fell prey to Kallar's attacks seconds later.

As soon as the adult dragon hit the ground, Karn plunged his spear into a soft spot in its chest, killing it. Then all three men ran for the downed adolescent.

Alísa's breath caught—they would capture it for training, just like always. Her heart ached for the little dragon, whose wonder she had felt only moments ago. If they would only kill it now and end its suffering! She wheeled

Sassy around and kicked her into a run, only barely catching Trísse's exclamation of surprise.

By the time Alísa made it to the group of warriors, L'non already had a rope around the young dragon's neck. The adolescent looked larger now than it had in the sky beside its parent—perhaps four feet at the withers. Kallar had dismounted and now held it in a mind-choke, keeping its emotions from reaching her. She could only feel Kallar's triumph and her father's surprise.

Karn's eyes narrowed. "What are you doing? You shouldn't be here."

Trísse rode up from behind. "We were already out here, chief."

"Papá, p—please, don't take it back t-t-to camp. Just k-kill it now; don't torture the poor thing!"

Movement in her peripheral caught her attention. The dragon had shifted its head ever-so-slightly to regard her with deep amber eyes. She shivered; it seemed as though it were staring through to her soul.

"Help me, Singer."

Alísa froze, the unfamiliar male voice resonating in the depths of her mind. It trembled with weakness and perhaps fear, yet also held certainty, as if the dragon had no doubts she could do as he asked.

Kallar rushed to stand between her and the dragon, breaking their eye-contact. He must have felt the brief connection break through his mind-choke—indignant rage practically dripped from his every pore.

"Stay out of her head," he growled. "For that, I'll make sure you suffer!"

Someone gripped her shoulder and pulled, and she swung around to see her father.

"What did the foul creature say to you?" The intensity of his stare spoke anger, but there was fear rippling under the surface. He wasn't angry at her, but at the dragon who'd spoken to her. "What did it say?"

"He asked me for help," she whispered.

He didn't break eye-contact. "Kallar?"

"I didn't catch the message; it was too fast. But it won't happen again!" The dragon slumped as Kallar tightened his hold on the dragon's mind.

Karn frowned. "Its words, Alísa. What were its exact words?"

Alísa's mind raced. It—he—the dragon—had spoken to her as if he were a person, not just an animal. And his voice was almost human, not at all like what she had imagined after hearing the tales.

He had even given her a name, and though she didn't know why, it felt intensely personal.

She met her father's eyes.

"He said, 'Help me.' P-please, Papá, don't t-t-torture him."

Karn searched her eyes for a moment, and she trembled under his intense gaze. Then his eyes softened, and he pulled her close.

"Don't worry, you won't have to see or feel it."

She pulled away. "That's not what I mean. He didn't hurt anyone; all he did was b—be in the wrong place."

Karn's eyes hardened. "We've been over this. It will grow to kill our people, and the boys need to learn."

"But he—"

"Enough, Alísa!" She tensed at his tone; she had taken it too far. "Your mind is susceptible to them. You must learn to recognize their tricks!"

Her throat clamped shut as she fought back tears. She looked to the young dragon and pressed her lips together. There was nothing she could do.

"Karn," L'non spoke quietly as he and her father forced the dragon to rise, "it's been a while since I've had the boys work on stamina. I suggest we have them hold it for the night and kill it in the morning."

The slumping dragon crawled along the ground between the two men. Alísa's heart ached and twisted.

This was wrong. Terribly wrong. She had always hated the way they killed hatchlings, but, minus her empathic connection, it was in the same way she hated when a foal was stillborn or a chick fell from its nest to its death.

Now that she had heard the dragon's voice, now that he had given her a name and pleaded for help, he felt like a child.

She studied the dead dragon and a tear fell to the grass. *A child whose parent was just murdered in front of him and knows he's next.*

Kallar slid his arm around her shoulders. "Don't cry, Lísa."

"Alísa." She shrugged him off. It was his fault the child fell from the sky into the hands of its captors.

She turned to Sassy, but Kallar stepped between them. He placed a hand on either shoulder and held her in place, his eyes earnest.

"You don't have to be afraid—it won't speak to you again. I won't let it."

She looked down, staring at nothing. She should say something—that she was angry, not afraid. That the young dragon didn't deserve death. But anything she could say could be refuted by the same argument her father just used. She was susceptible. Shapeable. Weak.

"Let me go," she whispered.

"Alísa—"

"She said let go, Kallar." Trísse's tone was dagger-sharp.

Kallar glared at Trísse and lowered his arms slowly, as if to say he was only doing it because he wanted to and not because of Trísse. He stepped aside so Alísa could mount her horse.

Kallar and Trísse rode on either side of Alísa the whole way back to camp, but she barely noticed them in the midst of her swirling thoughts.

The dragon's sapience, his personhood, was clear in her head and heart. But if she was wrong and the dragon had tricked her, how could she ever trust her own mind again? Even if she were right, there was still nothing she could do.

Nothing but suffer her heartache in silence.

The alarm horn jolted Alísa out of bed before she knew she had woken. *Dragon attack!*

Her heart pounded as she fumbled in the darkness for her cloak and sword belt, yanking them from the top of her pack. How long had it been since the last attack on camp? A year? Two? Dragons were usually too smart to attack a wayfarers' camp.

She nearly collided with her father as they ran through the living space. Karn grabbed his weapons from beside the door and bolted outside to lead the defense.

Hanah and Alísa followed close behind, stepping from their dark tent into the chaos of camp. A tent was ablaze, lighting the scene in violent red. Women and young teens ran for tree-cover. Men scrambled to aim spears and arrows at the sky. The metallic sounds of swords sliding from scabbards were accompanied by deep roars.

Dragons—at least three of them crossed and banked over camp, perhaps more!

Eldra Branni, strengthen our warriors!

Hanah stopped at the edge of the grove and waved Alísa onward. As lady of the clan, it was Hanah's duty to make sure all the others got away before getting herself to safety. Alísa's heart sank as she ran on, as with every time she left her mother behind, but Hanah never allowed her to argue the point.

Alísa pressed deeper into the grove, where the trees grew thick enough to hide her from the dragons' eyes. A few women and young teens ran ahead of her, and more followed behind, all of them afraid, but not yet panicked. They knew what to do. Shouts of anger and pain came from camp, but though her heart ached and twisted, Alísa forced herself not to look back.

Maker, forgive my boldness, but please, protect my people! I can't do anything, so you and your Eldír have to do it. Please hear me!

An intense motherly instinct fell over Alísa as a roar sounded above the trees. One of the dragons. She stopped, her heart skipping a beat.

That dragoness was here for love of her child.

A battle raged within her. She should continue on with the women and wait out the battle. She should leave the men to defend camp and drop the beasts out of the sky.

Only, they weren't mere beasts anymore. And if the dragons were here to set the adolescent free, perhaps the battle would end as soon as he flew to them. The violence could end before anyone else—human or dragon—got hurt.

But the only way was to do the unthinkable.

She, Alísa, daughter of Karn, would have to free a dragon.

5

A DRAGON INSIDE

Alísa veered left toward the field where they picketed the horses. Hopefully, no one would notice her departure in the chaos. The squeals and shrieks of panicking horses filled her ears as she neared the edge of the grove.

Poor creatures. If they reared hard enough, they could pull free of their pickets, but until then they struggled. And right now, her mission only allowed her to help one of them.

Her heart raced, and she breathed low and deep, ignoring the roars and shouts of battle. Pressing peace into the air, she held out her hands and clicked to the gelding closest to her.

"It's okay. I'm going to set you loose. Then we'll both get to safety."

The animal quieted, and she hurried to untie it and mount. Together they flew along the outskirts of the grove. L'non and his slayers-in-training would be further back, where the trees were the thickest. They held the adolescent there to cut off the sightline necessary for telepathic communication. So long as he was hidden beneath the foliage, no dragon would be able to find him psychically from the skies.

Alísa closed her eyes to view the astral plane. The physical barrier of the tree trunks translated to blackness, but as she flew past she caught a glimpse of a bright brown glow shining between the trees ahead—almost certainly the boys and L'non.

She pulled the horse to a halt, leapt off, and sprinted. Brambles tugged at her cloak and night-dress, but she pressed on. She had to get to them. She had to stop the battle before anyone she loved got hurt, or worse.

Finally, the silhouettes of the boys guarding the dragon came into view.

They stood side-by-side, facing their charge, with L'non behind them.

"Uncle!"

L'non started and hurried to her side. "Alísa! What are you doing here? You should be with the rest of the women."

I'm already breaking the greatest rule of the slayers; what's one more? She reached out with her mind to spread feelings of urgency. If she did this right, he would listen to her without thinking through her words too carefully.

"Papá needs you and th—the boys. He says the dragon you guard is worth n—nothing if c-c-camp is lost."

L'non's eyes widened. "He's never made such a call in the past. Are you sure?"

Alísa pressed her energies harder. They had to leave for her to save everyone.

"There are too many of them. He needs your strength, Uncle. P—p-please hurry!"

L'non nodded, and Alísa held back a sigh of relief. He motioned to the boys.

"You heard her. Let's move!"

The boys ran ahead, Taer calling behind him. "Come on, Alísa!"

L'non grabbed her arm to pull her with him.

"No." She strained to push the urgency further. "I'll only slow you down. Go! I'm right behind you!"

L'non nodded and ran after the boys, leaving Alísa alone with the dragon. Anxiety trembled in her hands, and she rubbed the forming sweat on her skirt before turning to face the creature.

A rope tied the dragon to a tree, but without the boys' mind-choke it wouldn't keep him down for long. His wings had been sprawled out on either side of him while the trainees held him, but now he flexed them slowly. He raised his head and stared at her, amber eyes glowing bright in the night.

Alísa held her hands in front of her, as she would to a spooked horse.

"Do you r—remember me? You asked for my help. I'm here t-t—t-t-to give it. I'm not g—going to hurt you."

"I know, Singer." His voice came through clear, a rich tenor. With it came the strange sense of a name, as if she already knew who he was just by the

sound of his voice.

Graydonn.

"You're different from the others. Open. Kind. Afraid."

Alísa's heart raced. "Should I be? Afraid?"

"Not of me."

She took a cautious step in his direction, keeping her eyes fixed on his.

"I'm going to c-c-cut the rope from your n——neck. I know you could break it yourself soon, but there isn't much t-t-time." She swallowed, then raised her head higher, like a chief. "In exchange for my help, you will c——c——call off the attack."

Graydonn's tail thumped the ground. *"I sense my mother now——she's here for me. When I go to them, we will lead them away."*

His voice was steady and calm, not a hint of fear trickling through.

I wish I felt as calm.

"You can, Singer. I will not hurt you."

Alísa stopped. He heard her thoughts! He was in her head, just like with Bria! What if he was controlling her? *But I'm in my right mind. At least, I think I am. Could I tell if I weren't?*

"I've only connected to you so we can hear each other; hearing your thoughts like this is as natural to me as hearing with your ears is to you. It would feel much different if I were trying to control you, and I would never attempt such a thing." She could almost hear a smile in his voice. *"Remind me of your name?"*

She swallowed, "It's——"

"Alísa!"

Kallar! She nearly jumped out of her skin. The call came from far off, but he was looking for her. And he always found her.

Graydonn stood on wobbly legs. *"Quickly, Alísa. We have little time."*

Pushing her fear aside, she hurried to him——if he wanted to hurt her, he would have done so by now. He didn't even flinch when she drew her short sword from its sheath and slipped the point between his neck and the rope. Her father's dragon-scale armor was cool to the touch, but Graydonn's live scales radiated heat.

Fascinating!

Kallar called out again as the rope slid off Graydonn's neck. *He's getting too close.*

Graydonn shook his head, then pinned his eyes on her. *"Get on my back. I'm weak, but I'll do my best."*

She stepped back. "What?"

"Alísa!"

"You freed me; now I will free you!"

Free her? What was he talking about? Was this a pretense so he could take her away, like her father feared? She backed up another step, tightening the grip on her sword.

Graydonn tilted his head. *"You don't belong with them, Singer. You belong with us."*

Fear filled her heart, every part of her rebelling against his statement.

"No." She backed up another step. "No, I don't."

His glowing amber eyes dimmed. *"You don't know, do you? What you are?"*

Those words again, like Kallar and her father. "What are you t-talking about?"

"Why are you freeing me?"

"Alísa!"

Kallar's voice was so close; he must be at the edge of the grove by now. She slid her sword into its sheath and pressed urgency toward Graydonn as she had with L'non.

"Go! Go now; he will k-k-kill you!"

"And you?"

"Just go!"

"Alísa, get back!"

Kallar ran into view, only forty feet away now. She looked to Graydonn. "Go!"

"Maker shield you under his wings." Graydonn gathered his feet beneath him to launch into the air just as Kallar ran into sight-range.

"Oh no, you don't!" Kallar growled, a hand at his temple.

Alísa ran to stand between him and the dragon. "S-stop! The dragons will stop attacking if you let him g-g-go!"

Kallar pushed her aside, nearly knocking her over. Graydonn wobbled, nearly toppling under the mental barrage.

"No! Stop!" Alísa leapt at Kallar, dragging him to the ground. With Kallar's concentration broken, Graydonn shot up through the branches, his final words echoing through Alísa's mind:

"Call to me, Singer, and I will answer."

Alísa stared after him, making sure he was out of sight before backing off Kallar. He sat up and stared at her, their heavy breaths nearly drowning out the sounds of battle over camp.

This wasn't part of the plan. He wasn't supposed to be here, no one was supposed to know she had freed the dragon. If only she could make Kallar understand that she had done it to save the lives of their clanmates. She had to try.

"I'm sorry, but I had t-to—"

Kallar lunged for her, grabbing her arm with one hand and placing the other over her temple. She cried out more with surprise than pain as he pressed into her mind, his presence a heated tremor of fear and fury. He rifled over the surface of her mind, not digging for memories, but definitely searching for something.

"Why did you do it? Did it call to you? Force you?"

She trembled and pulled back, though she couldn't break his grip on her arm. "The dragons only wanted to free him. I j—just—"

The fear in Kallar turned to disgust, his lips pulling back in a snarl. *"It didn't force you. You wanted to free it, all on your own?!"*

He struck her with an open palm, her vision blurring to a mess of red as she fell back to the ground.

"How could you be so stupid?!" Kallar's voice rang savagely. *"Every man, woman, and child that dragon ever kills will be on your head! Do you understand that?"*

Alísa breathed heavily, fighting the pain. Tension clamped her throat shut. Explanations and reasons cycled through her head, but it was pointless. Even if she could speak right now, Kallar wouldn't listen. No one would, perhaps not even her father. They weren't supposed to catch her in the act!

Why couldn't Graydonn have just flown away instead of talking to her? Instead of trying to convince her to go with him!

Graydonn's voice echoed through her mind as Kallar let her go and whistled for his horse. *'You don't belong with them.'*

Her stomach clenched at the thought. She belonged with her people. Though many of them didn't believe it, she did. She had to.

Kallar stood as his horse walked into view. *"Get on."*

She trembled at his continued presence in her mind. He didn't belong there. "I'd rather walk—"

He grabbed her upper arm and pulled her up. *"Get. On. The. Horse!"*

She nodded quickly, not daring to disobey. As soon as Kallar let go, she mounted the horse. He mounted behind her, grabbed the mane with one hand, and wrapped his other arm around her waist protectively. Possessively.

She tried to speak in protest, but a fog rolled in over her mind, bringing a strange weakness. Was this fatigue from the multiple adrenaline-rushes of the night? Or was it a mind-choke? Would Kallar dare use his powers on her like that?

She didn't know.

Dragons retreated in the moonlight, just as Graydonn had promised. They headed for a mountain in the northeast, slowly disappearing into the night sky.

Wings. I want wings.

The all-clear horn sounded as Alísa and Kallar rode into camp. Torches lit the scene, revealing the results of a fierce but short battle. A single dead dragon lay in a crumpled heap just outside camp. A couple men nursed bloody wounds, one burned the length of his sword-arm. Three tents were completely destroyed, and a few more had been burned but mostly saved.

If not for Alísa's actions and Graydonn's promise, it would have been worse.

But she would be the only one who thought that way tonight.

"Kallar!" Her father thundered. "Where were you? We needed you here!"

His night-shirt was singed and blood-spattered, but there were no wounds to be seen. Praise the Maker.

"Tell him, Alísa. Tell him why I wasn't here to do my duty, to help our people!"

Alísa tensed as Kallar's words reverberated in her mind. His voice didn't belong in her head; his arm didn't belong around her stomach. And now that they were with her father, she no longer feared what Kallar might do.

"Get out of my head," she growled.

Kallar let go of her, both physically and psychically, and swung off the horse.

"She'll tell you."

Alísa's mind cleared——the final confirmation that he had indeed used a mind-choke on her. A gentle one, to be sure, but still a mind-choke.

She got off the horse on the side opposite Kallar, coming around the front of the animal to face her father. She stroked the horse's muzzle, trying to gain whatever comfort she could.

"Papá, I will explain, but p-p-please hear me without interruptions."

"Of course." His eyes softened as he met her gaze. What she wouldn't give to make sure they stayed that way through her explanation.

"Karn," Kallar stepped to him, his voice low. "This conversation shouldn't happen where others can hear."

Karn raised an eyebrow, but nodded. "Very well. Follow me."

The three of them walked from camp, out of the path the women would take to get back. Alísa stared at the grasses as a breeze rustled them, twisting them even as her own thoughts turned over and over.

She had done the right thing. Though it went against all her upbringing, releasing Graydonn had saved lives. She had to remember this——it was her only chance to get her father to understand.

Why did Kallar have to follow me? Why did he have to see what I did?

Finally, her father stopped and turned to face her.

"Now tell me, what happened?"

She breathed in deeply and let it out, allowing her throat to open and loosen.

"As I ran for cover, I was w——worried for the destruction of c-camp. For the d——deaths of our p-people. We are strong, but were c-c-caught off-guard. Then I sensed a mother's love in the skies above me, and I knew. I knew the dragons would leave if her child were released."

Kallar scoffed at her, and Karn's eyes narrowed. "Alísa, don't tell me——"

"You p-promised, Papá! Let me finish! My duty is t-to my clan, and I knew I could end the attack, so I ran—"

"So you saved slayers by putting everyone else at risk?"

Though outwardly he kept his fury at bay, it boiled inside of him like an active volcano and flooded over her. It was all wrong—he wasn't supposed to find out!

"We are called to fight them!" Karn lowered his voice. "To protect others by laying our own lives on the line. Your actions have not only set an adolescent free to grow up and kill, but by ending the attack early, you stopped us from taking down more of the beasts. Now all but one of the demons are still free to wreak havoc on our world!"

"Demons?" Karn and Kallar's anger churned within her. She didn't fight it, instead allowing it to fuel her courage to speak. They had to understand.

"You've always t-t-told me they're all evil, but when I s-set the dragon free he didn't attack me. He c-c-could—"

Karn shushed her. "Keep your voice down. Do you want everyone to know what you've done?"

"And it didn't attack because I was there to stop it!" Kallar interjected.

Alísa glared at him. "He c-c-could have easily hurt me b—before you got there." She turned back to her father, pleading him to listen. "If they really are all evil—if *he* really is evil—wouldn't he have k-k-killed me?"

Shame clouded Karn's eyes. "Why would it want a dead slayer woman when it can have one with a dragon inside her?"

Alísa staggered back a step, his response like another slap in the face. The night suddenly felt colder, and she pulled her arms inside her cloak.

"P—Papá..."

"Go back to the tent. Now."

Tears filled her eyes as his chief-voice replaced his father-voice. She spun and hurried away, putting distance between herself and the men. Her heart became a gaping hole in her chest, one that might pull her inside and never let her out again.

"Alísa!" Her mother's voice cried in the distance.

She must be worried sick that I never made it to the grove with the women.

Alísa tried to call back, but her throat constricted as tears fell. She pushed herself to run in search of her mother, dodging tents until the firelight revealed her heading for the grove, calling Alísa's name still louder.

"M—M—Mamá!"

Her mother ran to meet her in a tight embrace. Her relief washed over Alísa in waves, cooling the anger and sorrow bubbling inside her.

"Where were you?" Her mother tried to pull back, but Alísa held her fast, her arms trembling as she sobbed. "What's wrong, sweetheart?"

Alísa couldn't tell her. How could she have thought anyone would understand her decision? It had been wrong to release the dragon.

No, it hadn't been. Saving lives was never wrong. But a dragon's life was less than an animal's to her people.

No one would understand.

A third hand squeezed her shoulder, and Alísa pulled away from her mother to face her father once more. His eyes were sad, his anger seasoned with regret.

"Go now. We'll speak in the morning."

Alísa pulled away from her mother and walked toward the tent.

"What's wrong, Karn?" Her mother whispered behind her. "What happened?"

Her father's response was too quiet to hear as she passed between two tents and through the door of her own. Tears subsided as she entered her chamber and sat on the bed-mat.

What if her father was right and the dragon had tricked her? He had encountered dragons all his life—who was she to think she understood them better than he did? Better than all the slayers she had ever met?

She ran through Graydonn's words and actions. His plea for help. His calm assurance when she gave it. How he didn't take her away, even though he had wanted to. How he believed in the Maker, praying to him for her safety.

It all made sense now, why she had always felt their emotions even when other animals were hard to read—dragons weren't all soulless followers of the Nameless. They weren't animals, but *iompróir anam*. And, at the very least, this one dragon had chosen good over evil.

This changed everything! It meant that despite all the people her clan had rescued from dragons over the years, every time they killed a hatchling was like killing a human child! It meant that every time she stood by, she became an accomplice to murder.

And somehow, deep down, she had known it the whole time. Her empathy proved it.

Blood rushed from her face. *Is this why you hate me, Maker? Because somehow my mind understood they were* anam *and I still stood by and let it happen? What was I supposed to do?!*

She closed her eyes tightly, wrenching with sobs. She wasn't supposed to speak directly to the Maker, especially not like this, but how could Branni, shepherd and strengthener of slayers, understand this? Was he wrong too?

Why did you choose me *to bear this knowledge, this pain? What good does it do to give it to a stammering girl no one will listen to? What am I supposed to do?!*

She ran her fingers through her hair. *I can't do it again. If I stand by again, I'll never forgive myself. I have to convince them to stop! But they've never listened to me before, why should they now? And if I can't convince them—*

Alísa trembled. *I have to leave.*

She started at the sound of her parents entering the tent and swiftly slid under the cover of her furs. She couldn't talk to them right now, not with such radical notions in her head. She had to appear asleep.

Tears slid to her pillow, and she shut her eyes against them. This was too great a decision to make on a whim, just as releasing Graydonn had been. Her heart felt split in two, between the comfort and horror of all she had ever known and the dark unknown of tomorrow.

Between them lay the abyss of sleep, and, thoroughly exhausted, she fell into its quiet depths.

6

SEPARATE PLANS

"It's getting worse!"

Alísa sat up in bed. *Kallar's voice, in the main chamber.*

"She released a dragon, dammit. We need to teach her to protect herself!"

The voices lowered and became too quiet to understand. *Papá must have hushed him.*

She pushed back her furs and hurried about the room. They wouldn't talk about her behind her back again! She had to tell them what she had learned. She had to convince them that not all dragons were evil.

Her heart pounded. She had given herself an ultimatum last night— convince them to stop killing dragons or leave them.

She shook her head. *No. I was tired and not thinking clearly. I'm just going to explain what happened and it will be fine. After all, I'm not trying to tell them all dragons are good, just that some are and we shouldn't kill hatchlings before they've decided for good or for evil. It'll be fine.*

She tied her heavy green dress to her waist with a red plaid sash—the colors of the chief's family. Then, with a deep breath, she pushed into the main chamber. Three pairs of eyes shot to her—her parents and Kallar, all kneeling on the ground.

Karn cleared his throat. "Alísa, good. You need to know what's happening."

That didn't sound good. She stepped into the light, but before she could kneel beside her mother, Hanah gasped and stood, rushing to her. She placed a hand under Alísa's chin, turning her face. *There must be a visible bruise.*

"What happened? Was it the dragon?"

"The dragon did nothing." She glared at Kallar.

Hanah followed Alísa's eyes, anger flaring. "Kallar? Explain this to me!"

Kallar stood and took a single step closer, staring at the bruise. "I am truly sorry. I lost my temper when you stopped me from killing the dragon."

Her father stood, his eyes narrowed. "Kallar, this action toward my daughter deeply offends me. If you *ever* hit her again, my wrath will be swift and fierce!"

Alísa lifted her head high, harkening back to their argument only three nights prior. "It s—seems you have yet to d-decide which is more important to you—winning my affections, or your b—b-bloodlust."

Kallar's hands balled into fists and he growled under his breath. "I was afraid for you. Do you even understand what could have happened?!"

"Kallar, sit down," Karn ordered in his chief voice. Then he looked to Alísa, his eyes softening with sorrow. "He is right about one thing, my Lísa. What you did has put you in danger, and not just from the clan. Sit. We have much to discuss."

Alísa's heart quivered at the fear hiding in his words, and she did as he said, her parents following suit. Karn's somber eyes held hers a moment more before looking in turn to each of the others.

"There is now a dragon out there that knows about Alísa's connection to them. More likely than not, it will return to try and take her away."

Alísa cocked her head. "What do you mean?"

"As Farren's tale said, dragons are crafty creatures who like to strike at the hearts of slayers. But simply killing our women isn't enough for them; they tend to take those whose empathy connects to them because they are easier to twist and gain control of. Like Bria."

"But if I'm a p-p-prime t-target, why didn't Graydonn try to grab and t-take me away?"

Her parents' eyes widened, while Kallar's narrowed.

Alísa swallowed. She shouldn't have said Graydonn's name.

"You're on a first-name basis with that monster now?"

She glared at Kallar. "He's not a monster. He's——" Her throat constricted around the words *iompróir anam*, fear of the radical notion taking hold of her. "He was young and s-scared and innocent, and he didn't do anything t—t—t-to—"

"It was weak, and I was on my way, loudly making my presence known."

Her father's voice filled with urgency. "What else did it say, Alísa?"

"He said he would call off the attack once he was freed. Which he d—d—"

"We'd just killed one of the other dragons," Kallar broke in. "Of course the cowardly lizards would flee!"

She ignored him. "He c-c-could have k-killed me or t-t—t-t-taken me away. He even told me that I didn't belong with slayers and to get on his back—"

"See! It's after you and will be back!"

"And I refused!" She said louder, glaring at him. "And when I refused he didn't try anything. Not to hurt me, not t-t—to grab me, he just left and let me b-be." She looked to her father, her voice raising. "Is he really the monster you think he is?"

"It was trying to trick you," Karn said. "It was too weak to take you against your will, but will be back when strength has returned—perhaps with help. We have two options. The first is to march on their mountain and kill the entire clan, but if even one escapes you still won't be safe."

His sadness and fear outweighed Kallar's frustration and Hanah's confusion. "The second is to get you far away from here, somewhere the dragons that know will never find you."

Silence ensued, but inside Alísa's mind chaos reigned. Kill them all? He wasn't listening! Graydonn didn't deserve death, and there could be others in his clan who didn't either.

"The safest thing," Karn continued quietly, "is the latter. We can't guarantee none of the dragons will get away, no matter how good our men are."

Kallar's words were but a breath. "There is a third option."

"No." Karn glared at him.

Alísa couldn't pass up the opportunity. "What? What's the third option?"

Kallar glared back at Karn, but the chief ignored him. "One that will not work. Our best option is to get you far away."

Hanah took her hand before she could reiterate her question. "Where will we go, Karn? What of the clan?"

"L'non is fully capable of leading them, and there is a large contingency of slayers in Kannin. He'll be able to recruit more slayers to fill the gaps we leave." He looked to Kallar. "Or do I assume too much?"

Kallar nodded firmly. "I'm with you."

"I'm not." Eyes turned back to Alísa. "G—Graydonn isn't a threat to me."

"Are you so blind?" Karn snapped. "You *know* you are susceptible to their evil. You *know* what I speak of has happened before. You *know* I wouldn't leave the clan if I didn't think it absolutely necessary. Stop fighting me!"

"*You* stop fighting the truth! You're b—becoming like him" —she pointed savagely at Kallar— "blinded by your hatred. Perhaps it isn't the *dragons* I should guard against."

Alísa went rigid as the words echoed in her mind's ear. She wasn't sure which scared her more—that she said it, or that she meant it.

Karn's eyes were flames. "Don't you dare compare us, compare *me*, to them! They would take you away and use you. We're trying to save you."

"I don't n—n—n—"

"Calm down, sweetheart." Her mother placed a hand on her arm.

She twisted away, her throat closing up, her chest constricting. They weren't listening. They would never listen. They couldn't hear her.

She stood and ran out of the tent, ignoring her mother's call. She pushed on into the grove, past all the tents and stares and frowns. Who knew how much of the argument they had heard?

She pressed further until all sight of camp was gone before she finally allowed herself to breathe. She leaned against a tree, the rough bark digging into her palms.

It hadn't worked. They refused to believe her, their own daughter, and it stung to her very soul. If they wouldn't believe her, wouldn't even hear her, who would?

She trembled against the tree as the memory of Graydonn's words echoed in her head. *"You don't belong with them."*

"No!" she whispered fiercely. "I am a slayer. I am the daughter of the greatest chief the wayfaring clans have ever known. I belong with my people."

But did she? She, who had held the truth in the depths of her mind without even realizing it? She, whose father was too afraid to tell her why it was so?

"Alísa?" A soft, deep voice came from behind her.

Uncle. Alísa wiped her sorrows from her face and turned to see his concern. He must have seen her running, perhaps heard part of the argument.

Tension seized her as she remembered how she had used her powers the night before. She rose trembling to her feet, her chin lowered in respect. She couldn't take much more anger before her heart caved in, but she certainly deserved whatever L'non dealt her for this.

"I know what you did," he said simply. "You let the dragon go."

She nodded. The softness of his tone hurt as much as her father's harshness. L'non wasn't an outwardly emotional man, keeping his feeling firmly tucked inside his mind. Anything could be hiding behind the quiet. Anger. Disappointment. Betrayal.

He came closer. "I didn't realize what had happened until I was almost back at camp, when Kallar ran past me to get to you." He placed a hand under her chin and examined her cheek. "Was this him, or the dragon?"

"Him."

L'non nodded, taking his hand away. Anger flared past his defense only a second before he reined it back.

"Your empathy is strong."

She swallowed, looking down once more. "I'm s-sorry. I know it was w—wrong of me to use my p-p-power that way, but I thought I was serving the clan."

"I understand. You were wrong, but I understand."

Alísa studied his eyes. They too were soft. Gentle. So different than Kallar and Karn's reactions. Perhaps he could be convinced?

He pulled her into an embrace, causing tears to form in her eyes once more.

"Did I ever tell you about the time a dragon spoke to me?"

Her heart skipped a beat and she pulled back to look at him. "You t-too?"

"It happened a long time ago, when we still lived in Azron. The twins had just been born, so you must have been five or six at the time. Your father and I had seen two dragons nesting in a nearby mountain and knew we had to put a stop to it before a clan formed and threatened the village. We were young and foolish. Rather than wait for the wayfarers to come do the job, the two of us and our friend Palin decided to take them down alone, and we climbed the mountain."

He stared past her, eyes glazed over in memory. "We were about a mile from the cave when the male dragon noticed us. He was small, but quick. He zipped through the air faster than we could aim with weapons or telepathy, blasting us with fire on each pass. On one run, the fire hit Palin and consumed him. We tried to save him, but there was nothing we could do."

Alísa shuddered. There weren't many deaths worse than burning alive.

"Your father and I raged over Palin's death, and our anger fueled us so that on the next pass, we were able to wound the beast psychically. This slowed the dragon down until we were able to finish him off. We entered the cave. Unlike most animals, female dragons are relatively docile when they have eggs. Their bodies are weaker, and their telepathy is nearly nonexistent. She didn't stand a chance against us, and we mind-choked her together until she died. But near the end, she spoke to me, pleading with me for the life of her egg."

L'non had a faraway look in his eyes, and a tear glistened on the precipice but refused to fall.

"It was like my wife's voice. I could imagine the exact words coming from Elani in a desperate attempt to save our boys. And for a moment, I wondered if we were doing the right and honorable thing…"

Silence fell over them. Did L'non already understand what she did now? He still trained the boys against hatchlings, so how could he?

"D—do you think it was right? Or do you r—regret your decision?"

"This is war, Alísa," he said softly. "By our actions, we protect our families. I regret nothing but our stupidity that killed Palin."

He stopped and turned to her. "But I do know what it's like to have a dragon in your head. Those who say their voices are demonic are lying for dramatic effect. No. The true horror is that their voices are not so different from our own."

He placed a hand on her shoulder and gave a slight smile. "I understand why you did it. I'm not upset with you for one mistake made from confusion. I won't tell your father of your use of empathy, and the boys didn't catch on to what happened with the dragon, so no danger will arise from them. But learn from this, lest one day you find yourself in this position again with none to stand between you and the flames."

She nodded rapidly, trying to hide her quickening breaths and clenching heart. "Thank you, Uncle. I w——would like t-t-t-to be alone for a moment now."

He shook his head. "Your father asked me to watch over you, in case the dragons return."

"P-please." Her shoulders drooped. "Just stand back. I n——need to p-p-process."

He stared at her a moment before nodding. "Very well, but I won't let you out of my sight."

She nodded and he walked back to lean against a tree about fifty feet away. She turned her back to him and sank to the ground.

He knows, at least in part, yet he still hunts them! A sob wracked her body and she buried her face in her hands. *Graydonn was right—how can I belong with people who refuse to see the truth when it's right in front of them?*

She clenched blades of grass at her sides, keeping her head bowed. *Why did the Maker choose me to bear this burden alone? He could have chosen someone the clan would listen to—why not Papá or Kallar or Uncle—*

She shook her head and wiped the tears away. *But Uncle didn't see it. And so he chose me. For what, I don't know, but I know what I have to do.*

Alísa lifted her eyes and stood, pointing her boots to camp for the last time.

7

RUN

"You don't belong with them."

"Call to me, Singer, and I will answer."

The words stuck with Alísa in much the same way Farren's wisdom often did—words she kept coming back to as she worked throughout the day. Now, as she stuffed her day-pack beyond its intended capacity, they reverberated through her, drumming against her heart.

She had lived in fear among her own people for so long—fear of judgement, her future, insignificance. Now that she knew the judgement was wrong, the future could change, and somehow this curse of dragon empathy was truly a gift, new fears rose to the surface. Fear of the unknown, of being caught, of the creatures she had been conditioned to fear for so long.

Was this foolishness?

Probably.

Was it right?

Yes.

Alísa fingered her necklace as she surveyed her chamber in the last vestiges of the evening light. Her pack carried an extra set of clothes, rope, knife, wool blanket, food, water, and sewing kit, her precious song journal and graphite the only non-essentials. She would wear her cloak, with her short-sword and coin purse both on her belt. All she would truly leave behind were her bed-mat, furs, and about three more sets of clothing. A wayfarer's lifestyle didn't allow for many frivolous items, a runaway's even less so.

She pulled her necklace out to gaze at it. She should leave it behind too—it would be offensive where she was going, even dangerous. But how could she leave the most precious gift her father had ever given her? To leave it behind not only denied the slayers, but denied his love.

She stuffed it down the front of her shirt.

Her stomach fluttered nervously. She was doing it—running away and choosing to live completely by her own means and will, for better and for worse. No father to guide and protect her, no mother to check her work and support her, and no Kallar to control her.

"Alísa?" She jumped at her father's voice coming from beyond her chamber. "May I come in?"

She placed her bulging day-pack inside her main pack so it looked less conspicuous. She had actively avoided her parents and Kallar all day, but she couldn't avoid them now. Not if she wanted to make things seem normal. Not if she wanted one last evening with them.

"Yes."

He pulled the curtain aside and entered. His eyes were soft and his tone low.

"I wanted to apologize for my harshness last night and this morning. What you did was wrong, but so was my reaction. But you must understand, if other slayers find out what you did, they'll call for blood. Not *our* clan," he amended, "they wouldn't dare touch you. But most others would—it's that serious an offense."

Alísa nodded and lowered her eyes, feigning remorse.

"I'm afraid for you, my Lísa. I'm afraid that you're not. This isn't like the stories, where happy endings are tacked on to ease our hearts. No maiden has ever been recovered from the dragons."

Alísa looked up. "Not even Bria?"

He shook his head. "I've always hated the tale, a bard's romanticized story to deliver hope where there is none. If that dragon had taken you from me, I don't know what I'd do."

He stepped closer, opening his arms to her. With tears glistening in his eyes, she couldn't refuse him. She wrapped her arms around his waist, relaxing as his arms enfolded her. His love washed over her like water in a lake, refreshing her spirit, nearly drowning her resolve to run.

"Maker between you and harm," his voice cracked, "his hands a shield about you." He kissed her forehead at the end of his prayer, then pulled away quickly and left.

Hot tears sprang to her own eyes, her father's love and fear still palpable. *This is going to kill him. Kill Mamá. How can I do this? I can't do this!*

She lowered to the ground, face in her hands. *But if I don't, I'm stuck forever in a place I don't belong. Forever unsure, forever in pain, forever guilty.*

Her father's prayer for protection within the Maker's hands was one she had known since before she could remember. It was time to learn from someone who claimed the Maker had wings.

Alísa gathered her dark green cloak tighter around her neck and shivered against the warm, scratchy wool. It was colder than she had anticipated. The stars burned bright in a cloudless sky, while the half-moon cast its callous beams across the hills.

She silently made her way through the trees, avoiding the night watchmen who stood in the field scanning the astral skies for signs of their enemies. They wouldn't notice her, not unless her astral form decided to manifest the dragon inside her.

She shook her head at the thought. It wasn't a dragon inside her—merely a fire burning in the cause of truth.

Dragon-fire, perhaps?

She shook her head again. If the watchmen did see her astral form, they would assume she was going out to relieve herself. They wouldn't see the heavy bag slung over her shoulder, and she was too far away for them to sense her apprehension.

A twig snapped ahead of her and she froze, her heart first stopping, then racing. A watchman in the grove! But that didn't make sense—they couldn't see a dragon's astral form in the sky due to the leaves and branches above.

The nearest trees were too young and thin for her to hide behind, but perhaps they could hide her pack. It wasn't strange for her to be out here, after all, only to be carrying a bag. She placed the pack on the ground against a tree, summoned as much confidence as she could muster, and strode forward.

Her unexpected guest appeared out of the night—tall, lanky, and shivering from the cold.

"Alísa." Songweaver Farren nodded respectfully. "Terrible night for such excursions, I must say."

She smiled, willing her heart to settle. "At least it isn't raining."

His shoulders lifted in a chuckle. "Indeed."

His eyes fell from her face to her outfit and he squinted, his voice softening. "Heavy clothing for a quick relief."

He met her eyes once more and she fought to hold them.

"It's c-c-cold."

"And the sword?"

"I always t-take it at night," she lied. "Animals and highwaymen."

He nodded. "Yes, of course. Well, good night, my dear."

She dipped her head in return and resumed her steady walk. *Don't see the bag. Please, don't see it!*

"Alísa?"

She tensed, her chest constricting. She couldn't just run—her life was in that pack. She turned to face him as he held up her bag not twenty paces from her. His thick eyebrows pressed together, his voice barely a whisper.

"Where are you going?"

She pressed her lips together. It was his duty to alert her father. She had to knock him out before he could call. He wasn't a warrior, and she had basic training—she could succeed.

But she couldn't attack him. Not this man who had showed her compassion all her life.

"They know something about my connection to dragons," she whispered, stepping closer. "But they refuse to tell me anything. Instead, they want to take me away and keep me in the dark."

She stopped three paces away and held out her hand for the pack. "Please, Farren. I must seek the truth."

Farren fell quiet for a moment, then whispered back, "There's surely another way."

She smiled softly. He could have spoken up, alerting the watchmen to her presence, yet he whispered.

"Not here. I c—can't tell you much, but I found a piece of the truth. I have to follow it. I won't find it here."

He scrutinized her until his shoulders drooped. "But where will you— no. Don't tell me."

He dropped the bag and pulled her into a tight embrace. "I will miss you, dear one."

She relaxed against him. "I'll miss you too."

When she drew away, he gripped her arms and looked her in the eyes.

"Never run away, Alísa. The moment you do, fear will follow behind. Keep running *toward* the truth, and don't stop until you have it in your grasp. Then," he smiled, his eyes glistening, "come back and weave it for us."

At her firm nod, he bent down, grabbed her pack, and set it in her hands.

"Wait until the watchmen are distracted, then grab a horse."

Alísa blinked. "B—but they'll know you helped me."

"It isn't uncommon for me to encourage the watchmen in their long nights." He patted her shoulder and turned away. "Don't you worry about me."

Tears blurred Alísa's vision as she watched him go, heading for the field at an angle so it would look to the watchmen like he came from camp rather than the grove. *Not only letting me go, but helping me. What will my father do if he discovers it?*

She set her jaw and pivoted, blinking back tears until the world came back into focus.

Farren would do his part. Now she had to coax a horse without alerting the watchmen. She dug into her pack and found an apple, one of only two she had allowed herself to pack—one to coax the horse, and one as a reward at the end of her journey.

She shouldered her pack and stole to the edge of the grove, close enough to see the watchmen. The closest man was stationed about two hundred yards away. Farren already approached him.

She looked away from the watchman and further up the field. There were a few horses in that direction; the farther she could get from sight, the better.

Alísa crept along the edge of the grove, careful to avoid the twigs that had first alerted her to Farren's presence. Most of the horses she passed slept soundly, while a couple regarded her with little interest as they grazed. Finally, she found Sassy, who acknowledged her with a bob of her head and a blow of her lips. Even that quiet sound made Alísa tense, but a quick glance at the watchman showed Farren chatting with him amiably. Still, better to keep Sassy quiet.

Alísa breathed in deeply, imagining the cool night air as the soft dark green of peace. She pulled it into her and let it settle in her lungs, then blew it out slowly, simultaneously releasing her own calm into the air. She walked softly from the grove to the picket line, always breathing, always pressing. The horse blinked slowly. Too much more of this and Sassy would fall asleep.

She pulled the line and clicked quietly, holding the apple out and walking back into the cover of the trees. Sassy followed her quietly, her gentle footfalls hiding beneath the murmur of Farren's conversation with the watchman.

Maker bless him.

A few trees into the grove, Alísa gave the apple to Sassy and slowly reined in her empathy. The mare munched contentedly while Alísa mounted.

"Good girl," she whispered, patting Sassy's neck. "We've got a long journey tonight, you and I."

She kicked Sassy into a walk, fighting the urge to look back at camp one last time. At Trísse, who knew nothing of this plan. At Levan and Taer, who wouldn't understand why she left them. At her guaranteed future with protectors at her side.

A long journey, indeed.

They exited the grove on the north side, the trees still blocking the watchmen. They would continue north until they crested the first hill, then turn northwest once the watchmen couldn't see them. She would skirt the roads in a near straight-shot to Kannin, the village closest to the mountains where Graydonn's clan had gone. Then it was northeast on the seldom-trodden roads that marked the closest any human dared travel to the dragon-infested mountains. Northeast to Graydonn's mountain. Northeast to the most dangerous situation she had ever faced.

Northeast to the truth.

Miles of fields and hills opened up before Alísa as Sassy crested the hill. Now far out of view of the watchmen, the once-cold beams of moonlight became the Maker's provision—Eldra Reí lighting her way.

The snowy peak of Graydonn's mountain on her right glinted like diamonds, beckoning her to admire its strange and beautiful secrets. It lay perhaps forty miles away—she could conceivably reach the mountain before morning.

She shook her head and straightened. Walking into that situation with no sleep was far from wise. She would stick to the plan. Even accounting for the extra energy needed for the hills, Sassy could get her to Kannin before sunrise, leaving plenty of time to rest before her family discovered she was missing and got to Kannin themselves. They might not even find the tracks to point them to her. Best not to count on that, though.

Rustling grasses drew Alísa's eyes, but Sassy remained steady and calm. Just the wind. She would have to stay alert in case of wolves, but the mare would probably sense them before she did.

Alísa clicked her tongue and set Sassy into a trot. They wouldn't be able to keep up the faster pace for very long, but alternating between a walk and a trot would save some time. The sooner they reached Kannin, the sooner the wind would stop sending her heart racing.

She rubbed Sassy's neck as they slowed back to a walk. "Thank you for helping me tonight."

The mare bobbed her head as if she understood.

Alísa smiled. "What am I going to do with you when we reach the mountain? You certainly wouldn't be safe with dragons around."

Her chest tightened. "Of course, who knows if I'll be safe either. I think—no, I believe that I'll be safe with Graydonn. But the other dragons?" She sighed audibly. "Oh, what am I doing?"

Sassy swiveled her ears back as if to listen. Maybe Alísa *was* going mad, talking to a horse as if it were a person. But animals didn't interrupt, and talking eased her fear of every quivering blade of grass.

"Truth. I'm seeking truth. Graydonn knows something, something my family seems to know and won't tell me. I have to learn what makes me different. I can't just fade into the background like I'd planned anymore."

An owl hooted in the grove to their left, and Alísa glanced in that direction. Nothing but stillness.

"Maybe once I learn what I am, I can use it to help save innocents—human and dragon alike."

Sassy snorted and twitched her ears as another owl hooted in the distance.

She chuckled. "I know, a radical notion. Don't worry, I won't let the dragons eat you. I'll send you away long before I reach the mountain. You're smart enough to find your way back to a village on your own, right?"

Sassy swished her tail and began trotting without a command. A warning shot through Alísa at the unexpected change, and she opened her mind wider to gauge Sassy's emotions. Fear didn't sting her mind, but unease crept from the horse. Sassy changed course slightly, swinging wide of the grove to their left.

Where the first owl had been.

Hair rose on the back of her neck. Had it really been an owl?

"What's a pretty thing like you doing out here alone?"

The grinning male voice stopped her heart. *Highwayman!*

Alísa shouted to Sassy and they bolted into a gallop. Hoof-beats echoed behind them, sending her heart pounding against her ribs. He was pursuing her, and his horse was probably fresher than hers. But Sassy was used to battle and had stamina. There was no telling which would give out first.

Branni, help me! But would Branni even listen to his charge as she ran from his people? She wracked her brain for another of the Eldír to call for aid, but all names fled from her as a shadow reached for her.

She yanked Sassy's mane to the left as a second rider lunged for her arm. She threw a rapid glance to the grove on her right, where the men must have been waiting. Her eyes caught the second rider's and she tore them away, but not fast enough to avoid the intentions and emotions behind them.

Lust—for money, flesh, or blood, it didn't matter. It coursed through him, fueling him even as the chase did. It roiled her stomach and set jaws of fear clamping around her throat.

The unused names of Eldír still fled her mind. *Maker, please! Send someone! Anyone! Help me!*

Words spoken to her only the night before reverberated through her memory.

"Call to me, Singer, and I will answer."

Alísa shrieked as Sassy reared to avoid a third highwayman's horse as it leapt in front of them. She grasped at Sassy's mane and clamped down with her legs, trying desperately not to get thrown. The mare pivoted left and bolted from their pursuers.

"Call to me, Singer."

His mountain was too far away. He would never hear her. *Maker, send help!*

A sword glinted in the moonlight to her right from the first man. The third stayed on her left, Lust directly behind her. Her heart thudded against her chest.

"Call to me, Singer, and I will answer."

"Graydonn!"

8

FEAR'S FLAME

His name ripped from Alísa's throat in a long, desperate note, carrying through the night more like a song than a shout. One of the highwaymen laughed in response, or it might have been one of the horses stumbling.

A second glance to the man with the sword and she considered drawing her own. She could defend herself on the ground, but on a wildly-racing horse? Sweat seeped through Sassy's coat, making it harder for Alísa to grip—taking a hand off the mane to draw her weapon might be her undoing.

She pulled right as the swordsman slashed at Sassy, his weapon barely missing the mare's flank. Then a rough hand grabbed Alísa's right arm and yanked her from her seat.

Her scream cut short as the fall knocked the wind out of her. She couldn't even curl into a ball to try and avoid Lust's horse. It leapt over her in the darkness, then pulled to a stop alongside the others.

Get up! Move!

She pushed up with trembling arms, sucking in air. Her pursuers dismounted. Rough-Hands released a low chuckle as he strode closer, broad shoulders casting a deep shadow in the moonlight.

"Was that your husband you called for, sweetie?"

"The fool should know better than to let his lady ride alone." Lust's creaking voice came from the tallest of the men.

Alísa pushed her bag off her shoulder and forced herself to roll to her feet. Her right arm protested as she drew her sword, and she fought not to show her weakness.

"S-stay back!"

Swordsman stepped closer, his dark eyes staring at her over a hook-nose and amused smile. "I like a woman who can dance."

"Almost as much as one with a full coin-purse." Lust prodded her bag with his foot while Rough-Hands drew his sword.

Alísa's eyes darted from man to man. Her skills with a blade wouldn't be enough against three men, even two. She had been trained in defense, but almost always with the assumption that the other clanswomen would stand with her. She wasn't ready to be alone, and right now that's all she was. A lone, amateur swordswoman against three men who had chosen to make crime their living.

But she did have one weapon they didn't, and her state of heightened fear was just what she needed to utilize it. She grasped the terror pounding in her frantic heart and opened her mind wide, allowing it to flow from her in waves. Fear might cause her to make mistakes, but by using it against them, by taking it under her control, it just might slip them up too.

Swordsman lunged for her, aiming for her sword-hand. She parried, the clang of metal on metal ringing in the night and up her aching arm.

She re-gripped her sword in both hands—she wouldn't let herself go down easily.

Swordsman struck again, while Rough-Hands circled to her right. She blocked the attack and backed up a step, turning to keep both attackers in her line of vision. Then she lunged for Swordsman, pressing fear harder as he parried.

A tremor passed through him as he held her back. She pushed him away and pivoted to block Rough-Hands' swing at her side. His strength rattled up her arms, but his attack was clumsier than Swordsman's. She might be able to take him down and scare the others off long enough to get away.

Maybe. If she could steal one of their horses—Sassy was long gone now.

Fighting back tremors of fear, she swung at Rough-Hands. He parried and she pulled back quickly to attack again, unwilling to get into a test of strength. She pushed terror with her next swing, making his block clumsier. A quick second attack sliced the bicep of his free arm, drawing a curse from his lips.

She drew her sword back to swing again, but strong arms pinned her arms to her stomach before she could. She grunted and twisted in Lust's grasp, stamping the ground and trying to find his foot. He used his considerable height to lift her off the ground and stifle her attempts. Alísa let go of her sword with her left hand and dug her nails into one of his arms.

FEAR!

She surged it through the skin-contact as hard as she could, wrenching a yelp from his lips. He dropped her, and she stumbled as she tried to catch her balance. She pivoted and swung her sword to hit Lust in the gut, but Swordsman parried, nearly knocking her sword from her hand as he stopped her momentum like a rock wall.

Lust rubbed his arm and laughed. "Well, a slayer wench." His smile turned wicked. "Two can play that game."

There was no time to process before he struck with a psychic arrow to her mind. She screamed as it bored into her, barely noticing as she dropped her sword.

"Branni, help me!"

She reined in her empathic powers, trying to form any barrier she could against the attack. Hatred seethed in her heart—Lust was a slayer, a psychic who should be protecting the innocent, not preying on them! This man, this monster, was exactly why wayfarers took first-generation slayers from their parents and gave them a home with their own kind. They trained these boys, too confused and frightened by their powers to do good by them, and made them into honorable men.

But this man had never learned the code of the slayers, or else had turned from it. He had no honor, using his powers only to inflict pain and to take from others.

Lust pressed the attack, now clawing at her private thoughts and memories. Rough-Hands held her tightly around her waist, making her acutely aware of how badly she was shaking. No help was coming, no shining Eldra would appear to protect his runaway charge from the beast in front of her.

"Graydonn!"

The cry surprised her, once again ripping from her throat in a sustained note rather than a shout. Lust clucked his tongue as he rifled through her memories of just a few hours earlier.

"Slim pickings in that bag of yours."

Alísa jerked away as he ran a knuckle over her cheek, her insides clenching.

"Guess we'll have to find another way to make our trouble worth—"

An earth-shaking roar cut off his words. Then fire rained from the skies, engulfing Swordsman in its hungry blaze. Swordsman shrieked, the sound carrying into the night, then silencing just as quickly, his charred remains tumbling into the grass. The sight sent a chill through Alísa's veins.

Graydonn?

Rough-Hands dropped Alísa and took off, Lust directly behind him. They barely made it twenty yards when scales like storm-clouds blocked their path. The ground quaked as an eight-foot dragon landed in front of them.

Not Graydonn! Alísa stumbled as she tried to stand, her heart pounding, her body covered in cold sweat.

Another blaze from the attacking dragon's maw. Another chorus of screams from the highwaymen. Another deathly silence.

Then fiery yellow eyes trained on her. Her heart pounded into her throat. The horses were long gone, and the grove far behind her.

There was nowhere to run.

A shadow flew over her. *"Alísa!"*

Graydonn.

Shining amber eyes appeared as he landed between her and the gray dragon. He was half the other dragon's size, but perhaps he could save her, distract the dragon who'd just slaughtered the highwaymen without a second thought. Not that she felt sorry for them, but as the putrid scent of burnt flesh wafted into her nostrils and their screams repeated incessantly in her mind's ear, everything within her screamed she was next.

Graydonn came closer, ignoring the other dragon. His shining eyes dimmed as his concern cascaded over her in waves.

"Are you okay?"

That undid her. Sobs wracked her body as she released all the terror and sorrows of the last few days. Her chest heaved, and she wrapped her arms around her knees.

"You're safe, Alísa. No one's going to hurt you anymore."

His tone was so sincere, and his intentions set off no alarms, but she couldn't will her heart to settle. She was alone, by her own choice, and it had nearly gotten her killed. She would be dead if it weren't for Graydonn and this other violent dragon, one who could snuff her as easily as it had her attackers. Her blood pounded in her ears and her throat constricted as tears streamed from her eyes.

She should never have left.

Graydonn's concern became alarm. *"You're losing water through your eyes."*

"Are you sure this is the one, Graydonn?"

Koriana. Her name accompanied her voice like a light, unique scent, just like Graydonn's had. Her tone was low and skeptical, but not menacing, not like Alísa had expected from a dragon who had just destroyed three men.

"You'll hear it in her voice," Graydonn replied, though he kept his eyes on Alísa. *"Your fear is so strong. I can help you—do you trust me?"*

Did she trust him?

She had left in hopes that he would help her, and the only thing she had known for sure was that he wasn't her enemy. But now? Now that his eyes illuminated her in otherworldly light, now that the smoky stench of burnt flesh filled her nostrils, now that the moonlight shone off horns, spines, talons, and even a couple of teeth overlapping his lower jaw—

Did she trust him?

What other choice did she have?

"Yes."

Graydonn took a slow step, then another, until he was close enough to touch. Alísa trembled as he stretched his neck out to her, and when he pressed his muzzle to her forehead—

Peace.

Beautiful, powerful peace poured from him, ceasing the rush in her heart, the pounding in her ears, the trembling in her muscles. The only things it didn't stop were her tears, now sliding gently down her cheeks in relief.

"You are safe."

No doubts lingered in her mind, no nagging feeling that he was trying to trick her. Only the soft, dark green of peace. She breathed it in, letting it settle in her lungs, then breathed it back out as if it were her own. It *was* her own now, outweighing her fear.

Graydonn pulled away, and Alísa opened her eyes and smiled gently.

"Thank you, my friend," she whispered.

Bright yellow eyes blinked behind him. Alísa swallowed.

"Who is that?"

"My mother."

The strong maternal instinct she had felt the night before rose in her memory. This was the dragon whose love had spurred her to action. Not a monster, not a beast, but a mother.

A flame of fear still burned inside her, but she forced herself to her feet. She would have to get used to fighting fear among these new acquaintances of hers, letting go of all the lies and seeing past scaly hides to the *anam* within. To the friend who had come to her aid. To the mother doing everything she could to protect her son. Maybe one day she would no longer feel the fear, but until then, she had to keep moving.

Alísa stepped past Graydonn, willing herself to hold Koriana's burning gaze. "Thank you, K—K—Koriana, for s-saving my life."

The eyes blinked out and in again, slower this time, while a sliver of gratitude rippled. *"You saved my son. Though when he told me of the brave slayer woman who fought her people to aid his escape, you are not what I pictured."*

Alísa blinked. The dragoness' tone carried no aggression or mockery, merely an honesty seldom heard from humankind. Here, Koriana spoke her mind with no filters—simultaneously refreshing and off-putting.

"Why do you cower before those you called to your aid?"

"I told you, Mother, she doesn't know what she is. I doubt she even expected us to answer." Graydonn pawed the ground like an excited wolf pup. *"But you hear it too, don't you?*

Koriana looked Alísa over. *"I feel something, certainly. It's what I hear that worries me."*

Again, the words carried no scorn, but they stung. Alísa raised her hand to where her necklace should have been, then remembered it hid beneath her shirt. She gripped her upper arms instead, fingering the wool of her sleeves as she struggled with what to say next.

"I don't know what I am. All I know is I feel dragon emotions when n—no one else d-d-does." Alísa glanced between the dragons. "My father knew something, but refused t—t-to tell me. Will you tell me the t—t—t" —*breathe*— "t-t-truth?"

The glow of Koriana's eyes softened from blazing heat to warmth. *"Yes, little one. We owe you much—I will not keep the truth from you. I only hope the knowledge will help you rise to your high calling. But first, we fly. I cannot stand the stench of these serpents any longer."*

Venom laced the dragoness' words as she looked on the smoldering remains. *"May those who prey on the innocent never be mourned."*

Graydonn thumped his tail on the ground behind Alísa, agreement flowing from his mind. Alísa nodded once, silently. She certainly wouldn't mourn them.

"Come, little one." Koriana padded to her, and Alísa forced herself not to step back. The dragoness lowered to her belly and lifted the wing closest to Alísa.

Thrill and terror ran down Alísa's spine. An invitation to ride. Had a human ever ridden a dragon before? What if she fell? What if she dropped her pack? *Where is my pack?*

"D—do either of you see my p-p-p-p-p-p" —*breathe, redirect*— "my b-bag?"

Concern wafted from Koriana. *"Do you always do that? That stumbling?"*

Alísa tensed. Heat rose to her cheeks, while her throat tightened. She could barely manage a nod.

Graydonn prodded something on the ground with his nose. *"Here it is."*

She hurried to the pack, retrieving and sheathing her sword on the way, grateful to have something else to focus on besides the dragoness' insensitivity. She could feel Koriana's eyes on her as she shouldered her pack, and she hesitated to face her again.

"My query was not meant to be offensive. I merely wish to know what we're working with. The human voice is foreign to me."

Alísa pressed her lips together. Of course. Dragons spoke with their minds. They probably didn't know how personal her voice was, or how terrible it felt when it betrayed her every day. She could forgive ignorance.

She looked Koriana in the eye and forced a small smile to her lips. "It d—doesn't happen when I whisper. Or when I sing."

Alísa jumped as Graydonn made a guttural thrumming sound behind her, accompanied by the sweet tang of amusement. Was that the dragon equivalent of a laugh? Why was her statement funny?

Koriana's eyes brightened. *"Well then. Let us fly, Singer."*

Alísa blinked. "Graydonn c-c-called me that before. Why—"

"I promise, all will be explained at the cave. Step onto my muzzle and I'll lift you to my back."

Alísa breathed in slowly and let it out. *Right.* Her fear returned the closer she got to Koriana's large, angular face. Her head was easily three feet long from nose to ears—she could snap a human in two with those powerful jaws.

But she won't. I can do this.

She placed a foot on Koriana's muzzle, carefully putting weight on it before grasping one of the two-foot spines running down the ridge of the dragoness' back. Koriana lifted her head smoothly until Alísa could swing a leg over her back and settle between two of the spines.

A comforting heat radiated from the scales as Koriana breathed, each expansion of her chest allowing warmth to seep through the cracks in her armor. It combatted the cold of night and emanated a pleasant oily scent, tinged lightly with smoke. Alísa grasped the spine in front of her, her fingers easily gripping the slight ridges.

Koriana faced front as Graydonn took off. *"Stay low and hang on tightly."* Then the dragoness gathered her legs beneath her and launched.

9

WITHIN THESE WALLS

Alísa bit back a shriek as Koriana vaulted into the night sky. Her stomach dropped and she closed her eyes against the stinging wind, gripping Koriana tightly as each wing-stroke jolted them higher. The air yanked at her cloak, allowing the harsh chill of night to seep through her skin.

Would the whole flight feel like this? How long could she hold on?

Seconds felt like minutes until Koriana ended their ascent and Alísa dared to open her eyes. The dragoness' massive wings stretched in a steady glide under the gently-twinkling stars.

Alísa unclenched her aching jaw and exhaled softly as the ride smoothed. Cold air rushed past her, chilling and vitalizing. Koriana flapped her wings again, but the motions were smaller now, just enough to keep them at a steady altitude.

The land passed beneath them so quickly—hills, groves, and a lake, all barely illuminated by the moon. The tiny lights of torches shimmered from Kannin far to their left. Before them lay the mountain, its snowy cap sparkling, almost inviting.

How strange to think that way about the home of her family's enemies.

Alísa slowly loosened the steel grip of her left hand and spread her arm wide over Koriana's moonlit wing. She giggled as the wind caught under her arm.

She was flying! She had always dreamed of it, and now she was doing it!

A change in the wind drew a gasp and sent Alísa's hand back to the spine as the dragoness course-corrected. Maybe now wasn't the time to fling her arms wide and pretend she was the one doing the flying.

Alísa shivered against the wind and carefully took a hand off the spine once more, this time grabbing the flailing corner of her cloak. She tucked it over her thigh, then did the same with the other side, creating a better shield against the chill. Now only her face and hands felt cold, but that couldn't be helped.

"Get low," Koriana's voice entered her mind. "It will be much easier to get into the cave if no one sees you."

Alísa stared at the spine in her hands. *How on A'dem am I supposed to get low with these spines?*

"Do what you can."

Alísa tensed at the dragoness hearing her thoughts. Would it always be like this, never having a private thought again?

"I heard you because I'd already established a telepathic connection for you to hear me. And the particular thought I heard was quite loud." Koriana vibrated with a thrum, amusement rising as it had when Graydonn made the same sound. "We will work on telepathy later; for now, get low. I will do all I can on my end."

Alísa shook her head and scooted back against the spine behind her. She leaned against the other spine as far as she could, then reached up to pull her dark hood over her hair. If she ducked her head low enough, she could keep the wind from yanking the hood off.

Problem is, now I can't see.

A dragon roared nearby and she shivered.

Then again, maybe that's a good thing.

Minutes passed in tenuous silence, with only the sound of wings and the wind as her company. Then the wing-strokes sped, beating against their forward momentum and slowing them until Koriana skidded to a stop.

"It's safe now," Koriana said softly. "You may sit up."

Alísa pulled back her hood, her breath catching as she straightened.

A tunnel of ice glinted all around her, illuminated by a warm orange glow in the chamber ahead. The light bounced off the sparkling tunnel and shimmered across the scales of her companions. The dripping of water echoed through the tunnel, a counterpoint to the soft padding of the dragons' feet. Comfort and calm rippled from them.

This was home.

Feelings of safety and warmth clouded in around Alísa, the emotions drawing up images. Kneading flatbreads with her mother. Her father's cloak over her shoulders. The furs of her chamber. All things that weren't truly here, in a dragon's home. All things she may never see again.

They entered a chamber wide enough for two adult dragons with wings spread. Dripping stalactites speared from the icy ceiling, though none stretched low enough for Alísa to duck, even on Koriana's back. The glittering walls caught and spread the light of a glowing bed of hot stones against the back wall. A large lump of polished onyx only a little smaller than her torso rested in the midst of the stones. Where had they found such a stone?

Koriana lowered to her belly and Alísa slid down the dragoness' shoulder, slipping on the icy floor as she landed. Padding over to the hot stones, Koriana pulled the onyx forward with a scaly forepaw, then laid against an icy wall, her tail curling around the stone.

The maternal instinct from last night returned, this time a gentle warmth rather than the desperate heat of when she came to rescue Graydonn.

"Is that an egg?"

Koriana's eyes gentled. *"I suppose you've never seen a dragon egg before, have you?"*

Alísa shook her head, fighting back thoughts of the bits of eggshells warriors occasionally brought back. It wouldn't do for the dragons to read her mind and see that.

Then again, could they see it merely because of her fleeting thought? Who knew how much of her thoughts the dragons could see? How deep did their telepathy go?

"You may come touch it."

Could Koriana sense how badly Alísa wanted to do so? To feel the warmth and life of the hatchling inside the egg? To forget the way her clan murdered the precious little ones to prevent human deaths?

Her uncle's words echoed in her mind: 'This is war, Alísa.'

Could they see that too?

"Alísa?" Graydonn snapped her out of her thoughts. He stood beside her now, his neck arched around to look her in the eyes. *"Your mind is racing."*

Alísa shivered. "C—can you s-see why?"

He snorted slightly, sending a puff of vapor through the cold chamber. He didn't answer beyond that. Was that a no? What did dragon sounds and body-language mean?

"Alísa?"

She rubbed her temples. "It's j—just so much. I c-c-c-c-can't—"

"We haven't even told you anything yet."

"Exactly. I'm c—c—confused and lost and" —she forced in a trembling breath— "and I'm afraid."

She blinked back tears. Everything was happening too fast. It was her fault, to be sure—she had no right to complain about it—but she needed to slow down. *But how can I do that here? Trapped on a mountain with two of the enemy who aren't* my *enemies?*

"Do you want my help to calm down again?"

Yes. Desperately yes. But what if that was a crutch, one that would make her dependent? Or what if he was tricking her into feeling safe, when she actually wasn't? How could she ever know for sure?

"What's one thing we can tell you?" Graydonn said gently. *"What's the most important thing for you to know right now that will help you feel safe?"*

She shivered, the cold of the cave seeping into her bones and heart. Graydonn was wise—she just needed to focus on one thing at a time. But what? She wanted to know what she was, but right now that wasn't the question making her afraid.

"Tell me about dragon t-t—telepathy. Can you see all of my thoughts? Do you only c—c—communicate with telepathic words, or d—do your vocalizations have word-equivalents?" She blew out her breath in a rush. "How do I understand you?"

Graydonn blinked slowly, double-eyelids sliding smoothly over the dark, reptilian slit of his pupil. *"Come. Sit beside me, and we will explain."*

He ambled to his mother and laid down, facing Koriana. Alísa followed, breathing deeply to slow her heart-rate. She glanced at the egg curled in Koriana's tail before turning away. It still called to her, but the need for understanding called far louder.

She settled to the ground beside Graydonn's foreleg. Heat radiated from him, deep and inviting so close to the icy walls. She rubbed her forearms and met his eyes. Nothing dangerous glinted there, nothing that warned her against leaning into the warmth.

"Do you mind if I s-sit closer?"

"No. Please, warm up."

Alísa gave him a soft smile, but kept her eyes on his as she scooted back, watching for any hint of offense as she settled just behind his foreleg. Her back warmed instantly, making the rest of her feel that much colder. She pulled off her cloak and tucked herself against him once more, using the garment as a blanket. His chest expanded behind her with each breath, bathing her in blissful warmth. If she weren't so alert with fear, she might easily fall asleep.

"Thank you."

Graydonn made a clicking sound in his throat, slightly reminiscent of a cat's purr. *"You're welcome."*

Koriana arched her neck to see Alísa, intelligence shining in her eyes. *"I suppose the most important thing for you to know, little one, is that we cannot see all of your thoughts, even when we are connected for speech. You would feel a difference if we pushed deeper—a higher pressure, perhaps pain. As it is, I can only hear words you deliberately send to me, and sometimes very loud thoughts. Your deeper thoughts and memories are safe within your mind."*

Alísa nodded. Like the difference between her father searching her memories and Kallar speaking directly to her mind.

"Since most female slayers can't focus their psychic powers beyond empathy into telepathy, you cannot create a connection to send us thoughts and words on your own. But, if we initiate the connection, we will hear your words with our own telepathy."

Graydonn shifted, bringing his head around to look at Alísa. *"Do you want to try it? It would probably be easier for you than verbal speech."*

Alísa winced. Were all dragons so honest?

"I'm sorry. I've offended you."

She pressed her lips together. "I f—forgive you. It's just, a human's voice is v—very p-personal. Important. And mine is—"

Alísa swallowed. It hurt to say the words.

"Mine is b—broken. It's like my heart has so much that it wants t—to say, but when the words try to come out, my throat grabs them. Holds them c-c-c-captive. Then, when the words eventually c-c-come, their meaning remains c-c-caught. It takes work and p—patience to understand. It's far easier for people t-to ignore."

Steam huffed from Graydonn's nostrils. *"Seems to me like the problem lies with those listening, not with you."*

Alísa gave him a humorless smile. "Not in their minds."

She shook her head to clear it of the shifting eyes, clearing throats, and waves of dismissal. Now wasn't the time to feel sorry for herself.

"Okay. How do I speak in my mind s-so you can hear it?"

Koriana's eyes brightened. *"Look at the astral plane."*

Alísa closed her eyes, focusing until she saw Koriana's yellow form nearly burning with its brightness, while Graydonn's duller amber form radiated warmth. A rope of shimmering light extended from their heads and reached for her, glowing with their respective astral colors. Another rope connected Graydonn and Koriana, glowing a shining gold blend of their two colors.

"Those tether-lines show we are already connected to you, so you can hear our words. Now, imagine sending your own words to us through the lines."

Alísa shut her eyes tighter and focused on the line between her and Koriana. *"Like this?"*

"You're muffled," Koriana said. *"Be stronger, more deliberate."*

Alísa pictured a bird flying from her head to Koriana's. *"How about now?"*

"Better."

"And Graydonn? Can he hear me too?"

"I can." He patted his tail against the cave floor. *"Since we're all connected, both of us will hear your words."*

Koriana's eyes brightened as a hint of surprise seasoned the chamber. *"It seems you're a natural—you will get along just fine among dragons."*

Alísa pressed her lips together. Did they expect her to stay? Did she want to stay? The thought of living with her family's enemies made her stomach clench with guilt. But a warmth filled her heart here, a feeling of home just as real and strong as in her family's tent. *How can this be?*

Her eyes landed on the egg once more and she studied the shiny oval. Though Graydonn's warmth remained blissful, a nagging urge drew her to the egg. She had seen so many broken eggshells, watched so many hatchling murders—the need to meet the little life called to her.

She glanced at Koriana. *"May I see her now?"*

"Yes." Koriana cocked her head. *"But I never told you her sex."*

Alísa shrugged. *"I just had a feeling."*

She stood, pulling her warm cloak back around her shoulders, and walked to Koriana's side. She knelt beside the great gray tail and Koriana uncurled it slightly, revealing the full size of the egg, about a foot-and-a-half long and a foot in diameter.

Alísa ran a hand over the glossy surface. Her fingers caught on tiny imperfections, divots in the surface. It radiated warmth, much like Graydonn and Koriana, calling her to place a second hand on its surface.

A feeling washed over her, a memory of when Alísa had gotten separated from her parents in the village when she was very little. Sadness, confusion, abandonment. Did it come from the hatchling?

Alísa looked between the gray dragoness and her green son. *"Is this your egg, Koriana?"*

"No. An egg must match one of its parents' colors. My mate D'lann was green, like our son."

Deep sorrow emanated from Koriana at the mention of her mate, wrenching Alísa's heart beyond the hatchling's feelings. That a dragon so great and strong could feel such sorrow proved her eternal soul even more.

"I'm sorry." She carefully rested a hand on the dragoness' flank. *"I was there when he was killed. He was a strong, brave dragon. It took three slayers to bring him down, and he protected Graydonn till the end."*

Graydonn nuzzled Koriana's cheek, and their combined grief shot through Alísa. They loved him so, and he had done nothing to deserve death at the hands of her clan. Tears threatened at the corners of her eyes, but she pushed against the dragons' sorrow threatening to take her.

If only the war could end! But who could stand between the races and be heard? There was no such person, human or dragon, and so the suffering of the innocent continued.

"Thank you for your kind words." Koriana's eyes softened. *"To answer your question, this egg belonged to a friend. She was killed when she came with me to free Graydonn. Her telepathy hadn't recovered enough to protect herself, but she came with*

me all the same. Her mate is Crakil, the clan's beta dragon, and he has no inclination to tie himself to an egg or a hatchling, so I took the responsibility upon myself."

Alísa looked to the egg again. *"Does the hatchling know her mother is gone?"*

"Dragonet," Koriana corrected. *"She hasn't hatched yet. And yes, she does. Dragons form a deep bond with their mother even in the egg. She misses her."*

Alísa reached out to the dragonet with her mind. She pushed peace and tranquility, but only lonely sadness returned. Her heart twisted in her chest. One so young shouldn't feel such grief.

She shut her eyes against the tears. There had been so many hatchlings she hadn't been able to help, and she wanted so desperately to help this one. She would help this one. As the dragonet's emotion continued to build inside of her, one of her mother's lullabies broke through her lips.

> Hush now, peace now, though the darkness falls.
> Peace now, sleep now, safe within these walls.

Her cheeks flushed as she sang—what a strange thing to do suddenly and unbidden. But to stop once she had already started would be stranger, so she pressed on.

> Though the daylight ends and fades into the night,
> Love will keep you safe, and hope will be your light.
> Morning soon will come, the sun will heal all,
> So sleep, my darling child, safe within these walls.

Sadness faded to sleep inside the egg, and Alísa's own heart stilled.

"There you go," she whispered, stroking the shell. "We'll make it through this, you and I."

Deep, contented breathing drew Alísa's eyes to Koriana and Graydonn. Their heads rested on the ground, their long necks arched so they pressed against each other.

Sound asleep—they must have been exhausted.

Now that I think about it, so am I. She stretched and yawned before reaching to the egg once more. Koriana's tail didn't hold the egg quite as securely as she had before. How warm did the egg need to stay? Should she wake Koriana and ask?

A glance at the toothy face sent that idea tumbling down the mountainside. No waking the dragons. She would keep the egg warm.

Alísa hefted the egg into her lap and scooted back to Graydonn. She wouldn't sleep against him—he would surely crush her if he tossed and turned—but she came close enough to gain some warmth. She took off her cloak and laid it on the ground as a barrier from the ice. Then she pulled the blanket from her pack, covered herself and her little charge, and nested the egg with her body.

She breathed slowly, surrounded by the dragons' peaceful sleepiness. Tomorrow would be filled with more questions and uncertainties, but for now she would sleep as a friend of dragons.

10

FLIGHT

Alísa dreamed of angry dragons, of tooth and talon and flame, and of dodging one only to be threatened by another. She awoke as a dream-dragon's roar threw her into the mountainside, and opened her eyes to a green, toothy face.

She pushed up and away with a yelp, only to collide with a wall of scales. Anger, discord, and unrest surrounded her, and she raised her hands up in defense.

"Alísa, it's me."

Graydonn. Her friend. She breathed in slowly to calm her rattled nerves.

A roar shook the cave, and Graydonn shot a concerned look to the entrance tunnel. He opened his mouth in neither snarl nor smile, perhaps preparing to use fire?

She sat up and held the egg to her stomach. "W—what's happening?"

"Speak with your mind. Your voice will only agitate them more."

"'Them?'" She shut her mouth. *"Sorry. What's going on?"*

"You are, Singer. I'm sorry. We should have told you last night—would have told you, if you hadn't sung us to sleep."

Alísa's heart pounded into her throat as Koriana's growls echoed through the chamber. She clutched the egg more tightly.

"Please, Graydonn, what's happening?"

"There was a better way to tell you. A story to inspire you, a plan, but—"

A flash of fire blasted past Koriana, melting pieces of the tunnel. Graydonn moved between the tunnel and Alísa, a low growl escaping his throat.

"*You are a Dragon Singer, Alísa, and a powerful one. You put us to sleep with your lullaby last night, and apparently the rest of the dragons within earshot slept too. When the alpha woke, he knew you were here——*"

"*Graydonn!*" Koriana's voice pitched higher than before. "*We only have one shot to get her out of here—get her ready, now!*"

The desperation in Koriana's voice nearly undid Alísa. Her limbs were lead, her lungs stone.

Too much. This was all too much.

Graydonn looked her in the eye, confidence shining in his own.

"*You are special, Alísa. You can end the war. This alpha and most of his clan would use your powers to destroy both slayers and innocents, and they would probably kill you in the end. My mother and I want only to save dragonkind from the slayers. We will take you far from here, where this alpha and your father cannot get to you, and we will teach you. But you must come with us now.*"

He pressed his muzzle to her forehead as he had the night before, but no empathic power escaped him. She couldn't feel anything from him—impossible unless he was purposefully holding back.

"*Please, Singer. I am not trying to trick or control you. You came because you wanted to know the truth. This is it, and we will tell you more. But now there is no time. Now you must trust us or face the hate-filled dragons outside.*"

Alísa breathed in a trembling breath and nodded. "*What do I have to do?*"

His eyes brightened. "*Empty your pack—you will carry the egg so that mother and I are free to use our talons.*"

Alísa scurried to her pack, shivering in clothing dampened by sleeping on the icy floor. She shoved back the questions pounding in her heart—delay would get them killed.

Heart twisting, she dumped the contents of her bag on the cave floor. The egg would fit, but little else. Food, blanket, clothing, rope, journal—what was most important?

Another roar, answered by Koriana. Her hands trembled with cold as she rolled the egg gently into the pack. Flying on Koriana's back would be even colder. She had to get out of these clothes.

"*Graydonn, turn around.*"

"*Why?*"

"I need to put on different clothes."

He snorted. *"This is hardly the time for fashion."*

She glared at him. *"These clothes are wet—I'm going to freeze if I fly, now turn around!"*

Graydonn's eye-ridges raised. *"Right. No fire to warm you. Hold still."*

He stretched his neck until he was directly in front of her and opened his mouth. Teeth and the glow of fire sent her heart racing.

"Wait!"

Hot, dry air streamed from his mouth, coursing through her damp garments and caressing her shivering form. She relaxed her shoulders, tight from cold, and closed her eyes. Even the smell of his breath was far more pleasant than she had anticipated.

"Did you really think I was going to breathe fire?" Incredulity filled his tone. *"When have I ever hurt you?"*

"You try being at the mercy of someone bigger than you and full of sharp, pointy things."

Graydonn hummed in his throat as the hot air faded. *"I suppose if you had the strong telepathy of a male slayer, I might feel the same about you. They haunt my nightmares now like they never have."*

A chill settled in Alísa's heart, though her clothes were now perfectly dry and warm. Graydonn understood what it meant to fear harm from another race—his father was gone, thanks to her people. She reached a hand for his muzzle.

"I'm sorry."

He pressed his nose to her hand, then pulled back sharply as another roar came from the tunnel.

"Finish packing. Hurry."

Alísa stuffed her blanket around the egg and examined the pack's former contents. She grabbed her extra set of clothes and pulled them on. The sewing kit and sheathed knife each fit uncomfortably into her boots, and she slid her song journal and water-skin into the bag.

She left the food on the cave floor. Accompanied by dragons, she would at least have meat to fill her belly. She slung the rope and bag over her head so the strap crossed her chest. Hopefully that would keep the bag from falling in the aerial battle they were about to face.

"*I'm ready.*"

A skitter of talons echoed from the tunnel. Koriana roared and snapped her jaws.

"*It's about time,*" the dragoness said. "*Graydonn, guard the front and be ready to fly. I will bear the Singer.*"

'Singer.' The word echoed in Alísa's mind as the dragons switched places. What troubles lay ahead of her due to that title? What did it even mean?

Koriana lowered herself to the floor at Alísa's side, eying the rope.

"*Will that fit around my neck and you?*"

Alísa grabbed it and threw one end over the base of Koriana's neck. "*I think so.*"

"*Do not get used to the rope. I am no beast of burden to be strapped. But avoiding the other dragons may call for quick acrobatics, and a fall will be fatal.*"

Alísa winced, her shaking fingers hindering her efforts to tie the ends of the rope in a good, strong knot. Then she reached for a spine and pulled herself up.

Once she had settled, she lifted the rope over her head so that it pressed against her back and held her to the spine in front of her. It wasn't the most secure method of tying herself to the dragoness, but it was better than nothing.

"*Hold on for the ride of your life.*"

Light flooded the tunnel as Graydonn flew out with a roar. Koriana ran after him, each step jolting Alísa harder than any horse's trot. Then they launched into the glaring morning sky.

Flames leapt from the mouths and nostrils of raging dragons. Alísa gritted her teeth and pushed against their anger as it burned like fire in her mind.

Three—no, four of them pursued Koriana with roars and snapping jaws, but all eyes trained on Alísa.

A great black dragon roared, drawing Alísa's gaze to his flame-orange pupils. Alísa looked away quickly, but his voice came through strong.

"*Join us now, Bria-born, or be destroyed!*"

Crakil. Alísa started and met the beta dragon's eyes. *Bria again?*

Power and authority bored from his eyes and wrapped a vice-grip around Alísa's heart. Her every muscle tensed as an impulse to jump shot through her and pulsed with every heartbeat. The tether-line between them spoke of safety, that he would catch her and give her a place of honor in their clan, but her empathy felt only hatred and violence.

"Jump, Singer!"

She sucked in a ragged breath, struggling against the compulsion, but she couldn't tear her eyes from his piercing gaze.

"Jump!"

A flash of green slammed into Crakil, breaking the dragon's hold and allowing Alísa to twist away. She regained her steel grip on Koriana's spine and breathed. *That* was what it felt like for a dragon to try and control a person, what her father feared Graydonn had done to her.

A roar of pain called Alísa's eyes to Graydonn, her rescuer, just as Crakil's talon ripped through the edge of Graydonn's wing. Graydonn fell from his grasp and twisted as he tried to right himself. Fire filled Alísa as Koriana roared and banked hard.

"Hang on, Singer. He will pay dearly for that!"

Alísa's knuckles turned white as Koriana dodged another dragon with incredible agility, then speared into Crakil. Alísa shrieked as the collision nearly sent her flying from her seat.

Koriana grappled with the beta dragon, clawing at his neck as they fell from the sky. Alísa grasped the bag to her side to keep it closed, her heart pounding like thunder against her ribs.

Koriana bellowed as Crakil landed a taloned blow just below her eye, and Alísa cried out with her. Above them, Graydonn caught himself and plowed into another dragon coming to assist Crakil. Other dragons trumpeted with alarm as they plummeted to the ground.

This is how I die.

Koriana latched her talons in Crakil's wing and yanked, spraying blood into the sky. With mighty shoves of her wings that burned with effort in Alísa's mind, Koriana twisted in the air until Crakil was underneath her. Then she pushed off him and rose out of her fall.

"East, Graydonn," Koriana shouted.

Graydonn banked, his wings pummeling the air. The other dragons paid him no heed as they dove to catch their commander. Koriana pointed her muzzle down, breathing a long, slow stream of fire just underneath her. Her wings caught the heat, and with powerful strokes buoyed by hot air, she rose quickly.

"You're about to gain a flight-partner, Singer."

Alísa looked up as they ascended to Graydonn. *"Won't that slow you down?"*

"By our combined wing-strokes, we will not slow. He will carry his weight, and I will push us forward. We'll stay very near my top speed and allow him a small reprieve."

Koriana continued her ascent until Graydonn rested on her back. He gripped the base of her wings with his forelegs, his head reaching just past Alísa. Graydonn flapped his wings in near-perfect sync with his mother, though his injured wing did not rise quite as high as the other. Though his pain throbbed in Alísa's skull, deep breaths could temper it.

We made it. It's going to be all right. We made it.

A deep, throaty roar echoed from the mountain, spreading chill-bumps over Alísa's arms.

Wry amusement radiated from Koriana. *"And now the alpha comes out to play."*

Alísa slowly unclenched her fingers. *"Why didn't he before?"*

"Because F'renn is as lazy as he is powerful. If his lackeys can handle the fight, he will stay and watch from his cave and boast to himself of the greatness of his clan. He prefers to fight only when his clan has failed, and he has the advantage of fresh muscles."

Disdain rose within Alísa. *"Then Crakil is more honorable than he. No leader should sit and watch while their clan fights. My father is the first on his battlefields."*

Koriana snorted smoke. *"Neither dragon is honorable."*

"Then why are you part of their clan?"

"F'renn controls the central part of the land north of the Prilune Mountain Range. If there were any place to learn of the next Dragon Singer, it was as his scout."

The words echoed through her mind. Koriana had waited for her among dragons she didn't trust or like. Why? What was so special about a Dragon Singer that she would endanger herself and her family?

Alísa twisted as another roar cracked through the air. A large red dragon fixed on them—F'renn, she presumed. Two dragons accompanied him, flying behind each of his wings, their brown and gray scales glinting in the sunlight.

Anxiety rose in Graydonn, tingling over Alísa's mind like flies. *"What will we do, Mother?"*

Koriana beat the air faster, Graydonn matching her speed with a grunt of pained effort. They rose higher and banked for a mass of clouds.

"First, we put distance between us and our former alpha."

Alísa braced herself to enter the cloud formation, and was enveloped in a cold, thick mist. Water droplets accumulated quickly, drenching her hair and clothing. Under other circumstances, she would have been miserable, but the antagonistic dragons riding their tail provided a more than sufficient distraction.

Alísa's breath caught as they rose above the cloud-line and were greeted by a sea of white. The sunlight glinted off the ocean of clouds, beckoning her to come explore its secrets, but its call was interrupted by the pursuing gray dragon.

Koriana swerved right and left, but the fresher gray quickly gained on them. It snapped at Koriana's tail, but she flicked it away just in time to avoid the teeth, then whipped it back. Blood spurted where tail-spine connected with flesh.

Koriana dove back into the clouds and swerved south. *"Be silent. Don't even think."*

Alísa stared at the spine she gripped. How did one not think?

She focused on the spine—a bone-like protrusion rising a little over a foot-and-a-half tall and ending at a sharp point. Little grooves ran its length, giving her hands something to grip. Spines ran along the length of the dragoness, starting just behind her head. Those along her neck started at about six inches long and grew longer at Koriana's shoulders, shortening again at the base of the tail.

After a few minutes of spine-contemplation, the cloud-cover ended, forcing them back out into the open. F'renn and his wing-dragons lagged perhaps five miles behind them.

Alísa started as Koriana trumpeted. *"What was that? I thought we were trying to lose them."*

"We won't be able to without help," Koriana answered, her tone determined and sure.

"We're about to pass into Rorenth's territory. One of the Nameless' followers."

A shiver ran through Alísa and settled in her stomach. With her revelation that not all dragons were evil, she had hoped the stories of dragons swearing fealty to the Dark One's forces in exchange for power were false.

"F'renn might decide not to follow," Graydonn continued, *"but his desire for you might make him foolish enough to ignore the boundary."*

"I'm counting on it," Koriana growled. *"They cannot catch us in the five minutes it will take to enter Rorenth's lands, yet they still pursue. It will be their undoing."*

"And ours?" The words slipped through Alísa's mind before she could stop them.

Koriana responded with another baying trumpet. Alísa shivered as a dragon answered the call from the north. Graydonn's uncertainty and Koriana's confidence crowded within her, choking out her own emotions. If only these opposite feelings would cancel each other out, instead of ringing in her mind like clashing steel.

She breathed deeply, in and out, trying to settle her mind.

"I can feel your struggle without trying," Graydonn spoke softly. *"Why do you fight so hard against the Maker's gift?"*

"These emotions aren't mine. It's my head, but I can't feel anything but you."

"It's because you're fighting it. Your empathy is a part of you, as under your control as your limbs. Own it, don't fight it."

Alísa shook her head, gritting her teeth as she pushed against the onslaught. Graydonn didn't understand. He couldn't know the way her empathy had tortured her ever since it emerged, how dragon emotions had brought such pain and misery to her. No. These particular dragons weren't evil, but their emotions still couldn't have control.

She wouldn't let them.

A flash of blue came from the north—a sapphire dragon's scales catching the sun as it flew perpendicular to them. They had perhaps a minute before it cut them off. It roared a long bass note, spiking Graydonn's anxiety.

Alísa shivered, trying not to imagine dark power cascading from the dragon. *"Is that Rorenth?"*

"One of his border guards," Graydonn said. *"That call was a warning. A second will call the alpha."*

"Is he"—even in her thoughts, she couldn't bring herself to say it—*"like Rorenth?"*

"We would not call him if he were."

"Hail, Sareth!" Koriana called. *"My son and I are being pursued—we will be killed by our alpha if we cannot escape."*

Alísa jumped as a roar came from behind, closer than she had expected. A new male voice entered her mind through her link to Koriana. F'renn.

"I pursue justly! My fight today is not with Rorenth, but with this rogue. It is my right to punish my clan as I see fit—then I will return to my land. Do not obstruct my justice!"

"Do not assume you have any rights in this land, F'renn." Sareth roared, his voice echoing like thunder.

Alísa's heart pounded as a roar answered Sareth from the south—deep, ferocious, and far too close.

"Rorenth comes to end all intruders."

11

EXPECTATION

F'renn's voice rang through Alísa's mind. *"Foolish serpent! You've marked your own hide—I will destroy you along with these traitors!"*

Alísa could almost feel F'renn's hot breath cascading over her, his wing-beats close enough to hear. She didn't dare look back, for fear that he would take hold of her mind as Crakil had tried to.

Sareth ignored the alpha, fixing his gaze on Koriana as he flew to intercept. *"You are a fool to come here. Did you think our occasional conversation enough to win favor in your trespassing? I am bound to my alpha, and his wrath is fiercer than F'renn's."*

"He pursues to destroy the Singer," Koriana said, the strength in her voice belying the fatigue rolling off of her. *"Feel her mind connected to mine—know the hope in my heart. I would not risk my son's life for mere possibility!"*

Sareth was close enough now for Alísa to see his shining emerald eyes. They locked on her own, his presence brushing her mind and bringing with it skepticism and indifference.

Alísa breathed in a ragged breath and fingered her necklace through the fabric of her shirt. Should she say something? What words could temper his rigid justice?

"Please, great Sareth. I wish no harm to you and yours, I only wish to learn who the Maker designed me to be."

A wry humor poured through their tether-line before Sareth pulled his presence back. He banked lazily above and behind them, circling like a bird of prey.

"You believe this frightened hatchling will end the war, Koriana? Her predecessors

met untimely demises, as will she."

Koriana rumbled in her chest. *"Not if I have a say in it. Not if you let me pass."*

"You are a fool." Sareth blinked slowly. *"But I trust how you would use her more than either alpha. Fly low. Rorenth will easily miss you as he deals with his rival."*

Sareth banked west and speared at the brown dragon behind them, knocking it off-course with a mighty blow of his talons. Koriana made good use of Sareth's distraction, pushing them into a dive and shooting forward with her remaining strength.

"Maker's wings lift you, Sareth."

Alísa twisted at a high-pitched trumpet behind them. F'renn and his gray wing-dragon now banked to face a monstrous red dragon bearing down on them from the south. Rorenth. It had to be. Though no dark energy surrounded him in the physical realm, his very presence darkened Alísa's heart. His scales were dull compared to F'renn's rubies, but his eyes glowed with a white-hot flame of hatred. The scars covering his hide and the tears in his wings spoke of a brute used to combat and hard-won victory.

F'renn fanned his wings out and roared, slowing nearly to a halt as he faced the second alpha. The gray trumpeted in alarm, tipping its wings to retreat west. It met with two dragons who dive-bombed it and forced it to the ground.

Their pursuers distracted and Rorenth's dragons occupied, Koriana slowed. They flew perhaps fifty feet above the rolling hills now, hopefully camouflaged from any other dragons by Graydonn's green scales.

Koriana's head drooped and her mouth opened to gulp air. Alísa placed a hand on her hot scales.

"You are incredible, Koriana."

Roars and growls raged behind them, and Alísa looked back at the two reds grappling in the skies. A spray of blood gushed from F'renn's neck, and Alísa wrenched her eyes away. Had they led F'renn to his death? What kind of world had she entered—had she only traded the violence of one race for another?

"What does it mean when a dragon swears fealty to the Nameless?" she asked. *"My people say that all dragons did it, and so their telepathy is stronger than ours—*

but your power is stronger too, and you don't follow the monsters."

A hum ran through Koriana, barely audible over the wind. *"Dragons have always had greater psychic strength than humans, but dragons like Rorenth gain even more. Their fire also burns hotter and they grow larger than any natural dragon will."*

"But Sareth doesn't follow? What of the rest of the clan?"

"Some follow the dark ones. Others follow Rorenth because he is strong. Others simply do not wish his wrath. I have never heard of a full clan turning."

Alísa pulled in a steadying breath and reached up for the comfort of her necklace before stopping herself. She placed her hand instead on the leather strap of her bag. It wouldn't do for the dragons to know what she kept around her neck.

The bag weighed heavily on her shoulder, but she didn't dare switch sides for fear of dropping the darling dragonet. She reached into the bag and set a hand on the egg, feeling the slight movements inside.

A questioning feeling melted through the shell, buzzing lightly as it filled Alísa's mind. She pressed back peace through her fingertips and the dragonet stilled. She smiled, then looked up again at the dragons.

"How long will it take to cross Rorenth's territory?"

Koriana's voice came quietly, *"Three hours."*

"But you're so tired——"

"I will do what I must. I always have. I've flown for longer periods before—albeit, at a much steadier pace and without passengers. But now is as good a time as any to begin your training. Would you sing something for me? A song to buoy our flight?"

Alísa blinked. *"I don't even know how this works, or what it means. What if I do it wrong?"*

"Then nothing will happen and I will continue to fly."

"You used your power last night without knowing it," Graydonn said. *"You can do it again. You are a wayfarer—there must be journeying songs your clan uses to keep up their marches."*

Alísa nodded and searched her mind for a song. She settled on the tale of the founding of their continent, Arran, and Koriana's wing-strokes steadied to the song's tempo.

Come the fifteenth century, unto a place so green,
Famine spread throughout the land and took away our means.
A desert place, a hopeless land, a country torn by war,
Until a man rose up to stand, until our Belinor.

With words of wisdom, light, and truth, our hero paved the way,
Setting hearts and minds aflame to find a better day.
For other lands so rich and green, untouched by famine be
So with a man from every clan, he sailed across the sea.

The sun above gives life to all, so head toward its rise,
And dragonkind and fairy-folk, too, followed one so wise,
Until the land of Arran rose above the seas so wide.
A place of hope, a place of rest, a country to reside.

Dragonkind claimed mountaintops, between the earth and sky;
The western hills, the mountain range, the clearest space to fly.
The fairy-folk claimed eastern skies, where heaven wets the land,
In forest glen they hid within from dragon and from man.

Belinor called to the folk who'd stayed within their space,
All who dared to dream of more and had the strength to chase.
Man and beast soon filled Arran and lived from shore to shore.
Peace prevailed upon the land under our Belinor.

But 'pon his death—

Alísa stopped. She had forgotten where the song would turn. It was history, remembered true by generations of songweavers, but how would her companions feel as she sang of war and slayers? Perhaps it was better to end now.

And she suddenly felt so tired—

"Why do you stop, Singer?" Koriana asked. *"You were doing well—I felt your strength multiplying within me."*

Alísa leaned against Graydonn and closed her eyes. *"I don't wish to sing of the war."*

Graydonn purred softly. *"Denying history's voice will not change the past, but remembrance may yet change the future."*

Alísa breathed a slow, deep breath, then straightened and began again.

But 'pon his death, the dragon clans decided in their strength
All was theirs under the sun to have, to kill, to take.
Bodies large and powerful, and minds so great besides,
Dragonkind did as they pleased on earth and in the skies.

Shield to flame and sword to claw, defended humankind,
But none could match the power and strength inside the dragons' mind.
Branni wept for soldiers lost and lifted up his cries;
Ne'er before had greater sorrow spilt from Eldra eyes.

And then the Maker interceded for his dying men,
Bestowed upon a blessed few a gift to help defend.
So now the slayers walk Arran and face the dragon clans.
So honor them who fight and die—the Maker's gift to man.

With her final note, Alísa slumped against Graydonn once more. Her eyelids drooped and her breath came heavily. Though the sun shone high, her mind was as foggy as on very late nights. She might just drift off here, on dragonback.

"Well done, Singer," Koriana's voice came through loudly. So loudly. *"I will not ask for more now, but you mustn't fall asleep. We can all rest when we make it to the forests."*

The words brought some sense into her, and Alísa straightened. She needed to stay awake.

She struggled to focus her thoughts into words. *"What is this Dragon Singer thing? How does it work? Why does it work? Will dragons be affected every time I sing? Can I—"*

"Calm yourself, Alísa." Graydonn thrummed good-naturedly. *"Mind-speak might be fast, but even we cannot keep up with your questions."*

Alísa smiled weakly. *"Sorry."*

Humor radiated from Koriana as well. *"There is a story I will tell you soon that will help this all make sense. Until then, I will speak simply. Your songs affect dragons. Every time you sing and a dragon is within earshot, they will recognize the voice of the Singer."*

"Which is why we're taking you east," Graydonn jumped in. *"The forests have few mountains for dragons to live in, and most do not dare venture near them due to the fairy legends."*

Alísa twisted toward Graydonn. *"So, fairies do exist?"*

There were many a tale about the tiny, mischievous creatures. They showed up in some of the history songs, but were only ever mentioned in passing. It was the tales of the fantastic where they mostly came out to play. Some painted them as benevolent spirits a little lower than the Eldír, sent to guide humans toward their destinies. Others told of glowing lights leading humans deep into the forests to never be seen again.

"It is superstition." Koriana hummed in her throat. *"Legends claim they favor humans over dragons and will attack dragons on sight. This alone is enough to keep some dragons at bay—for the rest, like Rorenth, the flat lands beyond the Nissen River aren't worth claiming. It is harder to hunt amidst the trees. All the forests offer dragons is kindling."*

"And solitude," Graydonn added.

"Yes. Solitude in which to train you, little Singer."

A small twinge ran through Alísa's heart. Koriana never used her name, only her title and adjectives.

"Many dragons have debated how a Singer's powers work," Koriana's voice jerked Alísa from her thoughts. *"I believe a Dragon Singer uses her voice to focus her empathy into telepathy, and then channel it to the dragons within earshot. A Singer can strengthen, weaken, call, calm, and fend off dragons through this song-channeled telepathy. All they need is intention—a purpose behind the words they sing."*

Alísa ran through the events of the last day. Her journeying song helped Koriana push through her fatigue. Her lullaby had put the dragonet in the egg to sleep, as well as all the other dragons who heard it. Even when she had called for Graydonn to rescue her, it had come out as a sung note, as if her body knew her true identity.

"What will I do once you've trained me?"

Koriana looked back, one glowing eye fixing on Alísa. *"So much, little Singer. You will bring so much good."*

Hope rose from Koriana, tempting Alísa's heart with its lightness, but with it came the knowledge that it all settled on her. Alísa shivered; could anyone, especially her, live up to such expectation?

Koriana faced front. *"I promise, more will be explained, but right now I fear choking you with too much information."*

The finality in Koriana's tone settled the words in Alísa's mind. The dragoness was right—with all that had happened and all the new information rolling around in her mind, it was time to slow down.

As hills passed beneath them, a sense of melancholy settled over Alísa. She had left home, family, possessions—and now she left behind the verdant green grasses of the hill country for a land of trees.

She placed her hand on the egg and ran her fingers over the tiny pockets in its shell. It was almost as comforting as her father's gift around her neck.

"Are you all right, Alísa?" Graydonn's soft voice entered her mind.

She couldn't hold back the truth as her beautiful hills passed below.

"I feel so empty now. I've given up everything I am and now, even with the answers you've given me, I feel like there's nothing left."

His response was gentle. *"Perhaps; but there is new beauty on the horizon. Lift your eyes."*

Hills rolled before them for perhaps only fifty more miles under a sky speckled with clouds. Beyond it all lay the darker green of the forests, its flat land seemingly reaching to the edge of the world. Everything unknown lived in that space, hidden amidst the trees. Even dragons stayed away.

She leaned against Graydonn, and he thrummed soothingly. All but these two brave dragons stayed away. If she was with them, perhaps she could be brave too.

12

CHOSEN

Alísa nearly toppled when her boots finally hit the ground, her aching legs asleep from the long, hard flight. She fell to her knees a bit too hard, then sat on the carpet of dead pine needles and twigs. After clutching rough scales and spines, and singing to help bear the exertion of travel, all she wanted was to lie down in the perpetual shade of the forest and sleep for years.

Koriana slumped over on her side, laying her sweaty muzzle in the dirt and pine needles. Graydonn flexed his ripped wing and flinched as light pain zapped through him. Alísa barely had the strength to flinch with him.

Graydonn padded to his mother and nosed her cheek. *"I'm going to find you some food. I shouldn't be long."*

Alísa's stomach growled loudly. She hadn't eaten since dinner the day before. Technically, she wasn't starving, but dragon-singing took so much out of her. She might just eat whatever Graydonn brought back raw.

She chuckled silently. *Maybe I do have a dragon inside of me.*

Anxiety wafted from Koriana as Graydonn dashed deeper into the forest, his gait clumsy, but determined.

"Will he be okay?"

Koriana was silent, and Alísa realized the tiny buzz of their connection was gone. The dragoness hadn't heard the question.

Alísa cleared her throat, and Koriana turned an eye to her. "W—will he b-be okay on his own?"

Koriana blinked slowly, establishing the telepathic link. *"Yes. He has hunted alone many times."*

"Then why are you anxious?"

The words slipped through before Alísa could consider them. Grief rose in Koriana and pulled Alísa's heart in on itself. *Idiot! How could you ask such a question of a grieving widow?*

"*Your question wasn't fanged, little one. I know you meant no harm.*" Sadness slipped into her voice, unguarded and so unlike the resolved Koriana of the last few hours.

Alísa wanted desperately to speak, but nothing would come. How could she heal a broken heart? Neither human nor dragon could be consoled by mere words.

She forced herself to her feet and went to the dragoness. Pushing back lingering fears, she knelt beside Koriana's head and placed a hand on her cheek. She held there for a moment, looking into Koriana's tired eyes. The dragoness blinked slowly, her inner eyelid opening just a hair behind the outer. So beast-like, yet there was no beast behind them anymore. Only a fellow *anam*.

Alísa gave a small smile and pulled her hand back. She set the pack on the ground and pulled out the egg and blanket. Koriana lifted her head and sniffed the egg as Alísa laid the blanket on the ground, a barrier against the dirt and pine needles.

"*Is she going to be okay? She's been in the bag for so long.*"

Koriana blinked slowly. "*She's perhaps six days from hatching—old enough to create some of her own heat. She still needs help, but not like a newly-laid egg.*"

Alísa looked up and down Koriana's splayed body. "*Should I place her in your tail, so you can keep her warm?*"

"*Here is fine.*"

Alísa nodded and placed the egg against Koriana before crawling back to her blanket, her eyelids drooping as she curled up. It had never felt so soft.

She woke only moments later to a large, gray nose prodding her legs. She jerked back instinctively, then forced a calm demeanor as she recognized her companion.

"What is it?"

"*The dragonet is anxious. She has been ever since her mother died. The only time I've felt her quiet is when you sang to her.*"

Alísa hummed quietly, then swallowed. Her throat still felt scratchy and raw from singing over the winds. *"I don't think I can sing to her right now."*

"You don't need to." Koriana rolled the egg to Alísa with her muzzle. *"She likes you more than she likes me. She will still with you."*

Alísa looked from the egg to Koriana and back again. *"Why? I'm not a dragon. Not her kin."*

"A dragonet cannot survive the hatching without a bond to a parent. It's her instinct to find a new mother-figure now that her mother is gone. She will not calm for me, but has twice for you. She has chosen you."

"But I don't know what she needs."

Koriana nosed the egg once more. *"You will learn, Singer."*

Alísa shook her head, but took the restless egg in her hands. The dragonet wiggled inside, like a human child refusing to settle for the night and just on the verge of a tantrum. Alísa closed her eyes and focused, drawing psychic power from her foggy, tired mind.

"Settle down," she whispered, pressing her empathy into the egg.

The egg stopped wobbling, and a warm feeling pressed back to Alísa. The dragonet's contentment raised a smile to Alísa's lips. She was so trusting and sweet; it was hard to imagine her growing up to be a hard-scaled dragon with fearsome teeth and talons.

Alísa laid back down with the egg against her stomach. The light, airy feeling of Koriana's expectation settled over her again, but not knowing what exactly the dragoness expected of her made a pit in her stomach. She closed her eyes and did her best to focus solely on the dragonet's feelings.

Content.

Calm.

Peace.

Koriana's voice entered her mind. *"Graydonn was successful."*

Stomach growling, Alísa pushed up on her hands and looked around. There was no sign of Graydonn. She eyed Koriana.

"How do you know?"

"He told me," Koriana said, like it was painfully obvious.

Alísa sat up fully and looked for him again. *"You can see him through the forest?"*

Koriana thrummed with amusement. *"So much to learn, little Singer. When a dragon hatches, it creates a deep bond with the parent it has chosen. This bond transcends the telepathic law of sightlines. So long as Graydonn is within forty miles or so, we can communicate despite physical barriers."*

A thrill of awe and terror ran through Alísa. Would this bond form between her and the dragonet? *Could* this bond form? She was human, after all, not a dragon. Dragons tended to be much stronger psychics than slayers—what if she couldn't handle such a powerful bond?

Dead pine needles crunched behind her, and Alísa turned to see Graydonn approaching with a limp deer hanging from his jaws. The animal—almost as tall as him—made his gait even more awkward than before. She hid her smile. Dragons were definitely not ground creatures.

Her stomach growled again, but as blood dripped from the kill wound on the deer's neck, all thoughts of eating raw meat fled from her. She wasn't starving yet.

Graydonn dropped his catch in front of Koriana with a thud. He nuzzled her cheek, then looked to Alísa.

"Hungry?"

She nodded slowly. *"It probably isn't wise to build a fire here. I don't have many ways of putting it out."*

His eyes brightened. *"Right. Humans flame their food. Allow me."*

He clamped down on one of the deer's legs and easily tore it from the rest of the animal. *"Take the rest, Mother. I'll eat whatever Alísa doesn't."*

Koriana snorted. *"Take another leg. You need your strength."*

"You stuffed me yesterday. I can make it a few days."

Days? How often did dragons eat?

Koriana apparently didn't have the strength to argue. Alísa cringed and looked away as the dragoness chomped the deer's head and neck in one bite. Bones crunched in Koriana's powerful jaws and Alísa winced, running her hand back and forth over the egg. This was something she would have to get used to with her new companions.

"Do humans eat the whole thing, just flamed?" Graydonn came up beside her with the leg.

Alísa smiled up at him. *"Not quite. Can you find me a large, semi-flat rock?"*

Graydonn set the leg down and padded back the way he came. Alísa dug her knife from her boot and went to work on the meat, cutting away the skin and slicing long, thin chunks. Graydonn returned just as she cut the last slab, and she placed the pieces on the rock.

"If you could cook those gently, that will be enough for me. You can have the rest."

She frowned at her bloody hands as Graydonn went to work. No water nearby to wash in. She could wipe them on her clothes, but that would ruin one of her sets, and she only had two. Maybe leaves would do the trick?

Graydonn eyed her. *"You look as though your limbs have betrayed you."*

She chuckled. *"I need to clean them."*

"Humans don't lick to clean?"

"Eww, no!"

Graydonn thrummed. *"I suppose a creature who doesn't eat blood would have that sentiment. I would offer to clean them for you, but I suppose you'd think that equally unclean?"*

Alísa shut her eyes. *"Yes. I need water."*

Images from Graydonn flooded Alísa's mind—trees and bushes passing by in a fast lope until a trickling creek crossed the path. *"It isn't too far."*

Alísa's mind went blank and she blinked several times. A wave of dizziness passed over her, and she nearly placed a hand to her head, stopping herself just before smearing blood on her forehead.

"Thank you, but please warn me before you do that again."

Graydonn stopped his flames, his eyes dimming slightly. *"How do humans give directions?"*

She laughed gently and stood—clearly, she wasn't the only one with a lot to learn. *"They point and say 'a hundred paces north.' I'll be right back."*

It only took a few minutes to find the creek and wash, and she returned to find the dragons already finished with their meals. The savory scent of cooked meat met her nostrils as she sat beside the cooking slab. The outsides of the pieces were black and tough, the insides hot and rare, but the first piece tasted better than anything she could remember.

The second tasted like charcoal.

Graydonn settled to his belly beside Alísa as she ground the third piece of overcooked meat between tired jaws. The dragons' peaceful sleepiness covered her like soft rabbit furs as their warmth radiated on either side. Her eyelids drooped, and, pulling the egg close, she faded into sleep even as her head settled to the blanket.

13

SHADE & SHADOW

Early the following morning, they woke and resumed their journey. Three hours of flight over nothing but trees and the occasional clearing brought them to the closest mountain in sight. It was small and double-peaked, with trees climbing up the rock face, their roots gripping through cracks in stone.

Alísa clung tightly as Koriana flew fast and low over the mountainside. Anything different might expose them to the village sitting just south of the mountain. Her shoulder grazed Graydonn's neck as they banked, his ripped wing still keeping him from flying long stretches on his own.

They passed the mouth of a cave on the southwest side, about sixty feet above the forest floor and guarded by tree trunks. The cave sat within walking distance of both the village and a large lake west of the mountain's base. Alísa couldn't have designed it better, but Koriana passed it by, spiraling up the rocky slopes in search of other options.

One other cave opened up where the two peaks converged, higher than any tree could climb, yet not high enough for snow and ice. The forest below Alísa's feet felt so far away. She would not be able to reach or leave the high cave on her own.

Satisfaction settled Koriana's voice. *"This is the one. The altitude will provide protection from any slayers in the area."*

Alísa's heart sank, and she searched for anything that might convince the dragoness. *"The lower cave is well-hidden from the ground. With so many trees surrounding it, people wouldn't see the entrance unless they purposefully came looking for it."*

"Perhaps, but it's better to be sure."

Alísa leaned to the side, trying to catch Koriana's eye. *"I would really be more comfortable closer to the forest floor."*

Koriana hummed. *"Safety is a higher priority than comfort."*

Alísa sighed and placed a hand on Graydonn's neck. He seemed more attuned to her than Koriana—if Alísa could get him on her side, maybe she could win this argument.

"I'll need supplies from the nearby village, access to water, time to myself. I can't fly to the floor in minutes."

Graydonn glanced at her. *"We will take you when you need down."*

"But what if you didn't?" The thought slipped through and Alísa tensed. *"I'm sorry. That's not what I meant—"*

"But you do." Graydonn's tone was soft and slightly sad. *"You are not our prisoner."*

"I know. I really do, but" —she forced herself to meet Graydonn's eyes once more— *"up here I would feel like one."*

Graydonn blinked slowly. *"Mother."*

Koriana hummed in annoyance. *"I don't like it."*

"It is the Singer's request. Let's feel it out, at least. If we smell humans or can see a village from the mouth, we can use the high cave."

Koriana snorted, but banked away from the mountain and began a descent. Alísa rubbed the dragoness' neck.

"Thank you."

Mere moments later, they approached the low cave. Alísa tensed and fought not to duck as Koriana flew through its mouth and skidded to a stop on the stone floor.

Alísa squinted, the cave barely illuminated by the morning light. Cool and pleasantly humid air greeted her, the moisture tempering an earthy scent that might have been dusty otherwise. A flow of water cut a winding path through the stone floor and ran out the cave's mouth. Stalactites and stalagmites speared throughout the cave, only barely concealing the flow's origin—a small pool of water fed by a fist-sized hole in the back wall.

Graydonn leapt from Koriana's back and sniffed the air. *"No human has been here in months. A bear lumbered through recently, but didn't stay."*

"It's far too large for an animal to feel comfortable." Koriana lowered to her

belly so Alísa could slide to the floor, then looked out the entrance. *"I will admit you were right, Singer—the trees and brush are thick between us and the ground. No one could see us accidentally."*

"We can stay, then?"

Graydonn thrummed at Alísa's remark, while Koriana turned shining eyes to her. *"Yes, Singer, we can stay. But at the first sign of trouble, we will leave for the high cave."*

Alísa nodded firmly. *"Right."*

Koriana ambled further inside, but Alísa and Graydonn stayed to stare out over the land. The only thing visible besides trees was a light line of smoke rising to the south, most likely from the nearby village. That was the surest sign that there were no other dragons in the area—in the west, none would dare build a village so close to a mountain. There might not even be slayers in the village, instead called to defend closer to the Nissen River and the mountains beyond.

Alísa crossed her arms against a chilly breeze and grimaced as her fingers found grit caked over her skin and clothes. It wouldn't do to go to the village for supplies looking like a runaway. That would invite far too many questions.

She patted Graydonn's shoulder to signal for telepathy. *"Do you remember where the lake is?"*

"Desiring a swim?"

"Yes." Memories of going to the lake with her mother or Trísse flooded her, leaving her with an acute need to not be alone. *"Do dragons swim?"*

He thrummed, a twinge of mischief in his eyes. *"Come and find out."*

Trees shaded them the whole way down, their thick lower branches providing hand-holds in the steepest sections. Alísa stayed watchful in this new land under cover of trees, shifting her gaze between the terrain and boughs. Only days ago, she had used such cover to hide from dragons, the occasional grove in the hill country holding the promise of safety. Now the once-peaceful greens constrained her, making the air thicker and harder to breathe.

Even Graydonn seemed apprehensive as he wove through the forest beside her. Ferns and brambles grabbed at their legs, sliding easily off his scales but pulling at Alísa's skirts. The ground crunched beneath their feet, a mixture of earth, dried pine needles, and leaves that was so different from the soft rustling of tall grasses. With the commotion of their own steps, would they even hear if something were stalking them? Then again, what animal would stalk a dragon?

Alísa sidled closer to Graydonn. How strange that the creature she had grown up fearing was now one she leaned into for protection.

As Graydonn led the way, the wall of rough-barked pines ahead slowly began to thin, making way for the wide, open space of the lake. Shimmering waters reflected the joys of the sky, calling to Alísa with promises of freedom and cleansing.

"I don't think I've ever been so happy with the prospect of a bath," Graydonn said, his pace picking up a little.

"Me either." Even now, the humidity of the forest added to her need to bathe.

Alísa stopped and placed a hand on Graydonn's shoulder. Would there be other humans already there, feeling the same way she did about the warm humidity?

"Let me go first, Graydonn. There may be people from the village."

"I sense only birds, fish, and two deer over there." He pointed with his muzzle. *"We're safe."*

Alísa blinked. Even the strongest slayers couldn't have told her that much detail about the animals in range.

"You can sense all of that?"

Pride wafted from him as he pressed past her. *"It's my gifting."*

"Then why didn't you sense the slayers the day I met you?" She bit her lip, immediately regretting the question.

His eyes dimmed as he looked back at her. *"We were far from any villages—there weren't supposed to be slayers nearby. We were focused on physical training, not the psychic realm."*

She hurried to him. *"Forgive me. The question slipped before—"*

Graydonn cocked his head. *"Why do you ask forgiveness? Your question was innocent, not fanged. Telepathy ensures intentions are laid bare, so there is no need for apology unless you truly meant harm."*

"Still, I didn't mean to ask it." She searched his eyes. *"How do dragons keep thoughts from slipping into communication like that?"*

"We don't. Not unless there's a secret we must protect, in which case we use our telepathy to block off that portion of our mind. But that is tiresome—better to speak the truth than veil our feelings."

Alísa shook her head. *"I guess dragons are more comfortable speaking their minds than humans are."*

"We always speak with our minds; how can we do anything but?"

She chuckled, stopping at the edge of the lake. *"I suppose."*

Graydonn waded into the water and submerged, taking to it like he was born to swim. Alísa watched for him to reemerge. In all her years of hearing tales about dragons, she had never once learned of their ability in water. She had discovered so much in only a matter of days, and still had much to learn.

A minute later, Graydonn came back up for air with a fish in his mouth and slurped it down. *"Hungry?"*

She cringed at the thought of raw fish. *"I'll cook one later, if you'll save one for me."*

Graydonn dove back beneath the rippling waters, and Alísa scanned the area. Though now free of the dark canopy, the strangeness of the forest still lurked around her. With Graydonn now in the middle of the lake, she suddenly felt exposed. There were just as many predators in the forests as in the hill country, perhaps more. And who knew what nasties might lurk beneath the surface of the lake?

Alísa jumped with a gasp as something shrieked above her, stumbling forward a few steps into the water. Several birds clothed in blues and golds burst from their perches amidst the boughs and flew in lazy circles over the lake.

Graydonn poked his head above the water, closer than he had been a few seconds prior. *"Are you all right?"*

She placed a hand over her heart as she caught her breath, watching the birds ascend up and away. *"Birds. It was just a few birds."*

Graydonn came still closer. *"I'm keeping watch, scanning psychically every time I come up for air. I won't let humans or a predator sneak up on us."*

"I know." She sighed. *"Branni help me, I need to relax."*

He cocked his head. *"You've mentioned Branni before, in the history song. Who is that?"*

"He's my Eldra," she said, sloshing back to the edge of the lake. Time to get out of her now-waterlogged boots.

"Your Eldra?" Graydonn's tone filled with incredulity.

"Yes. He's the shepherd over all warriors and soldiers." She pulled off layers of clothing until only her slip-pants and a single shirt remained, then marched back into the cool waters to scrub them. *"That includes all slayers, even me, though I'm not a warrior."*

She stopped mid-scrub, her heart suddenly feeling just as waterlogged as the clothing. Was it even true now? She had left the slayers, after all, and was a Dragon Singer, whatever that meant. Did Branni still care for her now that she was with the slayers' enemies? Surely he knew the difference between evil dragons and those like Graydonn and Koriana?

Alísa looked to Graydonn, who still stared at her like she had grown a tail. *"What? Don't you have an Eldra who watches out for you and who you pray to?"*

Graydonn shook his neck and head, sending a few glistening drops of water over Alísa. *"No. My family and I pray to and follow only the Maker."*

The way he said it was somehow both cautious and resolute, as though he were speaking a necessary but ground-shattering truth.

In a way, it was. The Maker was high and holy, majestic and mighty. There were humans who prayed directly to him, certainly—she had even done so herself before—but only prophets, oracles, and some songweavers ever claimed to always pray directly to him without an Eldra as their go-between.

Apparently, dragons felt differently.

Graydonn fixed his eyes on her, a hesitancy filling his voice. *"You do follow the Maker too, don't you?"*

"Of course I do." She wrung out her clothes and began placing them on a rock jutting out of the lake. *"I certainly don't follow the Nameless."*

"Then why not just pray to the Maker directly? Why claim an Eldra?"

"It's easier this way."

A jolt flew through her heart, shame for the anger bubbling inside and threatening to surface. *"I mean, I've always been taught that the Maker placed certain Eldír over his people. Branni to guard and strengthen warriors. E'sall to bridge the gaps between nature and those who work in it, like hunters and farmers. Dinann to bless the work of artisans' hands. Ignoring this hierarchy would be disrespectful to both the Eldír and the Maker, who established it."*

Graydonn watched as she waded back out and began scrubbing the grime from her body and clothes. His confusion shifted into curiosity, salted with a little humor.

"It seems rather complicated. What if you change vocations? Or if you, who follow Branni, need help as you hunt? How do you remember them all?"

"That's why we have songweavers. Teaching songs stick in children's heads and follow them into adulthood."

"So you never pray to the Maker directly?"

Alísa sighed lightly, thinking back to the darkness of her chamber the night she freed Graydonn. *"I do. There are some things even an Eldra doesn't know. Some things I would never ask Branni."*

She paused slightly, feeling Graydonn's eyes on her and questions forming within his mind. A part of her didn't want to elaborate—if she couldn't talk to Branni about this, why could she tell Graydonn? But Graydonn was someone who could respond in words and ideas, while the Maker and even Branni had only ever responded in silence.

She swallowed. *"Questions like how my people could be so wrong about you. And why, for all that is holy, did the Maker choose me? Broken, frightened me?"*

As soon as she said it, she regretted it. Saying the words, even psychically, seemed to bring all the emotions to the forefront, where they heated behind her eyes and threatened to reveal themselves in tears. She turned away and splashed water on her face to cool it.

Graydonn's voice was quiet but clear. *"Sometimes strength is best shown in the midst of fear and brokenness. What we do in spite of these shows who we really are."*

She looked at him. *"Like you. Helping me even in your sorrows."*

"And you in yours."

She smiled softly, his sincerity making it hard to wave it off. He believed in her so strongly, and they had only known each other a few days. It was so new and foreign, like everything else in her life right now. What other changes lay ahead?

She shook her head and set her mind on the task at hand, flipping onto her back to let the water work through her hair. Graydonn watched as she gently ran her fingers through the matted curls, a humored curiosity wafting from him.

"I've never before thought to thank the Maker for how quickly I can bathe. Your process is much more involved than mine."

She laughed, glad for a lighter topic. *"I'm almost finished."*

"Then I should find you a fish."

Ripples sloshed against her as Graydonn made for the deeper water and disappeared under the surface. It only took Alísa a couple more tries before she was able to run her fingers through her hair without snagging. Then she paddled back to shore. Wet hair and soaked clothes weighed her down as she walked up from the water, but she had never felt so clean. She pulled her hair over her shoulder and began wringing it out.

Graydonn emerged with a limp fish in his jaws. *"Ready?"*

"Almost."

Water slid easily off Graydonn's scales as he pulled himself up from the lake, leaving him unburdened by the extra water weight. Pushing an odd jealousy aside, Alísa pulled on an uncomfortably waterlogged skirt, stockings, and boots.

Graydonn cocked his head. *"Clothing seems awfully cumbersome."*

"We get used to it. We don't have fire inside to warm us, or scales to protect us."

"As if those thin layers can protect you from anything."

Alísa shook her head and walked past him, unwilling to explain the need for protection from others' eyes. Though Graydonn tackled each new topic with a respectful curiosity, this was something a dragon wouldn't understand.

Koriana's eyes were the first things Alísa saw when she and Graydonn reached the cave. They glowed with their eerie inner light, floating high above Alísa as Koriana watched for their entry. She held the egg in the nest of her tail, harsh scales and spines curling gently around the precious shell.

Warmth filled Alísa's heart, her arms aching to hold the sweet dragonet. She hurried to hang her extra clothing over stalagmites, freeing her to take the egg.

"Do you want me to flame the fish now?" Graydonn asked as she passed.

She shook her head. Though a dull pain of hunger settled in her stomach, the work of deboning a fish would keep her from the dragonet. *"Soon."*

Alísa stopped before Koriana. *"I can take her now."*

Koriana regarded her, her bright eyes blazing with intelligence. It almost hurt to look into them, but as Alísa averted her eyes, Koriana placed the edge of her wing on Alísa's shoulder.

"Look at me, Singer."

Alísa's heart trembled as she met Koriana's gaze once more. She tried hard not to shiver. Though no pressure indicated Koriana was reading her mind, it seemed as though those eyes saw everything.

"What's wrong?"

"I merely wished to see if fear still lingered in your eyes. It has lessened." Koriana purred deep in her throat. *"Our journey is over, and my mind is strong. Are you ready to learn?"*

Alísa grinned. *"Yes!"*

Koriana's eyes brightened, and she lifted her wing from Alísa's shoulder. *"I will tell you a tale. Take the dragonet and sit."*

Alísa embraced the egg and hurried to the opposite wall, where Graydonn lay. He pulled his wing close so that she could sit against his side, and his warm scales banished the chill of her wet clothing.

Contented happiness wafted from the dragonet as Alísa held the egg against her stomach. Somehow the thought of being a surrogate mother wasn't as strange as it had been before.

"Close your eyes and open your mind," Koriana's voice flowed gently like shallow waters over stone. *"I will tell you a tale of the first Dragon Singer, passed to me through the Illumination by my mother, and her mother, and her mother's mother, who saw much of it firsthand. This is the story of Bria."*

14

BRIA'S TALE

P'laenn snorted smoke as she stared at the captive slayer woman on the cave floor below. Twenty-one other dragons sat on their respective perches, some in small side-caves, others on rocky ledges. The only dragons on the ground were P'laenn's parents—the alphas standing in judgement over their prisoner. Growls and grumbles echoed through the spacious main cave, but all telepathic communication was silenced in respect for the alphas.

The young woman stood tall, her nearly-black eyes reflecting the light from a small fire burning between her and the alphas, a concession to the prisoner's weak night vision. Fluffy curls sat behind her head in a mass resembling clouds of fire, cascading down over a fir-green cloth. The cloth covered the woman's deep brown skin just past her thighs, fitting tightly on top and loosely below.

How could a creature fight with that material swinging around her legs?

Bright metal armor protected her torso, decorated with swirling patterns of tangled vines. Black dragon scales wrapped her forearms and shins—spoils of war stolen to protect the parts most vulnerable to flames splashing around her shield.

P'laenn added a growl to the echoing chorus of her clanmates—vermin didn't deserve to wear the proud scales of her kin.

Still, the woman fascinated P'laenn—so few human females entered the battlefield. But this woman was indeed a warrior. She and her tactical partner were strong together and had killed at least two dragons by sword and mind in the last skirmish.

But now, separated from partner and weapons, this woman would crumple before P'laenn's parents, the mighty Moresh and Harna—alphas of the clan. While their clan sat to watch the proceedings above, the alphas stood on the floor, where their strength could best be seen by the vermin before them.

P'laenn's mother, Harna, stalked toward the girl. Bright red scales matching P'laenn's glinted in the firelight as the alpha breathed steam into the woman's face.

"Your sins have finally caught up with you, human. Your weapons are gone, your psychic defense left behind with your partner, your people unable to reach you." Harna's amber eyes narrowed. *"What does the mighty warrior have to say now?"*

The woman stared at Harna, unmoving. Fear emanated from her, but was overshadowed by something else. Defiance?

"Nothing?" Harna mocked. *"Not one word of defense before your judges?"*

The woman lifted her head high. "It is better to die in the service of my people than beg before my enemy."

Moresh advanced, his deep brown scales blending with the shadows flickering over the wall behind him, making him appear larger, almost otherworldly.

"Brave words, vermin. But your emotions are unguarded—we know your fear."

The woman's teeth flashed in a snarl. "Fear doesn't diminish my bravery; it merely fans the flame. Whatever you have planned for me, dragon, I welcome it."

P'laenn cocked her head. How could one so defenseless speak such words to her executioners? They could, and would, snuff her out with a breath, but instead of cowering or merely awaiting the flames, she now rose with the same confidence she displayed on the battlefield.

"Songs will be sung of my sacrifice, and my clan will rally under my name. The name Bria will haunt your caves until my people end your reign of terror over these lands, and I will rest while you burn!"

Growls and hisses echoed throughout the cave, but thrums added to the cacophony. Emotions clashed in the astral plane—outrage and wrath, humor and surprise.

P'laenn accessed her Illumination bond to her mother, tightening her focus on it to speak words only they could hear. Harna accepted the connection and P'laenn immediately felt her mother's humor—she was entertained by the woman's bold words.

"*Lae,*" Harna's voice softened. "*I sense confusion in you. Tell me, what do you think of this slayer girl?*"

"*I wonder at her words and the spirit behind them.*"

Harna didn't respond as Moresh looked up from the prisoner. His red eyes brightened as he broke off the communication link to the woman and spoke only to the clan. "*The fire within this girl amuses me. With my mate's agreement, we will keep her alive for a time. We shall enjoy this mouse with the heart of a panther a few days more!*"

Growls and hums clashed against tail-thumps and thrums. The clan seemed as divided as P'laenn's own heart and mind. This woman, pitiful though she was, troubled her. Her father had spoken her own thoughts, but in words far less damning.

This slayer, this Bria, bore the *anam* of a dragon.

It was five days since the capture of Bria. Five days since Moresh and Harna had stayed her execution. Five days of confusion for P'laenn.

The more she saw of the slayer woman, the more the dragoness became convinced that humans—or, at least, this human—were more than vermin who had developed psychic abilities. They were enemies of her race, but they weren't animals, nor were they completely depraved.

Bria had a way with hatchlings, keeping their attention with songs and tales. The clan quickly discovered that leaving Bria to entertain the youngest members of the clan allowed more efficient use of their time and energy. The task of watching the hyperactive hatchlings usually took at least three dragons. With Bria, only one was necessary—to watch her, rather than the hatchlings.

Two days after Bria's capture, when P'laenn had been assigned monitor duty, she had seen images from Bria's stories in her mind. Similar images formed when dragons told stories, but the human's singing voice combined emotion with story in a deeper way than a dragon's projection. It reached into the soul, pulling it in a dance like currents amidst the clouds.

This second watch-duty, P'laenn worked to keep her guard up. The hatchlings could enjoy the stories, but as monitor she needed to keep her head, in case the slayer woman tried to fill the hatchlings with evil.

Bria seemed comfortable with the four young dragons, even happy. She sat on the floor with them, an arm draped over one of the more adventurous hatchlings, while the youngest curled up at her feet. Tails twitched and muzzles bobbed to the beat of the song. P'laenn thrummed as one hatchling became so entranced that his jaw dropped and a sliver of drool formed at the corner of his mouth.

Today's song told of two lovers who had grown up together in the same village. Both came from poor families, she a weaver by trade, he a carpenter.

The song was full of sentiment and scenes that disinterested P'laenn—gift-giving, walking through the forests, heart-fluttering. P'laenn had never been in love, and she quickly learned from Bria's stories that humans placed a much higher value on the experience than dragons. Dragons loved, certainly, but they were not so weak as to be swayed by their passions like humans.

The song shifted, the joy of young love turning to sorrow. The young woman's parents had arranged for her to marry a rich man to help their poor family. The young woman cried in agonized poetry, torn between love for her young man and her family.

P'laenn huffed a cloud of smoke. Humans were so weak. No female dragon could be forced into a mating she did not desire. It was good for the hatchlings to hear this story and learn their enemies' shortcomings—it would make the beasts seem less intimidating when their time came to join the battle against the slayers.

The lovers now met in secret at their favorite spot. Salty sea-mist sprinkled lightly over P'laenn as she watched them discuss their options at the cliff's edge. The honorable thing would be for them to forget each other and for the young woman to marry the rich man as planned. But neither felt they could live without the other.

The lovers joined hands and closed their eyes, breathing in the ocean vapors and fearfully wondering what it would be like to fly—

P'laenn shook her head hard and roared, halting Bria's song. *"Hatchlings, to the yard, now! Stretch your wings and prepare for flight-training!"*

The hatchlings growled and hummed in protest, but obeyed their alphas' daughter. As they marched past her with drooping heads, P'laenn's heart twinged. It wasn't their fault they had to leave. She nearly growled at Bria, but stopped herself. There would be plenty of time for that once the little ones were out of earshot.

The hatchlings glided awkwardly down to the nearly-flat flight-yard. It was a mere sixty feet down a cliff from the cave, but that was enough to keep Bria from trying to reach it. Even if she tried and succeeded, there was plenty of mountain to traverse before she could make it to the ground. Escape was a fool's option.

P'laenn bared her teeth at the woman. *"What possessed you to tell that kind of tale to hatchlings? Would you bring sorrows to ones so young?"*

Bria smirked and stood. "You seem rather sorrowful yourself, P'laenn. Don't tell me you're growing soft?"

"Mind your words, human," P'laenn growled. Bria was right—she had been ensnared by the story—but she would not let the captive see her weakness. *"I am as likely to sympathize with humans as you are to fly."*

"I suppose I should jump, then." Bria sauntered to P'laenn, an amused smile growing. "You should know better than to lie about your feelings to an empath."

P'laenn huffed. *"Perhaps you would prefer death, vermin? To release yourself from captivity as the heroes of your tale did?"*

The amused light in the woman's eyes fanned into a flame of anger. "It's Bria. Not human. Not slayer. Not vermin. Bria."

Defiance flared in the woman's gaze as she stopped mere feet from P'laenn's face. "And I don't run from my problems. I face them, head-on."

P'laenn locked eyes with the impertinent human, her hot breath swirling Bria's tight curls. Not a drop of fear emanated from her. Fascinating. Though essentially helpless in the claws of her captors, the woman's fire never seemed to diminish.

P'laenn pulled her head back. *"Perhaps one day you will earn the right to have a dragon address you by name. If you live long enough."* She stalked to the cave entrance, flexing her wings in preparation for flight. *"Do not jump."*

The following evening, P'laenn and Anatoss, a flight-trainer, scouted for enemy movement in a ten-mile perimeter of their mountain. A trumpet from the alphas pierced the quiet night sky—a call for all dragons to come to the main cave.

P'laenn opened her mind and accessed her Illumination bond. *"Do you wish the scouts to return as well, alpha-mother?"*

"Yes. Come quickly."

"By Maker's wings." P'laenn cut off the connection and swerved in the direction of the cave. *"Anatoss, by alphas' orders, we must make haste."*

Without a word, the gray dragoness followed P'laenn. Though older and higher in rank, Anatoss was respectful to a fault and never so much as hummed at her alphas' daughter. She was a loyal dragoness, an excellent warrior, and an esteemed mentor. A pity their scouting time would be cut short.

They made it to the cave in minutes and flew through the entrance one after the other. Despite their speed, they found only a few open spots in side-caves near the entrance. P'laenn perched in one silently, Anatoss taking another directly across from hers.

Growls and hums echoed through the cave, and P'laenn braced herself for spiking anger as she reached out with her mind to enter the conversation.

"—the images are strong," one of the betas insisted. *"Stronger even than some dragons'! She cannot be allowed to put such things into the minds of impressionable hatchlings."*

A scout thumped his tail on the ground. *"I even caught two of them diving off a precipice—play-acting a story of two humans jumping to their deaths!"*

P'laenn hummed with her clanmates. Did humans tell stories of suicide to their own hatchlings? Irresponsible, annoying little creatures, even if they were *iompróir anam.*

Moresh thumped his tail on the ground and roared, silencing all sounds and telepathic communication. *"Harna and I listened to one of her stories this evening. Together, we saw the truth behind your statements. We had thought the girl a mere empath. We were wrong."*

P'laenn lifted her head. Not merely an empath? But all female slayers were—

"She is a telepath, like her slayer brothers, but her abilities seem to only manifest through song. We doubt she knows her power."

Dragons stood and roared, some flaring their wings out. A cacophony of telepathy bombarded P'laenn:

"Of course she knows. She's been using her power all this time to harm our hatchlings!"

"I told you we should have killed her days ago."

"Perhaps she can do us good."

"This is unheard of. How quickly are the slayers evolving?"

"SILENCE!" Harna roared across physical and astral planes.

One of the betas approached the alphas, his sapphire head hung low. *"Permission to speak, my alphas?"*

Moresh and Harna thumped their tails on the ground in unison and the beta spoke again.

"What is past cannot be changed, but we must think of our future. She cannot be allowed to find out the truth. The fire in her spirit and power in her mind may prove our downfall, whether she is in our caves or with her people. We must end her."

P'laenn stood now. This wasn't right. Perhaps she was dangerous, but if they killed Bria they would be killing a kindred spirit! She prepared to speak out against the beta, but her mother spoke first.

"You are right. We have enjoyed her spirit long enough. Now——"

P'laenn did not hear the rest as she raced out the cave entrance. She beat her wings as hard as she could, rising up the mountain toward Bria's prison. An insistent buzzing at the back of her mind indicated her mother trying to reach her, but P'laenn closed off her end of the bond. She couldn't fully hide her intentions if they connected, and secrecy was of the utmost importance.

P'laenn beat her wings for balance at the entrance to Bria's cave, the gusts of wind startling her awake.

"P'laenn? What are you doing here?"

"Saving your life. You are special, Bria."

Bria's eyes widened at the use of her name, and P'laenn couldn't help but brighten at her surprise, illuminating the chamber with her eyes.

"You are a human, but have the anam *of a dragon. The others seek to kill you, but I cannot let them."* P'laenn lowered herself to her belly. *"Come with me now.*

I am your only chance."

Without a word, Bria ran to the dragoness and jumped, grabbing two spines and pulling herself onto P'laenn's back. More fear emanated from her now than when she had faced the alphas the first day of her captivity, but with the fear came excitement and anticipation.

What would come of this unlikely partnership?

P'laenn made for the skies.

Darkness enveloped Alísa as the story paused, but she kept her eyes shut. Koriana's own voice broke past the historical characters she had been presenting.

"Eventually, Bria and P'laenn became good friends, and they altered each other's perspective on their races. Yet the war continued in their absence, and when they couldn't stomach the slaughter of innocents anymore, they flew from dragon clan to dragon clan, gathering together those who detested violence against villages and desired to end the slayers' vendetta against the dragon race. Eventually, my ancestor Anatoss joined them as well. Under the leadership of the Dragon Singer and P'laenn, their clan established their own territory, clearing it of slayers and ruthless dragons.

"But as word of the Dragon Singer spread, the slayer clans gathered together to face the threat to their way of life."

P'laenn's wings burned as she banked hard to avoid a flying spear, the pain echoing the raging flames covering the once-peaceful village below. Bria's order for the dragons to avoid breathing fire for fear of harming the villagers had been in vain, the slayers igniting home after home as they sought to eradicate the disease of dragon-friends.

Shouts of courage and cries of pain carried through the smoky battlefield as villagers fought the slayers. At the beginning of the battle, there had been pitchforks and walking sticks wielded alongside swords and spears—every able-bodied man and many women fighting to give the children and elderly a chance to escape. Now those who had never been trained in combat were either dead or retreating, while the few more capable warriors still stood their ground.

A mixture of pride, guilt, and sadness rippled through P'laenn. There had been a time when she had considered all humans vermin, but each of these villagers held an *anam* just as strong and real as a dragon's.

Above the din of clashing metal and crumbling homes, Bria's song carried from her position on P'laenn's back into the night. Though strained by hours of battle, its power continued to enter the minds and hearts of the few dragons left in the sky. It burst from her like fire, fueled by rage against the slayers. She had returned to her clan once since learning of her powers and tried to convince them of the truth. All they had seen was a traitor, and now they saw villages under her spell. There was no convincing creatures so blinded by hatred, *anam* though they may be.

A cry of pain called P'laenn's gaze to the ground, and rage filled her gut as she caught sight of one of the few villagers left locked in battle with a slayer. A scrape of metal against metal, and the villager fell to the ground under the slayer's onslaught.

Bria tensed above her. *"Lae—"*

"I see them."

P'laenn banked hard and dove for the combatants. Locking eyes on the slayer, she pulled air into the chamber of fire in her belly. She held back her roar of fury until she was right on top of him, then ignited the attacker.

She circled as the slayer screamed his agony, watching to be sure he didn't use the last of his life to end the villager's. She needn't have worried, the flames snuffed him almost as quickly as his sword would have their friend. The villager's face became recognizable now—a hunter, who had been one of the first to befriend Bria and her dragon clan.

A dragon screamed a death cry, and Bria's pain and anguish echoed P'laenn's. They could not stand against the slayers much longer.

Bria ended her song just long enough for her to call to the rising hunter, grief thickening her voice. "Follow your people into the wilderness and protect them. Tell any others you find the same. The dragons will cover you. There is nothing more to be done here."

Conflict showed in the man's eyes, but he only hesitated a moment before standing. His eyes flitted between Bria and P'laenn. "Maker between you and harm."

"*May his wings shield you,*" P'laenn answered, giving him a slow blink of her eyes. Then she rose, her wings again protesting as she fought gravity's hold. P'laenn's heart twisted as Bria's voice, too, protested—cracking, breaking, and cutting out as she tried to press on. She wouldn't last much longer.

P'laenn's mind raced. The clan had known the potential cost of this battle, known the odds were against them, yet they had decided to fight. Honor demanded they fight to the end; friendship demanded they guard the villagers' retreat as long as they could. This battle would end in the clan's death, where they would awaken in the Maker's eternal sky.

In previous battles, the thought brought her a warm peace, but something within her resisted. She was ready to die. The clan was ready to die. But Bria...

P'laenn stopped her ascent and dove after the retreating villagers. She couldn't let the Dragon Singer die. Without her, the hope of peace would end.

Bria's grip tightened and she stopped singing. "*What are you doing?*"

"*You have to go with them.*"

"*No.*"

"*You have to live and continue the fight.*"

"*No!*"

P'laenn didn't slow. Bria was a warrior—she had come to this battle prepared, even expecting, to pay the ultimate price. But P'laenn couldn't allow that.

Bria pounded a fist against P'laenn's scales, surely bringing herself more pain than she inflicted. "*I can't leave, not when my family are the monsters wielding the sword against you. Not when our friends' blood stains their blades! You above all know I cannot leave now!*"

P'laenn's former clanmates flashed through her mind's eye. She and Bria had fought a similar battle mere months ago, when dragons left Moresh and Harna's clan to join the Singer. The alphas hadn't taken kindly to the desertion, nor to the woman they had once deemed worthy of death. So many lights had gone out that day, some by P'laenn's own tooth and talon.

She had known what had to be done then, just as Bria did now.

With a roar borne by grief and determination, P'laenn tore back into the sky. Bria's renewed song granted her speed, and she rushed the slayers, breathing a long stream of fire—the last of her stores. It would be a few minutes before she could flame again.

Fire glanced off shields as she speared back into the sky and out of range of blade and arrow. Though she couldn't see them, she still sensed the presence of Anatoss and two male dragons—their only remaining clanmates. Perhaps if they could join together, they could—

Her body seized.

Vision blurred.

Sounds of battle fled.

Wind slipped from beneath her wings.

Mind-choke.

PAIN!

The next thing P'laenn knew was Bria standing over her. The Singer shook P'laenn's head with her tiny hands, begging her to wake up. Somehow they'd made it to the ground, where smoke and blaze obscured her from the slayers and their mind-choke.

P'laenn blinked, then bellowed as searing pain shot through her wing. A backward glance confirmed the worst—her right wing had broken in the fall. Her fate was sealed.

"Lae," Bria choked out through a fit of coughs, "they're coming. You must stand."

P'laenn's legs were heavy as stone. Now that the song had ended, the exhaustion of hours of battle finally caught up with her. She strained to rise, ashamed by the moan that escaped her throat in the effort. Even if she made it to her feet, she wouldn't have the strength to fight. After blacking out for who knew how long, she had perhaps one small blast of fire within her, and if she tried to swipe with tail or talon, she would surely fall again.

"Bria, you must leave me now."

"No!" Bria snarled. *"We started this journey together, and that's how we'll finish it!"*

Stupid woman. She bore the stubbornness of a dragoness, and it would kill her now. The slayers' voices were close, searching. They would soon find their quarry.

"You must live, Bria. Without a Dragon Singer——"

"There will be others."

Bria said it so simply, like saying the sun would rise in the east, as if it were guaranteed. But it wasn't—how could it be when only one had ever existed? Yet hope, even faith, shone on Bria's face, dancing in her eyes like the flames surrounding them.

Bria reached out and set a hand on P'laenn's muzzle. *"But you are right about one thing, my friend. Someone has to live. Someone has to carry the story and begin the search for the next Singer."*

P'laenn blew a weary puff of smoke. *"I will not last——"*

"We see you!" Anatoss' rich voice entered their minds. *"We're coming! For honor and death!"*

Two more dragons roared, their voices joining hers. *"By Maker's wings!"*

Bria's eyes slid back down to P'laenn's. *"But they will."*

The Singer stood, her body battered and scraped, and lifted her eyes to the night sky. Her shoulders drooped and her legs trembled, but purpose filled her eyes, and through coughs and cracks she sang once more.

> The wings that lifted me are gone,
> Fear has won its prey.
> Torn in two, body and heart,
> By family betrayed.
>
> Dearest ones, who'd fight and die,
> Tonight is not your time.
> Though fire calls to come and burn,
> Now throw away your pride.
>
> It is harder to live for peace
> Than die for honor's sake.

Bria fell to her knees as power flowed from her, draining her stores to silt and sediment. Anatoss and the others ended their approach, but rebellion coursed through the connection. Each of them would rather give their lives for the Singer than obey her command. But if they died, so did Bria's hope.

Bria coughed through the smoke and clenched her fists against the ground, fighting to give strength she no longer had. Such courage, such resilience.

Sister. Friend.

Every muscle trembled as P'laenn stretched her neck and touched Bria's forehead with her muzzle. *"Take from me. Finish your song. Give them a reason to live."*

Bria breathed raggedly, but she did as P'laenn asked, pulling psychic strength from her to fuel the song. Their last act as partners.

The Maker leaves no work undone;
His plans will see the light.
So search and find another who
In song will give you flight.

The battle here must end for now,
Until that new day's dawn.
By Maker's wings, fly fast and true
So hope is never gone.

It is harder to live for peace
Than die for honor's sake.

Memories flooded P'laenn and spilled into Bria. They went with the song, giving Anatoss and the others the full story. A trumpet of grief and sadness told of their obedience. They would pass every word, every image, every feeling to their future hatchlings through the Illumination. In them, a flame of hope would burn, kindling the search for the Dragon Singers Bria was so confident would come.

The slayers neared, the song ended, and the last thing P'laenn saw was Bria rising and pulling her sword from its sheath. A warrior dragoness to the end.

15

TO END A WAR

Alísa shivered as the scene in her head faded to black.

"After a time of mourning what was lost, Anatoss and the other survivors found mates and had hatchlings, each one gaining the memories of Bria from their parents. The task of finding the next Singer has passed from generation to generation. We believe you are to be Bria's successor and lead us in the war against the slayers."

Alísa drew in a ragged breath. Her stomach clenched and her throat closed. She clamped a hand over her mouth as sobs threatened to wrack her body.

Too much. This is all too much!

She squeezed her eyes shut against the tears, but visions of battle and loss cycled through her mind until she forced them open again. Her vision blurred with fear and sorrow, but she could feel the dragons' gazes on her, their light burning through her. She stared at the ground.

They waited for her now. Their expectation coursed over her, threatening to carry her away into a place she didn't recognize, a place she didn't want to be. A place of frontlines and blood and commands that drew the lines between life and death.

That power couldn't be hers. Shouldn't be hers. Wouldn't be—

"Alísa?"

"No." Her voice surprised her as she cut off Graydonn. It echoed through the cave and into her ears with a sound she had barely heard since learning to make the dragons hear her mental words. She kept going.

"I c-c-c-c—cannot be what you w—want. I am not strong. Not a warrior. Not c-c-c-c-c—c—c—" *Courageous! Spit it out!*

She couldn't.

She needed air.

Stumbling as she stood, Alísa scrambled for the cave's entrance. She clutched the egg, holding it to her more out of instinct than decision.

"*Stop!*" Koriana ordered. Alísa didn't slow, looking back just in time to see Graydonn scurry between them.

"*Mother, wait. She needs to process. Let her—*"

Graydonn's words cut off as Alísa rounded the cave entrance and broke their sightline. Her heart pounded into her throat as she ran across the mountain slope. Trees offered shade from the afternoon sun, but right now she would give anything to see the unimpeded sky.

With her escape came a strange calm—welcome in the midst of her roiling emotions, but unnatural. *Graydonn?* She stopped and looked back.

Nothing.

She breathed and searched for the source of calm. It started at her fingers and trickled up her arms and into her mind, where it soothed over her swelling panic.

The egg. Somehow, the dragonet echoed back the comfort Alísa had given her over the last few days.

Alísa breathed, sinking to the ground and running her fingers gently over the glossy surface of the egg. Divots became patterns as she worked to ground herself. Panic would do her no good.

"What do I do?" She whispered to the dragonet. "What am I going to do?"

Light confusion pressed through with the calm now—a questioning, as if the dragonet were asking her what was wrong. Could she understand, even within the egg? She certainly understood that something troubled Alísa. At the very least, putting her anxieties to words might help them settle.

"I've left everything behind, all to find out why I am the way that I am—and now this? How can they expect me to fight my own people? Leaving them and their violent ways is one thing, but I am no traitor!"

Tears welled once more. "Then again, maybe I am. If father knew where I'd gone, what I'd done to get here, he would be so—ashamed." Her throat tensed around the word, barely allowing it to squeak out. She half-sobbed, half-laughed. "And Kallar, he would erupt if he saw me sitting here with a dragon's egg in my lap."

The dragonet shifted inside the egg, and the very real life within the shell twisted Alísa's heart into knots. "Oh, little one, if they were here they would destroy you."

She pressed a hand over her mouth. So many little ones dead, so many widows or children missing parents like Koriana and Graydonn, so many lives ruined by this war. When Graydonn had said she could end the war, it had sounded so wonderful. But now she knew the cost—the Dragon Singer would end the war by fighting the slayers and ending the eradication of the dragon race. It was a bloody calling, one that Sareth had said could only end in death. And if she accepted it, she would take both the lives of her followers and of her enemies into her hands.

"I can't do it. I can't be the one to make those decisions and lead the charge. Father said war would break me, and he knows me better than anyone."

Grandfatherly eyes rose in her mind. "Except possibly Farren." And hadn't he warned her of this? *Sometimes we must be stripped of all we know in order to become our true selves. It is the Maker's way.*

She clenched her fists against the egg. "Why does it have to be me? Why not another Bria—fierce, strong, and able?" She ran her hands down her face. "Holy Maker, what have you done?"

Concern wafted to her, but it didn't run through her fingers like the dragonet's feelings. She twisted back the way she came and met amber eyes. Graydonn. He stood three trees away. They stared at each other, his eyes dimmed.

"I'm sorry." His voice was so gentle, as if afraid he might scare her away. *"I didn't mean to interrupt your prayer."*

Alísa sighed. "It's okay. My p—p-prayers are more incoherent q—q-q-questioning of the Maker's w—wisdom than respectful requests for more."

He thrummed wryly, grief seasoning his words. *"I know a bit about that."*

"I'm sure you do," she whispered.

They sat in silence for a moment. Graydonn watched the leaves being tousled by the breeze, while Alísa looked down at the egg. Her breathing smoothed and her heartbeat slowed. What now?

"May I approach?"

Alísa nodded. "Yes."

He padded to her and lowered to his belly five feet away. *"You stopped using telepathy."*

"I d—don't want anyone in my head right now."

He squinted at her. *"Speaking isn't the same as digging through your mind."*

"I know. This just f—feels safer."

"You are in no more danger from us now than before we told you Bria's tale."

She looked back at the egg. "W—what if I refuse t-t-t-to be what you want? Will I be s-safe then?"

Alísa's heart seemed to pound louder with each second of Graydonn's silence. It took at least ten counts before she dared to look him in the eyes.

"Will I?"

"I would never want to harm you." He spoke carefully, weighing each word. *"But a lie is as harmful as serpents' fangs. If you refuse and live as though you never knew the Maker's gift, you will be safe from us. But if you turn against us and use your power to destroy alongside the rest of your kind..."* His eyes dimmed. *"We cannot allow that."*

She nodded, his honesty oddly comforting. "I would never want to harm you, either. Or s-see harm come to this little one."

Graydonn's hope kindled as Alísa stroked the egg. The expectation still sent chills down her spine and clamped around her stomach.

"B—but I'm not what you want me to be. Bria was a f—fearless warrior. She impressed dragons with her fiery words and s-spirit. I possess n—none of those things."

Graydonn snorted. *"I've seen your strength. You wouldn't be here without it. You are capable of being what she was and more."*

Alísa tensed, ire rising. "No! Leaving in p-protest is one thing, but fighting against my own people? My father?" She shook her head. "I can't do it. I won't do it!"

Graydonn's voice rose to match hers. *"But you left because of their atrocities—why do you hesitate to stop such things from happening? Think of the dragonet you now hold; you cannot tell me you don't care!"*

Alísa glared at him. "You speak as though all dragons are innocent, and all slayers monsters. I've seen your k-k—k-kind's atrocities too—villages burned to the ground, widows b-burying their children. There is no right answer, and I would rather run to the edge of Arran and throw myself into the sea than p-p-p-pick a side!"

Her breath trembled out as this declaration reverberated through her. Though more forceful than anything she would normally speak, it was the truth. She couldn't be the slayers' bane any more than she could have continued to live among them. And so here she was, stuck in-between two worlds with no room to breathe.

Silence ensued as Graydonn stared at her. No breeze rippled through the trees, no animals chittered around them, even the trickle of water running out the cave entrance seemed to barely whisper.

Then, with far more calm than Alísa expected, Graydonn spoke. *"Then, what do you want, Singer?"*

Alísa stared at the ground. How could such a simple question have no simple answer?

She wanted to be safe. To stay far away from the frontlines, live in peace, and forget she had ever heard the title, 'Dragon Singer.' It was all she craved right now, the thought calming her racing heart and settling her nerves.

But was that really what she wanted? If so, then why on A'dem had she ever left the safety of her father's tent? Even a life spent as Kallar's wife would have been more comfortable. She would have been safe in his arms, so long as she never helped the dragons again.

And that was the key. She wanted to help the dragons. Not just 'the dragons,' though. She wanted to help innocent dragons who had been marked as evil. She wanted to stop the slayers from killing hatchlings and smashing eggs, from choking fathers out of the skies in front of their children.

She wanted to make the slayers know better, to convince them to be what they once were—the Maker's shield to protect humans, not his sword to annihilate dragons. She wanted to be that shield, to use whatever the Maker had given her to protect humankind from those dragons who would see them burn.

Alísa's heart sank. She wanted too much. She wasn't strong enough to shield anyone, wasn't eloquent enough to sway, wasn't wise enough to lead.

Tears filled her eyes as memories swirled around her. All the times she had tried to speak and was ignored. All the times she hadn't spoken and watched injustice take hold. All the times she had shivered in fear—even this very moment, trembling against a tree, too terrified to move in any direction that may or may not be the right one. If there was one thing she knew, it was that she wasn't enough.

But perhaps, more than anything, she wanted to prove herself wrong.

"I want to end the war." Each word, formed carefully and purposefully, seemed to fuel a fire in her heart. Her eyes shot to Graydonn, making him start. "Not to w—win it for the dragons, or for the slayers. I want to end it."

Graydonn blinked. *"What?"*

She grasped onto the psychic connection carrying Graydonn's words and sent her own, no longer afraid of what he might see. *"I want to convince dragons and slayers to stop the fighting. No more murdered hatchlings, no more burned villages. I want to end it all."*

He closed his eyes. *"You do realize that this is many times harder than what you've refused? Dragons would rally to you to fight the slayers—so many that you could leave behind those who would harm the innocent and still have a clan large enough to rival the slayers. But this? How could so many hearts change?"*

Alísa shook her head. *"I don't know. All I know is there are slayers out there who would turn if they knew what I do now. I cannot abandon them to die for a lie without first showing them the truth."*

Lumbering footsteps lifted Alísa's gaze to Koriana. The dragoness approached with none of the caution Graydonn had shown, apparently unconcerned that she might spook Alísa. *"And what of those who still will not turn, little Singer? Those who continue to prey on the weak? What will you do with those slayers?"*

Alísa gritted her teeth. *"And dragons."* She let out a breath full of tension. *"I don't know. I don't know how I'm going to do this, or if it's even possible."*

In fact, the more it ran through her mind, the more impossible it seemed. It would require convincing dragons to follow her without promises of revenge. It would require speaking to slayers, hardened warriors who had never before given her a second look. An impossible task, but with the greatest reward, should she succeed.

"It might be impossible, but it's the only option I can truly run toward."

Alísa stood, lifting the egg with her and holding it close as she approached Koriana. *"I can't make it there alone. You've seen my heart, you know I care for dragons as well as humans. Train me in how to use my powers, and I will seek guidance as to how to bring peace. I trust you, and I want you at my side."*

Koriana stood still, fixing glowing eyes on Alísa. They were like lightning amidst her storm-cloud scales—fiery, dangerous, and beautiful.

"Slayers are known for their ruthlessness, not their willingness to change. I fear you are being naïve, Alísa-Dragon-Singer."

The title sent a chill down Alísa's spine, yet kindled her hope. Koriana had used her name.

The dragoness dipped her head. *"But by Maker's wings, I will serve and counsel you in your journey."*

Graydonn got to his feet, lifting his wings lightly as a man might draw himself up tall. *"By Maker's wings."*

Alísa nodded to herself. To make this desire a reality, she, too, had to trust that the Maker knew what he was doing when he made her—daughter of a slayer chief, stammerer, and Dragon Singer, all. She had to let go of her anger, of the thought that he must hate her, no matter how long she had held onto it.

"By Maker's wings."

16

HOLDERS & SLAYERS

Ferns and brambles tugged at Alísa's skirts as she hiked along the southeastern edge of the lake. Birdsong, chittering squirrels, and the occasional rippling of the water were her only companions. Though alert to sounds of possible predators, she kept a relaxed pace, reveling in the peaceful sounds and silence of nature. It wouldn't last much longer—soon the bustle of the nearby village would overtake her, and she would have to play her part.

Three days of staying with strangers lay ahead of her, days of lying about who she was and why she was there. But the story she had woven for herself was believable enough, and she would only stay at the Hold until her metalwork orders were filled. Then she would go home to the cave.

Her heart ached as the little dragonet filled her thoughts. Would she be afraid that Alísa would never return, like her mother? Alísa had tried to explain it to her, but Koriana said a dragonet could only understand emotions. Language came after hatching, which should be in about five days.

Wary anticipation sent a chill through her. *Five days until my world flips upside down once more.*

She shook the anxious thoughts from her head. Better to focus on the task before her.

A large, two-story building slowly came into view through the trees, one with a door on each of its walls. The village Hold. Inside waited the first and most important people she had to convince, and likely also the most tiresome.

She breathed, forced her shaking hand into a fist, and knocked.

A tall young man answered the door. He was incredibly clean, in true holder fashion, with unwrinkled tan pants, a dark green tunic, and clean-shaven face. Despite his polished appearance, a mess of brown curls on top of his head seemed desperate to escape the short style.

"Welcome!" He flashed a smile.

"Hello." Alísa's voice came out more quietly than she intended. She swallowed and raised her voice. "My name is Alísa. My f—father hunts nearby and I'm in need of a p—p-p-place to stay."

She fought not to wince as she tripped over the formalities. Telepathic speech was far preferable to fighting against her stammer. This would be a long few days.

"Of course. Come in." He swept his hand inside. "My name is Falier."

She dipped her head graciously. "Eldra Nahne bless you, Falier."

"Eldra E'sall guide your paths."

Alísa nearly started at the customary blessing. *'Eldra Branni strengthen your hands'* was the greeting she normally received from holders. The greeting for E'sall's people settled hard in her chest, lifting her unanswered questions to the surface. Had Branni disowned her? Could she go straight to the Maker, as the dragons did? Was that even what she wanted?

"Are you hungry?"

Falier's voice brought her back to the present. Smells of savory stew and freshly-baked bread filled her nostrils and made her stomach growl.

"Very."

"Good." He gestured to one of the many tables. "We've only got a few minutes' wait before lunch is ready. Let me take your bag?"

Alísa slid her heavy bag off her shoulder, leaving her laden with only the short-sword and coin-purse on her belt. She settled into a chair, then looked in surprise as the stairs creaked lightly under Falier as he took the bag up to her room.

Wood. The entire Hold was made of it, from the support beams to the outer walls and ceiling. In the west, a wooden building was considered both foolish and a poor use of resources, but here—where dragons were rare and trees plentiful—it made sense. It certainly had a warmer, more welcoming feel than the stone and brick of her hill country.

Falier hurried gracefully back down the stairs and took the chair across from her. "I've never seen you before. New to the area?"

She nodded silently, fingering the tassels of the green and gold plaid table-runner.

"Welcome to Me'ran. Where are you from?"

"The hill country."

"Really?" His deep blue eyes lit up with interest. "How far have you come?"

She forced a smile. *Nosy holder. You're the reason I thought through everything beforehand.*

"I c-c-couldn't" —*breathe*— "tell you the mileage."

"I bet you've seen some interesting things in your travels."

I couldn't tell you the half of it…

A rich alto voice singing loudly outside interrupted the interrogation. Breathing a deep sigh of relief, Alísa glanced over her shoulder to see a petite woman about her mother's age coming through the southern door. Most of her blond hair was pulled half-up in braids, but a few stray curls stuck to her sweat-glistened brow. Her dress was a red plaid, much like the garb of a chief's wife except for the discolored white apron hanging about her waist. Her skirts swayed as she danced into the room and filled the space with an unfamiliar folk-tune.

> —My daughter saw a welcome sight:
> There's travelers a-coming.
>
> So run and tell your brother, oh,
> Make the stew and rise the dough.
> Run and tell your brother—Oh!

The woman stopped suddenly, then smiled warmly at Alísa. "I'm sorry, I didn't realize we had company. I usually ask before serenading my guests."

Alísa returned the smile. "P-please, don't stop. I've never heard the song b—before."

The woman dipped her head graciously and continued. The tune was simple and repetitive, allowing Alísa to pick it up quickly. She hummed a harmony, while Falier tapped the table rhythmically with his fingers.

> A holder stoked a fire bright,
> Keeping flames against the night,
> My son, he saw a welcome sight:
> A messenger's a-coming.

> So run and tell your mother, oh,
> Make the stew and rise the dough.
> Run and tell your mother, oh,
> A messenger's a-coming!

> A holder stoked a fire bright,
> Keeping flames against the night,
> When I saw a welcome sight:
> The bards, they are a-coming.

> So run and tell your father, oh,
> Make the stew and rise the dough.
> Run and tell your father, oh,
> The bards, they are a-coming!

Alísa applauded the holder's performance as a bellowing voice came from the kitchen.

"How's a man supposed to bake with all that singing going on out there?"

Alísa's eyes widened, but the woman merely smiled and rolled her eyes. "Don't mind my husband. His brand of humor needs time to grow on people. I don't believe we've met. What's your name and where are you from?"

"Alísa. My f—father is a hunter roaming the area. And you are?"

"Katessara, but everyone calls me Kat. The loudmouth in the other room is Parsen."

Alísa chuckled half-heartedly, eying the door to the kitchen and not entirely sure she wanted to meet said loudmouth.

Kat looked about the room. "And our eldest is somewhere nearby."

"She's out," Falier supplied, a slight sadness tilting his eyes. "Taking the last of the supplies to the wayfarers."

A jolt ran through Alísa, and she gripped her skirt under the table.

Wayfarers nearby. Were the dragons in danger?

Settle down. She forced herself to breathe slowly. If they were gathering supplies from the village, they were probably heading out. Me'ran was the closest village to the mountain, so they were likely heading away. Everything would be fine.

Kat slid into the chair across from Alísa. "Will your family be joining us?"

"No, they're back at c—c-c-camp." She swallowed back a lump forming in her throat. That bit wasn't a lie, yet it was the hardest thing she had said yet.

"You came alone?" Falier's eyebrows lifted. "What of your wares?"

Alísa's heart skipped a beat. She hadn't thought of that—hunters typically brought skins, antlers, meat, and the like for trading.

"We—we're still establishing ourselves in the area. P-P-Papá is learning the animals and t-t-terrain. We've used much of our c—c—c" —*no, don't get flustered! Redirect—* "k-k-kills for ourselves."

Kat and Falier both nodded silently, Falier with a sympathetic half-smile. Heat rushed to her cheeks and she looked away. *So it begins.*

A hand covered hers, and Alísa started and looked into Kat's deep blue eyes. "No need to be embarrassed, dear. I understand. My brother stammers, and I did a little myself when I was young. Don't fret about it."

Hope warmed Alísa's heart and she searched Kat's eyes, her voice coming in a whisper. "It can go away?"

"Mine did—"

"How?"

"—but my brother's didn't. Mine went away with practice when I was eight. I can't tell you yours will, just that I understand, and you needn't be ashamed."

Alísa sighed as her heart came back down to earth. She was well past eight years old—there was probably no hope for her now.

At least that got us off the wares path.

"I heard you harmonizing before," Falier said. "Are you a musician?"

And here we go again. "I really only sing for m—my own p-pleasure. But I enjoy music a lot."

"Falier!" Parsen called from the kitchen.

Falier jumped up to answer, making eye-contact with his mother as he left. "Tell her about the céilí."

Kat's eyes sparkled. "Oh yes, you should join us tomorrow night. The whole village gets together once a week for a night of dancing and story-telling."

Alísa fingered the fabric of her skirt as images of the last celebration she had attended filled her head. The raucous laughter and conversation, all of the emotions ringing through her head, and the taunting man-children.

"I'm not much for large social g—gatherings. Plus, I d-don't céilí dance."

Kat smiled. "We can fix that last part. Think about it."

Alísa nodded, more to appease Kat than anything else.

She started as two doors opened simultaneously. Falier stepped through the kitchen door with a large pot, while a blond young woman in a deep green dress came in from outside.

The young woman was obviously Kat's daughter, with a similarly petite frame and wavy hair only a shade darker than Kat's. She could be only a few years older than Alísa, but her brown eyes seemed to hold a wisdom beyond her years. They held melancholy in their depths that quickly disappeared when her gaze landed on Alísa.

"Hello."

"Just in time," Falier called, setting the pot in the middle of the table. "We were going to send out a search party."

The sadness returned to the young woman's eyes, and Falier's brow creased. He hurried to his sister and gave her a hug, which she returned fiercely. He held her for a few seconds, and when they pulled apart, Falier whispered something that put a genuine smile on the young woman's face.

The sight warmed Alísa's heart. There was something about a brother's love that had always made her jealous of Trísse and her brothers. Sure, they got on each other's nerves frequently, but Trísse's brothers would protect her to their dying breaths, and Falier comforting his sister was just as beautiful.

The kitchen door opened once more as Falier and his sister came to the table, and Parsen emerged with steaming hot bread and soft cheese for spreading. His smiling brown eyes matched his daughter's, but peeked out from under thick brown eyebrows. His hair pulled back in a half-up ponytail, and his strong jaw was clean-shaven.

Kat began dishing out the stew as Parsen set the heavenly-smelling bread on the table. "Welcome to our Hold, young lady. I'm Parsen."

"Alísa." She dipped her head in respect. "Eldra Nahne bless you."

Alísa turned to the daughter for introductions, but the young woman sitting across from her didn't notice. Instead, she stared into space just above Alísa's head and to the right, leaving Alísa at a loss.

Falier's mouth quirked as he nodded at his sister. "That's Selene."

Selene shook her head quickly and met Alísa's eyes. "Sorry. Yes, I'm Selene." Her voice was high and airy, as if made of clouds. "It's nice to meet you."

Falier leaned toward Selene. "Color?"

Selene answered him with a hard pinch to his arm, eliciting a yelp. Alísa pressed a finger to her mouth to keep from laughing, but Parsen and Kat didn't hold back their chuckles.

"All right, let's not let this get cold." Parsen reached for his wife and Falier's hands.

Selene and Kat held their hands out to Alísa and she quickly took them, trying to not show her surprise. Her family would hold hands when blessing food, but never with strangers.

Parsen's deep voice echoed a blessing Alísa had heard many times: "For what the Maker has provided, we are grateful. May he and his Eldír bless the faithful unto strength of body, purity of heart, and commitment to our word."

"So be it," the others responded.

It took Alísa a second to notice that all eyes were now on her. Her cheeks heated—as a guest, she was expected to take the first bite. She had never been the sole guest in a Hold before. Her father had always gone first, as the head of the family and chief of the clan.

She grabbed her spoon quickly and lifted the savory stew to her mouth. A smile came to her lips unbidden as the tender meat practically melted between her teeth. Certainly different from the charred meat of the last few days.

The others began eating as well, Parsen breaking off a piece of bread and passing the loaf to his wife before dunking his piece in gravy. The bread tasted just as divine as the stew.

"So, Alísa," Falier spoke between mouthfuls, "did my mother convince you to come to the céilí tomorrow?"

Alísa swallowed. "Maybe."

Selene's voice floated over the table. "Come for the music, if nothing else. It's wonderful to listen to, even if you aren't dancing."

"You won't be able to sleep through it anyway." Parsen pointed at Alísa with his spoon, only to be smacked on the arm by Kat. "It's held right outside."

Alísa pushed a potato across the bowl. *Good. I'll still be able to enjoy the music while avoiding the social aspect.*

"I'll think about it."

The corner of Selene's mouth quirked, and she made brief eye-contact with Alísa before returning to her food. She knew it was a lie.

Silence settled over the table for a few precious seconds before Falier began again. "What brought your family over the river?"

Parsen raised his eyebrows. "You're from the hill country?"

Alísa nodded once. "My father was bored with the same old game and t-t-terrain and decided to look for a new challenge. We've m—moved a lot."

"I've always wanted to travel." Falier leaned on the table. "What's it like in the hill country?"

Everything she could say seemed too obvious to voice. But perhaps it wouldn't be obvious to people from the forests.

"It's far more open. There are g—groves of trees here and there, a few shrubs, but mostly just grasses as far as the eyes can s-see. The sky feels so much c—closer, always t-touching the earth on the horizon, and the winds are harsher than here. Sometimes I could lean b-back against it and the wind would hold me up."

She laughed as memories swept over her—had it really only been three days?

Alísa jumped as the southern door swung open behind her and she twisted to see three adults enter. The first man held the door for the couple behind him, and Alísa's heartbeat quickened. Everything about him screamed 'slayer.'

He was perhaps in his early thirties, but held himself high as a man who'd earned the right. Two small warrior's braids twisted amidst his sandy hair, and the hilt of a sword just barely stuck out past his deep brown cloak.

The couple behind him were perhaps in their late fifties. The man leaned heavily on a staff, compensating for a missing left leg. The woman—his wife, Alísa presumed—stayed just behind him with ever-watchful almond-shaped eyes. Silver strands of wisdom framed her face, beautifully contrasting her tan skin. She moved with the strong grace of the female warriors of old, her flowing red dress dancing gently about her legs.

The husband held a dignified countenance, belying his plain tunic and pants and the sweat glistening on his brow. His salt-and-pepper beard was neatly trimmed, his long hair pulled back in a low ponytail, and his bright blue eyes held the pride and vigilance of an eagle.

"Namor," Parsen said, standing. "I thought you'd be seeing the wayfarers off."

The older man nodded gravely. "They are on the road. I've called a meeting of the elders—the rest will be here shortly."

His eyes landed on Alísa, then moved to Falier and Selene. "This conversation isn't suited to young ones."

Alísa blinked. The only one to call her young in over a year was Koriana. By slayer standards, she, Selene, and Falier were all adults. Even without the status of future chief, Alísa had been privy to 'adult' meetings.

Parsen looked back to the table. "Alísa is a guest in our Hold. She will leave when she is ready. I cannot send her away for a meeting you called without notifying me."

The slayer shut the door behind them. "We won't take more than an hour. Surely she will understand the needs of the village outweigh her own."

"Yarlan—"

"No, it's fine," Alísa interrupted Parsen, placing her spoon into her empty bowl. There was no way she would get on the slayer's bad side, nor that of the elders. "I have errands t—t—to run, anyway. I can c-c-come back later."

She stood to leave, and Falier and Selene stood with her.

"We'll go with you." Selene smiled. "We can show you where the shops are."

"Thank you."

Selene nodded, then walked past the couple and paused as Yarlan opened the door. Alísa smirked inwardly. *At least he's not a completely awful representation of our people.*

"Excuse me, young lady." Namor's gravelly voice came as she walked past him.

Alísa turned. "Yes?"

"I haven't seen you before." He squinted at her, not unkindly. "Where are you from?"

"M—My father hunts in the area, b-but we c—c—c—"

"Don't hurt yourself," Yarlan mumbled.

Alísa tensed. *Ignore it. Redirect.* "Hail. We hail from the western hill c-country."

Namor nodded slowly. "You came here recently?"

Alísa nodded. The fewer words she could say, the better.

"Have you seen evidence of dragons past the Nissen? Footprints? Burning sections of forests? General senses of unrest in villages?"

She shook her head quickly, fighting to keep her anxiety at bay. "Why?"

"A few days ago, I thought I sensed the presence of a dragon."

Alísa's heart skipped a beat. His missing leg and eagle-like gaze now made sense. She did her best to rein her mind in. If Yarlan or Namor realized she was a fellow slayer, there would be trouble.

"It passed by so quickly, I wasn't sure I was right, or if it was just the imaginings of a weary old warrior. None of the wayfarers or even Yarlan here noticed anything, but a hunter in the middle of the forests might spot something."

"I'll k-keep my eyes open. My father, t-too."

He nodded firmly. "Good. Thank you, dear girl."

She gave him what she hoped was a smile and made for the door. She hurried past Yarlan without giving eye-contact, sighing as Falier shut the door behind her.

"Don't mind Yarlan," Falier said. "He's a good slayer, but kind of a lousy human being."

She chuckled mirthlessly. "I'm used to it."

He gave her an almost sad smile. "Well, you won't get it from me."

"Us," Selene corrected, swinging around to smile at Alísa. "Now, where are we headed?"

"B—blacksmith, p-please." She tried to smile back, but it might have been a wince. Her empathy pounded against her skull, begging for release, and she let it go until it gently wafted around her like a cloud. It was safe now.

Anxiety still raised chill-bumps over her skin. She wanted to end the war? How could she, if fear took hold at the first sign of trouble? How could she—frightened, trembling Alísa—ever accomplish such a task if the sight of slayers made her want to run?

No slayer would listen to her like this. *She* wouldn't listen to her like this. She needed to be braver, step out, build an alliance.

Alísa sighed to herself. *And the first step is going to the céilí.*

17

THE CÉILÍ

Alísa couldn't help but smile as she twirled through the céilí steps, now barely needing to watch Selene mirroring the steps as Falier called them. The last half-hour had flown by as she learned from them in the safety of the Hold's walls, her apprehension of tonight's festivities slowly melting away.

There was a comforting structure to céilí-dancing, as the dancers merely followed the caller's steps. Dancing also didn't require talking—another point in its favor. In fact, the hard work of keeping up with the caller discouraged conversation.

Falier ended his step-calling with a small round of applause.

"Those are the basic steps." Selene smiled, placing her hands on her hips. "Everything else stems from them and, with a good lead, will be easy enough if you keep moving your feet."

Falier approached Alísa. "Now we'll show you how these steps work with a partner."

He took Alísa's hand lightly in his, and a light pain pulsed through their point of contact. It felt like a headache or the beginnings of a migraine, but the feeling soon faded, lost to the movement of the dance.

Embarrassment and panic shot through her the first time she tripped up. With her hand in Falier's, she couldn't pause and catch up on the next step as she had done earlier.

He gave her a small smile and pulled her along with him.

"You're doing fine. Keep your feet moving in that same basic pattern and use the connection to your partner to keep you on track." He squeezed her hand lightly to emphasize his point, then with a quick pull and push sent her into a spin that hadn't been called. She missed a step but did her best to keep moving, and Falier grinned as he pulled her into the next step. "There you go!"

Soon Parsen and Kat joined them, teaching Alísa a two-partner dance. Falier and Selene switched places, Selene taking Alísa's hand and Falier calling while drumming on a *bodhrán*—a wide, flat drum held in the left hand and played with a double-sided mallet in the right.

A few people joined the dance, seemingly out of nowhere, and on the next partner-swap Alísa moved from Selene to a man she had never met before. Her face reddened, but she forced herself to focus on Falier's calling.

Advance. Retreat. Side-sevens. Side-sevens. Advance. Retreat. Spin.

Soon she found herself with another new partner and allowed herself to smile and enjoy the dance. A flute joined in the song, and Alísa nearly tripped as she swung her head to look. Selene's eyes laughed from behind the wooden instrument, but the young holder didn't miss a beat.

Selene and Falier ended the song with a long, low note and a drum-roll. Alísa joined in as the dancers clapped, her heart pounding out its own applause. She had done it! She had made it through the dance with minimal tripping, and she actually wanted to do it again!

Parsen waved a hand at the growing crowd. "Unless you're wanting to jump over tables and chairs, I suggest we move outside."

The small crowd followed the holder's instructions, chatting and laughing as they exited the building. Their excitement bounced through the air and pounded against Alísa's tightly-controlled empathy. She could fight it, but it would take focus to keep the pounding at bay. The other option was to accept it, let it join to her like her own pulse, and see where it might take her.

With a deep breath, she loosened her hold and let excitement spread through her.

Kat threaded her arm through Alísa's as they stepped into the cool of the evening. "Having fun?"

Alísa grinned. She didn't need the others' excitement to truly mean that.

"Good." Kat smiled back. "Enjoy yourself tonight. And, fair warning" —a twinkle shone in her deep blue eyes— "I may ask you to teach us a folk-song from the hill country."

Alísa's throat closed up, excitement suddenly swallowed by anxiety. Sing a song for a large group of people? She had barely ever sung in front of anyone but Farren. Even her own parents had only ever caught bits and pieces as she went about her chores in perceived solitude. She had only ever felt comfortable in front of Farren—even singing to Graydonn and Koriana had been difficult.

And teaching? Teaching required talking. To a large crowd of people. Loudly. With her stammer evident to all. It would form many people's first impression of her.

Still, she *was* here to build bridges. How could she if no one knew her? Singing for them would allow them to see her face and know her. And she didn't stammer when she sang. Maybe—

Kat's brow furrowed. "If you'd rather I didn't put you on the spot—"

"No, I'd love to s—sing a song of the hill c-c-country. But K—K-Kat?" She lowered to a whisper. "Can I just sing? I don't want to talk in front of people."

Kat's eyebrows raised. "Oh! I'm sorry. Of course, you can just sing. I'll do all of the talking."

Relief swept over Alísa, and she smiled to herself. Kat hadn't thought of her stammer as an issue. She had even forgotten about it!

A breeze chilled Alísa's skin as Kat left to join the rest of her guests, but the cold couldn't wipe the grin off her face. Joy filled her, lifting her heart into the sky, where the stars laughed with her. So many people thought her fragile, even unintelligent, due to her stammering. But not Kat.

The light of the bonfire pulled Alísa back to earth. The villagers gathered in a space cleared of trees just outside the Hold and began partnering up for the next dance. Six instrumentalists gathered near the fire—Falier, Selene, a man with a low-fife, a woman with a fiddle, and two other drummers.

A freckled teenage boy—probably fourteen or fifteen years, yet slightly taller than she—offered his hand to Alísa just as Parsen began introducing the next song.

Here I go! She took his hand with a polite smile and he led her closer to the fire, where the other partners assembled. Parsen explained a few peculiarities about the coming dance, while the instrumentalists spread out around the fire, alternating between percussive and melodic instruments.

They began a fast jig that made Alísa's stomach drop, but as her young partner led her through the steps she began to relax and let herself flow with the music. It surrounded her, like rushing waters spinning her effortlessly through the steps. The beating of the drums became her heartbeat, energizing her and bringing life to her body and soul. The flute's strong melody lent her its grace, the low-fife served as her anchor, and the fiddle—Oh, the fiddle! So vibrant, melismatic, and dissonant—became her life.

The song ended far too soon.

Alísa clapped for the players and returned a bow to her partner. A new partner, one of the men she had danced with inside the Hold, snatched her up before the next reel began. Soon the music had her in its embrace once more, spinning, weaving, and flying her through its story with ease.

She nearly fell over as she bowed to her partner, laughing as her head spun for a few seconds after the music ended. He grabbed her elbow, gently supporting her as she found her balance.

"Next time, keep eye-contact through the spins." Kat walked up to them. "Or watch his shoulder if you don't feel comfortable. It will help."

Kat's eyes wandered somewhere beyond Alísa, first squinting, then smiling. She laid a hand on Alísa's shoulder and pointed.

"We have guests."

Alísa twisted to follow Kat's finger, and her heart skipped a beat as lights glimmered in the treetops. They glowed in pairs of blue, green, red, and many other colors, all shining like a wildcat's eyes when they caught the moon. It was eerie, yet no fear rose from Kat.

"What are those?" Alísa whispered.

"Dreki. They've been gone a couple of months. You're in for a treat tonight."

Kat left her, weaving through the crowd to the instrumentalists. Alísa backed up until she bumped into another woman. She breathed an apology, and when the woman turned, she saw the lights and laughed with delight.

"Come, let's give them space." The woman pulled on Alísa's arm.

Soon the whole crowd had cleared a path between the bonfire and the dreki. Only Selene and Falier remained in the path, Falier's excitement dancing in his eyes, while a ghost of a smile graced Selene's face.

Selene raised her flute to her lips and began a new jig, slower than the others, but with a solid downbeat and light attitude. Soon Falier joined the song, lightly tapping his hand on the *bodhrán* rather than using a mallet.

Alísa allowed a row of people in front of her, but as their eager anticipation filled her, she stood on tiptoes to watch for the awaited moment.

She gasped near-silently as a pair of blue lights darted from the cover of the trees and hovered before Falier and Selene in the light of the bonfire. Her heartbeat sped as she recognized the silhouette against the backdrop of the flames.

The dreki were tiny dragons!

18

DREKI

Alísa couldn't tear her eyes away. Blue baubles on each finger of the tiny dragon's translucent wings caught the firelight, flashing it over the crowd as they dipped and twisted. The creature's mane ran the length of its body, flowing and dancing like sapphire grasses in the wind.

Two more of the silver creatures swooped and spun near the flames, joining the aerial dance. Their manes and wing-baubles glimmered in ruby and amethyst, each matching the color of their eyes. They twisted through the air, coming so close it seemed they might hit each other, yet in their grace they never collided.

More joined in the dance, until six dreki dove and flipped around the bonfire, some even diving through the flames. Their bright bodies reflected the firelight in patterns that flickered over the crowd.

Other dreki stayed in the trees, their glowing eyes moving and flashing in the foliage like fireflies.

Three young children, each between four and ten years, ran to the light of the bonfire, giggling and dancing to the music. The six brave dreki wove around their new dance partners, radiating mirth. It spun into Alísa's heart like a dance partner, beckoning her to join it with the other dancers, but none of the adults moved. She filled her lungs slowly and breathed the mirth back out, forcing herself to hold back.

Falier took a cautious step closer to the dreki and began singing in a lovely tenor—a song of springtime and newness. The sapphire creature flew to him and hovered in front of his face. Its shining eyes stared into Falier's with an intensity that would have made Alísa turn away, but Falier didn't waver. The tiny dragon gave out a high-pitched trill and settled on Falier's shoulder.

Multiple trills answered from the trees, and Alísa laughed with delight as the rest of the dreki whisked into the dance. The woman beside her laughed too, swaying to the music, and across the way two adults began dancing again.

Slowly, the rest of the crowd began to move, free-dancing without a caller. The dreki kept their distance, but didn't retreat back into the trees until the song ended.

Alísa stared after them, bouncing from one pair of eyes to the next. *Are these creatures as intelligent as the dragons?*

A long note from the low-fife, answered by Selene's flute, drew Alísa's eyes from the forest. The song was a beautiful, melancholy ballad, the flute weeping in the night, while the low-fife provided a grieving counterpoint.

Some of the dreki flashed back out into the light of the bonfire, weaving together in swirling patterns, smooth and drooping, as though they understood the emotion behind the song. An emerald one settled on Selene's shoulder, watching the holder's fingers glide over the instrument. The other dreki seemed comfortable with her as well, dancing closer to her than to the fifer.

Selene herself remained steady, completely at-ease with the creature on her shoulder. The same part of Alísa that had always longed to fly, the part that settled when holding the dragonet's egg, now reached out for the dreki. Perhaps Selene could introduce them later.

The song drew to a close and Kat's hand found Alísa's shoulder. "Are you ready?"

Alísa's stomach dropped. *Right. The song.* "N—No. But let's go."

Kat took her hand with a reassuring smile and drew her to the bonfire. Her voice resonated over the crowd.

"Some of you may have already met or danced with Alísa—"

"If she danced well, I take full credit," Parsen quipped. "If not, you should know that Selene taught her, and I can't take any responsibility."

The crowd laughed as Kat shoved him. "What you may not know about her, though, is her family hails from the hill country. I've asked her to sing us a song of her homeland tonight, and she graciously agreed. Please, give her a warm welcome."

Heat rose into Alísa's cheeks as the villagers applauded. Her stomach dropped. She hadn't thought of a song to sing. Her mind raced through her options, immediately dismissing any songs about slayers or wayfaring, as well as anything so generic that it might be a song the villagers already knew. She ran out of choices quickly.

The last note of the previous song echoed in her mind over and over again until it slid into the first notes of a song she had written not too long ago.

Alísa drew in a trembling breath. She hadn't even sung this one for Farren, but at least she could be certain the villagers wouldn't know it.

A hand tapped her shoulder. Falier.

"Give me the meter and tempo and I'll back you up. The other musicians will too, once they hear the beginning. You've got this."

Alísa gratefully returned his warm smile. "It's a reel."

She tapped the tempo on her thigh. Once Falier picked it up, she turned back to the crowd and released the first notes into the night.

With graceful feet my maiden dances to the song;
Praise of would-be lovers who know they'd be wrong
If they ever thought my maiden would turn her eyes from me.
Her love and beauty deeper than the deepest sea.

The stars shine in her eyes, and the sun shines in her hair.
No one can compare to my maiden fair.
The stars shine in her eyes, and the sun shines in her hair.
No one can compare to my maiden fair.
No, no one can compare to my maiden fair.

The villagers clapped to the upbeat song and Alísa's courage rose. Selene joined with her flute, providing musical space between the chorus and verses, and Falier hummed a delightful harmony as Alísa came back in. They were obviously well-versed in the art of improvisation.

She launched into the second verse of the reel a bit louder.

> Every day my maiden, with legs so very strong,
> Sets out to face the day, with a joy that is lifelong.
> Though many men do praise her personality,
> They know that they could never take her love from me.

Dreki stopped and stared as Alísa entered the second chorus, each bright, colorful eye fixed on her. They hovered around her, looking almost mesmerized, but the magic of the moment quickly turned to uncertainty. What if these tiny dragons were affected in the same way as regular dragons? Would her singing expose her secrets to Me'ran?

Her breath squeezed in her chest, cutting off the air for her song. She missed her entrance for the third verse, and Falier nudged her.

"Go on," he whispered. "They like it!"

His words were so sure. Maybe this reaction had nothing to do with her gift. Maybe the dreki had done this before. Either way, if she didn't continue the song it would raise just as many questions as continuing. Perhaps more.

She steeled herself and began the third verse.

> With skilled hands my maiden works throughout the day;
> Mending, baking, building, her strength will never sway.
> The would-be lovers praise her virtuosity,
> Though knowing that my maiden has eyes for only me.

> The sweet voice of my maiden takes me far away.
> The quiet strength within her heals all my pain.
> She sings her songs with words formed specially for me.
> Her strength and beauty like the waves upon the sea.

> The stars shine in her eyes, and the sun shines in her hair.
> No one can compare to my maiden fair.
> The stars shine in her eyes, and the sun shines in her hair.
> No one can compare to my maiden fair.
> No, no one can compare to my maiden fair.

The villagers applauded as her last note faded into the night. She smiled graciously, but gasped as tiny, excited voices echoed over and over in her head.

"Singer!" "Singer!" "Singer!"

The voices clashed in Alísa's head, each bringing with it a name and an image, quickly overwhelming her outstretched empathy. Wonder from Falier and Selene assaulted her. She choked back her own fear as the dreki danced around them as though the music were still playing. Alísa pushed against their excitement and batted back the peoples' wonder, but the emotions rose up strong. Weariness fell over her like a heavy cloak.

Come on, Alísa. She swallowed hard. *Focus.*

A purple creature flew inside the circle of its brethren and hovered in front of Alísa. Her voice gave the distinct impression of lavender and a name—Chrí.

"Singer?"

The creature's eyes pulled at Alísa, deep pools of amethyst. She focused on them with all her empathic powers and formed her thoughts carefully, hoping Chrí would understand.

"Please calm yourselves. It's too much, and these people don't know about me. They can't know, not yet. Please."

Chrí let out a sharp chirp and a fleeting image passed through Alísa's mind—distraction.

The dancing suddenly stopped and the dreki flew into the crowd. The people laughed with delight as the creatures swirled around them before heading back into the trees. Alísa breathed low and deep as their pounding emotions and image-names left with them, though an echoing ring stayed with her.

Breathe. You're fine. It's fine.

Falier shot her a reverent smile. "They've never reacted that way before." Alísa lowered her eyes and began to shrug it off, but he raised a hand to stop her. "You have a gift—the voice of an Eldra."

Heat rose to her cheeks and she instinctively raised her hand to the chain around her neck before stopping herself. She couldn't finger the dragon scale without raising questions. She would have to hide it even here.

"You all right?" Selene spoke behind her, her soft voice breaking through the ringing. "They can be overwhelming."

Selene's had a similar experience? She turned to meet Selene's eyes. Genuine concern flowed from them, and Alísa smiled weakly.

"M—maybe it would be good to t-t-take a break."

Selene inclined her head toward the Hold. "Come with me."

Alísa followed, skirting along the edge of the crowd until they made it to the building. Instead of entering, Selene led her around the outside until the giant wooden walls blocked the light of the fire, leaving them with only starlight and a sliver of the waxing moon.

Alísa breathed deeply and stared into the night sky. It pulled her into its depths, bringing a sense of wonder and drowning out the noise of the last few minutes with its vastness.

Selene stood silent beside her, contentment and peace flowing from her in gentle ripples.

A flapping sound interrupted the night's calm, and Selene's giggle answered it.

"Haven't you caused enough trouble, little drek?"

Two points of green shone in Selene's hair. Was that the same green dreki—drek?—that had listened to Selene play?

"Singer!" A weight settled lightly on her shoulder. Chrí.

"Have you met the dreki before?" Selene spoke gently.

"No."

A psychic connection flowed between Chrí and herself, kept open by the drek. Alísa met Chrí's eyes. *"Thank you."*

The drek chirped and rubbed her tiny muzzle against Alísa's cheek. *"Yes."*

"Wow. It took a month of work for Laen to trust me." Selene raised her hand to pet the drek's mane. "And I'm one of the few they'll all speak to. Ska waited a few months before sitting on Falier's shoulder, despite his obvious interest in the *bodhrán*."

Alísa swallowed. She was treading dangerous ground, raising questions she didn't want to answer.

"You doing okay? You seemed a bit preoccupied, even anxious, even before the dreki swarmed you."

Alísa fingered the folds of her skirt. This wasn't exactly a comfortable topic either, but at least it didn't have to do with the dreki's attraction to her.

"I've never liked large c-c-crowds of p-people. And the louder I have t—to talk, the worse my stammer gets."

Selene nodded. "I'm not a huge fan of crowds myself."

Alísa raised an eyebrow. A holder who didn't like large groups of people?

"You seem so c—comfortable."

"I love the people, just not the crowd." Selene paused a moment, as though pondering whether to continue. "I can see sounds, and the noisier it gets, the harder it is to focus on what's really there."

Alísa must have made a face, because Selene laughed musically and continued. "I know—I've never met anyone else like me. But it's true. Every sound has a different color to me. For example, when I hear my own voice, I see flashes of lilac blue just before my peripheral vision on my left. When I hear my flute, I see clouds of pale orange."

Alísa leaned back against the Hold, careful not to crush Chrí between her head and the wall. "That's incredible. I've never even heard of that before. Is—"

She stopped herself from asking Selene if something was wrong with her. She of all people should know better than to ask that. "D-d-do you know why it happens?"

Selene shook her head. "It's been this way as long as I can remember. I didn't even know it was strange until I tried to teach Falier his colors by using the ones in the air and my parents became concerned. No healer has been able to find any detrimental effects to my health, though. The only real problem it causes is that large, loud groups of people can be overwhelming. But then I just come here for a while and center myself."

Alísa nodded. As an empath, she could relate more deeply than Selene knew. There was a part of her now that wanted to tell Selene just that— something that felt completely at-ease with the young holder even though they were practically strangers. But that was foolhardy and would endanger more than just herself, so she merely smiled and looked back up at the stars.

"It's very p—peaceful back here. Thank you for sharing it with me."

"Of course."

A new song began, led by the low-fife, and melancholy trembled from Selene. Her eyes danced over the stars as she absentmindedly stroked Laen's mane. Her ghost of a smile gave no impression of the sad thoughts flowing through her.

Alísa swallowed. Technically, she shouldn't know something was wrong, but such was the burden of an empath. Should she ask anyway? Would Selene even tell her what was going on?

"Selene?" Falier's voice preceded him around the corner of the Hold.

"Falier," Selene answered quickly. "Alísa and I were just taking a break."

His eyes widened slightly, then he relaxed. Apparently, he had expected Selene to be alone.

"Hey," he said, a smile replacing his surprise. "Is the crowd too much for you too?"

"A little." Alísa raised an eyebrow. "And you?"

"You kidding? This is my favorite event each week." He glanced at his sister. "I just wanted to check on Selene."

"I'm fine." Selene nodded quickly. "But I did want to talk to you. Alísa, you wouldn't mind giving us a minute, would you?"

"Of c-c-course. I think I'm ready t-to g——go back now."

Chrí launched off Alísa's shoulder with a tiny *"Bye,"* and Alísa hurried past the two young holders.

Falier reached out to touch her forearm. "Thank you. We won't be a minute."

His touch zapped pain through her arm, stronger than before, and she instinctively shrank back.

Falier pulled his hand away quickly, concern furrowing his brow. "I'm sorry."

Alísa searched his face. He couldn't know that she had just felt his pain. He must have thought his friendly touch had spooked her.

"No, you're fine," she breathed out, calling a smile to her lips to reassure him. "I'm j——just a bit jumpy. I'll save you a d-dance?"

His shoulders and brow relaxed. "Yeah, that'd be great."

Alísa wandered back to the céilí. She would have to be more careful, especially when she danced with Falier. She should be able to hide the pain of his touch as long as she was prepared. It was nothing compared to the agony of dying hatchlings.

She had barely made it back to the dancers when a man in his late twenties offered his hand, introducing himself as Breggan. She took it with a smile and he led her to the bonfire, his freckles and light brown hair standing out in the firelight.

"Thank you for sharing with us." He smiled. "Always good to learn songs from different villages. What brought your family out here?"

Alísa breathed low. "My father is a hunter. He's always looking f—f—for new g-game and challenges."

"Ah, a hunter." A woman behind Breggan leaned forward to see Alísa. "My husband and I are tanners. Be sure to bring your wares by us—we'll pay you well."

Alísa smiled. She would have to ask Graydonn and Koriana to try not to damage the hides of their kills in the future, both to keep up appearances and to refill her coin purse.

"Thank you. I d—d—didn't bring anything this t-t-time, b—but—"

"Are you all right, dear?" The woman's brow furrowed.

Heat rose to Alísa's cheeks. She breathed deeply again, trying to loosen her throat muscles.

"I'm f—fine."

"Do you need some water?"

"I'm fine," Alísa repeated, shaking her head. "I j—just s-stammer."

The woman's face scrunched in scrutiny before she spoke again, this time slowly, almost drawling.

"Well, dear, you tell your father to find us when it's time." She pulled back, ending the conversation.

Alísa closed her eyes, fighting back a tremor of anger. *Just because I can't speak doesn't mean I'm unintelligent. We spoke together just fine before that.*

How she missed Trísse. She had always been a good buffer in social situations, making some sarcastic remark that took the attention off of Alísa. Here, she was so very alone.

Breggan tilted his head. "You didn't stammer when you sang earlier."

Alísa pressed her lips together before whispering. "I never stammer when I sing."

He leaned in. "What was that?"

She swallowed. "I n——never stammer when I s-sing."

"Oh. Have you tried singing everything instead of speaking?"

Right, because that *will make people think I'm normal.*

Alísa breathed a silent sigh of relief as the musicians played the intro, swallowing up any need for further conversation. Breggan was careful with her, barely adding any extra spins and reaching for her hands quickly after a move separated them.

The song couldn't end fast enough.

At the final note, she nodded a *'thank you'* to Breggan and excused herself. Time to call it a night, before anyone else decided her broken voice meant the rest of her was broken too.

She reined in her empathy, drawing it around her like a cloak until the constant buzz of everyone else's enjoyment became a mere whisper. She ran her fingers over the weathered Hold wall, eager for the barrier between her and the others' emotions.

A bout of laughter turned her head back to the crowd and formed a hollow ache in her chest. She had been a part of it for a while—the fun, the joy, the people—but she had never truly belonged. Not with her clan, not with this village.

She lifted her eyes to her two-peaked mountain, barely visible in the sliver of moonlight, and smiled sadly.

I'm coming back soon, she thought, as though the dragons could hear her across the distance. At least to them, she was someone. Even if she wasn't sure she could be who they wanted, at least they saw her as more than an inconvenience.

"Hey." Falier's voice jolted Alísa from her thoughts. "You heading in?"

Alísa forced a smile. "Yeah. I'm tired."

"You owe me a dance." He reached out to her. "One more before you turn in?"

She stopped a sigh. She *had* initiated that conversation. "One more."

She steeled herself for the pain as she took his hand, but only a twinge settled in her temple. Either his headache was fading, or her hold on her empathy was a lot tighter than she had realized.

Falier led her to the firelight as Kat explained the next dance.

"This is one of my favorites," he said, a twinkle in his eyes. "The steps are simple, but it's easy to add steps and spins. You up for a challenge?"

Apprehension zapped through Alísa, but she nodded. At least this dance promised to be more fun than her dance with Breggan.

Selene's flute sounded the introduction, and Alísa caught her eyes just briefly, a smile wrinkling the corners. Then Falier pulled her into the dance, the same smile gracing his features, and as he spun her effortlessly through the steps, she grinned back.

Maybe she didn't belong with the village, but maybe—just maybe—she had made a couple friends.

19

MASKS

The door to the kitchen shut behind him and Falier finally allowed himself to wince. He set the pile of dirty breakfast dishes on the counter gently, praying they wouldn't tip over. Tumbling plates would only increase the headache pounding in his skull with all the enthusiasm of a toddler with a goblet drum.

He rubbed his hands over his face, pressing fingers to his eyes to allow himself a moment in quiet darkness.

Too many people. That's all it was. Too much noise and not enough sleep last night. A little extra rest would help release all the tension building inside him.

But rest wasn't the way of Eldra Nahne's people. Theirs was the way of service, whether as holders, healers, or songweavers. Others always came first. He and his family were the hosts, so they were the last to blow out their lights and the first to lift off their covers. It was that simple.

He growled to himself as he scraped the first of the dishes. *What kind of holder am I if I can't handle ten extra people in the room?*

Of course, he usually could, just not after a long night of keeping the crowd happy.

"I'm trying, Nahne," he prayed silently. *"I'm trying so hard. Help me be what I need to be."*

The prayer didn't lift the throbbing in his skull, but it lessened the ache on his heart. His Eldra had come through for him so many times—an extra measure of strength here, a friend sent to comfort him there. She would come through again. After all, the Eldír knew the Maker's ways better than their charges. Nahne understood why he had to suffer in silence, and she would help him perform his duties.

"Falier?" Selene's quiet voice slipped through the crack between the door and the frame.

Falier straightened and steeled himself as the door moaned on its hinge. Selene stayed silent until the door shut behind her, then fixed him with her concerned-older-sister stare.

"Are you okay?"

"Yes."

"Liar."

"What are you, a telepath?" He turned away and scraped another plate. It wasn't fair—she could literally see his lies.

She snorted. "Wouldn't that be something."

He kept his eyes on the dish. "At least you'd be with Taz and the wayfarers instead of stuck here with me."

He cringed as his own insensitivity entered his ears. He shouldn't have mentioned Taz. The sadness tainting Selene's eyes made his heart sink.

"I'm sorry. I didn't mean to—"

In two steps, Selene had her arms around him. "I know. It's the headache talking."

Falier set the plate down and returned the embrace. His sister was so small, her head barely reaching his chin, yet her hugs were almost as comforting as their mother's. He relaxed into it, hoping he reflected some comfort back to her.

"I'll be okay. I'll take a walk in the forest once they're gone, allow myself to relax, then I'll be fine."

She nodded against his shoulder, then pulled back to look him in the eyes. "They're already starting to filter out. I wanted to let you know that Alísa's about to leave too."

He nodded in thanks. The rest of those here for breakfast were villagers, or else regular visitors from Soren, the village closest to Me'ran. He could and did see them anytime. But hunters and their families were notorious loners, rarely coming out of the forests and into civilization. Maker knew when they'd see Alísa again. All of the holders should see her off and make sure she knew she was welcome in their village.

Plus, she was cute, in a lost wolf-pup kind of way. Skittish around people, yet wanting to be included—a total hunter's daughter.

He breathed in deeply and let it out through his mouth. Then he straightened once more, lifting his head and forcing his tight shoulders down. Time to go back to work.

Selene shook her head. "You wear the mask too well, brother."

He gave an exaggerated bow, coming back up to the same professional, not-a-care-in-the-world position.

"And you are too kind, dear sister."

His chest deflated as he met Selene's eyes. Her smile was still too sad, but perhaps her melancholy would now be fixed on him, rather than Taz. The wayfarers had taken their best friend six years ago, and each time he returned less and less like the Taz they knew. And so the heartache grew.

He breathed out a quick puff of air. "Okay, let's go."

Gently guiding Selene to come with him, he strode to the door. His hand stopped on the handle only a moment as he braced himself for the noise, then he pushed through into the main room.

Two men, a woman, and two girls still occupied one of the tables, chatting and laughing about the tall tale his father had told to wrap up the céilí's festivities. These were the Sorenites. If they held to past practice, they would leave before the sun was much higher.

All of the other tables were empty, though muffled voices from outside signaled that not all of the guests had returned home. His father cleared a table of plates and extra food, quipping back and forth with the Sorenites. His mother was nowhere to be seen, nor was Alísa.

"I see them; they're outside," Selene said quietly, heading for the northern door.

Falier hurried to follow her. "I wish my ears were as good as yours."

Her lips quirked, containing a laugh. "No, you don't, Chief Headache."

There we go, a real smile. "At least I'd be getting something cool out of the deal."

She lifted an eyebrow at him. At least, *he* thought it would be cool. Despite the problems the sound-lights caused Selene, they certainly came in handy from time-to-time, like distinguishing muffled voices.

"You never did tell me what Alísa's color is," he prodded.

Selene stopped at the door and twisted to face him. "White. It's actually really hard to ignore—I could pick out her voice in the middle of the crowd last night."

"See? Cool."

Selene shook her head and pulled open the door to reveal their mother and Alísa. Alísa wore her green cloak over the clothes she had purchased two days prior—a deep forest green shirt over a dark brown wrap skirt, perfect for blending in amidst the trees.

Hunter's daughter.

Her bag crossed her chest and sat on her hip, the top flap barely closing over the tripod metal stand she had ordered with the pot at her feet. A short-sword hung from her hip. It made sense for her to wear it when she was out in the world by herself, but she carried it with the grace of a musician with their instrument—barely conscious of it, but never letting it hit anything as she moved.

Alísa smiled at Selene, then gave him that same smile. Her light freckles became more pronounced as her cheeks lifted, her storm-blue eyes sparkling in the cool morning light.

"Thank you," Alísa said. "I had a lovely t—t-time."

"Good." He returned her smile. "I hope you'll come again."

His mother touched Alísa's arm. "Yes, whether you need supplies or just want to come to another céilí. They're every Friday evening. Bring your family too."

"Oh." Alísa spoke so quietly Falier could barely hear her. "My family isn't very musical."

"Well, we'd love to have you either way."

Alísa nodded quickly. "Thank you."

Selene brushed past Falier and clasped Alísa's arm. "We mean it—be it next week or months from now, alone or with family, we'd love to see you again."

Alísa seemed to grow a bit taller with Selene's reassurance. Selene must have seen something in Alísa's voice that he hadn't heard, some disbelief or insecurity.

"Eldra Nahne b—bless you," Alísa said, looking first to Selene, then to Kat and him. "All of you."

"Eldra E'sall guide your paths," his mother said.

Alísa pressed her lips together and nodded firmly, her curly ponytail bouncing lightly behind her. Selene bent down to grab her pot and hand it to her.

I should have done that. The pounding in his head was no excuse for him to forget chivalry.

With a final wave goodbye, Alísa strode northwest into the forest. There was no path there, barely even a trail created by wandering deer, yet she didn't hesitate as she disappeared into the brush. She seemed so confident in where she was headed; so confident in everything but herself.

It didn't make sense. She was a traveler, comfortable coming to a new village by herself, a quick study in dance, a wonderful singer, and had even captivated the skittish dreki. Could so many wonderful things really be overcome in her mind by a stammer?

Had Uncle T'ron felt the same self-doubt as Alísa? He came across confident in his high position as one of Soren's holders, but perhaps he suffered insecurity when he was younger. Was even the confidence he now exuded real?

Maybe wearing masks well was hereditary.

Selene touched his arm and swung her head to the door. "Just a little bit more."

He nodded firmly. They still had work to do. He faced the Hold. Head high, shoulders loose, smile ready. *Just a little bit more.*

20

ILLUMINATION

"Bring your family."

The echoes of Kat's words trembled through Alísa like the wind through the leaves. Her rushing mind nearly blinded her to her path. If it weren't for the guiding landmark of the mountain, she would surely lose her way.

"Bring your family."

Had it only been five days? Five days since she felt her parents' embrace and their love rippling over her? What hell was she putting them through? Had they been unable to sleep the last few nights? Could they stand to lose their only child?

Was it really worth saving her own conscience at their expense?

Grief and worry choked her heart and squeezed tears from her eyes. Sobs wracked her, bringing her to stop and lean against a tree. She dropped the pot at her feet and pulled her father's necklace from under her shirt, running her fingers over the grooves in the scale.

"Eldra Branni, please hear me just once more. Tell them I'm okay and I'm sorry I've hurt them. Please, tell them!"

She breathed slowly and deeply. She had to get a grip on herself. It wouldn't do for the dragons to see her like this. They wouldn't understand her feelings of loss. Her father was a slayer—a hatchling-murderer—and her mother his accomplice. How could they empathize with her for missing them?

Truly, she had missed humanity. After only two days alone with dragons, she had soaked up the interaction with humans like a woman dying of thirst. At least, until they learned of her stammer. *That,* she hadn't missed.

But then, not everyone had treated her badly. She had never imagined she would feel so at home with holders, but they were a wonderful family.

She glanced back at the village. What if she didn't return to the cave? Graydonn had said they wouldn't come after her if she promised not to use her power against them. Since she wasn't yet trained, that didn't seem a likely threat. And there was little danger of the war coming this far east.

She could call Me'ran home.

Was that what she wanted?

Right now, yes. But later? Overall?

She shook her head, ridding herself of leftover tears before grabbing her pot and setting out for the dragons' cave once more. Somehow, her purpose lay with them. They weren't her kind, yet the Maker had created her mind and heart to reach out to them. Though that ability had wounded her time and time again, she couldn't deny now that there had been a purpose in it.

She sighed to herself. The stammer made no sense, but everything else the Maker had done—the empathy, the sorrow, the isolation from her people—all led her here, to this moment and this task. Perhaps Farren had been right; she had to lose everything in order to find her true calling.

"Alísa!"

She whirled, searching the forest as Graydonn's agitated voice echoed through her mind. He had to be within sight to speak with her telepathically.

She grasped for the telepathic line. *"What's wrong?"*

"She's trying to hatch, and you're not there!"

Amber eyes grabbed hers as she spun once more, Graydonn's head rising above the brush maybe thirty feet away. Alísa ran to him.

"But Koriana said I had five days when I left!"

"It was her best guess." Graydonn spread his wings. *"Climb on—you must be there for her, or she'll die!"*

Alísa's heart pounded into her throat. How had she even considered leaving the dragonet behind only moments ago?

She gripped a spine and pulled herself into position on his withers. *"Are you sure about this? You've never flown me before."*

He shifted from one foot to another. *"Sing for me and I will be strong."*

"But how? What do I sing?"

"A song for strengthening." He flexed his wings and the ripped one zapped

through Alísa. *"And for pressing through pain."*

"I don't know a song with words like that."

"Then invent one," he urged. *"A dragonet's life is on the line. I'll do my part, Singer, but you must do yours!"*

Alísa tensed as Graydonn trotted for a spot of sun on the forest floor. She closed her eyes and pictured Farren. He had never judged her when she wove new songs. His warm encouragement spurred her on.

'Sing it,' he had whispered. *'No one else is here.'*

Only, someone else *was* here now—a dragon who knew how this whole Dragon Singer thing was supposed to work. A dragon who would know if she did it wrong.

A new image faded into view, pressed into her mind by Graydonn. The egg, trembling with tension, exuding fear and loss.

Alísa's heart twisted like it might break in two. The dragonet thought she had been abandoned by her mother again.

No, dear one. I'm coming!

A melody flooded her mind and heart, filling her as Graydonn leapt for the gap in the trees. Alísa's heart, too, leapt, opening wide to release a song woven for Graydonn and the dragonet.

> Dearest dragons, don't give in
> To pain and fear which hold you down.
> Find strength inside you, deep within;
> Shake loose the pieces and break out.
>
> For I, dear dragons, am held too—
> Claimed by fear as easy prey.
> So hear these words I sing to you.
> May my song help you find your strength.

The song flowed from her lips, power surging with it from her mind. It circled them now, winding around them, surging under Graydonn's wings like the wind. They rose higher and higher until they broke through the canopy.

Alísa laughed as Graydonn banked toward the mountain, her heart lifting into the sky with them.

"*Well done, Singer,*" Graydonn said, his own joy gushing from him and entwining with hers. "*Keep going, we're almost there.*"

She sang again, drawing in every drop of his joy and pushing it back out in her strength song, a cycle so right she never wanted it to end.

Graydonn speared for two trees on the mountainside. "*Hang on.*"

Alísa gripped a spine with one hand and held the pot against her side. Graydonn twisted sideways, his wings parallel to the tree trunks as he dove between them. On the other side was rock, and with a mighty flap of his wings, Graydonn pulled up and gripped the mountainside with his talons, bringing them to a halt. Then they slid backwards, his talons scraping against the rock and sending chunks of dirt down before them.

He flapped his wings for stability. "*As soon as we're down, get to her.*"

Alísa whipped her head around. The cave entrance sat ten feet below them. *I'm coming, little one!*

She swung a leg over Graydonn's spine to sit sidesaddle, then launched herself from his back as soon as he hit the little path leading to their cave. She hissed as she fell to her knees with a painful jolt, her bag and pot clattering beside her, then pushed back to her feet and ran inside.

Koriana's bright eyes guided Alísa through the dark. "*Her heart is rending, Singer. I've done all I can to calm her, but only you can heal her.*"

Alísa dropped to the ground before the dragoness, sending another shock of pain through her knees as she crawled. Squeaks and growls penetrated the darkness, muffled by the dragonet's egg. It shifted and writhed in Koriana's grip, tendrils of panic slipping from the pocketed shell and grasping for Alísa's unguarded mind.

Visions of slayer ceremonies rose as fear and pain drummed against her, beating her back and raising hot tears to her eyes. Her protective desires fled from her. If she touched that egg, it would all happen again—all the pain, all the suffering would come rushing into her just like at the ceremonies.

"*What are you waiting for? She needs you, now!*" Koriana pressed the egg toward her, the shell scraping across the stone floor.

No! Alísa held a trembling hand over her mouth, where her fingers met a steady stream of tears. She had felt the fear too many times before. The sorrow. The death. She didn't want this. Not again!

The dragonet cried once more in its confines—a desperate plea echoing through Alísa's scarred memories. She had never been able to answer that cry. Doing so now would tear her apart. It already was, love and fear waging fierce battle in the confines of her mind.

I can't do this.

I have to do this.

Alísa blew out a final sob, then lunged for the egg. Fear and heartbreak pierced her like white-hot talons in her skull. She cried out as it reverberated through her and mingled with the strength song still floating in her mind. They pulled at her heart, rending it and wrenching another cry from her lips.

But the pain didn't end in death.

Deep affection burst from Alísa's innermost being, a love that overcame the pain pounding in her mind. She lifted the egg into her lap and ran her fingers over the shell. Pain continued its assault, but her moans shifted into a melody she had never heard. Then the words came, lifting from her lips as though she had known them all her life.

> Where fear and heartbreak once arose,
> Replace it now with peace.
> Your nighttime ends, the light now grows,
> The darkness soon will cease.

The pounding emotions from the dragonet shifted. Panic fled and pain eased, but in their place grew desperation. The dragonet growled and scratched at her confinement, and Alísa continued her song.

> What once was home is just a shell,
> A prison for your soul.
> Now hear my voice, let it dispel
> Your fear, and make you whole.

A crack formed under Alísa's hand. The dragonet's anxiety poured from the opening, and Alísa instinctively jerked her hand away. She shook her head and replaced it, her fingers just below the crack. She had to help the little dragon fight!

> The world outside was made for you
> To leap, to dance, to fly.
> So come to me and breathe anew,
> And make your joy my sky!

A loud crack halted Alísa's song. She lifted her hands from the shell and the pieces fell away, leaving behind their ebony charge.

The world stilled, as though a refreshing breeze had swept through the cave to carry away all fear and noise. Two black wings and a tail flopped over Alísa's thighs as the new hatchling shook herself.

A sense of longing rippled from the hatchling, and she nearly tripped over her own feet as she turned. Emerald eyes locked with Alísa's, and the rest of the world faded around them. Warmth entered Alísa's mind—no words, only a sense of presence so strong they knew they would never truly be alone again.

Memories flashed before their eyes, their inner selves touching. The hatchling's short life raced before Alísa—

The safety of connecting with her mother.

The warmth of being held or sitting amidst hot stones.

The feeling of suffocation as her wings grew and pressed in around her face.

The loss when she realized her mother wasn't coming back.

The peace found in Alísa's lullabies.

The fear and wonder of seeing light for the first time.

The joy of finally being with the surrogate mother she had chosen.

As the feelings flashed through Alísa they blended with visions of her own life, whirling around and past her like dandelion seeds on the breeze. Most memories flew past with barely a second to contemplate, but a select few slowed as they went by, as though she, the hatchling, or both of them together were choosing which were most vital.

The bards coming to Azron when she was four, and the way she had freely danced with the other children that week.

The first hatchling murder she had witnessed, and the fear it kindled.

The following day when her parents had told her to slow down and speak more clearly.

Flashes of moments when the other children laughed at her lack of control.

The day she and her parents left Azron to join a clan of wayfarers.

The pride she had felt when her father took his place as chief.

The first time she connected to dying hatchlings.

The joy of finding friendship in Trísse.

The confusion brought by her father's new apprentice.

The day she met Graydonn and everything changed.

Joy collided with joy, fear with fear, each important moment of their lives converging and forging a bond more powerful than Alísa had ever imagined possible. Then, like mists clearing before the sun, the memories faded and only she, the hatchling, and the sweet warmth of trust remained.

The hatchling's vivid green eyes brightened, the light stark against her shiny black scales.

"Hello, Alísa." Her voice was small, but deeper than a human child's, and, as with every dragon Alísa had met, it came with a name.

Alísa smiled back. *"Hello, Sesína."*

A gust of wind from the entrance blew Alísa's hair into her face as Koriana flew inside, followed by Graydonn. One of Sesína's wings caught the air and she yelped as it nearly knocked her over before Alísa steadied her. Koriana held a dead deer in her jaws, which she dropped in front of Alísa. Alísa hadn't even noticed them leaving, and they had gone hunting? How long had the mind-share taken?

"You should both eat," Koriana's voice entered their minds. Somehow Alísa perceived that Sesína heard Koriana as well, almost like she heard through both their minds at once. *"The Illumination is exhausting."*

Illumination. The bond all hatchlings formed with their chosen parent. It lingered at the corner of Alísa's mind, feeding her a stream of Sesína's feelings and thoughts.

Right now, they focused on the deer with a deep, aching hunger.

Alísa's own stomach growled. *"Thank you. Would you mind——"*

Koriana chomped down on the end of a leg and ripped it from the bloody carcass. Sesína winced as tendons snapped, looking away until Koriana began breathing fire over the hunk of meat. Then she stared at the flames rippling over Alísa's food and licked her chops.

"*You don't have to wait for me.*" Alísa pressed her words through their connection.

Sesína spoke matter-of-factly. "*I have to wait for Koriana to finish. I can't breathe fire yet.*"

"*Dragons eat raw meat—*"

Sesína grimaced and stuck her tongue out with a gagging sound, the expression so undragonlike Alísa couldn't help laughing.

"*What are you waiting for, little one?*" Graydonn stretched his snout to Sesína. "*You need your strength.*"

"*It's raw.*"

Graydonn blinked and cocked his head, and Koriana stopped her flames with a coughing sound.

Koriana looked to Alísa, then back to Sesína. "*The blood will give you the strength and nutrients you need. All dragons eat it.*"

Sesína shook her head, her snout swinging clumsily back and forth. "*It's gross, and I won't eat it.*"

Alísa bit back a laugh. She completely agreed with Sesína's assessment, but hearing it from a dragon was so strange.

Koriana's flaming eyes fixed on Alísa. "*You're her mother, tell her.*"

Mother. Right.

Alísa touched the warm scales of Sesína's shoulder and the hatchling faced her. "*I know it looks bad, but Koriana's right. You need it.*"

"*It repulses you,*" Sesína argued. "*Why would you ask me to eat it?*"

After a beat of silence, Graydonn thrummed. All eyes turned to him as his eyes brightened.

"*It's the Illumination.*" His tone was so light, contrasting starkly with Koriana's vexation. "*She's learned everything from Alísa, just as she would a mother dragon, including what's good to eat and what isn't.*"

Koriana's head swiveled between them. Then her eyes dimmed. "*You're right.*"

The dragoness stood and began pacing.

Alísa shook her head. *"But I know what a dragon is supposed to eat—shouldn't Sesína know too?"*

Sesína raised an eye-ridge. *"There's a difference between knowing and liking."* Her tail swished, throwing her off-balance. Alísa caught her before she fell off her lap.

Koriana growled to herself as she paced. *"Her eating, her movement, her perception of her body in space. What have I done?"*

"You did nothing, Mother." Graydonn grabbed the half-cooked deer leg and began breathing fire over it again. *"Sesína chose the Dragon Singer—you couldn't have forced her to change her mind. The Maker knows."*

Koriana settled to her belly, placed her head on the ground, and studied Sesína. Melancholy rippled from her, overtaking the annoyance and ire. *"The Maker knows."*

Graydonn's flames ceased and he pushed the meat to Alísa. The scent made Alísa's mouth water and caused a tremor of excited anticipation in Sesína. The hatchling climbed off her lap and promptly fell on her face, her light pain washing through the bond.

Koriana closed her eyes, while Graydonn thrummed.

Sesína pushed up and shook her head as if to clear it. *"Stupid extra limbs."*

Koriana groaned as though the statement caused her physical pain. A twinge of chagrin rippled from Sesína, but was quickly overcome by hunger. Alísa grabbed a knife from her pack and set to work cutting the cooked skin from the meat.

She gave Sesína the first bite, which the hatchling took eagerly from her fingers. Enjoyment spread through the bond and made Alísa's stomach growl again. She cut off a piece for herself and chewed the tough meat as she cut multiple chunks for Sesína, placing each piece on her thigh.

Sesína reached for a second piece with her talons and drew it to her mouth like a human would. So strange. A part of Alísa wanted to laugh. The other part knew Koriana, though perhaps overreacting, wasn't wrong. Sesína was a dragon, not a human. Eating this way was probably harmless, but moving and acting like a human in other ways might hurt her, or at least get her into trouble.

Sesína reached for a third piece and Alísa stopped her with a hand. *"Uh-uh."*

Sesína drew her talons back, her eyes dimming. *"But I'm still hungry."*

"You can eat," Alísa said quickly. *"But you need to eat like a dragon."*

The hatchling studied the meat for a second, her eye-ridges scrunching. Then her emerald orbs slid up to meet Alísa's eyes, pleading that she change her mind. They nearly undid Alísa, but she fought the urge to give in.

"Grab it with your mouth."

Sesína grumbled in her throat—almost a dragon's hum, but not quite. The Illumination bond told Alísa that Sesína planned to walk away, but a rumble in the hatchling's stomach overcame her pride. Sesína stretched her neck for her third piece.

Alísa shook her head. *This one's going to be a handful.*

"I heard that."

Alísa winced. This would be worse than the other dragons' mind-reading. She had finally figured out how it felt when she was connected to them, so she could hide her private thoughts. But the Illumination bond was different—were all her thoughts and feelings open to this hatchling?

The thought should have repulsed her. A mere day ago, it would have. But now, the constant hum in the back of her mind soothed her. They could keep no secrets, but nothing within her balked. She trusted the little hatchling completely because she knew her completely. Sesína wouldn't judge her stammer or her fears, and Alísa wouldn't judge the dragon's impulsive nature or small size. The mere fact that she knew Sesína was impulsive without yet witnessing it proved their deep bond.

A rush of sleepiness grazed the back of Alísa's mind as Sesína yawned, now stuffed with all the deer meat her stomach could hold. The hatchling crawled close and placed her chin on Alísa's thigh, double-eyelids drooping.

"I think I need to sleep now."

Alísa grinned. So small, so young, so cute. She stroked Sesína's warm scales and Sesína closed her eyes and sighed, contentment wafting from her in gentle ripples.

"You should rest while you can, Alísa," Koriana said, a slight mirth rising above her distress. *"When Graydonn woke from his first nap, he played from sunrise*

to mid-morning the following day."

Alísa jolted her head up. *"Without stopping?"*

Koriana's eyes brightened. *"Welcome to parenthood."*

21

WRESTLING

Alísa collapsed to the ground against the wall of the cave, her breath coming in gasps and leaving in laughter. Sesína had woken her in the middle of the night with the boundless energy Koriana had warned her of, and so began what would be one of the longest days of her life.

So far, it was also one of the most fun.

Graydonn and Koriana helped, each of them taking shifts entertaining the insatiably-curious hatchling. They'd had to stop her from leaving the cave at least six times now. The first time was easy—Sesína hadn't quite gotten the hang of running on four feet at that point—but her attempts had become increasingly harder to stop. She made it out the entrance last time, but a sharp reprimand from Alísa brought her back, as if she knew she wasn't supposed to go, but couldn't control her impulses.

Now Sesína wrestled with Graydonn a few feet away, much like a wolf cub might wrestle with an adult—snapping at his tail and batting his paws and face.

"Wings up, Sesína," Alísa reminded, wincing as the hatchling stepped on a flopping limb. They kept tripping her up. Koriana had tried to help her learn to keep them pinned against her back during their last bout, but it seemed the only voice Sesína listened to was Alísa's.

"The stupid things won't stay," Sesína grumbled through their bond, pulling her wings against her back for perhaps the hundredth time. Frustration simmered within her, brewing feelings of inadequacy Alísa knew all too well.

"You'll get it," she encouraged. *"You just have to get used to it. Focus on it while you get Graydonn's tail. Ignore the rest of him so you can practice."*

Sesína whipped around to face her, the hatchling's eyes brightening. *"Or, I could get you!"*

Alísa braced herself as Sesína charged her at full speed. The hatchling plowed into her and nosed her way under Alísa's arm. Her wings flopped uselessly at her sides, forgotten in the excitement.

Alísa pushed the hatchling back. *"Wings."*

Sesína pulled them up, then got in close so Alísa could push her away again. It had only taken one moment of Alísa's pain for Sesína to realize she couldn't play quite as hard with humans as she could with dragons. She had done better controlling herself after that.

Now if only she could apply that same control to holding her wings in place.

Sesína pushed against Alísa again, over and over until Alísa's arms burned from the exercise. Then she switched to running in circles.

So much energy, much like Alísa's young cousins. She had once told Taer that he made her dizzy just watching him run through camp, weaving around tents and tumbling with the other children. The phrase had never been truer than now as Sesína's feelings rippled through their bond.

Alísa put a hand to her swimming head. *"Okay, stop now, please."*

"Chase me!"

"As if I can stand without falling over right now."

Sesína stopped and fixed pleading eyes on Alísa. *"Chase me?"*

Alísa's heart melted and she forced herself to her feet with a grunt. *"Go on—just not out the mouth of the cave."*

Sesína took off for the back. *"I don't know what you're talking about."*

Alísa followed at a slow jog, then sped up as splashes echoed through the space. *"And don't get in the water, either! You'll muddy our drinking source!"*

Alísa's eyes adjusted to see Sesína splashing in the little stream overflowing from the pool and out the cave. *"Okay, that's fine."*

"I know." Sesína rolled over the stream, then shook the water off her scales. *"It's so cold! I want to go to the lake where it's warmer."*

Alísa sighed. *"Someday, but not yet."*

"But I want to chase the fish!"

"No."

"Chase me!" She took off again, carving a wide arc through the cave. Graydonn swatted at her playfully, and Sesína pivoted to avoid him. Her flopping tail continued her original course, pulling her off-balance and sending her to the ground with a yelp.

"Are you all right?" The shock of the fall came through their bond, though after the initial jolt it became apparent Sesína was fine.

Sesína shook her head to clear it. *"Stupid tail."*

Koriana hummed lightly. *"Your tail is meant to help you* keep *balance, little one. Not knowing how to use it doesn't make it stupid. Keep it under control and purposefully twist it to the outside as you turn."*

Sesína stood and pulled her wings in. *"Why does playing have to be so much work?"*

Alísa saw her chance. *"You could rest for a little bit. Catch your breath, settle your heart, then come back fresh."*

"But that's boring!"

Koriana thrummed. *"You probably couldn't do it anyway."*

Indignation rose up in Sesína. *"Yes, I could! I just don't want to."*

"An excuse to cover your inability."

Sesína stamped a foot and Alísa stifled a laugh. Koriana's effort to goad the hatchling into resting was obvious to Alísa, which probably meant Sesína recognized the tactic as well. Still, a flame burned inside the hatchling, one that spiked higher each time she was told she couldn't do it.

The Illumination bond tightened, focusing to a finer point where Sesína's voice came through like a whisper, just as P'laenn had done to speak privately to her mother in Bria's tale. *"How long do you think I have to stay quiet to prove Koriana wrong?"*

"Ten minutes?"

"That's so long!"

Alísa chuckled. *"No, it really isn't."*

Sesína grumble-hummed and opened her communication to Koriana again. *"Teach Alísa something about dragon-singing. I'll rest and listen."*

Koriana thrummed again.

Sesína snorted and settled to her belly. *"Watch me."*

Alísa sat beside her, and Sesína placed her chin on Alísa's knee. Alísa rubbed her fingers under the hatchling's jaw, eliciting a contented sigh. She let the contentment flow through her and mingle with her own. Her gaze moved from dragon to dragon, and even the lingering fears from her upbringing didn't surface, all of those doubts silenced at Sesína's hatching. This was right where she was supposed to be.

Alísa looked to Koriana. *"We have ten minutes. What will you teach me today?"*

Koriana flexed her wings, then settled them back to their resting place. *"You've already shown your strength and power as a Singer—now you must learn to hone and focus it. So far, your songs have affected all dragons in earshot, the most obvious case being your lullaby in F'renn's mountain. But if you are to fight dragons, you will need to target your songs to strengthen specific dragons to the exclusion of your enemies. Look at the astral plane."*

Alísa drew in a deep, calming breath and closed her eyes. She focused on her breath, keeping it steady and slow. As all else faded from her mind, Sesína's breathing, too, came into focus. The hatchling breathed faster than Alísa, with a flame of energy slowly building up inside of her as she forced her limbs to stay still.

Soon all three dragons' astral forms came into focus, as well as the shimmering lines of telepathic energy connecting them. Graydonn and Koriana's tether glowed a golden yellow, while Alísa and Sesína's tether shone as a bright teal line.

A tendril of yellow energy reached from Koriana to Alísa, and as soon as it attached, her voice entered Alísa's mind—

"Do you see it?"

"Yes."

"Good. Now sing and watch what happens."

Alísa searched her mind for a song. It would need to be one with a specific purpose, so she could watch as it affected the dragons.

Sesína's vivid green head lifted. *"How about the strength song you sang for Graydonn?"*

The memory of the melody flowed between them, making Alísa smile. *"Thank you, that will work."*

She breathed a low, calming breath and allowed words to pour out in song. Not two lines in, a mist wafted out from her—storm-blue, matching her eyes rather than an emotional color. It started as a thin tendril, but grew thicker as the song progressed, much like it did when she spread her empathy. The dragons' forms each began to brighten, Sesína's emerald shining the brightest of all. Koriana flexed her wings, Graydonn straightened with alertness, and Sesína's tail and hind leg began twitching with her growing energy.

That might have been a mistake.

Sesína bared her teeth in a grin. *"But it is a glorious mistake!"*

Alísa shook her head at the hatchling, then lifted a hand to her temple. Despite Sesína's energy bouncing around in the back of Alísa's mind, the song was beginning to drain her.

"That's enough, Alísa," Koriana said. *"Save your energy."*

Alísa stopped and opened her eyes. *"The song looked like strong emotions."*

Koriana blinked slowly. *"As with most female slayers, you are used to using only empathy—raw, unfocused psychic power. But your songs are meant to channel your power and give you the focus of your male counterparts."*

Alísa nodded slowly. *"Farren taught me a focused voice allows a singer to project further."*

Koriana's eye-ridges creased. *"No. I mean that you are used to releasing your empathy to the winds. Female slayers cannot give direction to their powers or focus it into the points needed for communication or attack."*

Sesína wiggled under Alísa's hand, her energy building. She would burst soon. Alísa scratched the top of her head and whispered through their bond.

"Soon, dear one."

Koriana droned on, unaware of Alísa's distraction. *"But the combination of your psychic powers and your songs will allow you to press past those limitations, focus your psychic abilities, and use them like a telepath."*

Alísa stared into the nothingness past Koriana's head. All throughout her psychic training, she had known her limitations—how the Maker had made psychic powers to work differently in male and female slayers. But now she could move past it? Through song? It sounded impossible.

Yet, female dragons could use telepathy just fine. They had no such limitations. Maybe there was something to the *'dragon inside'* idiom. Not a mind that was possessed by dragons, as the slayers feared, but a mind made like a dragon's.

But then, why was that accomplished by song?

"Are you okay, Alísa?" Graydonn stretched his snout to her. *"Your mind is racing."*

So it was, and Sesína's expanding energy wasn't helping. Alísa shook her head to clear it.

"I just can't understand how song has anything to do with psychic powers. Why does it work that way for me and no one else? Well, besides Bria."

Graydonn tilted his head in a movement reminiscent of a shrug. *"The Maker knows."*

The finality in that statement grated Alísa. Yes, the Maker knew everything, yet what little he shared didn't feel near enough. No Eldra had ever come to tell her his words, no prophet had ever spoken over her. Even Farren had never been given a direct message for her. The Maker had given her a gift, then left her to figure it out on her own!

She shook her head at herself. Just yesterday, she had said the Maker's plan for her had been good, despite the pain that accompanied it. So why did her anger linger like this?

"All we know is if he made you to do this, you can." Koriana's chest expanded with a steadying breath. *"All that remains is your choice."*

Alísa gave a wry chuckle. *"As if there is a choice in the matter."*

A strange sadness crept from Koriana, tinged with longing and an anger not directed at anyone in their cave. *"There is always a choice, little one."*

Koriana's emotions twisted Alísa into confusion. Bria had chosen the dragons too. Why would such a choice make Koriana feel like this? Unless...

Alísa looked between the dragons. *"Was there another Dragon Singer before me?"*

Koriana shook herself and snorted steam. *"Never mind that."*

"There was, wasn't there?" Alísa shifted to sit higher, displacing Sesína's chin and eliciting a grumble from the hatchling. *"One who didn't choose the dragons?"*

Koriana looked away and Graydonn lifted his wings, resettling them against his back. Koriana hummed in her throat, now turning away from him.

Were they talking right now, whispering through their Illumination bond without her?

"P—p-please tell me." She winced at her voice, so loud compared to telepathy. If they were speaking without her, they had probably cut her off from telepathic communication.

"What happened?"

Graydonn swished his tail as if indicating Alísa to his mother. Then, slowly, Koriana looked at her again.

"There was another, yes. A dragoness discovered her gifts and too eagerly took her from her people, in hopes that she would be the next Bria."

Koriana's eyes flashed. *"The slayer woman hadn't proved herself, hadn't shown any care for dragons outside of her uncontrollable empathy, and yet the fool dragoness told her what she was. Armed with knowledge, the slayer woman sang the dragons to sleep, and slew nearly half the clan as she made her escape."*

Alísa's heart skipped a beat. How could she have done that? Morally, perhaps she had reason, having just been kidnapped by the enemy and expected to fight for them. But physically? The pain it would have caused her would have been excruciating!

"She made it home and told her clan what happened, and they turned on her, afraid she would betray them like Bria. Yet she and her husband and child escaped and found refuge with another clan—one that saw her as an effective weapon rather than a liability."

Koriana's eyes dimmed. *"My mate D'lann's clan was peaceful, yet they were attacked and slaughtered by her people when he was barely a hatchling. He, two others, and their nurse dragon escaped only through great sacrifice."*

At D'lann's name, Koriana and Graydonn's grief hit Alísa like a gust of wind on the plains. She fell to her knees, her teeth grinding as their loss clamped around her heart and squeezed tears from her eyes. So much pain within her friends, frequently hidden behind their walls, but no less potent. She pushed against it, fighting the pain it brought her.

Sesína nosed under her hand. *"You don't have to hold it alone anymore."*

The touch of her scaleless muzzle seeped away some of the heartache, but Alísa recoiled. She was the mother in this relationship. Sesína shouldn't be the one to take on her pain.

Sesína stood and reached her muzzle to Alísa's cheek. *"I already feel it through you—you can't stop that. At least this way I'll take some of it away."*

The hatchling's touch lifted the grief's vice-grip, cutting the pain and uncontrolled sorrow in half. Alísa's breathing evened and her heart rate slowed until she could gather her thoughts into words and speak.

"When you began this story, I had hoped this Singer targeted only the violent dragon clans."

"No," Koriana said. *"She sang to every clan she came across, calling dragons from cave after cave into the waiting spears of her people, until she was finally destroyed."*

Graydonn scraped a talon on the ground in front of him. *"Do you see it now, Alísa? Your plan to get slayers to join you won't work. The slayers killed Bria, and Allara's first clan—"*

Koriana growled. *"I do not wish to hear that name from you, Graydonn."*

Graydonn hummed deep in his throat. *"Her first clan wanted to kill her, not help her. And the only reason the second clan rallied to her was because she sided fully with them in destroying the dragons. You cannot reason with them."* His eyes dimmed and his tone pleaded with her. *"They will only harm you."*

Alísa stroked Sesína's neck and back, running her hand over the smooth, spineless scales. Her spines would probably start growing in after a month or two. She had seen many hatchlings before their spines grew in.

Tears sprung to her eyes, hot with anger. So many little ones. How could a Dragon Singer stand for it, especially one who was a mother herself? Did Koriana and Graydonn really fear that she would do the same?

"I see your heart, Alísa," Sesína whispered. *"I know you couldn't do that. Show them now."*

Alísa stared into those shining emerald eyes, so sure and ready to ignite. Confidence flowed through the bond, and Alísa latched onto it, drawing it into her own heart.

"Why did you hesitate to tell me, Koriana? Are you really afraid I would become her?" Alísa stood and approached the dragons. *"I told you before that I am not Bria. Hear me now—I am less Allara. Search my thoughts, know my heart and rid your own of this fear."*

Koriana fixed her eyes on Alísa's and stretched her neck. Alísa stood tall, refusing to tremble under the dragoness' gaze. This would be painful and more vulnerable than anything she had done before, but she couldn't end the war alone. She needed the dragons' trust.

Koriana's hot breath cascaded over her and Alísa closed her eyes, releasing her empathy, trying to keep as little resistance as possible. She nearly jumped when Koriana placed her muzzle to her forehead, yet the touch did not come with psychic pain. All she felt was a slight vibration as Koriana thrummed in a near-purr.

"I do not fear that you would become her, little Singer. I simply do not wish to continue giving her story life by speaking it. She deserves no accolades and no remembrance. Though you may be foolish in your desires to win your people over, you have never given me reason to doubt your sincerity."

Alísa's heart warmed. She lifted her hands to Koriana's chin and pressed against her. Her thumb grazed a tooth overlapping Koriana's lower jaw and she gave a breathy laugh. There was no fear here anymore, only contentment.

"What are you doing?" Koriana's confusion pressed into Alísa.

Alísa smiled. *"It's called a hug. Or, pretty close—you're a bit too tall for me. It's what humans do to show affection."*

Alísa let go and looked into Koriana's brightening eyes.

"You have become braver, Singer. You may yet have a dragon's anam." Her muzzle gently brushed Alísa's cheek. *"And I care for you too."*

"Can I play yet?"

Alísa laughed and glanced down at the fidgeting hatchling. *"Yes, you've been more than patient."*

Sesína stuck her tongue out at Koriana. *"See? I told you!"*

Koriana hummed, but her eyes brightened. *"Are human hatchlings all this impertinent?"*

Sesína bolted for Graydonn, and the adolescent allowed himself to be tackled, thrumming as she pounced on his limbs and face. Sesína's joy and energy rushed through Alísa and lifted her spirits, but it couldn't take her to the sky. In her mind's eye, the playful swipes of Graydonn's paw became a sword in the hands of young slayers, and Sesína's bouncing became the desperate dodges of hatchlings in the circle. Her heart sank with sorrow as her love for Sesína collided with love for her family, for those boys who didn't know any better.

For Levan and Taer, soon to be old enough to enter the ceremony circle.

For L'non, who believed horrific sacrifices were necessary evils in this war.

For Graydonn, whose father was taken by the swords of her family.

Alísa raised a hand to her mouth as her heart clenched within her. She wanted so much. Too much. Even Graydonn, her now-dear friend and perhaps the most level-headed *anam* she had ever met, didn't believe it possible.

Perhaps it wasn't, but the alternatives were abandoning her people completely and becoming the next Bria, or living with the knowledge that she could have tried to help the dragons but didn't. Those weren't options, especially with the ebony ball of energy bounding throughout the cave and into her heart.

In times of stress and anxiety, her parents would often tell her to take the journey one hill at a time. The hills of slayers and battle would come later. Right now, the hill before her was coming into her powers as a Dragon Singer. For now, that was enough.

22

FLIGHT TRAINING

The night air chilled Alísa's face and hands as it swept past her. She loved this part of dragon-riding the most—the way the air filled her lungs with vitality and swirled over and around her like the winds of the hill country. She had dreamed of flying so many times there, and now she reveled in its reality.

Sesína's joy mingled with hers, tinged with anticipation. She had waited nearly three weeks for a night as dark as this one, where the dragons could fly slowly without fear of being spotted. She lay on Koriana's back and spread her little wings wide, pumping them up and down as Koriana flew over an uninhabited area of the forest west of their mountain.

The sliver of moon left the forest a shapeless blob beneath them. Sesína's body, too, had almost no definition, but her outstretched black wings were easy to see against Koriana's gray. Sesína had already doubled in size, now standing a few inches shy of two feet at the withers, but her wingspan barely stretched past the base of Koriana's wings.

While Sesína enjoyed prime seating at the base of Koriana's neck, Alísa sat a few spines behind her. She curled her legs tightly beneath her, but couldn't avoid being bumped by Koriana's wings on the upstroke. Each jostle, small or large, made Alísa tighten her grip on the spine in front of her, her hands and gravity the only things holding her to the dragoness' back. But it should be enough—tonight's flight promised a much smoother ride than when they raced to escape Crakil and F'renn. No sharp turns or aerial acrobatics necessary for Sesína's first night of flight training.

Graydonn flew beside them, his wing almost completely healed. He had offered to carry Alísa, but Koriana insisted Alísa ride her. The last thing

Graydonn needed was to injure himself again just at the cusp of recovery.

The dragons beat their wings in a slow, steady rhythm, Sesína's movements nearly a full second behind Koriana's—a far cry from Graydonn's synced wing-strokes the day they fled. Apparently, an Illumination bond was deep enough to allow perfect synchronization. Without such a bond to guide her, Sesína had to rely on her view of Koriana's wings and the feeling of the wind.

Every day it seemed they found another disadvantage to being Illuminated by a human—Sesína's diet, mood-swings, hygiene, and now flight were all affected.

Koriana banked to the left and Sesína followed, over-compensating for the sudden change.

"Straighten out a little, Sesína," Alísa said gently. *"You're veering too far to the left."*

Sesína tried to correct herself, over-compensating in the other direction.

"Back the way you came, but only a little."

Sesína huffed, more at herself than her trainers' demand for precision. As she repositioned her wings, her emotions plummeted from confidence toward hopelessness.

"There, stop there. You're perfect—great job!"

"Don't patronize me," the hatchling growled. *"I had it wrong far too long."*

Alísa rolled her eyes. *"Give yourself a break. It's only the first night."*

Koriana straightened out and Sesína did the same, once again lagging behind Koriana's movements.

Graydonn flew into view. *"Alísa speaks truly. Don't be hard on yourself simply because you and my mother are not connected by Illumination. You are disadvantaged, but not without hope. Listen to the wind as it pulls on your wings."*

"Easy for you to say." Sesína grumble-hummed. *"It would be so much easier if I could watch myself from outside my body, like if there were two of me. That would be excellent."*

Alísa shook her head. One sassy, overactive hatchling was definitely enough.

Koriana thrummed and looked back at her passengers. *"Sesína, that is indeed an excellent idea. Time for a telepathy lesson."*

A confused excitement rippled through Alísa's mind, a mixture of Sesína's emotions and her own where it was impossible to discern where one of them ended and the other began.

Koriana faced front once more. *"An Illumination bond allows for many things other psychic connections do not, including vision-sharing. To accomplish this, both parties must be completely willing and their minds relaxed, no telepathic walls or tight empathic control. Can you do that?"*

Alísa raised a hand to her temple as Sesína's dizzying enthusiasm washed through her, then immediately replaced it as an upstroke jostled her.

"I think so. So long as relaxing my mind doesn't cause my body to relax and lose its grip."

She tried to say it lightly, but Koriana wasn't amused. *"You should know by now that the two aren't necessarily connected. This will be good practice for you, Singer. Now, both of you relax your minds."*

Alísa breathed deeply and closed her eyes, allowing the brisk air to settle in her gut before breathing it back out.

"Alísa, keep your eyes open while Sesína closes hers."

Alísa did as she was told, noting that the constant hum of Sesína's mind had quieted.

"Sesína, remember how it felt to access Alísa's memories during Illumination. Bring it to the surface and reach for it. It should be light and airy—you're searching for memories just being formed, rather than ones already buried in her mind."

The bond opened wider as Sesína pushed inward. A light pressure filled Alísa's mind and sank into her, as if their two minds occupied the same space.

"I see me!" Excitement rippled through Sesína, followed by palpable disgust. *"Your night-vision is terrible. How can you live like this?"*

Alísa scoffed. *"I have great daytime vision. The Maker didn't intend for humans to fly through night skies."*

"No kidding."

Alísa tried to emulate her mother's commanding tone in her mind-speech. *"Hush. Focus on your wing position."*

"I know what you're doing, Hanah."

"Hush." A growl escaped her lips and heat rushed to her cheeks—she had

been hanging around dragons too long. *"Focus."*

Koriana banked to the right and Sesína matched her movements near-perfectly, slightly over-compensating at the end, but quickly correcting herself.

"Nicely done. Keep going!"

Koriana began flapping her wings, taking them into a gentle upward spiral, and Sesína matched the dragoness' wing-strokes. The cold air tugging at Alísa's clothing and swirling through her bound curls brought a broad grin to her face.

"We're going to ascend rapidly," Koriana said. *"Get ready to speed your wing-strokes."*

Graydonn surged past them up toward the clouds, Koriana racing after him. Sesína joined Koriana's fight against gravity, struggling to match her teacher's wing-strokes. The rhythm of rising was faster than that of steady flight. Fatigue and discouragement began to take Sesína, and Alísa whispered through their bond.

"You're doing so well. Keep going—take us to the clouds!"

Sesína beat her wings harder, the effort flooding through Alísa and trembling down her arms. Alísa ignored the pain, pinning her focus to Sesína.

"Just a little bit more."

Finally, just as Graydonn speared into the clouds ahead of them, Koriana stopped, her wings spread wide. Momentum pushed them up just a little higher, until Koriana and Sesína's heads disappeared into the fluffy clouds. Sesína squealed with delight as she experienced the cold wetness for the first time. The sound made Alísa's heart soar, and she grinned as gravity caught them before she herself got wet.

"Sesína, I'm so proud of you."

Sesína's heart swelled. *"That was so fun!"*

"Oh, the fun's not over yet." Koriana thrummed as she sank back from the clouds. *"Hold on!"*

Graydonn trumpeted from above, then burst through the cloud cover in a dive. Alísa's stomach pushed up against her heart as Koriana gave a mighty wing-stroke and dove. A jolt of anxiety zapped through Alísa, while Sesína felt nothing but excitement.

Alísa clung to Koriana, tired arms wrapping around the spine, legs clamping to the dragoness' sides. Their speed threatened to lift her off Koriana's back and Alísa strained to keep herself from flying on her own. The air stung her eyes as they sped like an arrow toward its target, but she fought to keep them open. She couldn't leave Sesína in the dark.

Trees rushed up to meet them, and Koriana counted down. *"Three…two…one…"*

Both dragons fanned their wings out and flapped hard, jerking Alísa against the spine. Catching the air, they turned gravity's pull into forward momentum, rushing them over the treetops.

Sesína filled with exhilaration and gave a quiet trumpet of delight, while Alísa burst into laughter. Joy emanated from Koriana as well, her bliss gliding silently with them through the night. They followed Graydonn as he banked left and right, swerving like the wind between the hills.

As suddenly as Graydonn's previous burst from the clouds, anxiety spiked from the dragons. A trumpet echoed from the west, sending lightning through Alísa's bones. There weren't supposed to be other dragons here!

"Scouts!" Graydonn said. *"I sense two. What do we do, Mother?"*

"Alísa, get low," Koriana snapped as Sesína ended the vision-share. *"There will be too many questions if—"*

"Hail!" A female addressed Koriana. Rossi. Her green eyes were all Alísa could make out as they blinked out and back in somewhere to the west.

"Hail!" Koriana echoed, authoritative but not confrontational. *"This is our territory—explain your presence. What is your clan?"*

A new male voice answered. *"We are of Rorenth and have nothing to explain."* Lotann. He roared, indicating his presence behind them. *"Least of all to a human-bearing serpent."*

A rattling inhalation came from behind, and Koriana pulled her wings in and dropped just as flames shot from Lotann's maw. Alísa gasped as the fire caught the end of her hair, and she clapped at it to snuff the flames.

Koriana surged forward, nearly throwing Alísa. Her knuckles turned white as they swerved to avoid Rossi. Graydonn banked until he flew above Alísa, protectiveness washing over his fear.

"Alísa," Koriana said, *"Remember your training. Focus your energy and sing for*

the strength of your clan."

A hot knife of anxiety cut into Alísa's stomach. She had only just started training to focus her songs that way, and her technique was nowhere near perfect. What if she made it worse? What if she strengthened the enemy as well?

"You have to try." Sesína's strong tone quavered at the end.

The hatchling's fear mingled with Alísa's own, bringing her back to the cave where a frightened dragonet thrashed about in her egg, searching for the mother-figure who had disappeared. The scene fueled an instinct, a burning need to protect the hatchling before her. She couldn't lash out at their attackers with tooth or claw, but fire stoked in her belly—one that spewed out in words and melody.

The air within our lungs, the fire in our heart,
When strength within us fades, my song shall be the spark.
For hope is never gone, it takes us to the skies,
The wind beneath our wings. Together we will rise.

Lotann snapped at the air. *"It cannot be!"*

"But it is," Rossi's voice purred. *"She is untrained, but I feel her power."*

Alísa's heart sank. It wasn't working—she had to focus harder. She checked the astral plane. A direct line of psychic power connected her and Sesína, but as her song reached for the others it became fuzzy and trickled into a mist that fed both them and the enemy.

"What a prize for our alpha!" Rossi lunged at Koriana.

Graydonn roared and veered for Rossi's wing, slicing at it with his talons. *"Mother, take her strength and go. I'll hold them back as long as I can."*

A wave of motherly instinct slammed into Alísa, and Koriana banked to turn around. *"Never!"*

Alísa squeezed at her power as she sang, trying desperately to channel it. Her head ached. Her stomach clenched. Blood pounded in her ears.

Maker, help us!

The astral plane was a mess of dragon-shaped lights, glowing tendrils of energy, and red and orange empathy mists. Then, out of nowhere, a bright white mass rose into view. The sight raised stories of blazing Eldír to Alísa's mind and choked her song to a stop. She had prayed for an answer, but this…

Branni?

"*Mother?*" Graydonn's voice trembled. The growls and roars halted as all dragons looked to the light. "*Is that—*"

A chorus of barks, like a pack of wild dogs, pierced the night. Alísa opened her eyes to hundreds of tiny flashing lights rising from the trees and rushing closer.

Not an Eldra.

"*Fae!*" Lotann cried.

"*Fly!*" Koriana's fear ripped through Alísa, drawing a cry from her lips. Koriana and Graydonn broke off to the east, while Rossi and Lotann veered west.

Alísa's head and heart pounded as the lights split into two groups, half following Rorenth's scouts, the rest following Koriana.

Following, and gaining.

23

RUSHING WATERS

Fear pounded in Alísa's skull, racing over her like a raging river. Every instinct told her to run, but all she could do was hang on as Koriana darted away from the threat.

The creatures—fae?—barked again, echoed by multiple answers. An intense hostility emanated as they gained on the dragons, but the emotion flowed from them as though they were one being rather than many.

Lightning shot to Alísa's extremities as a few of the lights flew right through a tall tree to follow them.

"Did you see that?!"

"They can fly through anything," Koriana hissed. *"Graydonn, prepare your flames! Alísa, sing for speed!"*

Graydonn's eyes glowed brighter and Koriana's scales grew hot as the fire within them grew. Alísa reached for words and melody, but they failed her in the cacophony of fear and agitation. She pushed back against the feelings, watching as the lights ascended past them until their silhouettes met the sliver of moon and revealed tiny draconic shapes.

Alísa sat up straight. *"Wait! It's the dreki!"*

Sesína perked up. *"Dreki?"*

Graydonn looked back to catch a glimpse of their pursuers. *"Perhaps dreki is the proper name for fae?"*

"I don't care what their name is. They hate dragons, and they are powerful." Koriana growled. *"Graydonn, blast them when I give the signal. Sing for us, Singer. Protect your clan."*

"But they know me—there's a better way."

Dreki came in closer on all sides, nearly thirty of them now in pursuit. A voice like a raging river boomed in Alísa and her companions' minds—

"*LEAVE!*"

A mental shockwave pounded through Alísa and the dragons, making Koriana waver.

"*Sing, Alísa!*" Flames jumped from Koriana's nostrils as she moved closer to Graydonn. "*Do it now and we will fend them off!*"

Alísa's thoughts raced. She had to protect her clan, but the dreki had been so peaceful in the village. Why were they upset now? Why were they threatening her clan? She had to let them know it was her—surely if they recognized her they would stop!

"D—don't attack," she called aloud, hoping the dreki might also listen. "My song is for p-peace, not battle."

"*Alísa…*" Koriana warned.

Alísa ignored her and reached for a melody the dreki would recognize, lifting her voice in the song she had introduced to Me'ran, the one that had caused the dreki to dance.

As the song penetrated the night, the dreki's hot emotions simmered, turning from hostile to angry-but-curious. Alísa glanced at a trilling chirp beside her, catching the gaze of bright purple eyes. Patterns sparkled over translucent wings capped with amethyst baubles.

"*Singer?*"

Alísa grinned, ending her song and reaching for the psychic connection. "*Chrí!*"

The drek remained serious. "*Safe?*"

"*Yes,*" Alísa said quickly. Was Chrí asking if she was okay? Or if the dragons weren't dangerous? She needed to ensure understanding. "*I'm safe, and we mean no harm.*"

The drek chirped a command to the others and the anger melted away from the group. Wing-lights faded out to black until only dreki eyes shone in the night.

Koriana's wrath turned to surprise. "*I don't know what just happened, but now I sense the individual creatures instead of a single presence.*" The dragoness hummed, but her tone was soft. "*Well done, Singer.*"

Alísa smiled. *"I wish to speak with them and introduce you all. We need to avoid such misunderstandings in the future. Let's go to the cave."*

Koriana hummed. *"I do not want them in my home or near my son. Tell them to go away."*

Graydonn swooped nearer. *"I don't sense hostility or anger anymore. I think it's safe."*

Koriana growled. *"We are* not *taking them home."*

"Then land," Alísa ordered. *"We need to speak with them."*

"You put your clan at risk."

"You know I wouldn't do that," Alísa scolded the dragoness, surprising even herself with her conviction. *"Land. Now."*

Koriana grumbled, but began her descent.

Sesína directed a wide, tooth-baring grin at Alísa as she whispered through the bond. *"You told off Koriana!"*

Alísa ignored the hatchling and focused on Chrí, who still flew beside her. The buzz of connection was gone now, so she spoke aloud.

"We're going to land. I wish t-to introduce you all. We c-c-can be friends."

Chrí trilled to her companions, then settled on Alísa's shoulder, uncertainty flowing from her.

"What's wrong?"

"Land."

Alísa tried to get more out of her, but Chrí stayed silent.

Koriana and Graydonn soon found a spot less thick with trees and landed. As soon as they hit the ground, Koriana tensed.

Alísa put a hand on the dragoness' back. *"It will be okay."*

The dreki came near and hovered around them. Alísa twisted to slide off Koriana, but the dragoness lifted her wings, blocking Alísa's way.

"Do not get off. We may need to take flight quickly."

Chrí hissed from Alísa's shoulder and a few of the other dreki hissed as well, calling out to the group, *"Release!" "Singer!" "Free!"*

"It's okay, Koriana. You and the others stay ready to fly just in case, but the dreki obviously want me unharmed. I'm getting down—we need to reach an understanding."

Koriana silently lowered her wings. Chrí loosely wrapped her tail around Alísa's neck and gripped her shoulder as she slid down Koriana's side.

Alísa raised a hand to pet Chrí, walking toward the hovering dreki. Chrí purred with pleasure, but kept an eye on Koriana as they passed the dragoness.

Why was she so untrusting of the dragons? Shouldn't such similar creatures like each other?

Sesína fixed her eyes on Alísa, the green light illuminating her form before the audience of dreki. *That's like saying wolves and foxes should get along, simply because they're the same shape. Their minds are foreign, different than either of ours. Can't you sense it?*

Thirty dreki and three dragons stared at Alísa. As she neared the dreki, their emotions flooded over her—confusion, skepticism, and protectiveness. Though hostility was sprinkled throughout as well, all malice was directed at the dragons, not her.

"It's nice to see dreki again," she began aloud, unsure how to reach so many with psychic words. "The w—welcome your k-k-kind gave me in Me'ran was unexpected, but b—beautiful. I would like to c-c-count you all as friends."

Happiness wafted over Alísa, joy so great it nearly knocked her over. *"Friends!" "Singer!" "Return!"*

She smiled. "Good. I'm glad. These d-d-dragons behind me are my friends t-too. They r—rescued me from other dragons who would have k-killed me and have t-t—t-taken care of me. They are my clan."

At these words, the dreki's happiness dulled. Doubt and concern entered the mix, and the creatures were silent. Even Chrí seemed skeptical of her words.

"Why don't you believe me?"

The simple question prompted an overwhelming jumble of words and images. Alísa could pick out a few words in the mess—*"Crafty!" "Using!" "Murder!"*—but the pictures were too much. Her vision blurred to white as multiple images tried to fill her brain.

"Stop!" Dizziness took her and she toppled to the side. Chrí gripped her shirt and tried to keep her upright, while a green blur reached out and caught her under her arm.

"Are you all right, Alísa?" Graydonn asked, his neck supporting her weight.

The visions ended as the dreki surrounded Graydonn and Alísa. Some emanated concern, but most were angry, hissing and barking at the dragon.

Koriana roared, flames flying into the air. *"Stay away from them!"*

Dreki started to glow again, anger quickly growing amongst them. Some turned to Koriana and Sesína, while others kept their eyes trained on Graydonn.

"RELEASE!"

The mental shockwave ripped through Sesína and surged over Alísa through the Illumination bond. They cried out in tandem with Koriana and Graydonn.

"STOP!" Alísa screamed, standing up straight and throwing her arms into the air. The dreki stilled and faced her.

Chrí hovered in front of her, the drek's piercing gaze holding Alísa's.

"Chrí, p—please d-d-don't hurt my c—c-c-clan." She reached a hand to the drek to place her fingers on her nose like she might to a horse or the dragons. Chrí didn't move, but when Alísa's fingers hit her muzzle there was no physical contact. "What—"

A shock ran through her, from her fingertips at the drek's insubstantial nose through her arm and up to her head, where it became like warm waters. The presence of the dreki—a psychic presence greater than any she had ever felt—entered and enfolded her, pulling her gently into its strong grip. She couldn't fight it, but she didn't fear it.

The presence was riddled with confusion, troubled by her cry. Many voices joined together in a simple question.

"Pain?"

An image of her screaming as the dragons roared accompanied the word. The presence was near-overwhelming. Every breath she took was like trying to catch air bubbles underwater as it rushed around her.

"I felt your attack on Sesína, the little one. I Illuminated her." She couldn't hold back the anger stirring within her. *"You attacked my clan! Why? They've never hurt you!"*

They showed her pictures of dragons breathing fire on a village, of a man burning alive in the flames, then of Laen perching on Selene's shoulder.

"Protect."

"But these dragons are with me. With Singer. Why don't you trust me when I tell you they're safe?"

A picture of a dragon mid-flight filled her mind. *"Desire." "Crafty." "False!"*

Alísa winced as the presence heated. *"You sound like the slayers. But these have proven true. Sesína can hide nothing from me, and Koriana and Graydonn have had many chances to hurt or control me, yet never have. They will not attack the humans."*

The dreki regarded the dragons, who stood unmoving. *"Perhaps."*

"I cannot prove it to you beyond their past actions. But I believe them. I trust them. Please, do not harm them. Give them a chance to prove themselves to you."

The dreki turned back to Alísa. Their expressions softened and their emotions calmed. An image of Chrí on her shoulder, while she stood next to Koriana, entered her mind.

"Watch."

"Understood."

The lights on the dreki's wings began to fade and their presence pulled away while simultaneously separating into individual minds. Alísa gasped in a breath and Sesína rushed to her side.

"Are you okay? I couldn't connect to you."

"I'm okay. I'll tell you about it soon."

The dreki regarded Sesína curiously. Chrí flew to the hatchling twice her size and hovered in front of her. *"Illuminated?"*

Alísa nodded, kneeling down to eye-level. "Yes, this is Sesína."

Chrí trilled. *"Friends."*

A few dreki ventured nearer to Koriana and Graydonn, curious and cautious. Graydonn stayed still and calm, but Koriana shook her head and backed away. Alísa suppressed a laugh. To see a mighty dragon so unnerved by such little creatures was humorous. But now they knew the dreki were not so harmless as they appeared. They had to be sure they stayed on favorable terms.

"I do not like this," Koriana said to Alísa alone. *"What did you tell them?"*

"To give you a chance."

Koriana snorted, eying the few dreki nearing her. *"Does this 'chance' have to include them flying in my face?"*

Alísa suppressed a giggle, but it broke free as she glimpsed Graydonn, his head turned completely around to look at the six curious dreki sitting along his back. The creatures' hostility was gone, replaced by a wary curiosity. Hopefully, her friends would prove true to them soon.

Chrí sat on Sesína's back and the two of them sniffed and stared at each other. The sight warmed Alísa's heart—she had just brought peace between two races without bloodshed.

Sesína whirled her head to look at Alísa. *"I never thought I'd meet fairies before I met humans."*

"You haven't," Alísa chuckled. *"Fairies are magical, probably mythical creatures. These dreki seem to have an advanced form of telepathy that allows them to meld their minds together, but it's hardly magical."*

"And the lights on their wings? Their mind-meld? Their ability to turn insubstantial?"

Alísa had no answer.

More chirping and barking came from above and Alísa stiffened along with the dragons. The rest of the dreki. Would she have to convince them too?

The dreki under the tree canopy glowed and chirped back. Their collective emotion was difficult to ascertain—a mixture of joy, love, satisfaction, and sorrow. But no anger, even as more glowing dreki descended and caught sight of the dragons. Apparently, their fellow dreki had already caught them up on the situation.

Chrí jumped from Sesína's back to Alísa's chest, and Alísa instinctively lifted her arms to support her. Chrí snuggled up under her chin.

"Safe."

"Safe?" Alísa glanced over the rest of the dreki, their wing-lights slowly fading out once more.

An image shot through Alísa—two large dragons in uncontrolled descents into the forest. The bright green eyes of the smaller one solidified their identities in Alísa's mind.

"The scouts. You killed them."

"Safe." Chrí chirped happily.

Alísa swallowed and nodded once. For such a small, cute creature to be so happy over two deaths was unnerving.

Koriana lowered her snout to Alísa. *"This is good news. If the scouts had returned to Rorenth, he surely would have come after you. He counts all humans as vermin and would like nothing more than to kill a human claiming to stand as an equal with dragons."*

Alísa nodded again, stroking Chrí's mane. This was war. Death was normal. Growing up with slayers, she should be used to it by now.

Then why did her stomach clench so?

Koriana's eyes dimmed. *"Yet, it's concerning there were scouts here at all. Their failure to return may be enough to keep him from trying again, or he may just send more next time. This land makes little strategic sense for a dragon. I cannot tell you his motive for sending them. We should stay alert."*

Alísa stared at the ground. What if Rorenth did decide to send more dragons? She had failed to use her powers to defend her clan against the scouts. If the dreki hadn't come, she and her friends would probably be dead. She would have to work harder and learn faster. Only a full-fledged Dragon Singer could protect her clan.

For the first time, it seemed time was not on her side.

24

A HOLDER'S WORTH

Holders had a saying: *'A pint loosens the tales of bards, and quiets the woes of slayers.'*

As Yarlan's agitation traveled through the solid oak kitchen door, Falier pulled down two of their largest tankards. It couldn't hurt to try.

"I'm telling you, Parsen, it wasn't thunder I heard last night! There are dragons in the forest."

His father's voice stayed even, too quiet to make out through the door. Falier filled the mugs and hurried out, not wanting to miss the conversation.

Namor's response came softer than Yarlan's outbursts, yet carried a weight of authority held by no one else in Me'ran. His years as a wayfaring chief had shaped him into a great leader, one who needn't raise his voice to be heard. If Namor weren't a slayer, Falier would have loved to sit at his feet and glean from his wisdom. As it was, however, he kept his distance.

"The sounds weren't ones I could mistake, Parsen." Namor nodded to Falier as he took his tankard. "Years of being village-bound cannot dull senses cultivated on the front lines. Last night, dragons did battle."

Yarlan took a long swig of his mead and brought his mug down on the table with a thud. "I told the wayfarers they should leave another man or two here. Twi-Peak is too tempting a home for wandering dragons. If they come, Me'ran will burn."

Falier winced. He hated to agree with Yarlan, but Me'ran and its surrounding villages had become complacent, believing the war would never extend this far into the forests. They had a dragon shelter, built of stone with room to hide underground, but nothing to defend the village itself—nothing that could pierce scales except the swords and minds of their only two slayers.

'Dragons don't like forests,' the wayfarers would say, *'your young men would serve better near the Nissen.'* In the past, even Namor had said as much. Now all the boys who had shown potential were gone, taken to the front lines with the wayfarers to guard the border of the eastern forests.

Apparently, they hadn't done a very good job last night.

Namor squeezed his mug between his hands. "We should send out messengers to the villages west of ours to discover which village was attacked."

"We don't even know there *was* an attack," Parsen said. "Segenn's wayfarers traveled west—the sounds you heard could have been the sounds of battle and victory."

Parsen voiced Falier's own thoughts. Segenn's wayfarers—the clan Taz had joined—had only just headed back for the border. They could have caught the dragons who had broken past the Nissen River before they made it to a village.

Yarlan shook his head and took another swig, while Namor stared at his mead.

"I pray you are right, Parsen, but for the dragons to happen to fly over the wayfarers' camp would be a miracle of great proportions. It's more likely they flew right past the slayers with neither party aware. When the messengers go out, they must be prepared to find casualties."

Anxiety knifed Falier's stomach. Namor was so sure, his tone so dire. Falier swallowed and spoke quietly.

"What can we do, then?"

Namor didn't look up from his tankard. "You can do your job, young holder. Keep the peoples' spirits uplifted and leave the battle strategy to us."

Falier clenched his fists at the dismissal, his heart sinking into his stomach. The flippant words carried him back to the worst day of his life— six years ago, when the slayers had tested the young people of Me'ran. He and Taz had been thirteen and fifteen, both so scared and so excited to be tested. To be found with the slayers' gift meant a life of adventure and honor, but it also meant leaving behind everything they knew and facing danger every day for the rest of their lives.

"We'll stick together," Taz had said, sweat glistening over his rich brown skin as he swung a wooden sword. "Brothers-in-arms, facing the flames and always having each other's back."

"We'll be heroes," Falier had agreed as he parried. "Strengthened by Eldra Branni himself and serving the people with every breath."

How naïve they had been. They couldn't choose anything—the Maker decided who to bless with the gift. Taz had proven a strong slayer and was given the honor of serving alongside the wayfarers. All Falier could do was hold Selene's hand and watch through unshed tears as their best friend disappeared into the forest with his new clan.

A light breeze tousled Falier's hair. Somehow, he had gotten outside— the memories had distracted him so much he couldn't remember walking out. Hopefully, he hadn't stamped off like a child. He crossed his arms and leaned against the wall, shivering lightly in the cloud-cover.

The ache of that day had never fully healed. If only the Maker had blessed him too. Or, better yet, if only he hadn't blessed Taz with the gift. Then Falier would be fully content to serve here in the Hold with his family.

Now, though? Now Taz was out there, risking his life to serve and protect, while Falier was left to dance and drum and serve mead. A happy life, to be sure, but while the rest of the world was at war?

"Falier?"

He glanced at his mother, who had just crested the slight hill on which the Hold rested. She carried a bread basket, now emptied of its former contents and filled with flowers. Each step she took held a purposeful grace, as though every step were exactly the one called for in her dance of life.

"Is it the headaches again?"

He shook his head. "No, nothing today."

It wasn't exactly a lie. The headaches never really went away, except after a good, long sleep, and even then they always cropped back up. But today's headache was light and manageable, and he barely noticed it.

She gave a half-smile. "Just resting, then?"

"Yeah."

That was closer to a lie. His mind was anything but restful. Taz, dragons, slayers, death, and his own role in the midst of it all—or, rather, outside of it all—swirled and curdled within him like a bubbling pot. As danger closed in on his village, what good did holders do?

His mother nodded once, apparently satisfied with his answer, and headed for the door.

"Ma?"

She stopped, her expression turning to concern once more. "Yes, love?"

He hesitated. Being a holder was all his mother had ever known—to ask this question would be to devalue her work as well as his own. How could he do that to her?

"Nothing."

There. A full lie this time. But this answer didn't satisfy his mother. She returned to him, one eyebrow lifted.

"Lies do not belong on my children's lips."

He scoffed and looked away. "My whole life is a lie, Ma."

"Not so." In two steps, she was in front of him again, balancing the basket on a hip and turning his head to face her once more. "And you cannot lie to me. What's wrong?"

He sighed quietly. "Tell me I'm doing good here. Tell me again that my life isn't a waste."

The basket fell to the grass, and Kat wrapped her arms around him. He leaned into her, soaking up her love and strength like a rag in a bucket of water. She held so much of that strength in her heart, and she always gave of it willingly, not just to her family, but to every villager and traveler who came through. It vitalized him once more, reminded him of the good they did for the people. Such everyday good was needed, even in the midst of war, and if it was good enough for her, it would be good enough for him.

"I am so proud of you, Falier. You are a good man in a world filled with pain and misery, and that is so very valuable." Kat pulled away, a tear rolling down her cheek and an apologetic smile on her face. "Does that answer your question?"

Falier gave a half-smile and bent to retrieve her basket. Then he gave her his arm and pointed his boots to the Hold door. There was work to be done.

25

SHINY

Alísa wove through the cool shade of the forest, attempting to keep Sesína's long, black tail in sight. Now forty days old and three feet at the withers, Sesína was old enough to start hunting for herself. In fact, Koriana insisted she fend for herself and Alísa, rather than depend on her and Graydonn to provide. The trees hindered the older dragons' hunting, while Sesína could still weave about them with relative ease.

But neither she nor Sesína minded the extra time spent in the woods. Despite her rapid growth, Sesína retained her curious energy and took every opportunity she could to launch herself into the forest and explore. Though she had seen much of the world through Alísa's memories, Sesína had a keen desire to see it all for herself through playing, exploring, and generally making life challenging for her mother.

Alísa shook her head as the term *'mother'* entered her head yet again. While the Illumination came with certain instincts and feelings she could only describe as motherly, as Sesína grew and matured, their relationship became more of a sisterhood—Alísa the older, wiser, cautious one, and Sesína the younger, energetic, will-do-anything-to-draw-attention one.

"Do try to keep up, oh wise one."

A squirrel shrieked and climbed up a tree to Alísa's left, its sharp claws scuffling all the way to the top. Sesína didn't follow—she preferred birds to mammals.

"Any chance you could slow down until you actually find something?" Alísa asked, pushing through the burning in her thighs. *"I swear, one of these days you're going to get me hopelessly lost and* you'll *have to find* me."

"Because the mountain *isn't a good enough landmark for you?"*

A laugh broke through Alísa's lips and gave her a stitch in her side. She slowed as more tree-scratching came from the right. Sesína skittered up a fir tree, her wings helping to push her forward after a large bird with shiny blue and gold feathers. Sesína should be flying at this point, but the lack of draconic Illumination was proving detrimental in that area of development, despite her semi-frequent flight-training with Koriana.

Panting, Alísa leaned against a tree, then noticed the berry bush at her side. It had been a couple days since she had last picked and her store was almost gone. With only a wall of intense focus on the other end of the Illumination bond, Alísa turned to her own work, pulling a chunk of Sesína's eggshell from her pack and setting to work on the bush.

Branches cracked and fell behind her as Sesína clambered across multiple trees, the sounds punctuated by squawks from the bird. Alísa glanced back to see the bird fly out of reach multiple times, but it never flew up and away. Did it not understand that Sesína was a predator?

Finally, Sesína stopped, chest heaving and eyes dimming as she glared at her prey. The bird stared right back, cocking its head.

The mind link opened. *"It's mocking me."*

"I don't think birds think that way."

"This one does. It keeps waving its shiny feathers in my face."

Alísa squinted at her. *"You just want the feathers!"*

"Don't be ridiculous. They're just an added bonus." Pictures of Sesína's collection of glittering rocks, glossy feathers, and colorful beetles floated through Alísa's mind, and Sesína's voice came back, soft and longing. *"A beautiful, shiny bonus."*

Alísa let out her breath softly. *"Get ready."*

She reached out and shook the branches of the berry bush, first gently, then harder and harder, until the bird finally looked her direction. Sesína crouched, her limbs bunching underneath her, then leapt across the expanse. Her little wings unfurled as she glided toward the bird, and stretched her talons wide, reaching for her prize.

The bird jumped into the air and flew past her, so close Sesína could have caught it in her jaws, but the young dragon watched it fly past. Then she scrambled for a hold on the bird's previous perch, missed, and fell.

"Sesína!" Alísa dropped the eggshell and ran forward. The hatchling landed with a grunt, her outstretched wings softening her fall. *"Are you all right?"*

The question was reflexive—as soon as she asked it, Alísa realized that no pain beyond the hatchling's already-tired limbs flowed across their bond. Still, she hurried to Sesína and knelt beside her.

Frustration and anger flooded from Sesína, accompanied by growls and grumbles. She stood and shook herself as though she could rid herself of the memory as easily as water glancing off scales.

"Stupid. I'm so stupid!"

Alísa reached to still her. *"You aren't stupid."*

"I had it! Your distraction worked perfectly, the bird was in my reach, but I couldn't bite it! What kind of dragon am I?"

"There are worse things than not liking the taste of blood."

Sesína pulled away. *"Worse things? You mean like not being able to fly yet? Or breathe fire?"*

Alísa sighed, looking down. How had Sesína hit the moody-teenager point already? Yet Alísa's heart ached for her. She knew what it was like to not live up to one's own expectations of oneself. What had she needed to hear in times like this?

"You'll get there, Sesína. It's hard now, but it's what you were made to do." She reached out and touched Sesína's shoulder again. *"You know that my love for you isn't based in what you can and cannot do, right?"*

Sesína huffed. *"I know. Even a 'moody teenager' can see that."*

Alísa cringed. *"Sorry."*

A deep longing slowly covered over Sesína's shame. *"I just want you to be proud of me too."*

"I am."

Sesína shook her head back and forth, her long snout making her wobble. *"Uh-uh. Not parental pride. I want to bring something to the clan, and I can't do that like this."*

"You've hunted with just your talons before, and you'll do it again. You're still learning."

"But I lost the shiny feathers. And you shouldn't have to starve because of my ineptitude!"

"Koriana and Graydonn won't let either of us starve. Besides" —Alísa smiled and stood, walking back to the eggshell she had dropped, hoping to lighten the mood— *"I picked six whole berries."*

Sesína rolled her eyes. *"A veritable feast."*

She jerked to attention, sending a shock of nerves through Alísa.

"What is it?"

"Human," the hatchling said, staring south.

Alísa rose onto her toes and saw movement not too far away. *"Go, don't let them see you!"*

Sesína's tail twitched. *"What about you?"*

"Too close—they'll see me if I run. Now go!"

Sesína hesitated before darting into the undergrowth. The mind-link stayed wide open as the little dragon monitored her.

"Humans are bigger and clumsier than birds. I think I can get him."

Alísa cringed, turning to the berry bush and picking in a manner she hoped was inconspicuous. *"Let's leave that as a last resort."*

"Hey!" a friendly male voice called from behind.

She recognized it, whirling around to see Falier. He gave an apologetic cringe.

"Sorry, did I scare you?"

She let out a breath. "Only a little. I d—don't run into many p-p-p-people out here."

He looked around, as if reminding himself where he was. "No, I'd imagine not."

"W—what are you up to?"

"Out for a walk." He gestured to the trees and brush around them. "The forest is peaceful."

Alísa looked up at the canopy of green and smiled. Only a few weeks ago, the trees felt suffocating, keeping her from the joy she found in the sky. But no more. The boundaries imposed by the forest brought a strange comfort now—a reminder of her connection to the earth in the midst of creatures belonging to the sky.

"Is your camp nearby?" Falier looked over her head entirely too easily, hopefully missing any nervous twitch of her eyes or lips.

"On the north edge of the lake." The one furthest from them and least likely to be visited. "I'm g—gathering berries—"

She stopped herself too late. Falier's eyes drifted to the eggshell and squinted.

"That's an interesting bowl. Can I see it?"

Alísa fought to keep calm. Her façade was proving harder and harder to keep up. Why did holders always have to be so nosy?

"You're a lousy secret-keeper." Sesína broke into her thoughts. Then her tone softened, *"Relax. If he asks, just tell him you found it somewhere and don't know what it is."*

Alísa handed it to Falier. He slid his fingers over the surface of the shell, then felt the cracked edges Alísa had smoothed weeks ago. He held it above his head in a ray of light shining through the canopy, squinting as he examined it.

He handed it back to her. "I've never seen anything like it."

She pulled the shell close again. "Me either."

"It almost looks like an eggshell, but it's too large to be a serpent's..."

His voice trailed off and his eyes unfocused. Then he looked at her again and raised an eyebrow. "Where did you find it?"

Alísa's heart sped, but Sesína pushed calm through the bond. *"You found it months ago, when you were closer to the Nissen."*

"I found it months ago, when we were c—c—c—c-c—"

"Camping?" Falier said hesitantly.

Closer. I was going to say closer.

She nodded once and finished in a whisper. "Near the Nissen." She looked down at the shell, running a thumb over the lip. Falier finishing her word for her was embarrassing, but it was better than him telling her to *'spit it out'* or something similar.

Falier looked west, as if he could see exactly where she had found it if only he looked hard enough. His jaw worked as he looked at her again.

"Namor says there was a battle a couple of weeks ago, and that dragons were involved. That could be a dragon's eg—"

"No," she said entirely too quickly. She hoped he couldn't hear her racing heart. "I've seen d-dragon eggshells before, b—back when I lived in the west. They're always speckled."

Sesína snorted mentally at the fabrication. *"Speckled?"*

"You've seen a dragon's egg before?"

Alísa closed her eyes as memories flooded her. "Shells. Wayfarers would sometimes bring pieces back to the villages after their b-b-battles. You know slayers; they like to show off their c—c-c-conquests."

Sesína's sadness rippled to her, and Alísa clenched the eggshell more tightly. All those dragonets snuffed out before they'd even had a chance. Maybe it would be right for her to fight the slayers as Bria had. But for every murdered hatchling, she could think of another burning village or mourning parent. Evil, innocence, and everything in-between existed on both sides of this war.

Falier cocked his head. "Are you all right?"

She nodded in response.

"You seem sad."

Nosy holder boy.

"Why don't you tell him why?"

Sesína spoke as if it were the most obvious action to take. In reality, the best action was silence. Speaking up now would only paint a target on her back—one she wasn't ready to bear. Not again.

Sesína took a haughty tone. *"You said you want to end the war by bringing humans and dragons together. How will you do that if you don't talk to humans about it? At least feel him out."*

Alísa's heart rebelled. *"He and his family are the only human friends I have right now. I'm not going to alienate myself from them. Besides, it's slayers I have to convince, not normals."*

Sesína growled mentally. *"Fine. Be ashamed of me. I don't care."*

"That's not—"

"Alísa?" Falier's eyebrows knit together. "Is something wrong?"

"No." She sighed, looking at the ground. *For you, Sesína.* "I j—just don't like the thought of s-smashed eggs. I d-don't think it's right t-t—to kill dragonets b—before they've done anything wrong."

Falíer blinked. He opened his mouth as if to speak, then shut it again. Twice.

"See, Sesína? Now he thinks I'm crazy."

"I…" he drawled, as if unsure how to respond. "I've never thought of it like that."

Alísa looked away, watching a leaf twist in the breeze, clinging desperately to its branch.

"No one does," she whispered.

The leaf tore from its place and fluttered to the ground, and for whatever reason, a tear sprung to her eye. She turned so Falíer couldn't see it.

"I should go."

"Wait."

Alísa stopped, glancing at him out of the corner of her eye. His eyebrows pressed toward the middle, while his eyes searched for something.

"If your family has wares to sell—" He stopped and shook his head. "Or, really, just if you want to come be with people, our doors are always open."

Great. Now he thinks I'm going crazy because I'm lacking in human contact.

"You are *lacking in human contact."*

Alísa fought not to growl out loud. *"I'm not talking to you."*

"Touchy…"

"I mean, I guess our doors always have to be open…" Falíer rubbed his neck and laughed at himself. "But seriously, you and your family are welcome anytime. Céilí's on Friday. Come see us. Bring your family, if they want to come."

Alísa looked away. He had her up until that last part, but keeping up the appearance of being a hunter's daughter with her family somewhere nearby was exhausting. It would be easier to stay away and avoid the awkward conversations and the avoided eye-contact as she stammered along.

Memories flashed before her mind's eye, bidden by Sesína—learning dance steps with Falíer and Selene, clapping to the music, watching the dreki dance. The visions went by so quickly they made her dizzy, and she stumbled as she lifted a hand to her temple.

"Woah!" Falíer rushed forward and caught her elbow, and Alísa cringed as pain fluttered through the skin-contact and over the surface of her mind. It was lighter than the pain she had felt from him last time, but still present.

Did he always feel pain? The thought made her heart hurt.

"Sorry!" Sesína pulled the images back. *"I just wanted you to remember how much fun you had last time. It's been over a month since you've been with your kind. You need this."*

"Are you all right?" Falier searched her eyes, still steadying her by the arm.

Alísa let out a breath as heat rose to her cheeks. She straightened out of his touch and tried to laugh it off. "Yeah, I'm okay. J—Just a d-dizzy spell."

"You're sure?"

"Yes. Hopefully won't happen again."

Sesína's presence shriveled back, the psychic equivalent to covering her nose with her paws in shame. The feelings of inadequacy rose again, and Alísa's heart opened wide to her—she hadn't meant any harm. And maybe she did have a point.

Alísa gave Falier a small shrug. "Especially not at the céilí."

Sesína leapt from contrite to triumphant, her thoughts of victory bringing a grin to Alísa's face.

Falier grinned too, his deep-blue eyes sparkling. "Hopefully not."

There. She was committed, and there was no way she could back out. Not with Sesína around, or with the thought of wiping that joy from Falier's face.

Great Maker, where did that come from?

Sesína thrummed mentally. *"Seeing stars, are we?"*

"Hush," she scolded. *"He's still an annoying holder boy who asks too many questions."*

"Keep telling yourself that."

Alísa looked down and breathed silently, trying to hide and staunch the heat rising in her cheeks. The shell was still in her hand with only a few berries. That was her way out.

"I should p-p-probably get back to it."

"Right. I should head back too." He backed away a few steps. "I'll see you in a few days, then."

"Until then."

He waved, then headed back toward the village. Alísa let out a relieved sigh and rubbed a hand over her face. How could a conversation be so hard, awkward, and uplifting all at the same time? Of course, having interruptions from Sesína throughout the discourse hadn't been much help, either.

Sesína laughed aloud somewhere nearby, though it sounded more like a cough. *"You love me."*

Alísa smiled at Sesína's normal tone, devoid of shame. *"Yeah, yeah. Now, where are you?*

"Never far." Bushes rustled to Alísa's right and the black dragon emerged. She held her head high and deposited a flat, white rock at Alísa's feet. *"It's not a blue and gold feather, but look!"*

Alísa picked it up and held it in a ray of light. It sparkled in the sun like snow on a mountaintop.

"Lovely!"

Sesína winked, full of mischief. *"Now we've both found something shiny."*

26

FIRE BREATH

Alísa practically fell against the outside wall of the Hold. That last dance partner liked spinning her a little too much.

"He made me dizzy," Sesína laughed through the bond.

Alísa faced the fire, leaning back against the sturdy wood wall. She couldn't help but smile as the hatchling's mirth sprinkled over her, despite the three miles separating them.

"Well, you don't get to complain, since you're the reason I came."

A flash of mischief rose in Sesína. *"Not the only reason."*

She pulled up an image of Falier's grinning face, and Alísa shook her head. Ever since she had let that one thought slip, Sesína hadn't let it go. It was enough to make Alísa blush whenever he looked at her, despite the fact she wasn't sure if she actually had a crush on him or just found his smile attractive.

There *was* a difference, no matter what Sesína thought.

At least the hatchling was learning how to pull up memories and images without making Alísa feel faint. Then again, maybe that wasn't a good thing, as she had taken to this new ability like a child learning to swing their first wooden training sword, testing it out with every opportunity and sometimes hitting a little too hard.

"What did I say about distracting me today?"

"I said I wouldn't distract you from conversation. Unless you're planning on talking to the wall, I'd say I'm fulfilling my end."

"I just might, you little sass."

A new song started up, slow and melodic. The crowd still circled the musicians and the fire, blocking off Alísa's view, though the perfectly-tuned flute indicated Selene's playing. A fiddler joined in with long, drawn-out notes that spoke of peace and warmth. A lullaby, probably to calm the children enough for their parents to take them home before the night went too late.

Sesína's presence settled within her mind like a child snuggling under a blanket. *"I wish I could be there with you and see and hear it all for myself."*

Alísa smiled softly. What a world that would be, if Sesína could dance with the children like the dreki. If Koriana and Graydonn could listen to the music and converse with the elders of the village without fear from either party. The very thought brought tears to Alísa's eyes.

"Singer?" A familiar weight found her shoulders.

Alísa smiled. *"Hello, Chrí."*

"Hi, Chrí," Sesína spoke with a happy sleepiness.

"Sína!"

Alísa shivered; the telepathic pass-through tickled oddly. The astral energy ran through her mind like thread through fabric, pulling through it from one *anam* to the other. Hopefully these threads couldn't get tangled up like her first attempts at sewing.

"Safe?" Chrí nuzzled Alísa's cheek and pressed into her mind as though searching for evidence. The feeling sent prickles over her skin. She pulled away from Chrí's touch—as much as she trusted the drek had her best interests at heart, she also didn't want Chrí snooping through her mind. The only *anam* allowed to press into her memories without permission was Sesína.

"I'm fine." Her words came out a bit more tersely than she intended. *"Please don't read my memories without my permission."*

Chrí tipped her head to the side. *"Why?"*

"It's personal—"

"Secrets? Hiding?" Now the drek was really concerned. An image of Koriana flitted through Alísa's mind, followed by Graydonn. *"Safe?"*

"Yes, I'm safe."

"Perhaps dreki have no secrets?" Sesína offered.

Alísa hummed thoughtfully. With the way they had melded minds before, that did make some sense.

"Humans don't share everything, Chrí. Not like dreki. We pick what we share with different people" —she checked herself— *"different anam. I might tell my family more than I tell my friends, or my friends more than strangers. My thoughts and memories are my own—sacred and treasured."*

Chrí slumped her head. A small amount of remorse filtered in—more a courtesy apology than contrition—alongside a deep sadness, as though Alísa were breaking her heart.

Alísa's own heart twisted at her friend's ache. *"Chrí, I trust you. I know you care about me and will protect me. It's just not how humans interact. Or dragons. It makes me uncomfortable."*

Chrí nuzzled Alísa's cheek again, but didn't press in. Her sorrow lessened, though it still carried through her touch.

"That looks like a serious conversation."

A male voice caused Alísa to jump, and Chrí fluttered her wings to steady herself. The younger of Me'ran's slayers—Yarlan—stood beside her, though she hadn't seen or felt him approach. She had known a few slayers with such stealthy tendencies. A great advantage on the battlefield, but a little frightening in social situations.

Chrí wrapped her tail, soft with her silky mane of fur, around Alísa's neck. Wariness rose within the drek, and she leaned forward to monitor the newcomer.

Yarlan didn't seem to notice Chrí's response, his eyes on Alísa. She kept her mouth shut. Was it normal for the villagers to talk with a drek, or would conversing give away too much about her gift? She didn't know Yarlan, and Chrí didn't seem to like him. Better to keep silent as much as she could, and to rein in her empathy so he couldn't sense her mind reaching out.

His scrutiny relaxed and he leaned back against the wall beside her, watching the crowd.

"You do hear their voices, I presume?"

Alísa worked not to swallow or tense up, saying nothing.

"Do they frighten you?"

She shook her head, then realized Yarlan didn't see it, since he was staring at the people. Probably to get her to talk.

"No. D—Dreki don't f-frighten me."

He glanced at her. "Your voice says otherwise."

Heat filled her heart and face. It was a common misunderstanding, but that didn't make it any less irksome.

"I always s-stammer. Being frightened has n—nothing t-to do with it."

He nodded once but said nothing. Beyond them, the lullaby ended, and the crowd began to thin. Parents hoisted sleepy little ones into their arms, elders stood from their seats, and couples clasped hands as many began the trek down the hill to home.

A brunette in perhaps her late twenties approached them, a five-year-old in her arms and an eight-year-old at her side, both tired little boys. Yarlan's eyes softened for just a moment before he faced Alísa once more. Again, he kept his hawk-like gaze fixed on her, completely ignoring Chrí as she stood alert on Alísa's shoulder.

"They seem harmless, and their mental signatures are nothing like dragons', but I keep tabs on them nonetheless. If they ever do or say anything that makes you afraid, or even makes you uncomfortable, let me know."

Alísa nodded quickly, though Chrí's reaction and her own racing heart told her to do no such thing. Chrí was her friend, regardless of their mental and cultural differences, and slayers were not necessarily trustworthy.

How on A'dem will I convince them to join me if I think like that? And yet it was there, lurking in the corners of her mind and waiting to pop out at random moments. It could have been bias for her new friends, perhaps anger at her father and Kallar for their secrets, maybe a little of both.

Yarlan nodded respectfully. "Blessings be with you."

"Eldra Branni strengthen your hands," she whispered as loudly as she could.

As soon as Yarlan turned away, Alísa slumped, breathing a sigh of relief. The tensions of a first meeting between slayer clans were nothing compared to what she now felt. Then she bore a sword and stood with her people. Now she stood alone, unarmed, and bearing a heavy secret.

If only another human could know what was happening, maybe she wouldn't feel so afraid of Yarlan and Namor. But the thought of telling anyone, even Selene or Falier, set her heart racing once more. They barely knew her—she barely knew them. How could she trust them with such a secret? If word got out before she was ready, before she had a plan to keep slayers from turning on this village as they had in Bria's day, there would be blood on her hands.

Even a single drop would be too much.

Blond hair glinting in the firelight drew Alísa's eyes. Selene approached her with a smile.

"Did you have fun tonight?"

Alísa returned the smile. "Yes, it was wonderful."

"Good. I'm glad Falier convinced you to come back."

Alísa waited for Sesína to retort that she had been the one doing the convincing, but a prod at the hatchling's mind revealed the peace of sleep. Lucky for Koriana and Graydonn—they would get to sleep tonight too.

Alísa glanced at the leftover crowd. There were about twenty people left, many of them dragging logs or benches closer to the fire.

"Are there m—more festivities t-tonight?"

Selene inclined her head toward the fire. "Namor's agreed to tell a story from his days as a wayfarer."

Alísa's heart sank. She didn't want to hear such stories anymore. Perhaps she should call it a night and go to her room. But then, she couldn't avoid Namor for the rest of her life—or however long she and the dragons stayed near Me'ran—and if she was ever going to convince slayers to join her in ending the war, there would have to be a foundation of trust.

Chrí took off into the night, joining the rest of the dreki in the forest as Alísa followed Selene back to the bonfire. Alísa took a spot between Selene and Falier just as Namor began to speak.

Falier nudged her with an elbow. "Did you have fun?"

She nodded with a smile.

Despite her misgivings, Alísa enjoyed Namor's tale. One of the percussionists sat beside him, beating his bodhrán to add drama and emotion to the story—drumming slowly to build intensity, rolling in fast-paced moments, and beating short patterns to emphasize certain sentences. Namor displayed the energy of a man half his age, entertaining his audience with sweeping movements and facial expressions.

The tale itself was an exaggeration, the story of his single-handed defense of a village's cattle from three hungry dragons, while his clan was otherwise occupied protecting the village itself. In reality, Namor would have had to be more than twice as strong as her father to do what he claimed, and while Alísa had met slayers stronger than Karn before, none were that strong.

The audience applauded Namor's tale, and he bowed his head graciously. A freckled teenager raised his hand and Namor nodded his assent.

"Is this why they made you chief?"

"No, I was already the chief's second at that point. I didn't become chief until the dragons took him a few years later."

So, he invites questions? Maybe this is a chance to open a dialogue. Her heart raced at the thought, but if she waited for a better opportunity she might never speak. She didn't have to convince him tonight, just give him a nudge in the right direction.

Alísa raised her hand. "Have you ever encountered a d-d-dragon who refused t—to fight you?"

Namor chuckled. "I have met many cowardly lizards."

She shook her head. "I didn't mean that. Of c-c-course there were dragons who retreated before your might." She paused to let the compliment sink in, hoping it would make him more open to conversation. "But were there dragons who refused to fight or harm humans?"

"Ah, you're asking if there are good dragons out there. I would have thought a girl from the hill country would know the answer to this question," he mumbled, almost to himself. He sat up straighter. "I have seen many things in my lifetime, but the one thing I've never seen is a good dragon."

"But the Maker made them, just like he m—made us. How could something he made be c—c-c-completely evil?"

"There are some who say the Dark One created dragons—"

"They give him too much credit," Selene mumbled.

The corners of Alísa's mouth twitched, though she swallowed the smile. Those words wouldn't convince a slayer, but at least Selene apparently wasn't scared off by her questions. Perhaps people here could be convinced more easily than she had anticipated.

Namor cleared his throat. "It is better to overestimate the enemy than under, young lady. But" —he looked back to Alísa— "even if they are the

Maker's handiwork, don't forget he made serpents as well."

His brown eyes hardened with impatience, bearing a strong resemblance to her father's the morning she had decided to run. But this time, she didn't have to run—Namor had no authority over her, he couldn't force her to leave or act against her convictions. And she knew the answer to this argument.

"Serpents act only on instinct. They don't p-process thoughts like we do. Like dragons do."

"Their thoughts led them to sell their souls to the Nameless for greater power. Thought-processing proves nothing."

Alísa gripped the edge of her seat. That was an argument she had heard all her life as well, but it didn't make sense anymore. Nothing the slayers said made sense—the more she remembered, the more it seemed the arguments were mere excuses to allow for the extermination of the dragon race.

"P—Perhaps a clan might agree to s-sell their souls, but the entire race? How—"

"Tell me, girl," Namor huffed, his tone turning condescending. "Have you met many dragons?"

Alísa gritted her teeth and averted her eyes. She couldn't say anything to that—he might recognize lies in a denial. He was going to win this one.

"Take it from me. I have fought many dragons in my time. Not a good one among the demons."

The words awoke a fire in her veins. All the anger she felt at her father, Kallar, L'non, her whole clan, begged for release. No one called her friends demons. No one called Sesína a demon. No one!

"*They* might say the same about you. Tell me, how many hatchlings have you murdered, torturing and slaughtering them for sins not their own?"

Namor's eyes widened a brief moment before narrowing once more in contempt. Alísa lifted her head and stared back unflinching. She was right— he would back down, not she.

Finally, he broke eye-contact and looked to his wife, Tenza, who sat beside him. Her eyes glistened in the firelight, though they remained as proud as her husband's.

"I'm tired."

Without a word, Tenza wrapped her arm around his back and helped him stand. Namor was just as stubborn about dragons as her clan, choosing to take the easier path rather than pressing through territory that threatened to prove them wrong. Maybe Koriana was right. Maybe the slayers were the ones in the wrong in this war and she should fight against them as Bria had.

"What was that?"

She whipped her head around. Falier's forehead creased in a mixture of surprise and anger.

"How could you speak that way to a man who's sacrificed so much for his people? Do you realize how disrespectful you were?"

The words were like a slap in the face, jolting her out of her righteous anger. She stood quickly.

"I can't. I'm sorry. I'm t-tired too."

Alísa half-jogged, half-ran to the Hold without another word, hot tears stinging her eyes. Where had that anger come from? It couldn't have been her—she would never speak that way to an elder, especially one who had given so much in defense of humankind. Namor was surely a hero as far as their race was concerned.

And yet, somehow, the anger had been hers. All of the ire, all of the incredulity, all of the resentment toward her clan and their inability to change had been kept festering inside her.

The fire still burned, and rightly so. Namor was wrong and held stubbornly to his ways, just like her father, just like Kallar. How could she have thought she could bring the races together? Her words had even turned Falier—a normal—against her.

Alísa shut the door to her room in the Hold and kicked off her boots before curling into the bed, her clothing still on, wrapped about her like a shield.

She didn't belong here. Every day spent among humans proved she had never belonged with them. She had a dragon inside of her, and though she had wanted to find the balance between the two races, to find a way to fight for and live in both worlds, tonight proved there was none.

Sorrow swallowed her heart and squeezed tears to her pillow. She prodded at her bond to Sesína but found only the hatchling's peaceful sleep. She wouldn't wake her, not even in her desperate need for comfort. But who was left? Branni watched over slayers, like Namor—he wouldn't hear her anymore. And there was no Eldra for the dragons.

Her heart trembled. *"Maker, forgive me, but I don't know where else to go. I've been trying to do what you created me to do, but I can't. I just can't. Help me."*

27

A BEAUTIFUL FLAME

The world was white. A bright, blinding white that weighed on Alísa's eyes and stole the warmth from her body. Fire burned in her core alone, one that roiled within her like a bubbling cauldron. The silence was loud, and the lack of mental signatures ached in her mind.

Sure, steady steps echoed behind her, and Alísa whirled to face the sound. A tall, graceful figure draped in a blue cloak approached her, each stride filled with purpose. The cloak billowed behind, revealing black-clad legs and a broadsword on each hip, while the hood obscured all but wisps of tight, fiery curls.

Alísa backed up a step and reached for her short-sword. Panic gripped her as her hand found nothing, and she twisted to search for her weapon, her defense.

Nothing.

Her heart pounded as the figure drew one of their swords. They held the blade high and twisted it as though examining it, before throwing it to the ground at Alísa's feet.

"Would this make you feel safer?" a rich, female voice purred. The figure lifted off her hood to reveal glowing brown skin and a halo of tight orange curls.

"Truly, someone with your fire need fear nothing from me."

Alísa blinked as memory stirred. "Bria?"

Just a dream. She should have relaxed, yet a tremor settled in her heart. The warrior woman walked like a panther through the forests—not yet hunting, but ready to spring on a whim. Her lips quirked and her eyes were dark with secrets.

Bria looked Alísa up and down. "So young. I was worried it would take you years to lose your naïveté. I'm glad to see I was wrong—you've finally come to your senses."

"What do you mean?"

"You've finally realized that slayers can't be reasoned with. You've known it to be true for a while now, yet still you fought it." Bria lifted a hand and inclined her head. "A fine virtue, your loyalty, but misplaced. None of them listen to anyone but other slayers, and you and I aren't their kind anymore."

The argument with Namor flitted through Alísa's mind. *Right. Not their kind.*

Still, something about Bria's argument didn't feel right. A flaw somewhere in her logic sat in the pit of Alísa's stomach like a stone, but she couldn't put her finger on it, not as she shivered and squinted in the dreamscape, speaking to a woman long dead.

"They killed me for disagreeing with them, but you—you still have room to maneuver."

Bria stalked closer and placed a hand on Alísa's shoulder. Her touch was hot, near burning, and Alísa forced herself not to pull away. Bria was strong, and she was who Alísa had to become—pulling away would bring her weakness into the open and allow it room to grow.

Bria's deep brown eyes held Alísa's gaze. "Namor is broken in more ways than one—he won't move against you. Not yet. Find more dragons to bring to your cause. You can set Me'ran free and spread peace in the east. Their wayfarers are inexperienced, and the Nissen will protect you from the west long enough to complete this task."

Alísa broke eye-contact and stared at the ground. Bria's plan could succeed. But siding solely with the dragons? What about all the normal humans caught in the middle? Without slayers to protect them, dragons would be free to wreak havoc unchecked.

Bria's grip on her shoulder tightened reassuringly. "I know your fear, but with a strong hand, the dragons will listen to you. You can protect the rest of humankind even as you fight the slayers. Innocents don't have to die—

only slayers. Slayers, and those dragons who continue to kill innocents."

The words hit Alísa in the gut. That was what had rubbed her wrong earlier. Bria put a qualifier on dragons—only those who hurt humans have to die—yet condemned all slayers as though a full race could be turned to evil. If it wasn't true of dragons, how could it be true of slayers?

Guilt crept in, first cold as ice, then burning hot. How had she missed that before? Didn't that go against what she had told Namor, how it made no sense to condemn an entire race due to the sins of some?

"What about those who don't know any better, or those who kill only to protect?" Alísa pulled back, shrugging Bria's hand from her shoulder. "You would condemn them alongside those who willingly continue their evil? Did you even try before fighting them?"

Bria's eyes flashed. "Of course, I tried—even the man I loved didn't believe me. How much less old man Namor, or zealous Yarlan, or your family, who didn't hear you even when you agreed with them?"

Alísa stepped back and clutched for her necklace. It was ice to her touch—even where it had touched her skin was cold as death. She shivered as it sapped her strength, its comfort long gone. For a moment, she considered pulling it off and throwing it away, where it could no longer hurt her.

This was only a dream, after all. It didn't mean anything.

And yet, it did. Though her mind had swum with fear and anger last night, was she really ready to give up on her family? On her father, who had always tried to shield her and had given up a comfortable life to defend humankind?

No, she wasn't ready. It hurt to hold on, but she wouldn't let go.

Bria shook her head. "Perhaps I spoke too soon of coming to your senses. If you want to try, go ahead. Maybe two stories of failure will be enough to convince the next Singer."

Alísa's voice came in a whisper. "I won't fail."

"And how long will it take for you to succeed, to convince grumpy old men and the villagers they protect? Didn't Falier turn on you yesterday? And if you die before succeeding, who knows how long the world will have to wait for the next Singer? How many innocents will die in the meantime?"

Alísa swallowed, her chest and shoulders deflating. Convincing slayers would take time, time that she didn't have if Rorenth or any other clan sent scouts again. Yet if she moved too soon and the slayers found out about her before she was ready, they were in trouble. There were too many false steps and too few right ones.

Bria's eyes softened, and she placed a finger under Alísa's chin, tilting it until their eyes met.

"You're still young and afraid. I understand. But now is not the time for fear. Now is the time for action. You have strong, wise dragons behind you. Stop the slayers. Be what the Maker made you to be. You have it inside you."

The heat in Alísa's core burned hotter. *What the Maker made me to be?* Did the Maker truly make her to slaughter slayers as they had dragons, simply because it was too hard to turn them?

No. I can't believe that.

"It's true, Alísa. Accept it and move forward."

Stupid dream Bria, reading my thoughts.

"You aren't real," she said through clenched teeth.

Bria stalked to Alísa's left. "I'm as real as you want me to be."

"This is a dream. I need to wake up."

Alísa shut her eyes tightly and forced them open again, hoping to make her true, physical eyes open. It didn't work. She did it again. *Come on, wake up!*

Nothing.

Bria stood behind her. "And what will you do when you wake up? If I'm not real, then I'm a part of you. I'll stay with you, forever whispering in your ear."

"No."

"Yes."

"No!" Alísa picked up the broadsword at her feet and whirled to face the figment of her dream. The weapon felt awkward in her hands—too heavy and too long.

Bria drew her own sword.

"You aren't a warrior." She swung and clashed against Alísa's sword, sending a shockwave up her arm. "You'll only win if you allow the dragons to fight for you in their way. They won't follow you if you care for slayers."

Another shock and ring of clashing swords.

Alísa shook her head. This made no sense. Why couldn't she wake up? She reached for the Illumination bond.

"Sesína! Wake up, I need you!"

With a clang and a mighty twist, Bria disarmed Alísa and sent her stumbling back. A boot to the stomach brought Alísa crashing to the ground. She tensed for a death blow, but Bria lowered her sword. The warrior woman circled her once more, and though the corners of her mouth twitched upward, sadness tainted her eyes.

"I was rooting for you, you know. All last night I stood beside you, watching as you made your move against Namor. Your fire is beautiful—you can win the war by its flame."

Alísa breathed heavily, feeling the cold air filter into her core and become hot inside of her. Was this how dragons felt all the time—a fire burning in their chest and stomach?

"I won't breathe it on the slayers again. Not until they know the truth and have the chance to change."

Flames burned in Bria's eyes and seemed to steal Alísa's warmth. "Foolish girl! You condemn the innocent with your hesitation."

Bria lunged for Alísa, but just as the sword slashed at Alísa's middle, a shield of emerald light formed between them. The sword smashed into the wall of energy and shattered into dust.

The shield reshaped itself into a dragon—Sesína, taller now, as though she had grown up in the day Alísa had been away. The astral dragon bared its teeth and growled at Bria.

"Get out of here, serpent!"

Alísa clung to the voice and the warmth it brought her. She pushed out gratitude to the dragoness as she rose to face Bria.

"It isn't weakness to bring truth before the sword. You walked in your way, Allara in hers. Though I stumble, I will walk in mine."

Bria looked between Alísa and Sesína, her eyes brightening in what looked like triumph. Her image shimmered like the air above the road on a hot summer's day, and just as she faded away, she smiled.

"A beautiful flame, indeed."

Alísa breathed in a long breath as silence took the dreamscape once more. All that remained was Sesína's astral form and the comforting hum of their bond. She reached to stroke the dragoness' snout.

"Thank you. I know it was just a dream, but I felt I had to defeat her. Most everything she said had run through my head last night. I had to stop it."

Sesína accessed Alísa's memories, bringing her fight with Namor to the front and flitting through it. *"Looks like you had a rough night."*

Alísa sighed. "I have a rough morning ahead of me too. I have to repair the damage I caused. I can't bring our peoples together if the slayers and the holders are against me." She shivered. "It's a rare occasion that they have a common cause. I don't wish to be it."

"What will you do?"

Alísa swallowed and wrapped her arms around herself. There was only one way she could think of to pacify Namor, and it wasn't guaranteed to work. But, at the very least, it might soothe her relationship with Falier and anyone else who had witnessed her disrespectfulness.

"I will go to Namor and apologize."

Sesína's eyes flashed. *"Apologize? But he's wrong. He symbolizes everything you're fighting against. You'll never convince anyone to follow you if you back down from every fight."*

"Thanks, Bria." Alísa smirked, drawing a growl from Sesína. "I'm not apologizing for the truth I spoke. I will not back down from that. But I was highly disrespectful last night, and that will only push him away."

Falier rose in her mind's eye, his disapproving frown carving a hole inside her.

"It even pushed away someone who's been trying to be my friend at every turn. I'll never gain that back without humbling myself." She shivered and rubbed her hands over her arms. "I don't want to do it, Sesína, but I don't know any other way. I can't give up on my people, no matter how wrong they are."

Sesína nuzzled Alísa's cheek, zapping her lightly with astral energy. *"Eldra Branni would be proud."*

Warmth entered Alísa's heart, filling a hole she had felt all too often since running away. She had left her clan, yes, but she wasn't abandoning her people. She was following the Maker's call and doing so in a way that still honored them.

At least, she would be, if she got through the apology.

Sesína's calm affirmation washed over her. *"Do what you need to, then return to me. I miss you."*

Alísa smiled. "I miss you too, dear one."

Sesína shrank before her eyes until she stopped at her true height. The dragoness grinned. *"Being that big was fun. I should enter your dreams more often!"*

Alísa laughed. "You'll be that big soon enough, and what a frightening thought that is…"

Sesína chuckle-coughed. *"Wake up now. The sun is up, and the sooner you complete your mission, the sooner you can come home. I want to do more flight training."*

Slowly, the hatchling faded away until only the white of the dreamscape remained. Alísa closed her eyes and breathed, feeling heavier as she pulled herself from sleep into wakefulness.

28

APOLOGY

Alísa forced her eyes open. Sunlight illuminated the small, cozy room. A chest of drawers stood against the wall unused, her pack merely resting against it. A basin of water, filled the evening before, and a hand-held mirror lay on top. A wooden chair sat in the corner between the chest and the door, draped with a green-and-black plaid blanket. She certainly didn't need it, tangled up as she was in her clothing and the bed's blankets.

Trepidation weighed her body into the soft mattress and down pillow. It was time to move, but the warmth called her to stay just a moment longer. A little more sleep would allow her to think and speak better.

It would also allow her resolve time to melt.

She sat up slowly and unwrapped her warm bindings. No time for rest—she had to make this right.

Alísa forced herself to stand and changed quickly into fresh clothing, allowing as little time as possible for the morning's chill to seep into her body. She laced her boots loosely, distracted by the terrifying thought of humbling herself before Namor. Before a man who probably hated her right now. Before a man she knew was wrong.

She reached up to finger her necklace. It was warmer now than it had been in the dream, clinging to the life in her body.

"Move, Alísa," she spoke aloud to steel herself.

She forced herself to walk to the door, grab the handle, and pull. Every muscle moved slowly, mechanically. She gripped the stair railing tightly as she descended, leaning her weight against it in case she forgot how to catch herself as she stepped down.

Smells of eggs, ham, and fresh bread filled her nostrils, and her stomach growled. Yes, breakfast would be good. Food would allow her to think more clearly. Maybe she would see that she didn't have to apologize. Food would solve everything.

No! She told herself. *You will eat nothing until you've done what you need to do.*

Falier walked out of the kitchen. He avoided eye-contact, seemingly on a mission.

"Falier?"

He stopped and turned to her, his face devoid of emotion. "Yes?"

"C—Could you tell me where" —she swallowed and forced herself to finish her sentence— "where Namor lives?"

He huffed and kept going about his business. "So you can attack him again?"

"No—"

"The man has given so much in the service of his people," he said hotly, shoving a chair into position at a table and moving on to the next one. "He lost his leg to a dragon, nearly giving the ultimate sacrifice!"

Alísa clenched her fists. "I know—"

"You had no right to show the disrespect you did last night."

"S—s—s—s—" *Stop interrupting me!*

She couldn't get it out, but at the sound of her struggle, Falier stopped. His shoulders slumped as light remorse showed on his face. He shook his head.

"I'm sorry. Go ahead."

Alísa pulled in a shuddering breath and blew it out. "I j—just want to apologize t-t-t-t-to him."

Falier looked as though she had thrown cold water in his face.

"What I did was wrong." The words left a vile taste in her mouth. "Now, will you t-t-tell me, or will I have t-t-t-t-t" —*breathe*— "t-to find someone else who will?"

Falier leaned against the back of a chair and regarded her for a moment. His expression softened.

"I'm sorry again. I'll do you one better. I'll take you to him."

She let out a breath. "Thank you."

She followed Falier as he led her from the Hold to the southern end of the village. Some shops were already open and a few children played in the streets. Alísa fought the part of her that didn't want others to watch as she humbled herself. She had committed the misdeed before them—honor demanded she now apologize before them. Nothing less would satisfy a proud slayer like Namor.

Namor's home was a modest size, one of the few in the village built from stone rather than wood. *Of course, a slayer would build his home from fireproof material.* Only the door was made of wood, carved with intricate knotted patterns symbolizing honor, protection from evil, and the bond between mind, body, and soul. Many slayers from her own clan had these symbols stitched into their tents.

She stepped to the door, forced her fingers into a fist, and knocked, her mechanical movements creating a louder sound than she wanted. *No turning back now.*

She knocked a couple more times, more lightly than before, and backed away from the door. She acutely felt Falier's oddly-emotionless presence a few feet behind her. Colorful curtains in the windows of the other houses were pulled back to let in the cool morning air. Shopkeepers stirred behind open doors and under awnings, making their preparations for the day. Her apology would indeed be public.

Tenza opened the door, her silver locks pulled back in a loose bun. Her eyes hardened as she recognized Alísa.

"What do you want?"

Alísa bowed her head respectfully. "I w—wish to speak to Namor, p-please. Would you—"

"You wish to finish what you started last night? No, I think we've heard enough from you, young lady." She pulled back and began to shut the door.

"P-please," Alísa put a hand on the door. "I'm sorry. I want t-t-to tell him I'm sorry."

The door stopped and Tenza stepped forward again, squinting at Alísa.

"Tenza," Falier said. "Hear her out."

The woman nodded and slowly opened the door wider. "Very well. Come in."

"No," Alísa said quietly. "I need to do it out here. Where everyone else c-c-can hear me."

Tenza nodded once more. "I will bring him."

As Tenza disappeared back inside the house, Alísa began to shake. Her palms became clammy, and her throat threatened to choke her from the inside.

"Breathe," Sesína soothed. *"He can do you no harm."*

"Alísa," Falier spoke behind her. "Why do you want this public? You could—"

Tenza arrived back at the door, Namor leaning against her. He held his head high, and it was as if she saw him for the first time. He was like her father, a wayfaring chief who gave everything he could for the sake of his calling. He was proud, strong, and stubborn. If she couldn't convince him, what hope was there for her own father? But she had to go about it the right way, and right now, though every muscle in her body tensed to run, that meant apologizing.

She raised a fist to her heart in respect and bowed her head deeply, keeping it there for what felt like an eternity. She breathed in and relaxed as she lowered her fist and looked back up to him.

"Namor." Her voice carried through the quietly-stirring street, but she didn't look to see if any watched. The only way she was going to get through this was by focusing on him alone.

"M—m—my—"

"Spit it out, girl!"

Alísa tensed, her shoulders rising and stomach clenching.

Falier came up beside her. "Namor, please—"

"My words," Alísa interrupted sharply. This was her battle, not his. "And actions t-t—t-t-toward you yesterday w—were wrong. I d—disrespected you before others. You, who have given flesh and blood t-t-to protect the innocent. No matter our differences, n—n—nothing should excuse my actions. So I ask you, b-before all who will hear, p-p-p-please forgive me."

Namor stared at her blankly and she lowered her head once more.

"What is your name, girl?" he asked, softer than before.

"Alísa."

"I accept your apology, Alísa."

She breathed a silent sigh of relief. It was over—she had done it.

"Now, take my advice, lest you make such a mistake again."

Alísa looked up at him in wary anticipation.

"Such thoughts and statements will get you into trouble in the future. Guard your heart and mind well and watch over your tongue. No man wants a woman with a dragon inside her."

The statement was an arrow to her chest. Alísa clenched her teeth behind her lips and forced herself to dip her head politely one last time, swallowing the anger burning inside of her. She turned and marched away, past Falier and the few people who had stopped to listen. She needed to get away—somewhere out of earshot, where she could vent her frustration and pain.

Hot tears stung her eyes as Namor's words haunted her. Namor would probably say no man wanted a woman with a defective voice either, unless it kept her quiet. She had heard that one before, whispered and laughed about in moments people thought she wasn't listening. She had wondered in the darkness of her chamber whether it was true, whether she was lovable for any reason besides the promise of chiefdom.

She pushed past the edge of the path and into the forest, wiping a tear as soon as the foliage concealed her from Namor's front door. So, she was twice-damned in her love-life, so what? Twice-damned was no worse than once in this case, and she didn't need marriage to fulfill her purpose.

"Alísa, wait."

Falier's voice, though soft, made her jump. He had followed without her noticing? How? She hadn't felt his presence behind her. She shook her head and marched on, avoiding eye-contact so he wouldn't see her tears.

"Where are you going?"

Alísa opened her mouth to tell him to let her be, but her voice betrayed her, catching in her throat. Her chest squeezed in a silent sob. *Stop. You're fine—you're just fine.*

"*You are fine,*" Sesína soothed. "*Just breathe. You did it. You accomplished your goal, and it obviously worked, at least as far as Falier is concerned.*"

"*Then why does it hurt so badly?*"

"Alísa?" Falier's boots clumped through the foliage behind her. If he kept following, she would have to turn away from the mountain to throw him off, but all she wanted was to get home. She pushed branches out of her way and released them, not bothering to look back and see if they would hit him.

"Would you wait a second?" He grunted as she released a particularly large branch.

She tried to speak again, her voice squeaking. "L—L—Let me b-be." *Damned stammer!*

He caught her arm and pulled her to a stop, his grip light enough that she could break it, but strong enough she would have to pull hard. Light pain pricked from his touch, and her compassion rose to meet her ire.

"Look at me, Alísa."

"He wants to help," Sesína said. *"Let him."*

"I want you, not him."

"He's not leaving until you let him help you. This is what you wanted."

Alísa sighed and wiped the tears from her cheeks. She tried to keep her face stony as she faced Falier.

His eyes filled with concern, and before she realized what he was doing, he pulled her into a hug. She tensed as heat rose into her cheeks. What was he doing? He barely knew her. She reached out with her empathy, hoping to understand, but found only his pain. No compassion, no infatuation, no conflict.

Falier let Alísa go, but held her gaze. "You're right to be upset. Namor was unfair to you. I think you showed great courage and humility."

Alísa tried to smile, but while the words warmed her heart, she couldn't focus on them fully. This was the third time today she had noticed not feeling Falier's emotions. She couldn't remember whether she had ever felt them.

She opened her mind wider and reached out, her empathy spreading out from her like a fog. He was still speaking, something about how slayers treated women unfairly. She would have time to be offended by his stereotyping later.

Nothing.

There couldn't be nothing. The only way to keep his emotions from her was with a telepathic wall—

Hunger.

Deep, aching, consuming—and it didn't come from Falier. She twisted from him and searched for the source, her hand moving instinctively to her hip. Her heart went cold as she found nothing but the folds of her skirt, her sword left behind at the Hold.

Falier's eyes widened. "What's wrong?"

"S-something's out there."

As quickly as the hunger had washed over her, a warm sense of peace now coiled around her. There was nothing to fear here. No need to run or even move. Right here was the safest place in the world.

So safe.

So sleepy.

So…unnatural.

Serpent! Alísa shook her head hard and Sesína's alarm flooded through the bond, bringing with it the alertness of adrenaline. Alísa pressed against the foreign calm with her empathy and grabbed Falier's arm.

"S—s—s—ser—"

"Look out!" Falier yanked her aside, barely keeping her from falling as they dodged the strike of an eight-foot long serpent.

The creature coiled where it landed, its glossy green scales so dark they were nearly black. It pinned cold, emotionless eyes on them, its head rising high while two wings unfurled to launch itself at them again.

29

SERPENT

Alísa shivered with strain as she pushed against the serpent's empathic powers trying to lull her and Falier asleep. Falier, though motionless, didn't seem affected by the power—another sign that he was a telepath who could put up a wall against such things. Another sign that she had missed something vital.

But that was the last thing she needed to dwell on now, with death staring her in the face.

With no weapon between them, her and Falier's only hope was to run. But serpents were strong, and their wings made them fast. They couldn't fly like a dragon, but they could fling themselves at their prey. Though venomless, their fangs were large enough to do serious damage, and this one was large enough that if it got its coils around her or Falier, it would quickly be over.

"I'm coming!" Sesína's words echoed through Alísa's mind.

The serpent tasted the air. Sesína wouldn't be fast enough.

A twitch of the wings was all the warning they received, and she and Falier dove apart. Alísa rolled to her feet as the serpent advanced on its belly, its maw opened in a frustrated hiss. She didn't dare turn her back on it—at this range, she needed to watch for anything that might reveal its next move.

Falier shouted at the serpent as if to distract or scare it, but the creature didn't even glance at him. It struck at her legs and she dodged left, then right, the second strike ripping into her skirt and drawing a cry from her lips.

With another shout, Falier was there, clubbing the serpent's tail with a large branch. The serpent's whole body was thick with muscle and the attack only succeeded in turning the beast's attention to him instead.

"Run!" he shouted, backing away and brandishing his makeshift weapon. Beads of sweat covered his brow and fear clouded his eyes, as though he had never before seen battle.

She couldn't run. She couldn't leave him to die.

He swung at the serpent's head, and it pulled back, spreading its wings wide in threat. Even if he hit it, only a blow to the head would help, and it would only daze a serpent of this size. They needed a blade, or—

"Use your t—t-t-telepathy!"

Falier blinked in surprise, and a wave of cold rushed over Alísa as she realized her mistake.

Time slowed as the serpent flung itself at him. Falier swung the branch, missing the head and hitting what would have been its chest if serpents had such a thing. With a flap of its wings, the serpent course-corrected, coming around Falier's back and pinning his arms to his sides as the rest of the body wrapped around him. He fell to the ground with a strangled cry, and his fear blasted Alísa as though a dam had burst open, nearly knocking her over.

"NO!" She ran for the writhing pair, hardly aware of what she was doing, and reached for the part of the serpent closest to her. As soon as her hand connected with a wing, she shot all of her fear and terror through the skin-contact.

Falier gasped in a breath as the serpent's hold loosened, but then the creature jerked from Alísa's touch and turned its gaze to her. She fell over backwards as it struck, its snapping jaws missing her by mere inches. It flapped its wings to straighten again, Falier still in its coils, and pinned its eyes on her. The black orbs seemed to suck her in as the beast's unnatural calming coursed over her again. She pushed against it, gritting her teeth, but couldn't tear her eyes away.

A furious roar ripped from Sesína as she leapt from the brush onto the serpent, her talons tearing at its wings. The serpent let out a hissing scream that clamped around Alísa's heart, then released as the monster's empathic hold ended. Coils unwound from Falier, and he coughed and choked in breaths. Alísa hurried to his side and helped him sit up.

PAIN!

Alísa cried out as it shot through the Illumination bond, twisting to see the serpent pulling upright and Sesína snapping after it, one front leg dripping blood. She growled and spit at the beast twice her length, her back arched and wings spread to make herself look bigger.

Falier coughed and struggled to stand. "Come on!"

The serpent struck, and Sesína swiped at its face, both combatants swirling around to keep the other in sight.

Falier pulled Alísa up, sending shocks of his fear pulsing through her. "Let's go!"

Alísa wrenched away; she had to stay and help Sesína. She closed her eyes and breathed, focusing her tired psychic energies on Sesína and pushing them out in song.

> Dear young dragon, sister, friend,
> Brave one who protects us now.
> Strength will rise and pain will end,
> Hear these words and never bow.

Falier's surprise and incredulity came like waves. He tugged at her arm, stronger now than a few seconds ago.

"What are you doing? We need to run!"

Alísa pulled against him, locking her astral gaze on the combatants and watching as her tether-line to Sesína grew brighter, feeding the dragon's astral form. The serpent leapt at the dragon, its wings tangling with hers, its body flailing to catch hold of limb or middle.

> Arise, dear dragon, rise and stand,
> For your opponent stalks its prey.
> My song shall rise by Maker's hand,
> And Maker's wings shall fan your flame.

At the words, Sesína's eyes brightened, not with the light of happiness, but with the strength of a raging fire. The serpent's body now coiled once around her middle and it pulled back to strike at her face. Sesína opened her maw, matching the serpent's violence and fury, and with a rattling inhalation met its strike with flames.

The serpent's scream lasted only a second before the fire stole all moisture from its throat, its wings and tail pulling away from Sesína as it writhed in agony. Then it fell in a heap of smoking scales and crumpled wings, its eyes going vacant.

Sesína whirled around, her teeth bared in a grin. *"Did you see that? I did it! I breathed fire!"*

Alísa grinned as she ended the song, then stumbled, only now feeling the fatigue of her exertion. She unclenched clammy fists as tremors ran over her arms. Her legs quaked beneath her and her stomach churned. *I think I need to sit down.*

Sesína calmed down instantly. *"My turn."*

She pushed calm and strength back to Alísa through the bond. *"You're still not focusing hard enough to avoid the extra exertion. I bet Falier felt your powers too."*

Falier. He stood rigid, wide eyes flitting between Alísa and Sesína. His emotions flowed freely now—shock, fear, anger—reminding Alísa of the telepathic wall she had discovered around his mind.

Falier was a slayer, one who hid behind telepathic walls—a serpent in the grass, waiting for an unguarded moment to strike.

And now he knew her secrets.

Falier's heart pounded wildly against his aching ribs. *A dragon. A flaming dragon!*

His mind swam. Nothing made sense. The dragon should be attacking them now that the serpent was dead, not looking between him and Alísa.

Perhaps it was trying to decide who to kill first.

And Alísa, she should have run. Instead, she had started singing. Her voice had sent ripples over his mind, mesmerizing him, calling him to bravery and honor.

As if that would do any good. There was a reason Kerrik, the wayfarer who had tested him for psychic abilities, had left him behind. He was a waste of time as a slayer, barely able to keep walls up around his mind. Now he would die, despite all the effort of the man who had left him behind to keep him alive.

Alísa's voice still reverberated through his mind, her words encouraging him to stand his ground despite the odds. He couldn't win a fight with a dragon, even one so young as this, but maybe, just maybe, he could give Alísa the chance to survive.

"Run. I'll hold it off as long as I can!" He concentrated hard, trying to focus his powers into an attack on the dragon's mind. He had been told to picture a wall when instructed how to hide his powers from others. Now he pictured a sword.

The dragon barely flinched as his psychic attack landed, a mere wince on its beastly face. Its otherworldly green eyes locked on him, sending coils of fear around his heart. How long could he last against this beast?

The dragon's attention turned to Alísa, who rushed to stand between them. "No, Falier! Stop!"

Horror filled Falier's heart, sinking it into his stomach. There were tales of humans possessed by dragons and forced to do their bidding, even being driven mad. If that's what was happening right now, if the dragon was forcing Alísa to stand between them, then the only way to save her was to stop the dragon.

He couldn't stop the dragon, but maybe he could distract it. Perhaps an act of sacrifice would be enough to awaken her.

He had to try.

Falier took up the branch at his feet, discarded when the serpent tackled him. He dodged around Alísa and threw another psychic sword, but Alísa leapt at him, the force of her motion pulling him to the ground.

"Stop!" She placed a hand on the branch and gripped his shoulder. "She won't hurt you."

Lies! Falier tried to sit up, but Alísa pushed back. Anger pulsed through him, all directed at the creature forcing Alísa to hold him down. He could probably force her off him, but she was the victim.

Victim. Just thinking that about Alísa made his blood boil. He shot another psychic attack at the dragon, picturing an arrow shot from its bow.

"Let her go! How dare you possess her!"

The dragon didn't move, apparently content to let Alísa do its work for it. Maybe he *should* throw her off, knowing it would save her in the end.

"Falier, look at me." Alísa grabbed his tunic at the shoulder and shook him. "L—L—Look at me!"

The desperation in her voice made his heart hurt. He searched her eyes, trying to find his friend within them. If he could just find her and pull her out of this possession.

But he couldn't, not against a dragon. He couldn't do anything against something so powerful—even one this small. He was too weak. He would die a failure, unable to save even one person with his powers. Killed on his first battlefield, just as Kerrik had predicted.

His voice came out in a whisper. "What has it done to you?"

Her stormy-blue eyes fixed on his, sure and steady. "Nothing. She isn't p-possessing me. I'm acting of my own free will."

That was exactly what a possessor would make her say. But her eyes were so entreating, her pleas so earnest. How could an animal, even one in the service of the Nameless, fake such human emotions?

A terrible thought crashed over him. What if she wasn't possessed? What if she truly was acting of her own free will and had sided with the dragons? Some humans followed the Nameless too—what if she was one of them?

No, that didn't make sense either. She was too kind, too sincere, too humble for that. Even when she had a temper, she made things right. A human under the influence of the Nameless couldn't fake that.

Could they?

Alísa closed her eyes and sighed. "Reach out and feel my m—mind. She speaks to me, but she does not c-control me."

Falier swallowed. If there was one thing Kerrik had drilled into him it was this, to never use his powers on another human. The mind was too sacred, and even if he did do it, he didn't know how to control it. He would only hurt her more.

"I can't do that."

"Yes, you can."

Again, so sure, so kind, so Alísa. Everything about her manner screamed it was her. Even the way she defended the dragon evoked memories of the pain in her eyes when she had told him how she hated hatchling-killings, and the fire she possessed as she fought with Namor over the creatures' nature.

Was it really her in there?

She let go of his tunic and grabbed his hand. Light pain pulsed through their skin-contact, coursing into his mind and settling in his arm—where the serpent had bitten the dragon. Then Alísa pulled his hand to her temple, making eye-contact with him once more, serious as stone.

"I give you p—p-p-permission. Know the truth."

Falier breathed in a shaky breath. He couldn't do this.

He had to do this.

How did one do this?

He had never read someone's mind before. Feelings, sure, but thoughts? Memories?

Alísa must have seen his uncertainty, because her eyes softened. She pressed his hand against her temple more firmly.

"Picture a rope, extending from your mind to mine," she whispered. "You'll hit resistance, but push through it. It won't hurt me, not really."

Focusing on her eyes, he shifted the picture in his head from an arrow to a rope and did as she said. He felt the twinge of pain as he entered her mind, but she didn't even flinch. Warmth radiated from her like flames against the night, each memory so close, yet just out of reach, like stars in a cloudless sky.

A distinctly green voice echoed through the space—how could a voice sound green? Was this what Selene felt all of the time?—excited and fiery, though not Alísa's.

"I like you. You think I'm dangerous!"

Sesína. But how could he know that? Did her presence here prove that she did have control over Alísa? If so, why hadn't she killed him yet? And why did she seem so happy?

Alísa's laughter cascaded into words. *"As you can hear, she is here, but so am I. My mind is my own. I grant her access, just as I grant it to you now."*

A speck of light formed into a scene of another place and time as Alísa surfaced a memory. A black egg, warm with life and perfect in every way, sat on his lap—no, *her* lap—and cracked open to reveal a much younger Sesína.

Another image popped up, one of running and tumbling in a cave, accompanied by two other dragons, the sky-blue of joy, and no fear.

Then images of Sesína leaping away from a beetle in fear, a pile of brightly-colored rocks, chasing squirrels and birds, flying on the back of one of the other dragons, playing with dreki. More and more images swirled around him, and his anchor in Alísa's mind weakened rapidly.

"You don't need to protect anyone from her," Alísa said. *"Do you understand?"*

Falier's hold slipped, and suddenly he was back in his own body, staring into storm-blue eyes strong with certainty. If only he felt that way, but with this one new truth, everything else he had known about dragons, slayers, and the war was flipped on its head.

He gave a small, breathy chuckle, hoping it might hide the fear he still held.

"I understand."

30

HIDDEN SORROWS

Alísa kept her mind wide open, sifting through Falier's many emotions and searching for malice or trickery. He might be a weak and untrained slayer, but there were other slayers in the village whom he could warn. Namor and Yarlan would certainly attack first and ask questions later, if at all.

Awe emanated from Falier, followed by doubt and some fear. No malice, not even anger. Telepaths had the ability to hide ill-intentions, but she doubted Falier could manage it, short of blocking off all emotions behind his telepathic wall.

She backed off him, sitting on her heels. Sesína moved in the corner of her vision, bringing her wounded leg to her muzzle and blowing her hot breath over it—a tactic Koriana once taught her for stopping bleeding and staving off infection. How bad was it? Would she need more than that?

"Falier, I need to check on her."

Falier nodded, and Alísa went to Sesína.

Sesína pulled her wounded leg back. *"I'm fine."*

Alísa knelt by Sesína and reached for the leg. The dragoness backed up a step, grumble-humming.

"I said I'm fine."

Alísa grumbled back, hooking her hand under Sesína's elbow. *"I feel your pain. Now let me look."*

Sesína resisted her pull a moment more, then gave a steaming sigh. She stretched out her leg, revealing four red punctures just below the elbow. Apparently only the longest fangs had made it through the scales.

Sesína pulled back and breathed hot air over it again. Alísa grabbed the bottom of her skirt where it had torn during the attack, and began ripping it into a long strip with which she could bind the wounds. Two dark spots appeared on the fabric as her fear and relief poured from her eyes.

Sesína pressed her nose to Alísa's cheek and breathed a gentler heat over her. *"This is nothing. If the monster had caught one of your fleshy limbs, it might have torn clear off. I'm just glad I got here in time."*

Alísa sniffled and nodded before wrapping the fabric tightly around Sesína's leg, just in case the bleeding began again.

"You've tamed a dragon," Falier's voice came softly. "I never imagined that was possible."

Sesína snorted, causing Falier to flinch.

"What did I say?"

"I'll show him tamed…" Sesína said to Alísa alone. *"Did he not see me breathe fire?"*

"Hush. This is all new to him. Now is not the time to argue over specifics."

Alísa glanced back to Falier. "She doesn't appreciate you calling her 'tamed.'"

"Oh. Tell her I'm sorry?"

"Tell me yourself, dummy."

"Sesína!"

Falier's eyes widened. "Was that her in my head just now?"

Alísa stood. "Yes. I'm sorry for her rudeness. She's an adolescent. And she understands everything you say."

Falier nodded and spoke carefully. "I'm sorry for my poor choice in words, Sesína."

"Better."

Falier frowned at Alísa. "How did this happen? How did you come by a dragon egg?"

Alísa bit her lip. How much should she tell him?

"Alísa?" Sesína said, looking off into the forest.

Leaves rustled not too far away, raising the hairs on Alísa's arms and neck. Was there another predator out there?

"Alísa, there's something I neglected to mention."

Psychic words blasted through the astral plane, as though exploding from a mind in all directions rather than being sent in a direct line.

"Sesína! Where are you?"

Graydonn. Alísa's shoulders relaxed until Falier stood and faced the rustlings, gripping the branch once more.

"Something's coming."

Sesína scraped a talon through the dirt. *"When I ran to your rescue, he tried to follow me, but he was too slow winding through the trees."*

So much for introducing Falier slowly. She placed a hand on his arm. "He's a f-friend. D—d-don't freak out."

Falier tensed under her touch as green scales slowly became visible through the foliage. Amber eyes connected with Alísa's and glowed brighter.

"Alísa! Did Sesína find you?" He lumbered closer. *"She ran off without saying—"*

Graydonn stopped and pinned dimming eyes on Falier. His tail twitched and his wings lifted from his back, making himself look bigger. A wave of protectiveness ran over her like winds through the valleys.

Alísa swallowed and spoke aloud for Falier's benefit. "It's okay, G-Graydonn. F—Falier is a friend."

"What have you done?" Graydonn's mouth opened, releasing a hiss as he stalked forward. *"Do you realize he's a slayer?"*

Alísa fought not to shudder under Graydonn's fear and anger. She had never seen him truly angry before, but while his words spoke anger at her, his mind directed all rage and fear at Falier.

"Alísa?" Falier's voice trembled.

She squeezed his arm, whispering, "It will be okay."

"We're not ready," Graydonn said, desperation tinging his voice. *"If he tells his clan, they'll come for us. We can't let that happen."*

Alísa placed herself between Graydonn and Falier. Sesína limped to her side, lending her presence and strength.

"It was unavoidable, b—but regardless, Falier is not a threat."

Graydonn's tail thrashed. *"He's a slayer!"*

"Untrained. He has the p—p—power, but hasn't k-killed dragons. He stood down when I explained Sesína; he is my friend."

Graydonn stopped mere feet from Alísa, his eyes still dim and narrowed, his voice biting. *"You trust too easily. I know you wanted slayers to join us, but this—"*

"This is not what I expected of you." Alísa growled, taking a step closer to the dragon. "You, who showed me goodness in a r—race I thought was evil."

"They killed my father!" Graydonn huffed smoke. *"They killed him when he'd done nothing! They are monsters who haven't turned from their murderous ways in eons. How can you appeal to the heartless?"*

His sorrow and fear surrounded Alísa, choking her mind and springing tears to her eyes. Was this what he had been hiding under his calm surface? How long had he held back this fierce anger at those who stole his father from him? How long had he suffered in silence, helping her with all his heart, while suffocating under the weight of his own pain?

"The slayers who k-k-killed your father were my family, not his. Falier has done nothing t-to harm you. If he is your enemy, aren't I more so? I am a slayer. Bria was a slayer too, despite all she said and did. These p-people have p—potential t—t-to turn, but only if we give them the chance to do so."

She placed a hand on his cheek, barely seeing the teeth and tendrils of smoke she had feared not two months ago. His sorrow crashed over her in waves, raising sobs to her throat until she could no longer speak aloud.

"I know your sorrow. Feel it. Grieve. But don't let the sins of some get in the way of others who might turn."

She tried to give Falier a reassuring smile through the tears. Fear and awe dripped from him like rain collected on leaves until it was too great to hold.

"See how he stands, waiting, though he fears. He could run to the true slayers of Me'ran and bring them against us, yet he waits. He will listen."

Sesína sat on her haunches in front of Falier. *"He came to Alísa's rescue. I trust him."*

Graydonn looked between Sesína and the two humans, his motion full of tension. Then he sighed a puff of smoke and let his wings droop.

"Very well, Singer."

Alísa placed her hands under his chin and pressed her forehead to the bridge of his nose. A hug for a creature who didn't understand the gesture.

His emotions calmed at her touch, though his desire to protect her and Sesína stayed strong. He would be on his guard, but he wouldn't attack.

When she pulled away, Alísa placed a hand on Graydonn's neck and looked to Falier.

"Graydonn, this is Falier. I t-t—told you about him—the holder who helped me learn to c-céilí dance." She smirked at Falier. "Turns out, he has telepathy."

Falier rubbed his neck. "Uh, hi?" His eyes flitted from the dragon to Alísa. "You didn't raise him from an egg too, did you?"

Alísa laughed, while Graydonn made a cross between a grumble and an amused thrum.

"No. He's the first dragon I ever met. He and his m—mother have saved my life multiple t-times and taught me much in the p—p-process."

Falier tensed. "How many dragons live nearby?"

"Just the three." Alísa went to him. "I know the thought is frightening, but I swear, they mean n—no harm to Me'ran or the other villages. I wouldn't be with them otherwise."

Falier stared past her into the forest. "So, you're a slayer too? How did all of this happen? How are you here? *Why* are you here?"

"It's a long story." She pressed her lips together. "Are you sure you want it?"

Falier glanced at Graydonn. "So long as it doesn't make my life forfeit."

He smiled half-heartedly, as though trying to make it a joke, but his fear was still palpable. Truly, her own fear hadn't died until she had Illuminated Sesína. She had known in her heart that Graydonn and Koriana weren't going to hurt her, but there had been moments of panic. Falier would probably feel that way for a long time, even after she convinced him that Graydonn wouldn't attack him.

Though, Koriana was a different matter. If Graydonn reacted with fear and rage, how much more his hot-tempered mother?

Alísa raised her eyebrows at Graydonn, hoping to signal him to connect psychically. He didn't seem to understand the gesture, but Sesína caught her desires and became their bridge.

"Graydonn, has your mother been monitoring through your bond?"

He huffed. *"Yes. She'd be here now if she could make it without being spotted."*

"Is she—"

"Boiling with the flames of a hundred bellies."

Alísa cringed. *"What can I do to convince her?"*

"Convincing me would be a start."

Sesína grumble-hummed. *"Hasn't the Dragon Singer earned your trust?"*

Falier cleared his throat. "Are you trying to decide whether my life is forfeit? Or is there another reason you're all having a secret conversation?"

Graydonn eyed Sesína. *"She has."* He huffed smoke at Falier. *"He hasn't."*

Alísa groaned and swiveled to Falier. "You're safe. J—Just a s-second more." Back to Graydonn. *"What does he have to do to convince you?"*

"Release a dragon doomed to death by his slayer family, then leave his clan to join us."

Alísa gritted her teeth. *"You're being impossible."*

"You are *the impossible, Alísa. Slayers trust their own kind above all else, as do dragons. It's the way the world works. Nothing we do or say will override that in him— the only reason you and Bria did is that you were made with a dragon's anam."* A hum rumbled in his throat. *"This slayer was not."*

Falier forced slow breaths into his lungs, though his heart was in a panicked gallop. Not one dragon, but two. Three, though the third wasn't anywhere in sight. The green dragon's hum was only a fraction less frightening than his growl, and he was big—his withers were level with Alísa's shoulders. He could easily kill them all.

Yet there Alísa stood, mere feet from him. She had even hugged his toothy snout, though fire lived behind it. Would the contradictions in this girl, afraid of humans and friend of dragons, never end?

Alísa's memories said that Sesína was good, and as he sifted through the visions he had seen, he recognized Graydonn amidst them too. He had frolicked in the cave with Sesína and flown with her and Alísa in the night sky. Neither of them saw Graydonn as a threat.

Falier wiped sweaty palms on his pants and tried to relax his shoulders, tensed with adrenaline. Though his body told him to run, the logical part of him said that even if he was in danger, running would only make it worse. Another part of him—insanity, maybe—told him to trust Alísa.

After a few minutes of silent hand gestures, Alísa growled in frustration and turned away from the dragons, her eyes locking on his.

"C—Can you join our telepathic conversation?"

Him? Talk telepathically? Today was the first time he had ever tried to do anything with it besides put up a protective wall around himself! Talking sounded simpler than the attacks he had tried, but if the last twenty minutes were any indicator, it wouldn't be easy.

His face heated with shame. "I don't know how, or for how long I could hold it."

Graydonn grunted, the sound reminiscent of a wild boar. Then came his voice, a rich tenor, tinged with surprise.

"You don't know how?"

The unfamiliar voice echoed in Falier's head, reaching into the deep spaces and filling them with a strange warmth. He fought not to flinch at the feeling.

"No."

Sesína stood and stared at Graydonn, her tone matter-of-fact. *"She told you he wasn't trained."*

"But he hid himself from Alísa all this time. How?" Graydonn's head tilted to the side and his eyes brightened eerily, as though a fire burned behind them. Maybe it did. What was the sign a dragon was about to breathe fire? He looked to Alísa for reassurance.

She nodded gently, a corner of her lips twitching up. She exuded calm confidence, unafraid despite the beasts before them. He tried to stand a little taller and show the same confidence, but he doubted his mask would do any good in this company.

"I've only been taught one technique. The slayer who discovered me showed me how to put up a psychic wall to stop my powers from flowing outward. He said it would keep me from accidentally reading peoples' minds and keep other slayers from sensing me."

Sesína snuck closer, then settled back to her haunches, like a very large puppy craving play, but being told to wait. It was endearing, if one ignored the dragon's many pointy bits. Her eyes blazed with green flames, but her otherwise happy manner belied his thoughts of brewing fire.

"Why do you need to keep slayers from sensing you? Are you hiding?"

Falier rubbed his neck and sighed. "It's not quite as simple as that, but yes."

He really didn't want to reveal his shortcomings, especially to Alísa, another slayer and apparently a very gifted one. But when a dragon asked a question, one should probably answer.

"I'm a very weak telepath. No one else in my family is a slayer, so my powers weren't discovered until the wayfarers came and tested the children of Me'ran. The man who tested me was a friend of the family. When he saw how weak my powers are, he taught me to hold them back and kept me a secret."

Alísa tilted her head. "I don't understand. Even weak slayers can be t— trained to work together."

He looked away. "Apparently, my powers are so insignificant that I'd only be a liability, even with training. He was supposed to report me anyway, but he didn't."

Kerrik stood in his mind's eye now, strong and proud, just as the last time he had left all those years ago. Like most slayers, he had a fierce look. Talon scars sliced through his cropped brown hair and over his arms, but his eyes had always held compassion. They had been snuffed out far too soon.

"He saved my life," Falier said, "and taught me how to hide from Namor and Yarlan. He promised he would check in on me the next time the wayfarers came through—"

Graydonn's voice echoed in Falier's mind, halting his words. *"But a telepathic wall would do you more harm than good in the long run."*

"Don't interrupt his story," Sesína grumbled.

"But if the slayer's been checking on him, why hasn't he taught Falier better—"

"He's dead." Falier clenched his fists and shot a look at Graydonn. "Killed by a dragon before he ever made it back. His widow Serra lives in the village now with their two young children."

Graydonn drew back, the fire in his eyes dimming. *"I'm sorry."*

He actually sounded genuine—perhaps the antagonistic dragon had a soft side after all.

Falier cleared his throat and faced Alísa. "There. I've told you my story. Now you tell me yours."

Alísa's eyes shifted and she rubbed her hands up and down her skirt. "As I s-said, it's long. I'd feel more c—comfortable if I told it t-telepathically. W—Would it be okay if Graydonn established a telepathic connection? Would you be c-comfortable with that?"

No. That would allow Alísa and the dragons access to his thoughts, and right now those thoughts were all fear, uncertainty, and shame. But then, the dragons had already been in his head and Alísa could probably sense his emotions anyway. By not rebuilding his wall, he had already exposed himself.

What about his memories? Could they see and peruse those too, as he had with Alísa earlier? She had been able to guide him to specific memories, but he certainly wouldn't be able to do that.

"Will that open all my memories to you?"

"Only your direct words and general emotions," Graydonn supplied. *"Technically, I've already established a connection to you—"*

"I have too!" Sesína bared her teeth.

Falier took a step back and raised his hands. She had been so happy before, and her voice sounded happy still—why the aggression?

"She's smiling," Alísa said, laying a hand on his arm. She looked back at Sesína. "Your grins aren't as endearing to others as they are to me."

Sesína lowered her head. *"Sorry."*

Graydonn hummed at the hatchling, then his eyes returned to Falier. *"This connection is how you hear our voices now. This will merely open you and Alísa to telepathic communication as well."*

Alísa nodded. "It's true. I had the same f—fear at the beginning, but it's not an issue."

Falier eyed her. "You could be making all of this up and I wouldn't have a clue."

"True." She smiled playfully. "Do you think that?"

"No." He sighed. "I probably should—but I don't."

Alísa's smile widened, and she motioned for him to sit. Once they settled, he felt something shift in his mind, though he had no way to tell what until Alísa spoke.

"Can you hear me, Falier?"

"Yes." He hoped saying it aloud rather than simply nodding would prompt her to explain how to speak. The less he had to ask, the better.

Alísa obliged. *"To speak telepathically, think of your words as traveling a line from your head to one of ours. It doesn't matter which—since we're all connected right now, we'll all hear you."*

Falier looked from Alísa to the dragons, then back to Alísa. He imagined the energies that had once formed a wall now shaping into a line traveling from his head to Alísa's.

"Like this?"

Alísa's eyebrows shifted together. *"You're muffled."*

Graydonn grunted and looked to Sesína. *"I heard him. Did you?"*

Sesína shook her head. *"Just mumblings."*

Graydonn stretched his head closer to Falier. *"Try again, young slayer."*

"Think of your words like an arrow shot from a bow," Alísa said.

He nodded. He used to imagine using a bow and arrow with Taz all of the time—now he just had to imagine it coming from his head.

"Can you hear me now?"

"Focus," Alísa said. *"You can do it."*

Another failure, then. His temples started throbbing, and he pressed harder. *"Can anyone hear me?"*

"Yes," Graydonn said, while Alísa and Sesína shook their heads.

Falier cringed and placed a hand to his aching head. Just like Kerrik had said—he was worthless as a slayer. Why was he even here, speaking with dragons?

He jumped as Graydonn stood quickly and padded closer. Amber eyes fixed on him, the light behind them softening.

"I can hear you, Falier. Your mind is as clear as a starry sky, opening to show me your heart."

"Graydonn?" Alísa spoke quietly. *"What's going on?"*

"Hush." Sesína wiggled with excitement. *"I'm watching."*

Falier breathed evenly as Graydonn stopped and lowered his head directly in front of him. He should be terrified, but the emotion flowing from

Graydonn wasn't hostile. It was gentle, even soothing as it flowed from Graydonn's mind and reached into the recesses of his own, not pulling memories or taking control—simply present.

"*I am sorry,*" Graydonn said softly, his eyes now filled with sorrow. "*I was angry and afraid, but now I see. We are mind-kin, Falier, and we cannot be if our intentions are opposite.*"

Falier shivered like a cold man when a ray of sunlight hits his skin. "*I don't understand.*"

"*I don't fully either, but I know what I feel. My father taught me.*"

An image of a large green dragon flying through the sky filled Falier's mind. His scales were a shade darker than Graydonn's, his eyes a fiery orange. Graydonn's father.

"*He told me that psychic energy flows in waves, oscillating faster than anyone can fathom. It sometimes happens that two dragons' minds oscillate at the same rate, and if the two embrace it, it builds a deep bond between them. Sometimes this bond is between mates, but more often it forms between dragons of the same sex, like a brother or sister.*"

A second dragon joined the first, this one a sunset red. They flew together for a moment, then split apart and began dancing through the sky like dreki, coming close but never hitting, each mirroring the other perfectly.

"*I never would have imagined it was possible for a dragon and a slayer, but I felt the potential the moment I heard your psychic voice.*"

Falier breathed in slowly and tried to take it in. This morning, dragons were evil followers of the Nameless. Then they were creatures capable of friendships with people. Now Graydonn was saying they were supposed to be best friends on the level of mind and soul?

I guess that's better than him wanting to kill me for my nonexistent slayer abilities...

Graydonn drew back. "*You're hesitant.*"

Falier scoffed. "*Of course, I am. We just met, and I still don't know what's going on and why you're here.*"

"*It's normal for dragons to bond when they've just met—the bond establishes all of the trust you lack.*"

"*I'm not a dragon.*" Falier let out a sharp breath and pulled a hand down his face. *"I'm not saying I don't want to be friends with all of you, but I can't just take this on your word and psychic feelings I don't understand."*

Graydonn regarded him for a moment, his amber eyes searching. Then he settled to his haunches and blinked slowly.

"I understand. Like Alísa, you need time to figure this out. It is a strange thing that humans do not trust their own minds as readily as dragons do, but the Maker knows. Take what time you need. But in the meantime, you need psychic training. You cannot keep using that hatchling-level wall of yours. I will not let you hurt yourself further, my friend."

'Friend.' What a strange word to hear from a dragon he had just met. Yet Graydonn's sentiment and desire to train him sparked some warmth in his heart.

"Now, Alísa." Falier could almost hear a smile in Graydonn's voice. *"I believe we owe Falier a story."*

Alísa's eyes sparkled with joy, and Sesína flexed her wings excitedly.

"Four years ago, when my empathy was just developing, I attended a dragon-killing. And over all the excitement of my clan rattling against my mind, I felt the hatchling's sorrow..."

31

A SINGER'S LAMENT

Alísa hopped to her left to avoid a mass of falling pine needles and twigs. Some of the last batch still clung to her hair.

"You don't have to stand so close, you know." Sesína clutched a tree branch that looked entirely too small for her. She spread her wings for balance, now an impressive span of twelve feet. *"I'm too heavy for you to catch if I fall."*

"Call it a motherly instinct." Alísa scratched her head and pulled a piece of bark from her curls. *"If I don't keep an eye on you, you're sure to get into trouble."*

"Trouble? Me?" Sesína jumped to another tree, flapping her wings twice to reach it. Only a twinge of pain remained from the week-old serpent's bite—dragons apparently healed faster than any human.

Sesína's exasperation flowed to Alísa. *"If only we could go to that wide-open space north of the mountain. I can barely stretch my wings here anymore. How am I supposed to learn to fly if I can't practice properly?"*

"Be thankful for the trees. We wouldn't be able to stay out of sight without them. Slayers thrive in the valleys."

Mischievous mirth rose in Sesína as she crouched low on her branch. *"Speaking of slayers, I sense a young, handsome one coming this way. Think I can surprise him before he senses me?"*

Heat rose to Alísa's cheeks. *"I thought Falier was coming this afternoon."*

"He said he was coming when he could get away." Sesína pulled her wings tight against her body and shifted her weight like a wildcat preparing to pounce.

"I don't think that's a good idea. He's only seen you once now, and—"

Sesína leapt from her perch, bounced off another tree's trunk, and landed just out of sight. Her keening trumpet mixed with a surprised shout.

"Gah! Sesína!"

Alísa ran to them, stifling giggles spurred mostly by Sesína's mirthful pride. Pushing back the last of the brush separating them, she found Falier on his back with Sesína standing over him. He pushed Sesína's nose away, now apparently unafraid of his hands being so close to her teeth.

In fact, the only fear racing from him was tinged with surprise, not terror.

Sesína kept her forepaws squarely on either side of Falier and gave Alísa a wink. She whispered through the Illumination bond.

"See? I can handle slayers."

Alísa shook her head. *"Idiot. Let him up."*

Sesína backed off of Falier, who stood slowly, wiping the dirt and moss off his arms and clothing.

"Could you maybe not do that again?"

Sesína's eyes brightened. *"Serves you right, coming into our territory unannounced."*

Falier smirked, crossing his arms. "And you want what? Smoke signals? A messenger on horseback?"

"Hmm, I've never tried horse before."

Alísa laughed as Falier grimaced. He couldn't know that Sesína was equally as disgusted by the thought. She had seen too many memories of Alísa enjoying horseback riding to think of the creatures as food.

"I t-tried telling her it was a b—bad idea."

"And here I thought you were the commander of dragons."

"Not yet." She gave Falier a half-smile before looking away. He had made the statement lightheartedly, but it stirred the fear still clinging to her insides. She knew how to sing strength and courage into a dragon, but her control was still lacking, and the thought of calling strange dragons to rise and follow her was still a fantasy. Could she even keep Koriana calm long enough to meet Falier today? She would be relying heavily on Graydonn's help for that.

"What were you two doing out here, anyway?"

Falier's voice brought Alísa back to the present, where her hand clutched at the scale hidden under her blouse and a handsome young man's eyes studied her.

She shook her head, pushing away her thoughts of Falier. Only Sesína's teasing had put them in her head. "We were flight training."

Falier looked up and around at the tightly-knit trees. "In here?"

"That's what I said," Sesína grumbled.

"Where else?" Alísa raised an eyebrow at the mouthy dragon. "This is the only p-place she's safe from unwanted observers."

Sesína snorted at the word *'safe'*.

"What about the lake?" Falier tilted his head to the west. "People rarely go there at this time. They'd rather wait for the day to warm up a bit before doing chores in the cold water."

Sesína shifted from foot to foot with excitement, her talons digging into the soft earth. *"Yes! I knew I liked you, Falier!"*

She jumped at a tree and leapt from trunk to trunk to branch in a westerly direction, each landing bringing with it a small shock of pain. Alísa's heart pounded with anxiety.

"Wait! There's no cover there—if Falier's wrong, you'll be spotted for sure!"

"I need some real air-time. Don't deny me that joy!"

Alísa glared at Falier. "If she's seen, I'm blaming you."

"She won't be seen." He indicated the direction of the lake once more. "Come on. We'll stand between the lake and Me'ran and warn her if anyone's coming."

Alísa sighed. "Fine."

They ran after Sesína, hopping over fallen logs and pushing branches from their faces. The undergrowth thinned and the ground sank under Alísa's footfalls as the lake came into view. They slowed to a stop at the edge of the water, the sky turning the waters a silvery-blue.

The color of her mother's eyes, and perhaps just as wet.

Alísa pressed her lips together. If only there were a way to tell her parents she was alive and safe, without giving away her position. A messenger could certainly find Karn's wayfarers, but no messenger would respect a young, single woman's desire to keep her location a secret from her family. And when, not if, her family found her, disaster would follow. She had no choice but silence.

"Here I go!" Sesína launched from a tree and spread her ebony wings wide. She glided straight across, only wobbling with a couple wing-strokes that kept her from descending into the water.

Alísa smiled with pride, consciously choosing to focus on her current clan over her past one.

The young dragoness landed in a tree on the opposite side of the lake, shaking its top among the steady trunks. Alísa tensed. If a villager saw, it would easily call them to the lake.

"There are plenty of trees blocking this one from the village." Sesína leapt over the lake once more, this time banking around the outside. Her bank was wobblier than her straight-flying, and a change in the wind sent her flailing over the lake and nearly into the water.

"At what age do dragons start flying on their own?"

"Typically, when they're a little over a month old." She inclined her head, beckoned Falier to join her walking around the lake.

"And Sesína is…?"

"T—Two months." She sighed, hoping Sesína wasn't paying attention to their conversation; she didn't need to be reminded. "Apparently being Illuminated by a human has made it difficult f—for her to learn the skill. It was the same with b—breathing fire, though you saw her b-break through that block."

"I'm honored she chose to wait for me." He grinned, the corners of his eyes wrinkling with laugh lines.

She chuckled. "Yes, I'm sure that was why."

Across the lake, Sesína yelped and swung her wings wildly to keep from careening into a tree trunk. She braced for impact with all four legs and bounced off the trunk to continue around the lake, sending a fresh throb through Alísa's mind and down her arm.

"I'll get it—I will!"

"What's it like, flying on a dragon?"

"Terrifyingly exhilarating." She shook her head. "Or exhilaratingly t-t-terrifying."

"Descriptive."

She stared past Falier. How could one describe joy and terror joining together so completely?

"I used to love riding horses. The s—strength of the animal underneath me, the wind whipping against my face, the freedom to lead the horse wherever I wanted t-t-t-t" —*breathe*—"to go. Those were some of the few moments in my life I f—felt free. Riding a d-dragon, though…"

Sesína whooshed past them, lower than before as her wings' strength dwindled.

Alísa lowered her voice to a whisper. "A dragon's strength is greater than any horse. But that strength brings with it the feeling that I'm so small. Insignificant. The wind whipping my face is colder, harsher. I feel so alive, yet I can barely breathe."

She shivered. "The freedom of flight is greater than any I've ever felt— to be soaring high above the trees and into the clouds. But even in that freedom, I'm captive to the will of the dragon. I can't control where we go; they control me. All I can control is how hard I hang on."

Falier whistled low. "That could be poetry, with some deep, obscure meaning people debate for years to come."

She smiled through a throb in her temple. "But I know it's really just about horses and dragons."

He chuckled. "I've heard people debate the deeper meaning of poetry and songs for hours on end, but I've always wondered if that deep meaning is even there, or if people just see what they want to see."

Alísa laughed gently. "Me too."

Another throb in her head brought her hand to her temple. Was she getting a migraine?

PAIN!

She cried out at the shock, bending at the waist and stumbling.

"Alísa!" Falier barely caught her before she hit the ground.

"What was that?" Sesína yelped.

Alísa breathed heavily as the pain relaxed. *"I—I don't know."*

"I'm coming!"

Alísa started to stand, but pain ripped through her mind again.

Falier gripped her tighter. "What's happening?"

"I d-d-don't know. It's what I f—feel when a d-d-dragon is in p-pain, but it's n—not Sesína, and I think I'd know if it was K-K-Koriana or Graydonn."

The pain eased just as Sesína landed beside them. She nosed under Alísa's arm as Falier helped her stand.

"We should get you home."

Alísa nodded jerkily, her body full of tension. "P—P-Please."

Falier readjusted his hold around her back. "I don't think I'm strong enough to carry you up the mountain, but I can support you when the shocks come."

"Keep your hand on me, Alísa. I'll take as much of the pain as I can."

Another pang sent Alísa's knees buckling, but Falier held her up. She tried to pull her hand away from Sesína, but the dragoness nudged after it until Alísa finally stopped. The pain dulled as it seeped into Sesína, allowing Alísa to put her arm over Falier's shoulders. He took her wrist in his hand and the pain dulled again.

He gasped and let go. "Was that what you feel?"

Alísa nodded shakily, barely able to do more.

He reached up again and grabbed her arm where the sleeve kept them from skin-contact. "I'm sorry. I won't be able to support you if I feel it too."

She shook her head. "D-d—don't apologize." It wasn't his pain to bear.

The world blurred around Alísa. She barely felt her legs moving as Falier helped her trudge up the path to the mountain. Occasionally, her vision would fade into an image that came and left so quickly she only got a taste of emotion.

Fear.

Rage.

Sorrow. So much sorrow.

The next flash of pain came with a familiar psychic signature, one of rushing waters and fierce protection.

"Dreki," Alísa shivered as she tried to send words to her companions. *"It's the dreki. They're in anguish."*

They stopped, and Alísa flinched as Falier called up the mountain. "Graydonn!"

Seconds or hours later, Graydonn's voice soothed through her mind.

"I'll take her. Both of you, continue to the cave."

Falier guided her onto Graydonn's back and the dragon leapt into the air. The wind cooled her throbbing head and aching muscles, allowing her to catch her breath and prepare for whatever was to come.

"Your empathy surpasses my own, Alísa. I barely feel the astral disturbance."

"I didn't know I would feel dreki like this too. They're not dragons."

GRIEF!

Alísa shivered at the new wave of emotion as Graydonn landed at the cave entrance. She barely had the strength to push against it. The dreki had to be close now.

Graydonn hurried Alísa to his mother, who stood gazing at them with dimmed eyes.

"What's happening?"

Even thinking proved difficult now. *"I—I feel. The. Dreki. Some— something's wrong!"* She cried out as the sounds of tiny wings entered the cave. Her vision blurred and her head lolled to the side.

"Forgive me, Singer." Koriana spoke soothingly as a fog covered Alísa's mind. A mind-choke. *"But this will keep you conscious."*

Silence cooled her mind and she breathed in slowly. She could only feel Koriana, Sesína, and tiny remnants of the pain. She tried to slide off Graydonn's back gracefully, but stumbled when her feet hit the floor. Graydonn steadied her with a wing, and she rose to her feet slowly, weakened by the mind-choke but not hindered by it. Koriana's control was incredible.

Alísa glanced back at the cave entrance. About thirty dreki flew inside, some cutting corners by passing through the stone walls. Their lights faded as they entered until only their eyes glowed and they sank to the ground. Many had burned or singed wingtips and tails.

"Do you feel them, Koriana?"

"I do, but the strength of their emotions faded as they came apart. I think you might be able to stand it now. Do you wish to try?"

Alísa braced herself and placed a hand on Graydonn's flank. *"Do it."*

Pain and sorrow slowly reentered Alísa's mind as Koriana pulled back the mind-choke. The feelings were strong, but far more manageable than before. Alísa reined in her empathy. She could handle this.

She spotted Chrí and went to her. Carefully, she slid her hands under the exhausted drek and lifted her off the ground.

"What happened?"

Chrí's voice was weak but clear. *"Rorenth."*

Alísa's vision blurred as images entered her mind. A village built of stone but with flames inside each building. Fishing boats and docks turning to ash. A massive red dragon descending with more dragons in his wake.

Cold sweat covered Alísa as the images continued, breaking through her psychic defense. Men, women, children, all burning or bleeding on the ground. Dreki surrounding a dragon, making it fall from the sky. Charred dreki joining the dead villagers they wanted so desperately to protect.

Flames.

Sorrow.

Blood.

Death.

"D-d-did any escape?"

Grief hit Alísa like a battering ram. *"No."*

Sorrow swirled in Alísa's heart and stomach. It had been nearly a month since they had met Rorenth's scouts, a month with no further signs of aggression, and now he had destroyed an entire village.

Alísa lowered the drek to the ground and backed against a wall as Falier and Sesína loped into the cave. They stared, Sesína's eyes dimming and Falier's mouth dropping open. Alísa had no words for them, nothing but anger and grief burning within her.

She ran her fingers through her hair, grasping it as she sank to her knees. Breaths came in short, tight gasps. Hot tears fell to the stone floor one-by-one, trailing toward the cave entrance like the blood of the children who died in the streets of their village.

She had seen burnt villages before, lost people before, hurt for all the suffering before, but Chrí's memories seared her mind.

Her heart clenched for the dead. None had escaped, not even a songweaver to lament their passing. Farren's voice rose in her mind, and she poured out his words for the lost.

Why must the good die before their time,
And flames devour their prey?
When will our mourning be made right,
And smoke break for the day?

But in this world of suffering
The Maker holds us all.
His blessings follow those who stand,
Though some to home he calls.

Her final note reverberated through the cave and left silence in its wake. Empty, gaping silence.

Would Rorenth continue this rampage? How many more would die before they were ready to face him? Her powers were still new and unfocused, Sesína was unable to fly, and the dreki were wounded. She couldn't win a battle against Rorenth's whole clan with only two able dragons.

"K——K-Koriana?" Her voice was so small and frail. "I'm not ready. We're not ready. What do I do?"

Koriana padded closer and settled to her belly. *"We need more dragons, little Singer. I know you want slayers too, but there is little time. The old one wouldn't hear you, and this one"*—she indicated Falier with her snout— *"only did because he is untrained in their hatred."*

Alísa nodded once, unable to argue the point. She couldn't give up on the slayers, but she also couldn't afford to bring them into the fold yet—not if she was going to stop Rorenth before he destroyed another village.

"There is a clan neighboring Rorenth's territory, one I know has bad blood with him. Tsamen and his clan dwell high in the Prilune Mountain Range, where few slayers come, so their clan is large. We will be able to find help there."

A flicker of hope lit Alísa's heart. She didn't feel ready to lead a clan of dragons, but what other choice did she have? Wait until she did, while the rest of the world burned?

Koriana's eyes dimmed. *"But you still haven't mastered your telepathic focus—your strength song will bleed into enemies as well as friends, and leave you drained before the battle ends."*

Alísa's heart sank. Koriana was right. She had been working on this ability for weeks now, and she still hadn't mastered it.

Sesína nudged her cheek, having navigated the drek-covered floor. *"I'm behind where I need to be too,"* she whispered. *"I promise, I'll work harder than ever to be ready to go with you."*

Alísa leaned into Sesína's strength, resting a cheek against her warm scales. Beyond them, Falier and Graydonn stood at the edge of the scattered dreki, gazing over them. The poor creatures were exhausted, many of them sleeping or on their way. No great pain warned Alísa of death, though smaller sensations still rippled over her mind.

Koriana followed her gaze, her eyes dimming as they landed on Falier. *"Do you know for certain our secret is safe with this slayer?"*

Alísa nodded, wiping tears on her sleeve. *"Graydonn trusts him."*

Sadness and anxiety crept from Koriana. *"Yes. Mind-kin. I know."*

Alísa sat up straighter. *"What's wrong?"*

A near-imperceptible hum sat in Koriana's throat. *"Nothing you need worry about."*

Alísa sighed, not having the energy to press, and turned her attention back to Falier. He knelt at the edge of the dreki and scooped up one with sapphire highlights—Ska, if she remembered correctly. Falier was so gentle as he stroked Ska's mane and wings, so unlike the rough-and-tumble slayer boys she had grown up around. His life was surely better here, as a holder. Hopefully she wasn't ruining everything for him by bringing him in on her secrets. War loomed far too near here.

Thoughts of Selene and the rest of the holders, of the musicians and the people she had danced with, filled her with foreboding. She had to figure this out now, before anything could happen to them.

Her next lament wouldn't be for Me'ran.

32

SHIELD

Alísa crossed her arms and leaned against the outside wall of the Hold. The people of Me'ran communed inside and out in celebration of the summer solstice, and the air was spiced with the smells of berry pies and savory venison. The sun hung high in the sky, but currently hid behind scattered clouds, as if it too wasn't ready to be part of the crowd. At least out here the chattering and emotions had room to scatter, rather than pound against her skull.

Musicians and dancers gathered around the dormant bonfire in preparation for the first dance of the afternoon. All were dressed in light, airy clothing that allowed for greater movement. Selene conversed with the fiddler and two percussionists, while Falier still worked inside the Hold, cleaning up after lunch. He and the holders would be hard at work keeping the festivities going, though judging from the carefree smiles and laughter all around her, it wouldn't take much to keep everyone happy. What bliss ignorance was.

I shouldn't be here. It had been a week since the dreki brought news of Rorenth's attack. A week of singing until her throat was raw and trying to focus the psychic fog of her powers into direct lines of energy. It shouldn't be this hard! Graydonn said her powers were great. Why couldn't she make this adjustment?

Falier and Sesína had been hard at work too. Sesína continued using the lake to fly unhindered, each morning rising a little closer to the treetops before her tail twitched the wrong way or a change of air current sent her out of her desired path. Koriana had taken her to the other side of the mountain last night, so that she could start at a higher altitude without being seen in the light of the full moon. That had boosted Sesína's confidence, until this morning's flight when she had attempted to chase dreki around the lake, banked too hard, and fell into the water.

Falier had come to the cave twice since Rorenth's attack. Graydonn had been helping him rein in his powers so that other slayers wouldn't notice him, instead of building the psychic wall that left him battered by his own mind and the minds of those around him. He was probably practicing right now in the midst of the leftover throng inside.

Joy and excitement pounded in Alísa's head, creating the pointless desire to cover her ears, as if that could stop psychic noise. She breathed in deeply and imagined pulling it all in, then pushing it back out on the exhale while tightening the cloud of her empathy into a dense fog around her. It was the closest an empath could get to building a psychic wall, and sometimes the only way to keep her sanity in the midst of a crowd.

Falier emerged from the Hold and scanned those gathered outside. When their eyes met, he headed straight for her.

"You know, when you agreed with my suggestion of a day off, I kind of expected you to mingle and dance, not stand here sulking." He slumped beside her and raised an eyebrow. Though in range of her empathy, his emotions were subdued, barely there as he practiced the techniques Graydonn had been teaching.

At least *he* was making some progress in his telepathy.

"It sounded like a g—good idea at the t-t-time, but now…" The first song, a light reel, began and Alísa glanced at the dancers. "There's a very real threat out there, and I'm not ready to face it. Dancing and c—carrying on seems like a waste of time."

"Ouch. That's my life you're slaying."

She cringed and opened her mouth to apologize, but stopped when she noticed his smirk. She gave a sarcastic shrug in return.

"Well, if I can't slay dragons, I've got to find something else."

"And here I thought empathy made all slayer women kind and touchy-feely."

"Only for those who d—deserve it."

Falier clenched a hand to his chest in mock pain. "And who's more deserving than me? The discarded boy left to wait tables and entertain, while the true men run off to save damsels from fire-breathing beasts."

Alísa blinked. He had played it off as mockery, but very real pain accompanied his words.

"I thought you liked being a holder?"

Falier stared at her for a moment, the mirth draining from his eyes. Then he shrugged.

"I do. I like serving people and making music and hearing travelers' stories."

He settled back and watched the dancers, drumming his fingers against the wall. Alísa slumped; she shouldn't have said anything. They had only been having fun, after all. Now she had ruined it.

The song ended and today's caller announced the next dance. This was the worst part—the chaos as people changed partners and near-shouted to be heard over everyone else. It was loud, messy, and suffocating.

Thankfully, the chaotic moments didn't last long and gave way to fun and laughter and more music. But these were all things for normals without a care in the world, not for Dragon Singers who couldn't manage to solve the one problem holding them back. It was her duty to protect these people, and she couldn't even channel her powers correctly.

She started as Falier grabbed her hand. He pulled her from the wall.

"Come on. You can't bear the weight of the world forever."

I most certainly can. She drew her hand back. "I d-don't feel like dancing."

His eyes narrowed in concentration until the light buzz of a telepathic connection formed between them. *"Then train with me. The run Selene's practicing on her flute right now is for a dance that requires leaving your partner multiple times. It will help me learn to hold the connection without skin-contact."*

Alísa raised an eyebrow. *"You had that answer prepared beforehand, didn't you?"*

He flashed a grin. *"I'd hoped I wouldn't have to use it, but if you need some ulterior motive to dance with me, I'm prepared to give it."*

Heat rushed into her cheeks as the warm-but-sharp tang of flirtation prickled over her mind. Instinct loosened her grip on Falier's hand. She had only ever felt that emotion directed at her from Kallar, and only a few times, each a precursor to him trying to kiss her.

Falier's eyebrows pressed together. *"Are you okay?"*

She stopped pulling away, his concern a stark contrast to what her memories told her to expect. This wasn't Kallar. This was playful. This was fine.

"Yes." She gripped his hand once more and gave what she hoped was a convincing smile. *"Just a dizzy spell. Lead the way."*

His expression cleared and he pulled her to the crowd. Praise the Maker, Falier didn't recognize emotions yet. Maybe she should convince Graydonn to never teach him…

They slipped between the other pairs of dancers until they neared the fire. Almost as soon as they arrived, the musicians began a fast jig, too fast for psychic training. She could barely concentrate on anything but the caller and the push and pull of Falier's leading.

"We're going to separate soon. You ready?"

Apparently, Falier didn't need to concentrate for this dance.

"Left sevens," shouted the caller.

Falier raised his eyebrows and let Alísa go. As Alísa stepped closer to the fire and Falier away, it was as if a light fog rolled in between them. The psychic connection was still there, but Falier's voice traveling the line became as muffled as the first time she had heard him.

She caught his eyes on the way back to center, and as soon as they locked, his voice became clearer. *"—k of response means you couldn't hear me?"*

"No, I couldn't until we had eye-contact. That's normal—"

The crowd cheered and Alísa winced as she missed a step, fumbling into the next. Talking wouldn't be easy in this dance.

"That's right, keep going." He brought her into a spin. *"Let's try this again."*

"Right sevens!"

Falier kept his eyes on hers as they separated once more. *"Is it working?"*

She nodded, unable to do more.

He grinned. *"I guess eye-contact is a crutch too, but it's a step."*

She could barely form words as she kept pace with the calls. *"Step. Right."*

"No, left," he joked as they came back together.

She rolled her eyes. *"I need to focus on the steps now."*

Triumph lit his eyes and he gave her an extra twirl. *"If you insist."*

"I hate you."

But her heart lightened. Perhaps he had been right—this was something she needed after a week of sorrows and disappointment. An exercise of the body, and in fun. She laughed as she joined the exclamations of the crowd and grinned apologetically each time she missed a step and Falier had to catch her up. He was a magnificent lead.

As the song drew to a close, Falier added a few extra spins, twirling Alísa faster and faster until the final note. She wobbled as the world continued spinning and the earth tried to pull her feet out from under her. Falier grasped her elbows and held her up, a laugh in his eyes.

"Guess I got a little carried away. You all right?"

She giggled. *"Yes. Thank you. I did need that."*

Falier's eyes softened as he pushed a strand of her hair back into place. *"Anything to make your burden a little more bearable."*

Alísa's heart quivered at the affection coursing from him. A part of her wanted to run and hide like a twelve-year-old girl with a crush; the other wanted to embrace it. And him.

A force pushed between them—short, blond, and emanating anger. Selene grabbed the front of Falier's shirt and looked Alísa in the eyes.

"You two. Come with me. Now."

She pulled her wide-eyed brother away from the crowd, and Alísa followed, her insides clenching with anxiety. Had she done anything inappropriate?

They didn't stop until they hit the tree-line, far out of ear-shot of those at the Hold.

"What do you think you're doing, using your telepathy where everyone can see?" Selene whispered harshly. Her eyes turned on Alísa. "Do you have any idea what would happen if they catch him using it?"

Alísa swallowed. "You could t-t-tell? How?"

"How could I not, with your signals going back and forth?"

"Signals?" Falier crossed his arms. "Selene, dancers give signals all the time. There's no way anyone could—"

"I'm talking about the lines, idiot."

Alísa blinked. "Lines?"

"What lines?"

Selene opened her mouth, then shut it, her teeth clacking together. Her eyebrows rose higher as she did it once more. Finally, she spoke again, gentler this time.

"This is one of those 'Selene's brain works differently than everyone else' things, isn't it?"

Falier pinched the bridge of his nose. "Yeah. It is."

Alísa closed her slackened jaw. "You c—can see telepathy?"

Selene raised an eyebrow at her brother. "Why did you tell her about your powers?"

Falier's eyes shifted to Alísa and back to Selene. "It's complicated."

"I'm smart, most days."

The siblings drowned out as a shot of alarm flooded the Illumination bond. Alísa whirled to face the mountain.

"Alísa!" Sesína's voice came through high and panicky. *"Graydonn just sensed dragons approaching from the west."*

"No." Alísa's stomach dropped. *"Can he sense their intent?"*

"No. But judging by recent events…"

"Alísa? Did you say something?"

Alísa gripped Falier's arm, her heart beginning to race. "Does the village have a d-d-dragon shelter?"

Falier's eyes widened and he looked to the sky. "What—"

She shook him. There wasn't any time for mincing words. "Do you?"

He met her eyes, his own now filled with fear. "Yes. Are you sure?"

"What's going on?" Selene looked between them.

"Dragons!" Yarlan shouted from somewhere near the Hold. "Everyone to the shelter!"

The village erupted into chaos. People burst from the Hold's multiple doors. A woman screamed. Parents raced for their children. Young people ran down the hill to the rest of the village, while elderly people struggled to join them. Falier fixed his eyes on them.

"I have to—"

"Go," Alísa said.

"What will you do?"

Her heart trembled. "What I was made to."

With one last look of concern, Falier ran to the people. Selene stared at Alísa a moment more, then bolted after him.

Alísa stared up at the sky. *"Tell Koriana and Graydonn it's time. We need to defend the village. Does Graydonn know how many are coming? The whole clan?"*

"No. Three, maybe four dragons. Koriana says it's likely a scouting venture."

Alísa gritted her teeth. *"Let's make sure they can't take back a report. Tell the others to try and stop the scouts before they reach Me'ran. If they can slow two of them, it might be enough for Yarlan and Namor to defend here. I want you all to stay as far away from the slayers as possible. I'll do what I can from here."*

"Branni strengthen your hands."

Alísa breathed a steadying breath and remembered Graydonn's prayer. *"Maker's wings shield you all."*

Alísa sprinted over the dirt path for the center of the village, where the dragon shelter sat. She wouldn't hide in the shelter with everyone else, but the mass of people would make the area a target. By staying close to the structure, she would concentrate her clan's strength at the villagers' location.

Her heart pounded. This was it. Her ability as a Dragon Singer would now be put to the test, and the stakes were high. Even two dragons had enough firepower to destroy a town without slayer protection—especially one made of wood. Falier would be of no help, and Namor and Yarlan...

They might be our undoing if I can't get them to listen to me.

Young children cried as the people flocked into the stone structure, and Alísa's heart ached with their fear and worry. The shelter was barely the size of the smallest home in the village, but if it was anything like dragon shelters in the west, all it needed to do was cover the entrance to a larger, underground complex lined and pillared with stone.

Roars drew her eyes to the sky. One was Koriana's.

Yarlan already stood at the shelter, just letting go of an elderly woman as she entered. Namor hobbled in his direction, Tenza at his side. Her face was tight with worry, his set as flint.

Now to get them to listen. "Namor!"

He kept his eyes on the sky. "Get inside. We'll do whatever we can to make sure you get back to your folks."

"Namor, I need your—"

"Get inside," he repeated through clenched teeth. His voice softened as he looked to Tenza. "You too, my dear. Take care of them."

Tears fell down Tenza's cheeks. "No. I'm staying with you." She grabbed his hand. "Take what strength you can from me—we'll defend our people together."

More roars clashed as Sesína broke in. *"The scouts made it past. Everyone's headed your way!"*

Alísa knelt beside Namor. "I know the t-t-t-t-two of us didn't get off on the right foot, b—but you must listen to me now."

Namor continued staring at the sky, giving no sign of acknowledgement even to Yarlan as the younger slayer came to his side.

"I sense many. Perhaps too many." Yarlan fixed his hawk-like eyes on Alísa. "Do you have a death-wish? Get inside!"

Alísa stood up. "There won't be t-t-too many if you listen to me! There are t-t-two dragons c—coming to help d-defend us."

Namor's attention snapped to her. "Idiot girl! The only ones who—"

Falier ran to her side, out of breath. "She—she knows what she's talking about—Namor. Listen to her."

Namor's sigh was nearly a growl. "Has she gotten her claws into you, Falier? There's no such thing as a good dragon!"

Another roar sounded. Graydonn. Soon he would be visible and open to psychic attack.

Alísa grabbed Yarlan's arm. "Please, you must listen to me! I am the d-d-d-daughter of a slayer chief. An empath. There are two dragons up there defending us right now. Please! Don't attack the ones I p-p-p-point out to you!"

Sapphire scales flashed past them, followed closely by Graydonn.

Alísa's heart raced. "That one! Don't harm the green one!"

Graydonn wobbled and gave a high-pitched trumpet. *"I feel them; they aren't listening. Sing! Sing for us."*

His alarm wafted to Alísa. A black streak followed after him, emanating rage and bloodlust as it breathed fire on a shop. The emotions combined within Alísa, blurring and muffling everything as they drew her own fears to the surface. The sounds of the last of the fleeing villagers were muffled by the adrenaline.

Her throat clenched shut. *How am I supposed to sing when I feel this way? What if it doesn't work? What if it does? What will happen to us after the battle?*

"*I'm on my way. Be strong, dragon-heart!*"

Sesína. She couldn't fly into battle, and it would take her at least ten minutes to get here on foot, yet her voice was an anchor in the midst of the swirling emotions.

"*Sing, Alísa.*"

"*I can't! I'll only help the enemy too!*"

"*Then find another solution. You can do this!*"

Alísa closed her eyes and breathed. Perhaps seeing the astral plane would spark an idea. The tether-line between Sesína and her glowed brightly, as it did when Alísa sang strength into the little dragon's heart and soul, only this time, Sesína gave of herself.

Yarlan's brown energies shot after the black dragon, hitting the black's fiery orange shield over and over but doing nothing to slow it down.

Namor lit up a bright almond color as he drew hazel energy from Tenza. He pointed to the sky.

"Yarlan, the small one!"

Alísa's heart clenched. It was a common tactic to target the weakest dragon and thin their numbers quickly. Kallar had done the same the first time Alísa had seen Graydonn.

This time, she would do something. If she couldn't strengthen him or weaken his enemies, she would separate them.

She breathed in Sesína's calm, letting go of the tension in her body until her throat released.

> Branni, give me strength to stand against the flames;
> Maker, give us strength to rise.
> Let me be a shield against the slayer's rays,
> Opening their hearts and minds.

Alísa kept her astral eyes on the sky. A ray of teal light burst from her, fed by Sesína's green rays and her own blue. It spread out in the air above them and cascaded down to form a dome over her and the slayers. Their energy pelted her shield, each hit bringing a twinge of pain, but the shield held.

Namor's eyes widened as he turned them on Alísa. "It can't be..."

"What's happening?" Yarlan growled. "Why can't I break through?!"

"I told you she knew what she was talking about." Falier moved to stand between them and Alísa. "She won't let you hurt Graydonn. Target the other dragons, but leave the green and gray ones be."

"Falier, fight it! Don't let her bewitch you." Namor sounded genuinely concerned.

Koriana swooped into view with two dragons in pursuit, astral colors showing an emerald green dragon and a ruby red one, each larger than Koriana by at least a third. But Koriana was far more agile, zipping around her opponents to attack from behind and dropping just out of reach when they swiped at her.

Koriana could handle them for the time being, and there was nothing Alísa could do to help her right now. Better to focus on Graydonn and the slayers.

One of Graydonn's opponents—black in the physical realm, orange in the astral—flew back into view, its eyes fixed on the humans. An orange bolt of energy blasted toward Namor and spread harmlessly over Alísa's shield. No psychic power would penetrate it.

The aggressor roared, pulling the attention of its partner. Both turned flaming eyes to Alísa. Her heart skipped a beat—the dome wouldn't stop a physical attack. They dove at the humans from opposite sides, and Alísa opened her eyes as the black dragon's maw opened to reveal the harsh light of brewing fire.

33

TETHERED

Time slowed. Yarlan drew his sword and faced the blue dragon. Tenza screamed and wrapped her arms around Namor, her eyes tightly shut. Falier dove at Alísa and pulled her down, cradling her head as they hit the ground.

Then came the scream, raw and rage-filled as Sesína flew headlong into the black dragon. A loud snap cracked through the air as she rammed into its wing, folding it backwards at the joint. Flames rippled through the air harmlessly above the humans, and the aggressor let out a roar of anguish that roiled in Alísa's mind. Sesína pushed off its chest and landed beside Falier and Alísa.

A roar broke from Graydonn's maw. Alísa tensed as his pain entered her mind, and she pushed Falier back so she could sit up. Graydonn stood on his haunches over the slayers, his wings spread wide to block all three from the flames. The scaleless edges of his wings smoked, and as the blue flew back into the sky, he flapped his wings twice to snuff any lingering flames. Graydonn shook his head hard, wincing at the pain.

The humans stared in stunned silence, all except Yarlan, who gripped his sword tighter.

"No!" Alísa shouted, pushing up from the ground.

Sesína was faster, leaping into the air and knocking Yarlan to the ground with the back of her paw. She landed in front of him, her wings spread to block him from Graydonn.

"*Idiot!*" she scolded. "*Can't you figure out who your true enemies are?*" She pointed her muzzle to Namor and Tenza. "*Any of you?*"

Alísa rushed to Sesína's side. "P-Please. We're here to help."

Yarlan stood now, his face red with fury, his knuckles white on his sword hilt.

"Yarlan!" Namor called, pointing into the sky. "Focus on the immediate danger!"

The blue circled over them, and one of Koriana's opponents—another green—had broken off to help.

"I need to get back up there," Graydonn said. *"Give me strength to fly through the pain."*

Alísa shook her head. *"I can't. The other dragons will feel it too."*

"This is no time for fear, Singer!" He pointed his muzzle at Sesína. *"She flew to save you. Now you must fly to save us."*

Sesína leaned into her. *"Draw from me, like Namor does Tenza—together we'll find the strength to focus your powers."*

Alísa drew in a trembling breath. They were right—now wasn't the time for fear. She began singing again, weaving the strength song she had used in practice so many times before.

Graydonn took to the air with a mighty flap of his singed wings. His flight was steady as he rushed for the blue dragon. With her song, he would make it. But would Koriana? And would the enemy draw from her as well?

Rushing sounds of fire-breath came from the right, and Alísa turned to see multiple huts set aflame by the brown dragon. Koriana rushed after it, snapping at its tail.

Sesína stared at the slayers as Alísa continued her song. *"Now do you understand which dragons to attack?"*

Namor stared at the little dragon, his brow furrowed. Then he looked to the sky. Alísa closed her eyes to see his astral spears aimed at the brown dragon. Yarlan's blasts followed its path, both striking and spreading in a mind-choke.

Yes!

A roar came from far too close. Alísa swiveled to see the dragon whose wing Sesína had broken lumbering closer. Falier's dark blue form stood in its path and shot a single blast of energy at the beast. The dragon thrummed derisively and counterattacked with its mind. Falier crumpled to the ground with a scream that ripped Alísa's heart out.

"No!" She cried, her voice breaking.

The dragon lifted a paw to crush him, then shrieked as Yarlan came from the side and plunged his sword into its belly. It writhed and trumpeted until it slumped to its side.

Alísa trembled, the dragon's pain and her own fear for Falier colliding within her.

Sesína nosed her hand and siphoned some of the pain away, her voice soothing. *"You can't help him right now, but you can help them."* She lifted her head to the sky. *"Sing!"*

Alísa sang. Her throat and stomach constricted and halted her voice, but she pressed through it. Yarlan had Falier—she had to focus on Graydonn. She closed her eyes and set astral sights on him as he chased after the blue dragon. Mists of strength surrounded her and floated toward all of the combatants.

"Draw on me," Sesína said. *"We can do this."*

Alísa drew in a deep breath and allowed the dragoness' power to fill her. She channeled it, but the new burst of power acted differently than the rest. It stretched from her and twisted around the mists, drawing them in like a winding river and binding them together. The teal energy twirled around the loose particles and lifted them into alignment.

Alísa's mouth dropped open in a laugh of disbelief. *"So, this is what it's supposed to be. Not forcing it all out in a line of power, but weaving it together. It's almost like a dance."*

Sesína's tail twitched with excited energy. *"Now, find your partners."*

Alísa focused on the sky again until she spotted Graydonn. The power shot from her in a bolt, and as soon as it connected, she felt his essence pulsing at the end of the line. It was like when she felt his name as he spoke— unmistakably Graydonn. The blue dragon close to him bore a completely different signature, foreign and twisted. She rejected it and gave of her strength to Graydonn alone.

But then it wasn't Graydonn alone. He was connected to someone else...

Koriana. Unmistakably Koriana. She needed the strength too. Alísa's power filtered through Graydonn to Koriana, feeding both dragons and rejecting the others. Her companions roared with their newfound strength.

"You did it, Singer!" Koriana's voice dripped with pride. *"Now we shall finish it!"*

Alísa trembled with effort as her energies stretched further than she had ever tried before. Her breathing became ragged, as if she had just run for miles, but she couldn't stop now. Sesína lowered to her belly beside her, and Alísa followed suit, sitting on the ground so that even the strength she used to stand would travel the line.

"We've got this," Sesína encouraged, fatigue lacing her words. *"Keep going."*

Together, Alísa and Sesína pressed their energies again. Fueled anew, Graydonn put on a burst of speed, colliding with the blue dragon high in the air. They fell in a tangle of wings, tails, teeth, and claws, Graydonn fighting until he was on top of the aggressor. He kicked off the blue with all four legs, forcing the dragon down into the treetops. The blue screeched in pain, but Alísa's connection to Sesína and the others covered over the pain she would typically feel. Linked like this, it appeared she would only know the emotions and pain of her own clan.

Another cry came from the right—long and shrill, then suddenly silenced. Alísa's eyes found Koriana just in time to see the green scout's neck in her jaws. She shook it once, then dropped the limp body into the trees. The dragoness favored her right wing as she flew, and Alísa shook out the tension in her arms and hands as pain flowed to her from the dragoness.

Koriana banked for Graydonn as the blue dragon rose up from the trees. The aggressor fled west, pursued by a silvery mass. The cloud of silver was too far away to see clearly, but its presence couldn't be mistaken—the dreki.

"They will finish it," Graydonn's words flowed to Alísa, his voice low and tired. *"You can stop singing now. Your attentions are needed with the slayers."*

"We will be nearby," Koriana said, her tone strong and determined. *"If they try anything, we will come for you."*

Alísa nodded to the dragoness as she and Graydonn lowered into the forest. *"Sesína, run and find them. You'll be our bridge of communication—"*

Sesína hummed. *"No. Absolutely not. We're stronger together."*

Alísa sighed quietly. Sesína had a point, and after all she had done to help, she deserved the chance to make that call herself.

Alísa breathed a steadying breath and faced the slayers. Namor and

Tenza stared at her, Tenza's lip trembling and Namor's eyes narrowed. Yarlan knelt off to the side, his hand over Falier's temple.

"Falier!" His stillness sent her stomach churning and she ran for him, Sesína at her side.

In a swift motion, Yarlan dropped his hand from Falier's face and lifted his sword, pointing it at Alísa.

"You've done enough! Stay away from him."

Alísa's heart seized in her chest. She hadn't asked Falier to get involved—if she had been thinking more clearly, she would have told him to get in the shelter as soon as he came into view. Tears formed in her eyes and her whole body trembled with sobs.

"P—Please, just t-t-tell me if he's okay."

Yarlan's eyes were daggers. "Scared for your pet, witch? Whether he lives or dies, he won't be yours to manipulate anymore."

She drew in a ragged breath. "I didn't—"

Alísa stopped. Yarlan wouldn't be convinced with words, and right now Falier might be in more danger if they knew he had turned of his own accord. She stepped back.

"Just help him," she whispered.

Then she looked to Namor. He had stopped Yarlan from attacking Graydonn. Perhaps she had the chance to win him over, now that he had seen the actions of good dragons with his own eyes.

Breathing in slowly, she relaxed her throat and larynx. It was time to speak again. Namor's face held no expression as she approached. Would he hear her?

"Thank you for your help. I know it went against your life's t-t-training to not attack, b—but as I said, they're here t—to help."

Namor nodded. "You're right. It goes against all my training to not target that dragon standing behind you. You have some explaining to do, and you'd better do it fast."

She gave a silent sigh of relief. He might not understand, but at least he would listen.

Alísa glanced at the dragon shelter, still and quiet as the people waited to know they were safe. Though the thought of a crowd sent shivers of anxiety through her, it would be better to speak to everyone at once and get it over with in one fell swoop.

"I should explain to all of you."

"No."

Alísa tensed, turning back to Namor. His eyes were hard.

"It's my job to protect the village from dragons. You must first convince me that you yourself are not a dragon in human skin. You will not gain access to the others until you do."

She nodded slowly. He wanted to protect his people—she could understand that.

"How can I c—c-convince you?"

"Let me in. I need to see all your memories having to do with dragons to know if they've possessed or broken you."

A chill swept over her. She had never let anyone in that deep besides Sesína and her father. And now this grumpy, demeaning, hatchling-murdering old man wanted access to her deepest secrets? She didn't sense ill-intent, but he was powerful enough to hide it if he wanted, and once he entered her mind there would be no going back. And her relationship with the dragons, her connection to them, even the hatchlings she had never truly known, were all intensely personal.

"You may not be able to block him from memories you don't wish to share, but I can." Sesína's voice was steady and confident. *"He can't get one of us without the other. I'll protect you."*

"He's strong."

"So are we."

Alísa swallowed. "Okay. I'll d-do it."

Namor patted the bench. "Come, then."

Carefully, Alísa approached and sat beside the slayer. His eyes searched hers with an intensity that reminded her of a strong buck scanning the world around it for danger. He was scared too. He had more power than she did, but his vigilance outweighed his aggression. He merely wanted to protect his people.

Namor lifted a hand to her temple, then pulled back sharply and looked to Sesína. "That dragon. She's connected deeply to you."

"I hatched her from an egg and we c—connected. We're mind-sisters."

"I need to see only you."

Alísa shook her head. "We can't. We're bonded; you c-c-can't get one of us w—without the other."

His eyes narrowed with concentration. "I can, and I will. If that dragon is controlling you, the only way to know is by separating you."

Sesína's anxiety spiked. *"Alísa—"*

"I have nothing to hide. I can't let my own comfort and privacy get in the way, not when there's so much at stake."

She faced Namor. "I'll do it."

"But how will he separate us? What if he hurts you? What if we can't reconnect?"

Alísa made eye-contact with Sesína. *"It will be okay. Our bond is strong— nothing will stop me returning to you."*

She shifted back toward Namor. "Do it."

Namor placed his hands on her temples and locked eyes with her. She wanted desperately to close her eyes, but forced herself to keep them open.

She had nothing to hide.

Pressure surrounded her as Namor began. Weakness fell over her whole body—it took all her strength to stay upright. Her breaths came more rapidly.

Mind-choke. Of course, it had to be a mind-choke, there was no other way to cut her off from—

The tether-line snapped, sending a shockwave of white-hot pain to Alísa, and she and Sesína cried out in tandem. Alísa lolled forward, but Namor's hands at her temples kept her upright. The pain dulled, but now the world was cold. Lifeless. Hollow.

Was this how things had always been before Sesína's Illumination?

Namor's consciousness pressed in until his mind permeated hers, keeping Sesína out and granting him full access to Alísa's memories. She tried to pull the correct memories to the forefront of her mind, hoping he wouldn't see anything but what she actually needed to share with him.

"You're trying too hard," Namor's strong voice came. *"Relax and let me see."*

She breathed slowly and did her best not to fight him. Though she feared revealing parts of her mind that Namor had no right to, now that they were connected she could see the kindness hiding under his rough exterior. The war and his injuries had hardened him, certainly, but beneath it all he did what he did because he cared for humankind.

Including her.

Visions of ceremonies past faded into view, bringing pain, sorrow, and fear. Rather than skimming through, Namor lingered in these memories. A strange grief filled him, one so very different than the sorrows she herself had in the memories. It held longing and regret.

The tale of Bria as sung by Farren sparked guilt, and he jumped out of order, now racing from the song, to Koriana's retelling, to Alísa's dream before deciding to make amends with him. Bria's voice echoed through her once more: *"Namor is broken in more ways than one."*

Anger rose in Namor, but he deliberately pushed it aside and went back to the point in time he had skipped. She and Namor heard Graydonn's first plea for help. They released him from his bonds and faced Kallar's wrath. They were attacked by highwaymen and dragons and were rescued by Graydonn and Koriana. They felt Sesína's presence inside her egg and sang her gentle lullabies. Everything she had ever done with the dragons up until this moment was laid bare before the slayer.

Finally, the visions slowed, ending with the events of the day before fading to black. Alísa focused her thoughts into words.

"I'm not lying. I'm not under their control. I merely understand. Do you?"

Namor's hard warrior's eyes softened. *"I do, Alísa."*

Strength entered back into her body as Namor withdrew his mind-choke. Immediately, she sought Sesína, and as soon as their eyes met, their tether reattached, bringing warmth and joy with it. Sesína rushed to her, nearly bowling her off the bench. Alísa laughed and wrapped her arms around the dragon's neck, and Sesína wrapped her wings over Alísa.

"I missed you."

"I missed you too." Alísa kissed her muzzle.

A low groan came from behind, and all turned to see Yarlan helping Falier sit up. The young man held a hand to his head and said something to Yarlan. Yarlan responded gruffly, his words making Falier start, then wince from the sudden movement.

"You may go to him now," Namor said softly.

Alísa rose and hurried to him, but Yarlan pointed his sword at her again. Sesína growled at the slayer.

"Let her pass, Yarlan," Namor called, standing with Tenza's assistance. "She isn't a threat to him or any other villager."

"You can't possibly believe that."

"I can, and I do. Lower your weapon."

Yarlan's eyes widened and he stared at Namor, as if waiting for the elder to declare it had been a bad joke. Slowly, his snarl went slack and his sword-tip lowered.

Alísa pressed past him and knelt beside Falier, placing a hand on his shoulder. "Are you okay?"

He gave a weak smile. "Guess I'm really not cut out to be a slayer, huh?"

She wrapped her arms around him. "Please, don't scare me like that again."

He returned the hug lightly, shuddering with fatigue. "Believe me, I don't plan to."

Their eyes met and held as they pulled apart. His emotions were a jumbled mess of fear, relief, and affection. A part of Alísa wanted to look away, while the rest wanted to stay just a little longer, or maybe hug him again. The thought of him being killed or permanently injured by the dragon's attack had been far too terrible.

Falier broke eye-contact first, his eyes flitting to Sesína and back. "I'm guessing you won the battle, and won them over?"

She shrugged. "Yarlan still needs some c-c—c-convincing, but yeah."

He grinned wide, the corners of his eyes crinkling. "I knew you could do it."

She looked down to try and hide her blush. "That makes one of us."

"Two!" Sesína nudged under her elbow until Alísa's arm rested on her shoulders.

"Alísa."

A soft yet strong voice came from behind, and Alísa turned to see Tenza. The older woman exuded strength even through her fear of being so close to Sesína, standing tall against the gathering night. Her face was emotionless, her eyes set as flint.

"It's time to send the little dragon away, so she won't frighten the villagers." Tenza gave the slightest nod of her head. "You shall have your audience."

34

A VOICE

Breathe. Just breathe.

Me'ran gathered around Alísa and Namor in the Hold's main room, the space lit by lamps and a few wall torches. Occasional murmurs and crying children carried through the tense silence. The smell of fresh smoke and sweat permeated the space. Namor had told them they were safe, but fear and confusion reigned, coiling their tendrils around Alísa.

She glanced at Namor. He stood steady, firm and confident in what he now knew to be true. *But I'm the one who brought it to him, so why must I be swayed by the fears of the people? Why can't I stand unshakable?*

The answer settled in her throat, a weight tightening around her neck, threatening to drown her.

I can't speak. With Namor, I didn't have to. Now—

"You are not alone." Sesína's words flowed to her from the depths of the forest, where she now waited with Graydonn and Koriana. *"We stand behind you in heart and mind. You will make yourself heard."*

Alísa breathed and straightened taller, her knees quaking.

Namor leaned on his staff and hobbled in front of her, Tenza staying at Alísa's side and watching him closely. He needed to stand on his own, to be a rock for the people in the midst of their fear and the startling truth they were about to learn. Her father had taken that stance many times before.

Alísa's heart ached for her father. If only he were here right now, standing between her and the crowd. He would never let harm come to her. He would speak for her, like he always had, leaving her in safe silence.

She shook her head. *No! I have dragon-fire inside of me. It's time to act like it. By Maker's wings.*

"Today marks the first dragon attack on Me'ran in nine years." Namor's voice resonated over the crowd. "Praise the Maker there was no loss of life."

Murmurs of "Praise be" echoed from the people and Alísa whispered her agreement.

"The four dragons who attacked us were strong. Though Yarlan and I have experience and strength, we would not have been able to defend Me'ran alone. Today, our rescue came from an unlikely source—three other dragons and a telepathic girl."

Gasps rose from the crowd as Namor gestured to Alísa. She tried her best to smile, trembling under the weight of so many eyes on her.

No turning back now.

Namor lowered his arm. "It is up to us to decide whether to embrace this source or shun it. I've cleared her to speak to you, and while I have my own opinion, it is not my place to make such a decision for Me'ran. You must listen and decide for yourselves."

Namor nodded to Alísa—her cue to share her story. Alísa breathed in slowly and let it out, relaxing her neck and jaw.

"I am Alísa, daughter of K—K-Karn, a g-great slayer chief of the west. I g—grew up on the frontlines of the w—war. I know what it's like t-t-t-to grow up fearing for my life b—because of dragons. B—b-b-b-but—"

Her throat closed up again. Her palms were sweaty, her legs shaking, her mind swimming. She closed her eyes. It was too much.

She was going to fail.

"Graydonn and Koriana are urging you to sing."

"Sing? But I can't improvise in front of everyone like this!"

"Yes, you can. You've done it for us before, even today, praying for a shield."

"But that was for you!"

"Then do it for us once more! Without it, there will never be peace."

Images of the day Sesína hatched filled her mind. The song that practically ripped from her lips that day had been the power that joined two minds of different races. She could do it again.

Alísa breathed, lifted her eyes, and sang.

Daughter of hope, daughter of light,
A flower in a father's eye.
Daughter of war, daughter of might—
The slayers' weapon growing in her mind.

A world of grief, a world of shame;
The gift became a curse inside,
For hatchlings' fear and hatchlings' pain
Called her alone to weep for beasts that died.

As she sang, the people's eyes began glazing over. She glanced at Namor, then Falier, and saw the same was true for them. Soon the entire crowd either stared through her or closed their eyes, as if in a trance.

"What's happening?"

"Koriana says the same thing happened to you when she told you the story of Bria. They're seeing your tale."

"Everyone is seeing my life in their minds?" Alísa shivered. *"Everything?"*

"You're a telepath," Koriana's voice came, borne by Sesína's connection. *"You control the situation in the same way you control a verbal one. Decide what you will tell them and do so."*

Namor's trance ended and he arched an eyebrow at her. The others would soon come out too. She had to keep going.

They called her weak, they called her frail,
Not strong enough to keep at bay
The dragons' minds that pierced her veil.
They feared the beasts may spirit her away.

To walk in dark or walk in light,
The Maker gives all men a choice.
But scaly beasts could only bite
Until the slayer's daughter heard one's voice.

His voice was kind, his voice was good,
Despite the weight of slayers' chains.
Beneath the scales lived personhood.
His choice was light and now her choice remains:

To live with death, or die to life,
To silent comfort always known.
With trembling hands, she took the knife
To cut the bonds and forge a path her own.

A flash of silver flew through a window behind the people. Two dreki. Amethyst and emerald manes revealed the duo as Chrí and Laen. They circled Alísa as they had the day she had first met them, each trilling and chirping notes in harmony with her song. More dreki followed, dancing around her. Their presence buoyed her song, lifting her up on wings of joy.

A slayer girl, a dragon girl,
Two worlds will join within her song.
The war would see the world unfurl;
The Dragon Singer comes to right the wrong.

Are all men light, and dragons dark?
The Maker's love can fill each heart.
May voices join, ignite the spark,
And end the war that tears our worlds apart.

Her last note carried through the air, echoing off the Hold's high ceiling. The dreki ended their dance, most flying to the rafters, while a few fluttered to a favorite villager's shoulder. Chrí settled on Alísa, tangling her tail and a wing in her curly mess of hair.

The villagers' stunned silence surrounded Alísa, closing in on her, constricting her chest and breath. She longed to rush outside into the open air, away from the wide eyes and constant buzzing of their emotions.

Surprise.

Wonder.

Fear.

Disbelief.

A man whispered something to another, his actions sparking more murmurings. Even Falier leaned toward his father and said something inaudible. Alísa's knees shook. The emotions constricted around her in the tight space, nearly drowning out the continued debate.

She needed to go.

She needed to stay.

"This was no trick." Namor spoke like a chief, silencing the crowd. "What you saw was a piece of her story, as true as when I read her memories myself. The dragons of her story are the three who defended us today. One of them threw himself between me and an attacking dragon, even as I was still trying to attack him."

Alísa smiled. Graydonn's nobility could never be disputed.

"My friends and family," Namor continued, "what shall we do? Send them away as our gift of thanks? Or welcome them, knowing that what we do may seem treason against humankind? I open the floor to any who wish to make their case."

Alísa scanned the silent crowd, resisting the urge to wipe her sweaty palms on her skirt. Selene looked deep in thought, while Laen twisted her long neck to look Selene in the face. Selene reached a hand up to pet the silky emerald mane, then locked eyes with Alísa.

"The dreki say her dragons are safe."

Chrí nuzzled her cheek. *"Yes."*

Alísa gave a small smile, but it disappeared as murmurs rose from the crowd. One unfamiliar female voice rose above the others.

"The creatures are practically dragons themselves—who knows how trustworthy they are?"

A shot of determination hit Alísa like a sudden gust of wind as Falier stepped up and faced the crowd. Ska fluttered from his shoulder, surprised at his perch's sudden movement.

"I, too, can vouch for Alísa and the dragons."

Alísa's heart warmed. The words of holders, even young ones, were words to be trusted.

The villagers listened with rapt attention as Falier told of his interactions with the dragons. Kat raised a hand to her mouth as he told of the serpent's attack, and many eyes narrowed when he briefly spoke of his multiple visits to the cave.

"I trust them." Falier looked back at her with a smile. "And I trust Alísa."

Alísa returned his smile with a grin she couldn't scale back, her heart rising in her chest as if it might float away.

"Parsen!" A blond man in his thirties scowled, the anger in his tone bringing Alísa back to earth. "Your family kept this a secret from us?"

Falier raised his hands in defense. "They didn't—"

"My son," Parsen interrupted, his tone commanding silence from all, "has never kept a secret that would cause harm. Nor has my family." He glanced at Alísa before looking to Falier. "If we believed danger would arise, we would have made it known."

The accuser looked away, silenced.

A woman in her fifties spoke up, frizzy gray curls contrasting sharply with rich cacao skin.

"Where are the dragons now?"

"N—nearby in the forest. They will stay until they know whether they are w—welcome."

"Then there's no sense babbling on about them here," she said matter-of-factly. "I, for one, want to meet these dragons before I make my judgement. We can't call them here, so we must go to them."

Parsen stepped from the crowd to stand at her side. "Meira is right. I propose we and a few others follow Alísa to speak with the dragons. This company will make the judgement. Are there any objections?"

No one spoke.

"Then who will accompany us?"

A woman in her early thirties slipped through the crowd. One of the burned huts' residents—a widowed mother of two children.

"I will go if Namor comes."

Namor nodded. "I will go."

Sighs of relief sounded from the crowd and a few more people came forward.

"Sesína, you and the others had better be on your very best behavior…"

A line of nine humans faced the dragons. Some, like Namor, stood tall and confident, while others made valiant but unconvincing efforts to hide their fear. Selene cocked her head, deep in her own thoughts as she gazed at the creatures before her. Falier stood by his family, his presence lending Alísa strength.

She walked past the line to stand before the dragons. Koriana stood with one leg in front of Graydonn. The adolescent swished his tail in annoyance, but otherwise stood calm and collected—he was no longer a hatchling in need of protection. Sesína shifted her weight from leg to leg like an impatient wolf pup waiting for the signal to meet her new playmates.

Alísa faced the humans. "I would like you to meet K-Koriana, Graydonn, and Sesína. As I don't know all of you, p-p-please introduce yourselves to these who have protected your v—village this day."

Sesína chuckled mentally. *"Formal much?"*

"Hush."

Namor was the first to step up. "I am Namor, son of Lamik, and this is my wife, Tenza. As one who has fought many of your kind in his lifetime, to thank a dragon is not in my blood. But today I owe my life to Graydonn, and for that, I do thank you." He placed a fist over his heart and bowed his head in respect.

Graydonn thumped his tail on the ground and lowered his head. *"It is an honor to fight for you on behalf of Alísa-Dragon-Singer."*

Koriana lowered her head to Namor's level beside Alísa, eyes narrow, but voice even.

"As one who too has seen the atrocities of war, it is not in my blood to trust a slayer. Yet your humility with my son is moving. I am willing to call you ally, but know I will be watching you. You may be an ally, but these" —she raised her head, staring at Alísa and the younger dragons— *"are my family."*

Namor nodded. "The feeling is mutual. Perhaps we will surprise each other."

The woman whose home burned down spoke next. She lifted her chin high as she spoke, a defiant confidence in her tone.

"My name is Serra. My husband Kerrik was a slayer, killed in action."

Alísa blinked. Falier spoke of how Kerrik had kept his powers a secret. Did Serra know about Falier?

"He was a good and honorable man who didn't deserve to die by violence. But because he was honorable, I know his spirit thanks you from the Maker's halls for preventing death in our village. Before I welcome you, I have only one question for each of you: Have you ever killed a human?"

Sesína blinked slowly. *"I have not."*

Graydonn echoed her, but his eyes shifted toward his mother, worry rising.

Koriana's voice came softly. *"Dear woman, I too am a widow of this war. Too many good and honorable ones like our mates have suffered and died by its talons."*

Her eyes hardened. *"But so have many who deserved its justice. Yes, I have killed three slayers in my life, and three normals. One slayer raided my cave when I was barely older than Sesína, and I killed him in defense of myself and my family. The other two slayers belonged to a clan that purposefully tortured and murdered hatchlings. The three others were highwaymen about to harm Alísa. I do not apologize for any of these actions."*

Alísa's breath caught at Koriana's honesty. She could never fault the dragoness for the acts she claimed, but the thought chilled her to the bone.

Koriana's blazing eyes dimmed gently. *"The path toward justice and peace is filled with blood, but that blood should never be that of the innocent."* She eyed Namor, but her expression softened slightly. *"Nor of the repentant."*

Serra squinted at the dragoness. "Thank you for your honesty. Now I will be honest with you. I cannot trust mere words when my children's lives are on the line. They will be kept from you, but I will not protest your presence in my village."

Koriana blinked slowly. *"I understand the need of a mother to protect her offspring. I will keep my distance."*

Meira, the elder who had suggested the trek into the forest, held lightly to the arm of a man in his fifties with chiseled features and a stoic expression. She spoke for them.

"We welcome you to our village, good dragons." Her earthy eyes sparkled mischievously. "But know that if you sneeze your flames too near our carpentry shop, we will rescind our welcome."

The man's eyes widened in shock, while Falier snorted behind them. Koriana and Graydonn thrummed with mirth and Sesína chuckled mentally for all to hear.

"I like you."

The dragons thrummed and laughter sprang from most of the humans, some mirthful and light, some beginning nervously and loosening. Tensions eased, lifting Alísa's spirit from the mire of her darkened thoughts.

Parsen and Kat came forward hand-in-hand, Selene beside them, and introduced themselves next. Selene stood silently with an almost dazed expression, while her parents stood confidently and thanked the dragons for protecting their village.

"And you, Sesína," Kat looked to the smallest dragon, "Thank you for protecting my son from the serpent even before you knew him."

Sesína lifted her head high with pride. *"It was my great pleasure, dear woman."*

Alísa stifled a chuckle. *"Formal much?"*

"Oh hush."

Whispered chatter rose from the humans as Parsen and Kat returned to them, but Selene stayed behind. Her eyes cleared and latched onto Koriana, seemingly oblivious of the conversation behind her. She approached the dragoness and spoke so quietly Alísa could barely hear her.

"My name is Selene. Thank you for what you have done. It must be hard for each of you to lay your lives on the line for humans, especially so for you, Koriana. Even your laughter carries grief." She raised a hand to Koriana. "I thank you especially."

Koriana's eye-ridges raised, her bright yellow eyes dimming. She hesitated before reaching down and touching Selene's hand with her snout.

"Thank you for your kind words. If all humans were like you, I would give my life for all without hesitation. Then again, if all humans were like you, there may be no war in which to do so."

Selene smiled softly, then looked to each of the other dragons in turn before stopping at Alísa. Though the young woman regarded her only a moment, Selene's gaze seemed to push through to her soul. Alísa shifted uncomfortably, remembering the scolding she and Falier had received only hours ago.

Selene took a step toward her, but stopped when Namor's voice rose above the others.

"We have decided. In thanks for your protection, we will call you allies."

A flash of sky-blue joy flooded Alísa's senses, lifting her heart in its flight. Sesína nearly knocked her off her feet as she jammed her muzzle under Alísa's arm with a squeal.

Namor eyed Sesína with a mixture of concern and amusement. "For the sake of the villagers, though, I ask that you wait here until we tell them."

Alísa threw a warm smile at the dragons, watching as Koriana blinked slowly and Graydonn thumped his tail on the ground. Agreement. *We did it!*

It seemed all of Me'ran waited for them in the town square, half of them chatting quietly in the center while the other half stood as close to the door of the dragon shelter as they could. Yarlan stood closest to the tree line, his cloak gone and his sword prominent on his hip. Upon searching the crowd, Alísa spotted his wife and two sons among those waiting at the shelter.

Conversations ended abruptly as those who had visited with the dragons stepped from the forest, every eye turning to them.

"We have come to a decision," Parsen said. "Will you abide by our unanimous verdict?"

The people nodded and voiced their affirmation, while Yarlan narrowed his eyes.

"Then these three dragons are welcome in our village. They may fly overhead without fear. They are our allies."

Yarlan's eyes darted to Namor, as if seeking confirmation. His face darkened, though he made no move to speak against them. Apparently, his respect for Namor was enough to keep him at bay.

A combination of nervousness and wonder emanated from the rest of the villagers, punctuated with hints of understandable fear. She too had felt this way even after Koriana and Graydonn had saved her life. It would be a long journey until the declaration of peace intersected with feelings of it. But maybe she could help them along even more than she already had.

She placed a hand on Parsen's arm and whispered to him. "May they enter the village now, so the people can meet them?"

Parsen squinted in thought only a moment before turning back to the crowd. "Alísa would like to introduce you to the dragons. Since we have declared them allies, I see no reason why not, but if you wish to leave, the time is now."

Anxious chatter flared up from different places amidst the crowd, most from those already standing near the shelter. At Yarlan's glance, his wife took hold of their sons' hands and led them into the shelter, though he himself made no move toward it. A few others followed Yarlan's family inside, while others took steps back from the tree-line.

Then, when the crowd had settled, Alísa turned back toward the forest and reached out to Sesína. *"You can come now."*

"We're already on our way!"

Not five seconds later, three dragons flew overhead, passing over the village. Alísa's heart swelled at the sight of Sesína bringing up the rear, flying all on her own. Villagers gasped in awe as the dragons banked to come in for a landing near Alísa.

Koriana and Graydonn landed gracefully, their final wing-strokes sending a gust of wind into the villagers' hair and clothing. Sesína came in too fast and flailed her wings as she landed. Her talons scraped across the dirt path as she skidded to a stop, aided by Graydonn's extended wing.

Alísa covered her mouth as she tried to stifle a laugh.

"I heard that."

Sesína breathed heavily but held her head high as she faced the villagers, excitement coming off her in waves. Alísa set a hand on the scaly neck to convey a sense of safety to the people.

The crowd murmured, some staring wide-eyed, some gripping the hands of their loved ones.

"The gray one is huge!"

"Look how familiar she is with the little one."

"If Namor says they're safe, I believe him."

Alísa studied the older dragons' postures and emotions. *"Are you okay with them coming up to meet you?"*

Graydonn thumped the ground with his tail, curiosity wafting from him.

Koriana eyed the humans warily. *"I will do what I must."*

Alísa opened her arms. "These are your rescuers, Me'ran. K-K—K-Koriana, Graydonn, and Sesína. If you speak with them, you'll hear their v—voices in your head. D-d-don't be alarmed. The Maker made them d—differently than he made us, and they are n—not reading your minds. Please, c-c-come and meet them."

Most of those who had already met the dragons stepped aside, but Falier and Selene stayed, Falier moving to Graydonn's side, and Selene to Koriana's.

Selene placed a hand on Koriana's foreleg. "Would you like a friend to stand beside you?"

Koriana's chest rumbled in almost a purr. *"I would like that."*

What a strange, fast relationship. Selene's very presence was soothing to all who drew near her. Even dragons, it seemed.

Youthful voices came from the left, and Alísa turned to see a few children at the front of the crowd, staring at the dragons with wide eyes. These had danced with the dreki at céilís.

Alísa waved them over. "It's okay. C-come meet my friends."

A little boy of about six years strode up to Sesína, his face set like he had something very important to say.

"Does it dance?"

Alísa giggled and Sesína crouched down and spoke to the boy. *"I'm a 'she,' not an 'it.' And I just learned to fly, so I'll be able to dance soon."*

The boy grinned, while a little girl stepped in. "You're way bigger than dreki—we'll need to make more room for you on the dancing grounds."

Sesína began to grin, but stopped herself and allowed her eyes to brighten instead. *"Or maybe I'll just fly higher than all the dreki."*

This prospect delighted the children, who were now crowding around Sesína. Parents hovered nearby, some keeping a hand on their child's shoulder to keep them from getting too close. The children stroked Sesína's legs, neck, and wings, and Sesína thrummed happily, asking each one their name.

Alísa quirked a smile. *"You're a natural."*

About ten adults gathered around Graydonn and Koriana now. Some stood further back than others, and all stood erect with eyes constantly moving between the dragons. Falier and Selene alone stood at-ease, Falier gesturing to the few dreki hovering around them all. Alísa's heart warmed at the sight of the three races together and at peace.

This was what she was fighting for.

Koriana's eyes met hers, and a connection formed between them. *"This is all well and good, but it will end soon. Those scouts are a precursor to invasion. If we are to keep Rorenth at bay, we must form a clan large enough to do so. You've come into your powers, and Sesína can fly. Nothing holds us back now—we should leave in the morning."*

Alísa gave the dragoness a firm nod, though her heart ached at leaving just as a bond was forming. But they would come back to Me'ran—Twi-Peak was their home now, after all. The place from which they would change the world.

Breathing a sigh of resolve, she glanced over the crowd until she spotted Namor. He met her gaze, his former superiority softened with new respect. She pushed through the crowd to reach him.

"Where are you going?" Koriana questioned, though the hint of resignation flowing through the connection said she already knew the answer.

If it was time to recruit dragons to the clan, it was also time to recruit slayers.

35

A SLAYER'S WORTH

The village was quiet now; the attack and the introduction of the dragons had thrown off all thoughts of feasting and dancing the night away. Instead of celebration, there were quiet dinners in homes and scrounging through smoldering ruins to find heirlooms that might have survived.

The holders stayed busy caring for the newly-homeless, while the dreki had departed with a picture of Rorenth's mountain and a determined, *"Watch."* This left Alísa, the dragons, and the slayers out at the dancing ground in tenuous silence. The sun had yet to dip below the horizon, but the chill of night was slowly making its presence known.

Alísa stood close to Koriana, gleaning whatever heat she could while Namor and Yarlan waited for her to begin. A thought of Koriana doing the talking flitted through her mind, but left as quickly as it came. This speech couldn't be left to one who didn't fully believe in it. Perhaps Graydonn understood her desperate desire to have slayers accompany her, but even relying on him seemed unbecoming of the leader she was supposed to be.

"You're stalling," Sesína said. *"Speak up, or* I'll *do it."*

Now *that* was a bad idea.

"I've asked you here because there are things I d-didn't want t-to discuss in front of the whole village. I did not wish to frighten them. If you deem it necessary t-t-t—to tell them later, do so. But for now…"

She breathed in slowly, steadying her heart. "The dragons who attacked today weren't simply dragons seeking to inflict p—p—p"—*breathe*—"p-p-pain. They were scouts for a p-powerful clan just across the Nissen. They were a precursor to this c—c-clan expanding their territory."

Yarlan's eyes darkened, his hands fisting against the sun-bleached bench. Namor's were lightly glazed, as though he wasn't hearing her at all, though nothing about his usually steadfast manner supported that theory.

"This clan is a violent one—"

"Is there any other kind?" Yarlan grumbled.

She hesitated. He needed to hear her—how could she make him hear her?

"They have destroyed villages in their t—t-t-t-t—"

"Territory," Namor supplied.

She winced, but continued. "And they will likely do so again. I will not stand for it. They are the k—k-kind of dragons I wish to end."

Alísa paused, letting her words sink in before her entreaty. She gripped her skirt, allowing it to absorb some of the sweat.

"But we c—cannot do this alone. We are too few to press an attack, t—t-too few to even draw a meaningful boundary line." She swallowed. "We need more dragons."

Yarlan stood. "Three of these beasts in our mountain is one thing, but—"

Koriana growled in her throat. *"Mere 'beasts' did not save your sorry hides today."*

Yarlan glowered, but Namor spoke before he could retort.

"The last Dragon Singer raised an army of dragons who lived at peace with normals, yet slaughtered slayers and left violent dragon clans alone. I know this isn't your intent, Alísa, but how can you be sure this won't happen again as your clan grows and the dragons push their own agendas?"

The older man's words were slow, deliberate, and calm. The same fear flowed from him that had once flowed from her father. *'I'm afraid for you, my Lísa. I'm afraid that you're not.'* It was strangely unnerving, halting any response that might have risen.

Graydonn's head appeared in her peripheral. *"If I may, Singer?"*

She nodded once. His demeanor was just what was needed here.

"We are not calling for just any dragons—we are calling for those willing to fight for Me'ran and other villages. It's easy for dragons to follow a Singer who leads them against slayers. Only those who truly want peace between the races will fight for

justice against their own kind. Those are the only individuals we want."

His words provided the opening Alísa needed.

"It would make these expectations abundantly clear" —she glanced at Yarlan to make sure she held his attention— "if I entered their cave with a slayer at my side."

Yarlan's eyes widened a fraction, then became daggers. "You would have me step into a dragon cave in hopes that they will listen? All they will meet us with are flames!"

Alísa gritted her teeth behind closed lips. This wasn't how it was supposed to go. The same fire she had once used in her argument against Namor threatened to surface, and she choked it down. Anger wouldn't convince him. She had to keep a cool head.

"The dragons will hear me." *Though no human will, the dragons will hear me.*

"Oh yes, they will hear you. They will hear a girl who gives them power, force their wills upon her, and destroy any who would stop them. I am no coward, but I will not throw my life away on the naïve hopes of a mere girl. My place is here, protecting my family and my village in the way I have proved."

He turned from her, facing Namor. "I say send word to the wayfarers— tell them of this threat so they can bolster their defense at the Nissen and hold the dragons back before they invade again."

Alísa shook her head. "Their defense didn't hold before, so they have either failed or else are t-too far away to help. You need—"

"Do what you want," Yarlan growled, "but I will not die speaking peace in a dragon's cave—I will die on my feet, defending my people."

With those words and a hand on the hilt of his sword, Yarlan stalked into the night.

Alísa trembled with anger and cold and dying hope. Her hand rose to her necklace, then dropped. She glanced at Namor, who stared after Yarlan.

"I don't suppose *you* would come in his stead?" she whispered.

His eyes carried apology. "I fear I would not make the journey, dear girl. Not without a saddle to keep me secure, and such a thing would take time we apparently do not have."

Alísa looked down. Even if they had a saddle, Koriana wouldn't stoop to wear one. Graydonn might, but even that seemed a stretch.

"Then I go with only the promise of a single slayer who believes." She glanced up at Namor. "Or is that even true?"

Namor gripped his staff and hobbled to her. "I do not know that you will succeed in this mission. But I believe that if you do bring back other dragons, they will have been proved by your power and heart."

He placed a hand on her shoulder, a strange sadness flowing from him. Longing, regret, and self-loathing all clung to it, as though he hated himself for not going with her now, but this grief was deep and aged. His eyes moistened, and his next words were barely more than a whisper.

"I should have recognized that heart sooner—forgive me. Go with my blessing."

Her heart should have warmed, but instead it was her eyes, hot and stinging with his grief and her disappointment.

So, this was it. No grand alliance, nothing to show the dragons she was different from Bria.

Nothing but support from afar.

Falier shouldn't have been eavesdropping. Alísa had asked for a private conversation with Namor and Yarlan, and he already knew the gist of what she had to say. But then they elected to have the conversation just outside the kitchen's wall, he had been assigned dish duty, and he wanted to hear her make her case. The outside door hadn't even creaked when he opened it, as if it was meant to be.

How he regretted this decision now. Yarlan's angry refusals echoed through him, the words muffled and grunting, but the tone sharp as a cleaver. Yet it wasn't the slayer's response that haunted Falier, but the words that had incited it—

'It would make these expectations abundantly clear if I entered their cave with a slayer at my side.'

He left the kitchen in a daze, acknowledging the Hold's guests with nods and smiles so engrained in him they were automatic. He couldn't do any more with his thoughts so jumbled.

Lise's words were not aimed at me. I'm not a slayer.

Bright orange eyes reappeared in his mind, blazing yet so very cold, followed by an aftershock of pain. He reached for the edge of a table to steady himself. The dragon's attack had been an arrow to his heart which burst into flames over his entire body. He had blacked out after a single attack, and Yarlan—the man with the power to bring him back—was himself afraid and refusing to go.

Orange faded into the beautiful storm-blue that had captivated him mere hours ago. They entreated him. *'It would make these expectations abundantly clear if I entered their cave with a slayer at my side.'*

I am not a slayer.

He jumped as laughter erupted at a table behind him—his father entertaining with an exaggerated tale of a childhood prank. Falier watched as smiles overtook fear and loss in the eyes of these people who had just lost so much.

His people.

They were still in danger.

He shook his head. *But I can't help them. I'm not a slayer.*

"Falier?"

Selene's gentle voice broke through the noise. Even when they were little and he was crossing wooden swords with Taz and the other kids, the quiet voice of his sister had somehow always risen above the others in his ears. It had been irritating then, but now he clung to that voice in the midst of the physical and mental clamor.

He met her eyes, and she indicated his room with her head.

"Come with me."

Without another word, she grabbed the lamp off the table and headed for the room. Falier hesitated. He hadn't asked for her help—he could figure things out on his own.

He shoved the indignation away with a sigh, then followed her. Out of the rest of his family, even the rest of the village, Selene knew him best, and she knew what it meant to be different. Perhaps her insight was just what he needed to silence the battle raging in his mind.

Selene placed the lamp on his dresser and plopped down on the edge of his bed, patting the woolen blanket beside her. He hesitated again, put off by her decisive manner, and grabbed a bodhrán off the wall. A single eyebrow quirked at him as he sat beside her and drummed his fingers lightly over the stretched goatskin. The feeling of resistance against his fingers, how it gave and pushed back with the exact sounds he wanted, settled him.

Selene's eyes focused on something in the air that he couldn't see. "Are you trying to distract me?"

"What shapes do the beats make?"

"An annoying little brother with questions he won't ask."

He raised an eyebrow. "I didn't say I had questions."

"Yet I heard them all the same." Her eyes focused on him, first hard with exasperation, then softening. "How long have you known? About Alísa and the dragons?"

He kept drumming. "Two weeks. A little more."

She nodded slowly. "Your headaches haven't been nearly as frequent since then. They've been training you?"

He shrugged. "Graydonn showed me how to keep my telepathy from reaching out without having to put up a wall."

"And how to speak with it."

He let out a breathy laugh as he remembered her confrontation. "I still can't believe you can see it. Do the colors match our voices?"

"This isn't about me." She gripped the green wool blanket in her fingers, her eyes hardening again.

So she was serious. Great. He drummed a bit faster.

"Falier, talk to me."

He drummed a bit louder. "You're the one who wants to talk."

He yelped as she cuffed him on the ear. "No, *I'm* the quiet one. *You're* the one who always wants to talk through his problems and anxieties. Yet now, when you're tense and jumpy, you refuse to speak. Why?"

He fisted a hand against the goatskin. "Gah. I don't know, Selene!"

"Yes. You do."

He looked away, his heart twisting. He began drumming again. The sound was that of an amateur, but at least it would hide his tense trembling.

"Give me the drum, Falier," she said softly.

"Bodhrán." He winced at his own childishness.

"Drum." Selene placed her hand over his, stilling his fingers, and gently lifted the instrument from his hand. She placed it at the end of the bed and scooted closer, rubbing a hand over his back. She was silent, but silence held its own sounds, ones she knew he hated. They filled the room, unhindered by the bodhrán, echoing in his mind until he could take it no longer.

"She needs a slayer, Selene. Yarlan and Namor won't go, so that leaves me." He raked a hand through his hair. "But I'm not a slayer. I can't fight. I can't even defend myself. I'd only be a burden to her and the dragons, just like I would have been to the wayfarers if they'd taken me all those years ago."

"Why does she need a slayer?"

"To show the new dragons she recruits that her plan to end the war includes both dragons and slayers. She wants to make sure the dragons who follow her are like the ones with her now—good and open to working with humans, to protecting them."

He shook his head. "But what will I show them? That only the weak will follow her? That she tried to convince true slayers to come with her, and failed? And what if dragons do follow her and we set out to fight the violent clans? They'll all have to watch my back as well as their own—I can't do that to them. To her."

His throat closed up at the thought. Alísa wanted to save everyone— what if his inability led to her injury or death? Or even one of the dragons'? Graydonn's? He couldn't do that to them, and yet the thought of letting them go without the slayer Alísa so desperately wanted seemed equally terrible. He had heard it in her voice—Yarlan's refusal had crushed her.

He hung his head. "What do I do, Selene?"

Selene slid off the bed and knelt in front of him, her earnest eyes locking on his.

"Do you believe in her mission?"

He nodded once.

"Why?"

He searched the air for the answer, as though it might pop into existence like the sound-lights did for Selene. It wasn't just that he liked Alísa—though

Maker knew that was true—it was the way the world had turned upside down when he met the dragons. It was Sesína's sweet and sassy personality. The fear that had turned to friendship in Graydonn's amber eyes. Even the tolerance in Koriana, despite the glares she still sent his way.

"They're my friends, Selene. Their kind are killing and being killed by mine, and Alísa thinks she can stop it." He sighed. "And if no one else will help her, shouldn't I? Useless though I am?"

A weak smile graced Selene's lips. "You aren't useless. You're kind and good and supportive. The world needs more men like you, willing to listen and learn, and then to stand even though the rest of the world says they'll only fall."

Falier shut his eyes and let the words sink in, let the pride in Selene's voice fill him. It was just what a sister or family-member *should* say, even if it weren't true, but Selene would rather be silent than tell a lie.

He opened his eyes as she stood, her smile becoming a smirk. "Besides, the fastest way to a woman's heart is to care about the things she does."

He rubbed the back of his neck. "Is it that obvious?"

"I can literally see it when you talk about her." She grabbed the bodhrán off the end of the bed and shoved it back in his hands. "Do you know when they're leaving?"

He hurried to his small window and pushed aside the curtains. No sign of the dragons or Alísa. No sign of anything, really, now that the sun had gone down. His heart pounded.

"I don't know. Maybe in the morning, but dragons can see in the dark. They could easily leave toni—"

Selene grabbed his arm and pulled him away. "Go to the cave. I'll start packing for you."

Falier bolted from the room, drawing the eyes of the guests and his parents. He hesitated for a second, his eyes resting on his mother, then made for the door. If he caught Alísa in time, he would insist they came back here first so he could tell his parents goodbye. Now, speed was key.

He yanked the door open and nearly barreled into a short redhead, herself reaching for the door. She jumped back and placed a hand over her heart. His own felt like it would leap from his chest.

"Alísa. Sorry." He gave a sheepish grin and rubbed the back of his neck. "I thought you had left already."

Her eyes glistened and the corners turned down with fatigue. Red blotches covered her cheeks, but any tears they had held were wiped away. She shook her head.

"I w—wouldn't leave without s-saying goodbye."

You won't have to. He was about to say the words when his mother's voice rang behind him.

"Aren't you going to invite the lady in, Falier?"

He sighed. He couldn't have this conversation in front of his parents. They would ask too many questions, and this wasn't the time. Soon, but not while he was pledging his support.

He flashed a grin at his mother. "Nope."

Falier stepped through and shut the door behind him. Confusion covered Alísa's face, tweaking her eyebrows and loosening her jaw. It was kind of cute.

"Come with me." He grabbed her hand. "I need to speak with you alone."

She let him lead, her slow movements speaking to her long day of ups and downs. Hopefully, this would end her day on a high note.

Queasiness settled in his stomach as he led her to the benches at the dormant fire pit. What if she didn't want him to come? He hadn't considered that yet. He had been under the assumption that she would want him to come, even if he were a burden, and that her kindness might be her undoing. But what if she was smarter than that?

Who was he fooling—of course she was smarter than that. He had finally overcome this hurdle of his own fear and gotten the courage to offer his help, but what if the support he had to offer wasn't worth the risk to her? What if she said no?

All the confidence he'd had at the door fled from him as he sat Alísa down at the benches. His brain was a jumbled mess, and he searched for a way to start the conversation.

"So, uh, where did the dragons go?"

She quirked an eyebrow as if to say, *'That's why you asked me to sit out here in the cold?'*

"I told them I wanted t-to say goodbyes, so they went flying for a few m—minutes." Joy lit her face, nearly covering the tiredness in her eyes. "Sesína's so excited she can do it now."

He smiled back. "She was amazing today. So were you."

She looked at her hands folded in her lap.

"Thank you," she whispered. Then she met his eyes again, pushing a curl from her face. "You were too."

He blinked. What had he done?

Alísa giggled musically. "The way you stared down that d—d-d-dragon. It was stupid, but incredibly brave. That's what, the third dragon you've stared down? Fourth, if you c—c-count Koriana, who stares you down all the t-t-t-t-time."

He chuckled. Could he have asked for a better opening?

"I'm sorry," she whispered, cutting off his response.

"Why?"

"You never asked for any of this. You had a p—p—p-p—" She stopped, wincing, then met his eyes again and tapped a finger to her temple.

"Is that a request for telepathy?"

She nodded once.

"You know I don't care if you stammer, right?"

Moonlight rippled over the tears reforming in her eyes, making his heart hurt. He was supposed to be fixing that, not causing it. He reached for her hand and she gave it to him. This time it only took him a couple seconds before the connection took hold.

"Can you hear me?"

"I'm so sorry, Falier. You never asked for any of this. You had a perfectly good life, one of laughter and joy and no danger whatsoever, and now I've taken it away from you. I've made people turn on you, I've given dragons opportunity to attack you—
"

He grabbed her other hand. *"Alísa, stop it."*

She did, wincing as his voice echoed through the connection multiple times. He hadn't meant to be so loud.

"Sorry. But none of that is your fault. The dragons would have attacked today

whether you were here or not, and it's only because you were here that no lives were lost. It's only because you were here that I've stopped hurting myself to hide my telepathy. And it's only because you were here that I've found the courage to stand before dragons."

Tears flowed down her cheeks and she shook her head. He grabbed her hand again and did his best to soften his expression, but she didn't look at him.

"I want to help you end the war, Líse."

Her eyes shot up, and he fought not to wince at the slip of the nickname he had only ever used in his own thoughts. Too late to take it back now.

"I know I don't have the strength of Yarlan and Namor, but if you think having a slayer at your side will help, then I volunteer."

Her eyes searched his, full of uncertainty. Then her shoulders started shaking, bringing his own to slump. He had made her cry again.

Her hands wrenched from his and she flung her arms around him. She laughed against his shoulder, joyous and nervous at the same time. His heart warmed, the feeling quickly spreading throughout his body. He returned the hug, awkwardly, as she pinned his left arm to his side.

"I take it that means yes?"

She pulled back and looked him in the eyes. He couldn't quite tell in the darkness, but her cheeks might have been red.

"I would take you over Yarlan any day. You believe."

He grinned, though perhaps the more amazing thing was not that he believed in her and her mission, but that Alísa believed in him.

36

UNSPOKEN

Alísa gripped Koriana's spine tighter as the air currents shifted with the setting of the sun. She shivered as the chill pressed in, and leaned forward to get close to the warm scales.

What I wouldn't give to truly have dragon-fire inside me right now.

To their right, Falier held loosely to one of Graydonn's spines, far more comfortable with flight now than he had been the first few hours of the journey. Those hours had been tough on both of them—Falier had never ridden a dragon before and Graydonn had only carried Alísa on a couple of flight-training sessions a few weeks ago.

Sesína adjusted her position frequently, sometimes out in front, sometimes high above, sometimes lagging behind to circle over something interesting. She reveled in the power and freedom of flight in a way perhaps no dragon had since the first Illumination. With no memories of a mother's flight, everything was completely new and fresh to her, and she eagerly drank it all in.

She flew in front of them now, bearing two sacks of rocks hanging by a leather strap over her shoulders. Weight-training was something she had insisted on, claiming it was her duty to carry Alísa, not Koriana's. When the clan had come to Me'ran to pick up Falier that morning, she had been trying to carry a boulder in her talons. Falier and Parsen had quickly come up with a better solution.

The clan flew south over the thickest parts of the forests, avoiding the larger clearings where villages sat, despite the distance it added to the journey. A giant lake stretched out just southwest of them. Russig Lake, if Alísa remembered her father's maps correctly. By Koriana's estimation and Alísa's own memories, their journey to Tsamen's territory was about two-thirds over.

Alísa's stomach tightened. Tomorrow she would enter his caves and make her case before a strange clan. Her last encounter with a dragon clan in their own mountain didn't go so well.

"*There,*" Koriana spoke to the full group, pulling Alísa from her anxieties. "*We'll stop at that little clearing for the night.*"

"*I wish I had a dragon's eyes.*" Falier searched the treetops. "*I can't see it.*"

His telepathic voice was strained, tired from the long hours of solely psychic communication. The dragons kept the group of five linked up with ease, but Falier had insisted he carry some of the load. He had come a long way these last two weeks, but the non-stop use was taxing on a first-generation slayer.

The clearing soon came into view, the sight of grass bringing a smile to Alísa's face. The eastern forest was a vast expanse of trees, only rarely broken up by villages or natural clearings. She gazed west as they began their descent, squinting against the sunset to see the rolling hills in the distance.

One day, I'll make it back to my homeland.

Graydonn thrummed a low, pleasant tone as he caught her thoughts. "*When we bring peace to the west, I'll fly low in the open spaces, riding the winds without a care.*"

Alísa smiled at the thought of riding Sesína in such winds. "*Yes, then I'll rest in the valleys surrounded by verdant hills and frolic in the flowers and grasses with the wind at my back.*"

Sesína spun around to descend closer to Koriana. "*I'll carry you from the lowest valley high into the snow-capped mountains. We'll explore the ice caverns together, then zoom back to the ground at top-speeds!*"

"*That all sounds wonderful,*" Falier broke in. "*I'd love to see it.*"

Koriana thrummed quietly, her nostalgia laced with sorrow.

Alísa rubbed the dragoness' neck. "*Are you all right?*"

"*Yes. Merely remembering.*"

Alísa nodded gently. Perhaps the memories of living there with her mate were too painful. Would she go back if they succeeded in ending the war?

Soon trees blocked the view west and the dragons landed in the tall grass. Koriana crouched and Alísa slid down her foreleg to the ground. Alísa stretched her tired arms back, popping her shoulders into a more comfortable position, then bent over to stretch her back and legs. The accompanying pain was oddly wonderful.

A soft giggle escaped her lips as she brushed the tips of the grasses with her hands, enjoying the tickling on her palms and breathing in the damp scent of home.

She turned to Sesína and found Falier already helping her unload the sacks of stones. Sesína crouched low so the sacks rested on the ground, while he lifted the strap off her shoulders.

Alísa smiled. Falier must have gone straight to her before stretching his own tense muscles. He was so considerate. And handsome, with his tall, lean physique, curly brown hair, and eyes like the twilight sky.

Sesína chuckled mentally, whispering through their Illumination bond. *"He just gets shinier by the day, doesn't he?"*

Alísa rolled her eyes. *"Isn't it your turn to hunt?"*

Sesína trotted to her and sat on her haunches. *"But all of the excitement is here."*

"What excitement? We're heading into danger—this is hardly the time for anything beyond camaraderie."

"This is the perfect time for it. We could all die tomorrow, who knows? Better to get your feelings in the open than die with love unspoken." Her eyes brightened. *"Hey! I just wrote your next song!"*

Alísa laughed and pushed her snout away. *"Get out of here. I'm hungry."*

Falier walked up behind Sesína, his pack over his shoulder and two nectarines in hand. Always the gentleman, he had insisted on carrying the heavier food while she carried the bread.

"What's so funny?"

"Sorry. T-too long to explain."

Sesína cough-laughed and pranced away, humming to herself. *"Get your feelings in the open, don't live or die with love unspoken."*

Though the 'song' was only whispered through the Illumination bond, Alísa had to fight to keep from blushing.

"She seems happy."

"Too happy."

Alísa rifled through her pack and pulled out the loaf of blackberry sweetbread. She inhaled the fading yet tantalizing smell. Though the loaf was now over a day old and beginning to dry, the contrast of the sweet and sour would still please her taste buds.

She and Falier settled at the edge of the clearing. Falier leaned back against a tree, while Alísa sat among the grasses. They exchanged food and ate in contented silence.

Koriana and Graydonn settled further up the clearing, their heads bobbing and eyes changing in private conversation.

"Do you think she likes me yet?"

"Koriana?" Alísa glanced over her shoulder at the dragoness.

"I get the feeling she doesn't, but I also get the feeling she's just that kind of person—err, dragon. One who's hard to tell except under exceptional circumstances."

Alísa shrugged. "She's brutally honest, is all. I actually w—wonder if all dragons are, Graydonn being the exception. He once t-t-told me that it took too much psychic energy to k—k-k-k-keep a s-secret, and dragons don't do so unless it's extremely important."

He gave a single, breathy chuckle. "Tomorrow will be interesting, then."

Tomorrow. A shock of nerves ran down her arms, settling in her fingertips. What would Tsamen's clan think of a Dragon Singer? Or of a dragon carrying a slayer man? Would they be curious? Frightened? Threatened? There was no way to anticipate it.

Bushes rustled far to her left and Sesína walked back into the clearing, a dead deer draped over her shoulders.

Falier cocked his head. "That seems a bad omen for a rider."

"She hates the taste of blood."

"It's all her fault." Sesína shrugged the animal onto the ground with a sickening thud. *"One poorly-cooked steak in her childhood and now I'm stuck paying for it."*

"Ah. I'd wondered why you've been eating the cooked stuff. This

Illumination thing is strange."

"You're strange," Sesína retorted, eliciting a snort from Alísa.

Koriana and Graydonn stayed on the far edge of the clearing while Sesína cooked the meat for everyone else. The other dragons had eaten a good meal that morning and wouldn't need to eat again for another day or so, despite all the energy expended in their travel.

Almost makes me jealous. Alísa bit into her nectarine and closed her eyes, savoring the sweet flavor. *Almost.*

Sesína took a leg off the deer, needing to replenish her young, growing body, and Falier and Alísa sliced off pieces with their knives. The meat was tough from dragon-fire, and unseasoned to boot, but it would be their only source of protein on this adventure. Who knew what opportunities for food tomorrow may or may not bring?

Falier wiped greasy hands on the grass before settling cross-legged. "I'd like to practice more without skin or eye-contact. Would you be all right with that?"

"Are you sure? You've been hard at it all day."

"Yeah, this was enough rest for me, and the food helps too."

She nodded and scooted beside him, about a foot-and-a-half away. She wouldn't make eye-contact with him unless he was having difficulty. The tether-line latched onto her as by threads rather than a strong rope.

"Can you hear me?" His voice echoed faintly in her mind.

"A little. C—close your eyes and focus on my mental signature only."

He did as she said, his brow furrowing in concentration. She got the sudden desire to touch his cheek and watch the tense lines fall away, but shook it out of her head. *Sesína, you've ruined me.*

"What was that?" Falier's voice came through, stronger than before as the connection took hold.

She ignored the question. *"You did it! Now, can you keep it there if you open your eyes without looking at me?"*

He did as she asked, and she watched as the tension left his face. Not quite what she had imagined, but she had still helped fix it.

"No fair, looking at me after telling me not to do the same!"

She laughed and looked away. *"Good job. You'll probably get tired quickly, but it's good practice. This will become second-nature to you soon."*

"I can't wait."

After a short pause, Falier drummed his thigh with his fingers. *"So. Tomorrow we'll be contacting the dragon clan. How do you feel about that?"*

"Nervous. Excited. Terrified. Take your pick."

"Do you know what you're going to say?"

She sighed. *"I've gone over what needs to be said more times than I can count, trying to figure out how many different ways I can say the same thing and thinking through arguments and counterarguments."*

"What if they won't come? What then?"

"I don't know. I don't even want to think of that possibility." She rubbed her palms on her skirt. *"Can we talk about something else?"*

"Sorry." He paused a moment. *"Okay. If you weren't a Dragon Singer, what would you do with your life? If you could do anything at all?"*

Alísa laughed. *"You aren't very good at small-talk. I'd have to think hard to answer that question."*

"Really? There's no passion of yours that immediately comes to mind?"

"Honestly? Before I met Graydonn, my only aspirations were to help lead my people. My life was already decided for me by my father's position, and I was okay with that."

Kallar flashed through her mind, and she rubbed her hands over her arms. *"Mostly okay."*

Falier looked at her, his eyes searching, analyzing her face, posture, hands. She shifted under his gaze.

"You aren't supposed to be looking at me."

He righted himself. *"You must miss them terribly."*

Alísa sighed, more faces whisking through her mind. *"I do."*

"Would you introduce me?"

She looked at him. *"Why?"*

He didn't move his gaze to her. *"I thought maybe you'd want to remember. And I'll have to meet them, eventually."*

He was talking about meeting her family? Her heartbeat sped up. *"What do you mean?"*

"Your end goal is to teach them too, right?" Mirth filled the tether-line. *"Or*

are we out of missions once we've drawn the line against Rorenth?"

So, he planned to stay beyond this mission. It made her warm and nervous and excited all at the same time, and she thanked the Maker once more that Falier didn't read emotions well yet.

She focused on an image of her father, standing tall in his red dragon-scale armor and chief's sash and holding his spear. Then she added her mother at his side, wearing a highly impractical white dress with intricate lacing and a sash around her waist matching the chief's.

"These are my parents, Karn and Hanah. He grew up a slayer, she a weaver. Papá married Mamá against his parents' wishes; they said he should marry a slayer woman so their children would grow stronger than him, but he believed in love and whisked her off her feet. He's now one of the greatest wayfaring chiefs in the west."

She continued through the people most important to her. L'non, Elani, Levan, and Taer. Trísse. Farren. She stopped there, and for a moment, silence took the tether-line. Then Falier drummed his fingers on his thigh again.

"And—the apprentice?"

Alísa sighed. So, he had seen Kallar too. She could refuse to give any information on him, but Falier would ask why, and she had no good reason other than, *'I don't want to show you my ex.'* That explanation would only lead to more questions.

She drew up an image of him returning from the battlefield. Dirt and grime still covered his armor, his half-head of hair blowing in the breeze along with his billowing blue cloak. War-markings ran from his forehead to his jaw, starkly yellow alongside unblinking azure eyes.

"Kallar came to our clan as Papá's apprentice when he was fifteen. Not every chief takes an apprentice, so his presence should have warned me of my future from that day. The clan wouldn't listen to a stammering girl, so the chief's daughter needed a strong man beside her, leading in her stead."

Falier shook his head. *"When were you betrothed?"*

Alísa pressed her lips together. *"I figured it out when I was fifteen. A band of highwaymen attacked camp while my father was away. About half the men were gone, and in the chaos of battle, I tried to command those still present."*

Tears filled her eyes at the memory. *"I couldn't get the words out. And those I could weren't heard over the din of battle. But Kallar could command them. He made the same orders I'd tried, and he led us to victory."*

"Oh, Líse."

Her breath caught. There it was again—that nickname he had given her yesterday. He said it with such affection and compassion it made her want to laugh and cry at the same time. Did he know she could feel those emotions, or how they affected her?

She pushed the thoughts away to finish her story. *"When it was all over, I was distraught, and he tried to comfort me. 'Don't cry, Alísa. That's why I'm here.'"*

She fingered the fabric of her skirt, taking comfort as it stretched and pulled against her fingers. *"That's when I knew I couldn't lead the clan, and why Papá had taken an apprentice. From then on, I lived as though I were betrothed. Everyone else in the clan already knew it, so there was no need for a ceremony. It just was. And now it isn't."*

Falier waited a moment before speaking, a twinge of anger and sadness rippling from him. Empathy—not the psychic power, but the potential connection available to every human interaction. She had felt pity for her stammering so many times in her life, but rarely this.

"What if he listens to you when you go back?"

She swallowed. What if. Could she love Kallar if he stopped hunting dragons and started fighting for peace? There was a lot she could like or admire about him, but love? His abilities were seasoned with arrogance, and his affections toward her with entitlement. Those emotions had built a barrier between them long ago.

She shook her head. *"I resigned myself to him for the good of the clan. When I go back, it will be to save them, not lead them. I won't go back to him because I don't need to. I would rather fall in love, or else become an old maid."*

A ghost of a smile crossed his face as Falier stared up at the first appearance of stars. How had it become so late?

"I can't imagine living without support from your family—having them be the ones to tell you that you can't do what you were born to do. I've had others tell me that, but never my family."

Alísa's heart twisted. *"Don't think little of them. They love me deeply. In that way, they did support me, and my father always encouraged me to exude confidence despite the stammer."*

"And then took away your chance to do so." Falier looked her in the eyes now, his own earnest and sure. *"You've done incredible things, Líse, I hope you know that. I hope you know you're capable of more, especially going into tomorrow."*

Tomorrow. If only she could stay here, in this moment, where she was safe. Her four closest friends beside her, never to let her fall. The man she might possibly be starting to love sitting beside her, looking into her eyes like she was worth something, and not because she was a way to the chiefdom or to win a war.

Tomorrow was coming far faster than she wanted.

37

DRAGON SINGER

Alísa stretched after sliding off Koriana's back at the edge of the Nissen river just outside Tsamen's territory. It had taken six hours to get to this spot, where they would wait for Koriana to make contact and gain an invitation into the territory.

The rushing of the water matched Alísa's racing heart. It was almost time. She would sing, and his clan would decide whether to attack, ignore, or join them.

"Stay close to Sesína and Graydonn," Koriana instructed. *"I know Tsamen, and I don't anticipate trouble, but if it comes you must be ready to fly."*

The dragoness took off alone, following the river as she rose, then banking west over the trees and out of sight.

Sesína paced along the bank, unencumbered by her rocky weights. Energy still coursed through her young body, despite the days of journeying. Alísa was tempted to join her and let out her own nervous energy, but it seemed better to save as much as she could for when it came time to sing.

Falier stood by Graydonn, locked in some private conversation. Though the young man still balked at the concept of psychically bonding to Graydonn, he seemed infinitely more comfortable with the dragon now. It probably helped that Graydonn was a patient teacher in telepathy and a gentle flyer.

It wasn't long before Koriana's trumpeting sounded in the distance. Alísa and Sesína hurried to Graydonn's side as multiple trumpets answered the call.

"Tell us what's happening?"

"She's made contact," Graydonn said. *"Two of their scouts are questioning her."*

Falier quirked an eyebrow. *"How far does your Illumination link extend? Have you two ever been out of range of each other?"*

"We haven't. She and her mother have. I would say it's about an hour's flight."

Alísa blinked. *"That's what? Thirty miles?"*

Sesína nosed under her arm, whispering, *"Let's never test that, okay?"*

Graydonn looked to the sky. *"The scout is sending word back to his alphas. We'll know soon."*

Nerves tingled down Alísa's spine. She needed to keep herself distracted. *"Does the distance diminish the connection?"*

"Yes. It diminishes until it is no more. It's a much kinder transition than when Namor separated you from Sesína. Many dragons have gone through it when they leave for other clans."

"And when they come back together?"

Graydonn cocked his head upward, as if the thought had never occurred to him. *"I don't know. I would assume they reconnect as you and Sesína did. But time apart could be a factor."*

More trumpets sounded. No roars, a good sign.

Graydonn thumped his tail on the ground. *"They are allowing us passage."*

Alísa fingered the chain around her neck, careful to keep the necklace hidden. *"Did she tell them about me?"*

"No. She didn't want to risk that Tsamen would be against you before hearing you. We'll fly within hearing range and then you'll sing. The song should intrigue them enough to allow us inside their cave."

"Should? She's banking a lot on her ability to predict what other dragons will do."

Graydonn lowered himself for Falier to mount. *"She's met many dragons in her time as a scout. She understands other minds better than anyone I know. I would follow her into any dragon's cave."*

Sesína swished her tail. *"Of course, you would. She's your mother."*

Graydonn thrummed as he rose to his feet. *"Yes. There is that."*

Koriana came in for a fast landing, the ground shaking under her weight. She crouched for Alísa, excitement flowing from her in waves.

"It's time, Singer."

Alísa drew in a steadying breath and hurried to Koriana's side, hoping she showed more confidence than she felt. She gripped two spines and hoisted herself to the dragoness' back.

Sesína launched into the air as Alísa situated herself. *"I feel light as a bird without those rocks strapped to me. I bet I'm ready to fly Alísa now!"*

Koriana gathered herself for her own leap into the air. *"Now isn't the time to find out."*

Gravity pulled Alísa against Koriana's back as the great dragoness launched. Take-off was her least-favorite part of flight. Her stomach dropped, her ears popped, and she inevitably ended up with bruises.

The sun peeked out from behind the clouds, warming her for a moment before going into hiding once more. She shivered in its absence.

The dragons flew toward the wall of mountains to the southwest—the Prilune Mountain Range, dividing Arran's green northlands from its harsher southlands. Stories told of a great mountain erupting and turning the southlands to ash centuries ago. People still lived there, but there were far fewer plants, and the animals that survived there were of very different types than those of the northlands.

Alísa shook her head and brought her thoughts back to the present. Maybe one day she would get to see the southlands, but today's mission was for the north and its *anam*.

Tsamen and Paili's main caves sat near the top of the first mountain west of the Nissen, before the river churned and wove between the other mountains with water white as snow. All three dragons flew straight and true, the solemnity of what they were about to attempt quieting even Sesína.

"Stay low, Alísa, Slayer," Koriana said. Falier visibly sighed at the lack of his name. *"There's no sense letting them see you before Alísa is ready to call to them."*

Alísa shivered. *Branni help me. Will I ever be ready to call them?* She realized too late that the others would hear this question of herself.

"Peace, Alísa," Graydonn soothed. *"The Maker will grant you words when it is time."*

"You've done this before," Falier encouraged. *"You can do it again. You are an incredible person."*

She pursed her lips and heaved a sob. The cold wind in her face stole any tears she would have shed. Their encouragement was simultaneously helpful and not. Their belief made her feel like she could move mountains, but her fear and knowledge of her own limitations told her she would let them down.

Sesína opened her mind wider to Alísa, allowing her presence to be felt more fully, yet saying nothing. Alísa grabbed onto that feeling with all her might, drawing on her sister's strength and confidence. They would do it. They would do it because they had to. Because others needed and believed in them.

Koriana led the group from their straight-shot into an arc, flying along an invisible perimeter a few miles from the alphas' cave. She slowed her flight, Graydonn and Sesína following suit.

"Now, Alísa," Koriana said. *"Sing for them. Sing into their hearts and souls."*

Lyrics ran through Alísa's head, jumbled and unrhyming. What was the most important thing to convey in order to gain access to the caves? Was it her story? The plight of the dragons against the slayers? Helpless humans against Rorenth? The possibility of alliance where once was only hatred?

Graydonn's words flowed to her again in a whisper that may have only been her own memory. *'The Maker will grant you words when it is time.'*

She had to have faith. This was what He made her to be. This was what He called her to do, and right now it required stepping out, even though she didn't feel ready. If the words hadn't come yet, then she would open her voice and wait for them to flow.

She breathed low and deep, expanding her ribcage as wide as she could, and began an "oo" vowel. She droned on a single note, breathed, and began again.

A melody came to her, swirling around her and shifting the tone from drone to song. Her voice resounded over the treetops, louder than she had thought possible, or perhaps only ringing in her own mind. She breathed in deeply, imagining the cold air transforming to lyrics in her lungs, and breathed out her song.

Young maiden, lost unto her own,
Now finds her place in dragons' lairs.
The darkest caves she now calls home,
Alight with songs and woven prayers.

Why does she feel so intertwined
With family's sworn enemies?
For though she's slayer by design,
Inside live dragon melodies.

In the distance, dragons rose from their caves. Some merely peeked out
to find where the song was coming from. Some took to the sky and spiraled,
keeping their eyes on the newcomers. Four or five flew from their caves and
trumpeted, dancing in the sky like dreki.

Koriana trumpeted, joy flowing from her and bolstering Alísa's own.
"That's it, Alísa! Keep going—ask for entry to their cave."

A Dragon Singer rises now
To find a clan to fly and fight.
Upon the wings of solemn vow
She asks you now to hear her plight.

To end the fight of claw and mind,
A war for hearts she must now fight.
A Singer asks to come and find
Dragons who in song take flight.

The loudest trumpet she had heard yet sounded from a dragon at the
entrance of the main cave. The call was long and deep as thunder, and soon
the other dragons joined. Those dragons who were still in their caves now
took flight, and all dragons of the clan made for the main cave.

All but one.

The sun peeked out once more from the clouds, its beams reflecting
brilliantly off a white dragon. Its scales shimmered in the sunlight like
diamonds, and its bright azure eyes shone like the clearest, deepest lake Alísa

had never seen.

The white flew fast, straight for their group until it seemed as though he planned to fly right through Koriana. Koriana kept her movements steady, and the white dipped under her at the last second. It climbed rapidly from underneath the dragoness and flew over the top of them upside-down, joy radiating from it.

"*It is an honor to welcome you, Singer,*" his tenor voice crooned as he made a second loop. Saynan. "*I am to escort your clan to the main cave; we will hear your plight.*"

Alísa's heart swelled with the white dragon's hope and happiness. "*Thank you, Saynan. Lead the way.*"

Stalactites and stalagmites lined the cave entrance, the expanse just tall and wide enough for two dragons to fly abreast. It opened near the top of the cave, then dropped off to the floor thirty feet below. Smaller alcoves lined the side walls of the cavern, each holding one or two dragons.

All thirty-some dragons poked their heads out of their caves to face a great fire burning near the back wall. Two massive dragons, one gray and one red, stood at the edge of a ten-foot precipice beyond the flames, likely Tsamen and his mate.

So many dragons.

Alísa's heart beat so fast it seemed it might explode. The slayer's daughter in her told her she should fear the dragons themselves, but in this moment her truest fear was that none would answer the call.

They said they would hear her, but would they listen?

Koriana's presence began tightening around her in a mind-choke, much like it had when the dreki's grief threatened to take her. The dragoness had warned her of the psychological dangers of a human allowing so many foreign dragons access to her mind at once. She would act as a shield for Alísa, keeping out all of the other dragons' voices and emotions—except for the alphas.

Of course, that meant for all the dragons to hear her, Alísa must speak verbally the whole time. Her throat constricted just thinking about it.

She trembled as they neared the cave floor, glancing back at her companions. Though their connection dimmed as Koriana tightened the shield, Alísa could still feel the remnants of their bonds. Graydonn held a mixture of nervousness and courage, the latter firming up around the tremulous former, covering for its frailties. His eyes brightened as they met hers, and he sent a pulse of peace through their bond. She breathed it in and allowed it to warm her as it had all those weeks ago, the day she had first entered a dragon's cave.

Alísa lifted her eyes to meet Falier's gaze. His brow furrowed as he smiled, visibly displaying the conflict inside of him. He was afraid, and well he should be, representing the slayers to a large clan of strange dragons. They didn't know his willingness to turn, or his bravery in the face of certain death. But now, more than fear or bravery, he radiated belief. He followed her into fire now with eyes wide open, settling her almost as much as Graydonn's calm.

Sesína brimmed with strength and confidence. Half of it settled within her, pulsing like the blood in her veins, while the other half bounded from her, as though she felt their little group of five could take on Tsamen's whole clan if they decided against her. Sesína's link to her was the only one undiminished by Koriana's shield, and Alísa clung to her mind-sister's strength, drawing it into her and allowing it to dance alongside Graydonn's calm.

She would make it. She would make it because she had to. Without a larger clan, they could only stand and perish against the onslaught of dragons and slayers.

It was time.

Saynan landed before them and thumped his tail on the ground, bowing his head to Tsamen and his mate. *"My alphas."*

He launched back into the air and joined another dragon in an alcove, a blue dragoness who matched his eyes. Koriana landed gracefully on the cave floor, Graydonn and Sesína slightly behind her in a V-formation.

She dipped her head in respect. *"Great Tsamen and Paili, I present to you Alísa-Dragon-Singer."*

Alísa's heart pounded as Koriana crouched to let her down. Now, more than ever, she wished to stay on Koriana's back—both for support and an easy getaway—but dragons would take her more seriously if she stood on her own two feet. Subordinates sat, leaders stood.

Tsamen thumped his tail on the ground as Alísa landed. *"At the sound of your voice, Singer, my heart leapt for joy. If you have come to seek sanctuary among your true kin, you will find it here."*

Alísa's thoughts raced through all Koriana had taught her of draconic diplomacy the last two days, bowing her head graciously. Politeness was necessary, but not at the expense of the mission. Tsamen's invitation to sanctuary steered the conversation—it was her task to stay on-target and not let him talk her into something she didn't want, or out of something she did.

"Thank you, great Tsamen. Your h—hospitality is appreciated. But as I said from the skies, I have not c-c-come to ask f-for sanctuary but to seek draconic aid. Your b—b-b-b—"

She stopped and breathed, but Tsamen interrupted before she could recover.

"I see. Am I right, then, in saying you have come to me looking for gifts with nothing to offer in return? You wish to take from my clan to build your army? Perhaps to even reign over my territory?"

There was no animosity in his voice—he wasn't upset yet. What was he doing?

Koriana closed off her mind-link to only include Alísa. *"He's putting words in your voice, hoping you lower your ask in a show of good faith. Stand your ground."*

"The opportunity for p-p-peace is the gift I bring. Your b—brothers and sisters bleed, as do my own, in a w—war that has gone on too long."

"Then make your case, Singer."

"If you can," Paili thrummed.

Thrums echoed hers throughout the chamber, and Alísa's cheeks flushed.

"Pay her no heed," Koriana said. *"She is an alpha and will try to make you look weak."*

Sesína's tail sliced through the air. *"Don't back down, dragon-heart. You are an alpha too."*

Alísa breathed slowly and addressed Tsamen. "My desire is t-to bring peace to the east and let it spread outward. I and my c-c-clan have already achieved m——much in the village of Me'ran. The v——villagers have welcomed these three d-dragons as friends. Even the three slayers of the village c-c-call them allies."

"*Ah yes,*" Paili growled, glaring at Falier. "*The abomination on the green's back.*"

Tails slapped the ground in agreement throughout the cave, causing Alísa's heart to sink. She was losing them to the overbearing alpha female.

"*Tell me, little green, what did she promise you in exchange for your demeaning task?*"

Alísa rose up taller. *Dragon-heart. I am dragon-heart.*

"Falier is here as a s——s——sign to you that I will succeed where B-Bria failed."

Growls echoed at her words, but she pressed on, almost strengthened by their ire.

"Already I have done what she could not. Already I have found slayers willing t-t-to f——fight alongside dragons. There *will* be more! But now I call on dragons t-t-to take their place as they did at the first. To lead the way in an alliance that will bring p——p-peace."

Tails slapped the ground again, this time in her favor, and for the first time since they entered the cave, a smile lighted on her lips.

Tsamen's deep voice echoed in her mind. "*And what would you call us to do in order to bring this about? How do you plan to spread something so sluggish as peace?*"

"By r——rising up and being the first t-to do what's right. By ending Rorenth's reign of t-t-terror over the innocent humans in his territory."

A cacophony of roars and growls mixed with trumpets and tail-thumps. The clan was divided. Paili's narrowed eyes brightened in a show of gladness more eerie than pleasant. In those eyes Alísa found for the first time what it meant to have an enemy.

Tsamen's roar shook Alísa to her core as he brought order to his clan.

Paili's harsh voice resounded in her mind. "*There, you see? This Dragon Singer is no Bria——she is another Allara, who fought only for the slayers. But while Allara stood and faced us head-on, this coward intends to pit dragonkind against itself! She seeks to make us bring about our own destruction!*"

Growls from the surrounding dragons punctuated Paili's words. Some even stood and flexed their wings as though preparing to take action.

Alísa's heart raced as she looked from one dragon to the next. "No! That's not t-t-true!"

Paili's pleasure at their agreement gleamed in her eyes as she stepped to the edge of her precipice. *"Allara burned in my flames for her insolence; how much more this stuttering serpent?"*

38

DRAGON-HEART

Ire and fear clashed within Alísa as dragons voiced their feelings all around her. Roars and trumpets, hums and thrums, tails swishing and thumping until she could no longer make out the individual sounds. Neither Tsamen nor Paili moved to silence them. None would hear her in the midst of this cacophony, even if she had the presence of mind to refute the alpha female.

Sesína stepped up and extended her wings. *"I've got you if flames come. Be strong."*

Paili thrummed loudly. *"And what's this I see? An Illumination bond connects the little black to the Singer."* Her tone turned to mockery. *"It's no wonder you fear for her, sweet thing. Without a proper mother's bond, you quake with a human's fear before true dragons!"*

Sesína yanked her head back as though Paili had physically struck her, more derisive thrums echoing through the room. Visions of her failures rose and traveled through the bond to Alísa. Lack of control over her wings and tail when she was little. Having to cook her meals because the taste of blood still disgusted her. Failure to fly and breathe fire at the normal age.

Alísa's blood boiled. To attack her was one thing—to attack Sesína was unforgivable. If only the dragon inside her would manifest itself and wipe that sneer off Paili's face. Wipe her face off her head!

No. Alísa shook her head. There was nothing she could do to convince a dragoness so completely bent against her, and her rage would do nothing to turn the other dragons either. As the world stormed and spun around her, she pulled herself to center and breathed in a tremulous breath. Another. Deeper and deeper, until she breathed out her anger toward Paili and her fear of the other dragons. These would do nothing but agitate her, diluting her message with the very emotions that sustained the war.

And as they left, a melody took their place, its lyrics wafting into her mind like strong emotion.

The time for speaking was over.

"Koriana, let me go."

As the dragoness released her protective mind-choke, Alísa prayed a silent prayer. *"Branni, and great Maker over all, give me strength."*

She opened her mouth and words poured forth without rhyme or repetition—a song somehow both her own and a gift from another.

Who will seek wisdom in an age of violence?
Only the quiet, who stand by nothing else.
Who will listen to the quiet in a time of chaos?
Only the ones who tire of the noise.
Who will stand with the weak through the storms?
Only the ones who too are affected.

None will listen. None will stand. None will seek the truth,
Until fire meets fire, and sword meets sword,
Until man gives life for dragon,
And dragon gives life for man.
Woe to the ones who will not stand!

She stumbled into Sesína as her last note reverberated in the silence of the cave. She had never reached out to so many dragons at once before. The stillness echoed her address to Me'ran, some dragons staring with glazed eyes, some standing with their eyes shut. Even Tsamen and Paili were entranced by her song.

Sesína's affection and pride were still tinged with her insecurities, and Alísa reached across their bond for memories. Running through the forests with grace and the skill it took to hunt without using her teeth. Her first fire-breath and how she had killed the serpent. How she had broken the wing of the black dragon attacking Alísa and Falier.

"You are a dragon-heart too, Sesína. You've never given up, no matter how

difficult the task, and you've always risen up strong when it truly counted."

Sesína's confidence bolstered, her eyes brightening to their most vivid green. *"Something we have in common. Finish it now."*

Alísa looked out to the rest of the cave, glancing from dragon to dragon, all still entranced. Even her own clan closed their eyes under her sway.

She breathed and spoke in a high and smooth tone, eliding her words together so they flowed into each other like a song. She rarely used this stammer-eliminating technique because of the airy sing-song tone it gave her, but in this moment, it didn't matter whether she sounded unintelligent. Stumbling over words might wake the dragons too early.

"I will not lie to you—there are dangers. And before we face the slayers, we must first face other dragons. If we merely send a dragon army to stop the slayers, none will turn and the battle will not end until extermination. I will not stand for that. The Maker will not stand for that."

She reached up and placed a hand on Koriana's wither, and the dragoness' eyes opened. She then walked to Graydonn's side to awaken him and Falier as well.

"But if dragons will be the first to rise—if they stand to protect humans from those dragons who will not see the light—then the slayers will turn and hear. I come to you now because I believe the dragons are strong and wise enough to be the first to take a stand. I have seen it firsthand in these three."

After waking Graydonn and Falier, Alísa returned to Koriana. *"Please, let me onto your back."*

Koriana lowered herself, and Alísa climbed into position. "If I am right about you, awaken and follow me." She reached for the Illumination bond. *"Fly, Sesína. Lead them."*

Sesína took to the air, followed closely by Graydonn and Falier. Alísa took one final look at the alphas, then patted Koriana's neck for take-off.

All was silent as they flew from the cave, nothing but the sound of wings beating air and her own heart pounding in her chest. She basked in the beauty of silence. She had done it. But who would follow?

The dark of the cave gave way to light as her dragons sped through the entrance tunnel into the open air. Clouds obscured the sun, but even then the light warmed her.

Koriana's words poured into her mind, her voice soft. *"Well sung, Alísa. You stood strong against the threat and stayed true to your plan. Now, see your followers."*

Five dragons flew behind Koriana, led by Saynan and the blue dragoness. Saynan flew directly beneath the blue, who clutched a white egg in her forepaws. Behind them flew a red adolescent, about Graydonn's age, and two browns took up the rear, one massive and muscular, the other an adolescent very near adulthood.

The newcomers caught up to Alísa and the others quickly, fresher than those who had already traveled for two days. Alísa twisted to look at them again and grinned, unable and unwilling to quench her excitement.

Five. Out of thirty, the number should have been discouraging, but pride still swelled in Alísa's chest. These were the five they needed. The five who cared about the true cause. The five who had awakened at her call.

Her clan.

Soon Saynan and the blue dragoness flew beside Koriana, and the white dragon's voice reached into Alísa's mind. *"If I may be so bold as to link myself into your communication, Singer?"*

"Of course. And that goes for all of you." She looked to the red who flew above and behind Koriana, then to the browns who flew beneath. They couldn't hear her request. *"Would you tell them for me, Saynan?"*

Saynan nodded and soon all except the blue dragoness were psychically linked to her.

"My mate, Aree, apologizes," Saynan said. *"She is still under the influence of ruby bark and cannot link up. I speak for her."*

"Ruby bark?"

Saynan gave a mental chuckle. *"No, I suppose you wouldn't know about that. Human women have no need of it, but a dragoness' body is unable to produce an egg without it. Unfortunately, it comes with side-effects of weaker telepathy and mellowed attitude. She should be back to normal in another week or so."*

"Fascinating. Please tell her no apology is necessary. Congratulations to both of you."

Koriana spoke up. *"Yes, congratulations. I was unaware that an ice dragon could procreate with a fire dragon."*

"Most are unaware. It doesn't help that my kind isolate themselves in the high mountains."

"Ice dragon?" Alísa voiced her curiosity.

"You don't know what an ice dragon is?" The young red male, Harenn, spoke from above. *"How long have you been among dragons?"*

She shook her head, glancing up at him. *"A little more than two months."*

"Harenn." The larger of the two browns, Faern, growled in a deep bass voice. *"You dare travel above the Singer and question her? You are not a prince here, young one."*

Koriana stopped Alísa's rising protest with a private mind-link. *"I sense Paili's psychic footprint on him. He is her son, but currently blocks their Illumination bond. He wouldn't have woken if his turn weren't true, but Faern is right to put him in his place—do not contradict this."*

Harenn's deep brown eyes dimmed slightly, and he lowered himself to fly beside Sesína.

Sesína winked at Alísa. *"I'll keep him in line."*

"An ice dragon breathes a burning cold instead of fire," Saynan answered Alísa's question. *"It isn't true ice as the name denotes, but it is close enough."*

The smaller brown dragon, Komi, remained silent, scanning from side-to-side and behind. No fear emanated from her, only a constant vigilance imitating her father, Faern.

They made a quick stop to pick up Sesína's discarded rock straps—no sense wasting the materials—and continued north until sunset with no signs of pursuit. Koriana led the group to land in a small clearing. Though the new clanmates could have continued flying through the night, the other three would need sleep to make it to Me'ran tomorrow.

As soon as Alísa slid off Koriana's back, Sesína bounded to her. She wrapped her wings around Alísa and pulled her to her side.

"You were amazing, the way you shut the alphas up with a song. I bet you made that stupid Paili so mad! You're the best alpha ever!"

Alísa wrapped her arms around Sesína's neck and laughed. *"And I wouldn't have made it this far without you cheering me on. Thank you, dear one. I'm proud of you."*

Sesína's chest rumbled in a purr, happiness pouring from her. Then she opened her wings, revealing Graydonn.

"My turn, Singer."

Alísa leapt to him, wrapping her arms around his muzzle as he thrummed pleasantly.

"I knew you had it in you. From the moment you begged for my death to be quick, I knew what you would become."

She giggled. *"Not many would take a plea for their death as a sign of goodness."*

"Your kindness shone even in your ignorance."

She kissed his forehead. *"And your kindness lit my way."*

Graydonn cocked his head. *"Another one of your kind's strange ways of showing affection?"*

"It's called a kiss."

"If I tried that, I'd burn you." He pointed his snout to something behind her and opened their connection to a third party. *"I guess I'll leave the kissing to Falier."*

Alísa cringed as heat rushed into her cheeks. The dragon had no idea what he had just said, but all the same it made her insides flip. Sesína rolled on the ground in a fit of coughing laughter, as if it were the funniest thing in the world.

Alísa didn't want to turn around, not with her face almost certainly red, but wouldn't that betray her just as much? She snuck a glance at Falier.

He closed his eyes and rubbed the back of his neck. "Dragons say the darnedest things."

"What?"

Sesína cough-laughed again, this time bounding to Graydonn and nearly knocking him over. *"Say it again, say it again!"*

Graydonn glanced between the humans. *"I don't think I should."*

Awkward shyness tried to burrow into Alísa's gut, but she pushed it away. It was ridiculous. She and Falier were friends. Surely they could survive something as simple as a dragon's accidental faux pas. She just faced a cave full of antagonistic dragons, after all.

She opened her arms. "How about a hug instead?"

"Yeah," Falier said through a laugh. "I could do that."

Alísa wrapped her arms around his ribcage, and Falier returned the hug lightly, as though he feared he might break her. His emotions were all over the place—embarrassment, joy, caution—but his pride in her overtook them all.

"I knew you could do it," he whispered. "You were incredible."

Surprise tears welled in her eyes. She pressed her lips together and tried to hold them back. Now wasn't a time for crying! The tension made her tremble, and Falier pulled back, concerned.

"Are you okay?"

"Yes." She cringed as her voice cracked. She looked him in the eyes just as a tear fell down her cheek. "I d—d-don't know w—what's wrong with me."

He searched her eyes, then his own softened. "Nothing's wrong with you, Líse. Come here."

He gently wrapped his arms around her again, then pulled her close as she gave in.

"You have people who support you now, and we aren't going to leave you."

A sob wracked her body, and he held tighter. His breath tickled in her hair, sending warmth coursing through her. Her stomach flipped, and her breath trembled. She couldn't decide if she wanted to pull away quickly in embarrassment, or to hold on and never let go.

After a time simultaneously too long and not long enough, Falier loosened his grip. She pulled back and looked at him. He had the stubbly beginnings of facial hair after the last two days of travel. Put together with the dirt and grime of the journey, he looked less like a holder boy and more like a slayer, except his eyes always shone with a kindness she had rarely seen from slayer boys. She noted their softness now, and the way he rubbed his hands over her arms reassuringly as they pulled apart. Something stronger than affection poured from him, and she wished he would voice it, but he let her go silently.

She pushed away her disappointment—now wasn't the time, standing here amidst her new clan. The dragons needed to see her as their strong alpha, not a sobbing girl falling in love too quickly. Alísa wiped the tears from her cheeks and sniffed, then blew out her breath through her mouth.

"Thank you."

Sesína and Graydonn stood facing the rest of the clan now, though Sesína looked back at Alísa. The young dragoness' mirth was seasoned with a quiet happiness. Her tail and wings twitched with pent-up energy.

"They asked if you were okay," Sesína whispered through the Illumination bond. *"I told them to mind their own business."*

Alísa cringed. *"More nicely than that, I hope?"*

"Such gratitude," she grumbled.

Graydonn swung his head around and connected to them and Falier. *"Singer. They want to know the plan."*

The plan. Such a good question.

She looked out over the dragons. Eight of them, plus an egg. How many dragons did Rorenth have? If Tsamen and Paili commanded thirty and they had to fight Rorenth for territory, then Rorenth's clan must be near that size. Thirty against her eight? Even with her ability to strengthen her clan, those were terrible odds. How could she lead these wonderful dragons who believed in her into a certain bloodbath?

No. They weren't ready to face Rorenth head-on. Not yet.

"Sesína, can you connect me to them?"

As soon as it was done, all the dragons perked their heads up and faced her. Her heart quivered. So attentive, so ready to hear her. But who was she to lead them?

Alísa sighed and lifted her eyes to the clan once more. She stood tall, her shoulders back and head high, and thought of her father and all the times he stood in authority over their clan. She may have rejected his way of life, but right now, she was the daughter of a chief.

"Thank you, dear dragons, for coming with me today. You've left your home, some of you have left family. I can't tell you what it means to me that you believe enough to follow and risk your lives in the cause of peace between our peoples."

She spread her hands, focusing on each of the dragons as she spoke. *"Today is only the first step. Tomorrow we head north and make our boundary at the Nissen. Tomorrow we draw a line against Rorenth and establish our own territory, one where dragons and humans can come and stay in peace. Where little ones can grow up without fear."*

Her eyes settled on the egg resting between Saynan and Aree. No more hatchling murders or egg-smashing. Not in her territory.

"From there we will continue the call to dragons and slayers until we are strong enough to cross into the dangers of the west, where fire will meet fire and sword will meet sword, until the war comes to an end."

Tails slapped the ground and growls rumbled in dragons' chests. She smiled, bolstered by actions she had once found frightening. Behind the scales and teeth lived *anam*, souls she now desperately wanted to know better.

39

THE RIGHT ONES

Alísa woke to the sounds of ground-shaking thuds. She lifted her head in the warm darkness and hit the soft underside of Sesína's wing. The dragoness woke just after her and lifted her wing to peer at the source of the disturbance. Faern and Komi stood in the middle of their tiny clearing, their wings shifting to their resting spots against their backs. Both dragons carried a dead deer in their jaws.

On the ground, it was obvious that Faern was the largest dragon in her clan, both in height and muscle mass. Komi was smaller, almost Koriana's size, but her mental signature clearly identified her as an adolescent—older than Graydonn and Harenn, but still a young dragon.

Sesína uncurled, allowing the last vestiges of heat to flee Alísa's dragon-wing tent. Rubbing her arms in the morning chill, Alísa stood and approached the father-daughter pair. "Faern, K-K-Komi. When did you leave?"

"At dawn, Singer," Faern responded, dropping his prey and dipping his head slightly at her approach. *"My daughter and I thought you and those who flew here with you might need sustenance."*

Sesína's hunger shot through the bond and Alísa's own stomach growled. *"Thank you. Go ahead, Sesína."*

The young dragoness shot forward and ripped at a leg with her talons until it came loose. Faern and Komi stared for a moment as she began cooking it, but quickly diverted their attention back to Alísa.

"We also scouted the area," Faern said. *"We must fly a bit further east today before heading north. We saw signs of Rorenth's expansion over the Nissen, but no signs of the clan itself. Where do you plan to draw the line?"*

Alísa stared at the ground. She hadn't thought of that. How much territory could her small clan protect? Was it better to carve out a large territory, even knowing she didn't yet have the resources to keep it, or to only claim what she could defend, then expand as they grew?

She didn't know.

She looked back up to the dragons and tried to come across with confidence. *"I will consult with Koriana on this. Thank you for your report."*

Faern slapped his tail against the ground. *"Singer."*

Curiosity rippled from Komi as she stared at Alísa, her head cocking to the side and her wings shifting against her back.

"Komi? Do you have anything to add?"

"No." She looked down quickly, embarrassed, while Faern thrummed.

Alísa looked from father to daughter. *"What?"*

Komi's voice came through softly. *"All due respect, Singer, but—you look different. The growths on your head are bigger."*

Alísa reached up to feel her tangled mess of hair. The tie had fallen on the ground behind her, and she bent over to pick it up. It must have come out in the night. With a full day's flight ahead, her hair would just have to be a wiry mess tied behind her until tomorrow.

"I've seen wildcats do that when they're surprised, and birds do it to scare things away. Why do humans do it?"

Alísa chuckled, reaching up to tame it enough to tie. *"It wasn't on purpose. It got messed up in the night."*

Komi cocked her head. *"Does it hurt when you do that?"*

"No." She sucked in a breath as her fingers caught a tangle, and laughed at herself. *"I mean, a little. If I do it incorrectly."*

"So, you don't control it like animals do?"

"I wish."

"Then what is its purpose?"

Alísa stopped. *"I'm not sure. To keep my head warm. To look nice."* She grunted as she wrapped the tie around the unruly curls. *"To teach me patience."*

Sesína's flames sputtered as she cough-laughed at the joke, but the others stayed quiet. Komi looked at Falier as he stepped out from under Graydonn's wing, yawning and stretching.

"His is shorter. Is that a difference between males and females of your kind?"

"Not necessarily." Alísa repressed her smile. *"I've seen men with hair longer than mine."*

"Then it's up to the Maker how long one's hair grows? Is length a sign of beauty?"

"I suppose length is a sign of beauty for some. Others, like Falier, cut it shorter."

Komi flinched. *"He must be very brave to suffer so."*

"Or very foolish," Faern rumbled.

Alísa stifled a laugh. *"It doesn't hurt to cut it."*

"Oh," Komi said. *"Thank you, Singer. I hope my questioning wasn't disrespectful."*

"Not at all. And please, call me Alísa."

Komi blinked slowly. *"Very well, Alísa-Dragon-Singer."*

Alísa giggled—Komi's respectful innocence would add a fun dynamic to dragon-human relations in the clan. *"Just Alísa will do."*

Faern pawed the ground. *"Perhaps among humans, but you are a leader of dragons now, Alísa-Dragon-Singer. My daughter and I will use your title."*

Alísa pressed her lips together, the simultaneously sharp and respectful refusal creating a strange ache in her heart. Couldn't she be friends with her clanmates, even though she was the alpha? Her father allowed his clan to use his given name, only insisting on his title for those being particularly disruptive, and it put the clan at-ease around him. Did dragons ever allow that in their clans? It seemed she hadn't scratched the surface of draconic social and political structure. She'd had two months. Would even two years be enough?

She turned away with a heavy heart and looked to Falier and Graydonn. A little food with friends would lift her spirits.

"Do you want me to smack Faern for you?"

Alísa snorted and glanced at Sesína. *"I'd say yes, but I think you'd actually do it."*

The dragons congregated in smaller groups, their massive bodies and flexing wings making the clearing seem even smaller than it was. Koriana now approached Faern and Komi, dipping her head in a silent *'good morning'* as she passed Alísa and Sesína.

Saynan and Aree lay on their bellies next to each other with their egg between them, Saynan draping a protective wing over his mate and offspring.

Alísa had never seen dragons in love before. Their affection wasn't over-the-top—a nuzzle here and there, a paw over a paw—but it ran deep.

Graydonn and Falier sat together. Falier rummaged through his pack, probably for breakfast, while Graydonn lifted his wings in greeting as Alísa's eyes met his. Yes, breakfast with those who already considered her a friend would be nice.

The only lone dragon was Harenn. He lay in the spot where he had slept, but held his head high and alert, watching the others as they interacted. He was the only one who had left the clan without a family member. Maybe he, too, needed a friend.

Caution spread through the Illumination bond. *"He's Paili's son, don't forget."*

Alísa eyed Sesína. *"Yes. And?"*

"Remember how he flew above you yesterday?"

"He came down when Faern told him to."

Sesína grumbled in her throat, the sound muffled lightly by the cooked deer-meat in her mouth. *"I just don't think you should encourage him to see you as an equal."*

Alísa shook her head. *"He awoke to my call; for now, that's enough for me."*

She pivoted to face him. "Harenn, c-c—come sit with us."

He started at her call, then stood, shuffling toward Graydonn as she continued walking that direction. *"What's the matter, Singer?"*

"Nothing. It's just, since you're not with anyone else, I want you to join my group."

He stopped. *"I don't need pity, Singer. I'm fine by myself."*

She raised an eyebrow. *"It isn't pity. I don't know you well, and I'd like to fix that."*

He gave a nod reminiscent of a shrug and made his way to Graydonn's side. His emotions were difficult to read, a jumble of independence and strength mixed with desire.

Alísa took the nectarine Falier offered and sat between him and Sesína, facing the male dragons. It suddenly struck her that she had nothing to talk about. All she could think of were yes-or-no questions that would do no good.

"What are you doing?" Harenn burst out, looking to Sesína, who had

started eating the deer leg.

Sesína raised an eye-ridge. *"Chasing butterflies. What does it look like I'm doing?"*

Harenn hummed. *"Why did you flame your food?"*

"Your mother explained the situation well enough," she hummed back, wings rising in her ire. *"I was Illuminated by Alísa. She hates the taste of blood and I inherited that taste."*

"Harenn," Falier spoke up quickly, perhaps breaking up a squabble before it occurred, *"I know next to nothing about dragon society. What does an alpha's son do in the clan?"*

Harenn hummed again. *"The three oldest dragons are trained in leadership to be future alpha and beta dragons. I am the sixth."*

Sesína straightened up. *"Six? No wonder your mother is so testy——"*

"Sesína!" Alísa slapped her forepaw, causing more pain to herself than to the dragon.

Sesína's tail swished. *"I just mean that being Illuminated to six other dragons must take an awful toll."*

Harenn thrummed derisively. *"You need to work on your knowledge of your own kind, little one."*

Sesína growled. *"Perhaps my next lesson will be what color blood flows through a dragon prince's veins!"*

Graydonn snapped his jaws in the air between the quarreling dragons. *"Enough!"* He eyed Sesína, narrowing his speech link to include only her and Alísa. *"You should know better than to let conflict escalate. Be the better dragon."*

Sesína hummed and looked away from the group.

"To answer the question," Graydonn opened communication to the group once more, his tone even, *"a dragon can only carry one such binding at a time. To carry more would tear one's mind apart. When a dragon hatches, their Illumination bond replaces the previous. In some families, the mother will Illuminate the first hatchling, then the father the second; in others, the mother will Illuminate them all."*

After a moment of silence, Falier spoke again. *"Then, Harenn, what was your role in the clan?"*

"I was training as a scout. I helped patrol our western border, but I was soon to be transferred to the northern border against Rorenth's territory. We——I mean, my

parent's clan—needed all the help we could get to hold our territory against him."

Alísa cocked her head. *"Why did so few come with us, then? If your clan was already fighting Rorenth, I'd expect more to follow me, if only for their own gain."*

Harenn gave a small huff of hot air. *"Your song called only to those who wished to be part of something greater than one's own battles. If you sang differently, I suppose more might have followed."*

Alísa nodded to herself and gazed at the blades of grass beside her. Of course. It was her fault so few came, that their strength was small.

"I think that was why I woke up, actually," Harenn's voice lifted Alísa's eyes from the ground. *"I have no special love of humans, but when you called only those who wished good upon the whole world—excluding those who might have followed you for their own gain—I realized I'd been waiting for your call. The bravery you displayed in limiting your strength only to those who truly believed is one I would follow against any odds."*

Alísa's heart soared as Harenn's words replaced her doubt. Yes, it was her fault that so few came, but, like with Yarlan and Falier, those who followed were the right ones.

"Your confidence moves me, Harenn. I'm glad to have you at my side."

Having finished her fruit, she rose to join the waiting dragons. Twi-Peak and Me'ran called to her, with only a single day of flight between her and home.

Home.

"Sesína, would you—"

"Linked."

Alísa smiled, feeling the minds of her clan once more. Her clan. *"It's time, dear dragons. Prepare to move out."*

The dragons still lying down rose to their feet, arching their backs and stretching their legs like giant felines. Wings flexed and chests rumbled pleasantly as Alísa walked to Koriana.

"Where are you going?" Sesína trailed behind her.

Alísa gestured to Koriana. *"It's time to fly."*

"Yes, and I'm strong enough now. There's no battle looming or reason to rush, so I should carry you."

Alísa stopped, a mixture of excitement and worry filling her. *"Are you sure you're ready?"*

"Only one way to find out."

Koriana moved to Alísa's side. *"Little one, today is not the day. You've only been flying on your own for three days."*

Sesína grumbled. *"It should be my job to carry her, not yours!"*

Saynan came up beside Koriana and stretched his neck to Sesína's level. *"We know your heart, Sesína, and that you would bear this responsibility with strength and joy. But Koriana is right—a long day of flight and combat training is not the day to carry the Singer for the first time."*

Sesína perked up, her eyes brightening. *"Combat training?"*

"Am I right in assuming you've never been in a combat situation?"

Sesína pawed the ground, her tone taking an air of nonchalance. *"As a matter of fact, I did save Alísa and Falier from a serpent. I was smaller then, but I managed."*

Saynan thrummed. *"Then I look forward to seeing your prowess in the sky."* He looked to Komi, then Harenn and Graydonn, swishing his tail through the air. *"You three as well. I know Komi and Harenn have trained and fought before, but one is never too good to sharpen their skills. Graydonn, I assume you plan to carry the young slayer in coming battles?"*

Graydonn and Falier looked at each other and psychically cut themselves off from the rest of the group. After a moment of deliberation, Falier pulled himself up onto Graydonn's back.

"We're ready."

Sesína looked to Alísa, her disappointment tempered by excitement. *"I suppose waiting another day won't hurt. Right?"*

Alísa grinned. *"Go. Learn lots and have fun."*

Saynan spread his wings. *"May I have your leave to leave, Singer?"*

Alísa nodded firmly and the ground shook as multiple dragons took off, Saynan in the lead. Pride rose within her as Sesína flew among them. She might be the smallest of the bunch, but she carried the most enthusiasm.

Maker help her training partners.

"I was about her age when I had my first flight-combat training," Koriana said wistfully. *"And only a little older when I had to use it."*

Alísa's heart clenched. Sesína in battle? A true, life-or-death battle with dragons and slayers? She was just a baby. How could Alísa send her out like that?

Maker, give us time. Please give us time.

40

COMBAT TRAINING

Falier ducked under a swinging red tail, grimacing as he slammed his shoulder into Graydonn's spine. After two days of riding and two nights on hard forest floors, it was a wonder he still had any muscles that weren't bruised or sore.

"Hold on!" Graydonn's voice echoed through his mind. Graydonn dodged as Harenn came back around, dipping under him and twisting to slap the red's underbelly with a wing.

"That's a win for Graydonn," Saynan declared through the group's connection.

Sesína's mouth hung open in a smiling pant. *"Nicely done!"*

Falier relaxed his grip on the spine as Graydonn pulled straight with the group once more. The younger dragons flew ahead of the adults and kept a steady pace as they paired off for aerial sparring.

"Your feint was excellent, Graydonn," Saynan said. *"But in a true combat situation a wing-slap brings more danger to you than your opponent. Your wings are your life, not mere tools. Instead, fly under your enemy and snap your tail up. The tail is sturdier and its spines are longer than your wing-claws."*

Falier shook his head. *"But how are we supposed to practice these things without hurting each other?"*

"Worry about yourself, Slayer," Harenn snapped.

"He is of the Singer's clan, Harenn," Komi admonished. *"You would do well to keep your mother's speech to yourself."*

Sesína cough-laughed several times. *"I like you, Komi."*

Komi's eyes shifted away, as though embarrassed, and she said nothing.

"Sesína, you're up next with Harenn," Saynan said. *"Try to be less enthusiastic*

this time."

Falier bit back a laugh. Sesína had flung herself into her first bout with such gusto that she overshot Graydonn on every pass. It was a very good thing she wasn't carrying Alísa right now—they might have to perform a rescue or two.

Falier glanced back at the adult dragons, his eyes landing on Alísa. She gestured with her hands to Faern, perfectly comfortable sitting on Koriana's back without a handhold. And perfectly comfortable conversing telepathically with a dragon.

Surely if the rest of the world saw them and how perfectly they treated each other as equals, they would understand. The war had to end.

Alísa looked up and met his eyes. Maker above, she was beautiful. Even with her wind-streaked hair matted behind her and days-old dirty clothing, her smile alone made his stomach flip.

There it was! Maybe once they were back in Me'ran and the clan was settled in the mountain, he would finally get up the nerve to tell her how he felt. Nothing had felt like right timing yet. He couldn't tell her when she was overflowing with emotions or should be focusing on the mission at hand.

Alísa cheered, her hands cupped around her mouth to direct the sound, and was answered by Sesína's victorious trumpet. Falier deflated, then laughed at himself—she had been smiling past him, at Sesína.

Oh well.

"*The training is before you, Falier,*" Graydonn said, his voice almost a laugh, "*not behind.*"

Falier righted himself. "*Right. Sorry.*"

Graydonn vibrated in his chest—was that the thrum sound Alísa had told him about, or the hum? "*She'll still be there when we've finished. Don't worry.*"

Falier sighed. He wasn't very good at hiding his feelings. Alísa probably already knew how he felt about her.

Who was he kidding? Of course she knew—she was an empath, and his emotions were all over the place. On occasion, he would remember to reel them in, but after years of boxing them behind his telepathic wall, the last thing his mind wanted was to be confined again.

It wasn't fair that she could read him so easily, while he couldn't yet recognize the psychic signatures of others' emotions. He had so much to learn.

"*Saynan.*" He reached out to the older dragon. "*You've said nothing of psychic attacks, only physical. Will we learn those as well?*

Saynan's eyes brightened. "*An excellent question, young slayer. Tell me, have you ever fought dragons with your clan?*"

"*No. I've never been part of a slayer clan.*"

"*Then, have you ever wondered how humans can possibly hold their own against dragons? After all, you are much smaller than us. Physically weaker. You have blades, but we have tooth, talon, and fire. Slayers have telepathy, but many dragons have greater powers than humans. How, then, do slayers do such a good job taking us out?*"

Falier shook his head, searching for an answer but finding none. Dragons seemed superior to humans in every aspect.

"*The answer is found in our mental make-up,*" Saynan answered. "*The Maker endowed dragons with great physical and psychic strength. But in his great wisdom, he gave humankind a way to protect themselves should we turn against them—our focus in the heat of battle can only truly be devoted to either the physical or the psychic. Splitting our attention between the two weakens both considerably, so if a dragon is going to attack to the best of their abilities, he or she must choose either physical attacks or psychic.*"

Saynan swung his head around to face Falier. "*Humans, however, are far better multitaskers. A slayer can throw his perfectly-aimed spear in one direction while sending a psychic arrow in the opposite. It is a difficult task, certainly, but far more accessible to humans than dragons.*"

Falier nodded. "*So, you won't teach any psychic battle tactics today?*"

"*I focus on the physical aspects of battle now because our most immediate enemy will be Rorenth, and dragons are more likely to fight other dragons on the physical plane.*"

Falier slumped as Saynan returned his attention to Sesína and Komi's sparring. That wasn't the answer he had wanted.

"*You're troubled, my friend?*"

Falier readjusted his grip on the spine. "*I have so much to learn, Graydonn. Riding you in these sparring exercises, I'm just dead weight.*"

"*Perhaps, but not forever. You heard what Saynan said. In a battle against dragons, they won't be using their telepathy much at all. That will give you an advantage.*"

Falier snorted. "*How much advantage can a flea have against a giant?*"

He shuddered as he remembered the fiery eyes of the dragon at Me'ran, and the pain coursing from his mind to his body when it had attacked him. He hadn't even known how to put up a shield against it.

"*The wall Kerrik taught you,*" Graydonn supplied. "*That's how you block telepathic attacks. It isn't meant to be used all the time, but it is scales around your mind. In fact, if you construct it like interlocking scales rather than a solid wall, it will hurt less when attacks ricochet off it.*"

Falier shook his head. Graydonn had heard his thoughts without him directing the words. This happened occasionally, probably a result of their minds vibrating the same way, or whatever being mind-kin meant. It was slightly unnerving.

Practice continued, each of the younger dragons pairing off and testing each other, with Saynan's instruction to guide them. For such a well-mannered dragon, Saynan certainly knew how to fight. He drew their attention to a dragon's weak spots—the underbelly, the base of the head, the tip of the tail, the muzzle, and the underside of the wings. Each spot was more susceptible to tooth, talon, and tail-spine.

Fire was usually a waste of energy against other dragons, though a good shot to the underwings or eyes would deal some damage. Saynan's ice-breath, on the other hand, could slow any fire dragon to a halt with a well-aimed blast.

After two full hours of practice, Saynan let the others go and flew beside Graydonn. "*You two fly well together. I had anticipated catching you at least twice, Slayer, but you understand Graydonn's movements well.*"

Falier shrugged. He just did it. "*Graydonn is good at looking out for me even as he flies.*"

"*We're mind-kin, Saynan,*" Graydonn said. "*We haven't bonded, but I feel it simmering under the surface.*"

"*A human, mind-kin with a dragon?*" Saynan's eyes brightened as he thrummed long and loud. "*Great Maker, what wonders you've made!*"

Yet what a mistake. Falier's stomach clenched as he realized the words echoed through his connection to the dragons. "*I'm sorry, Graydonn. I didn't mean—*"

"I know."

The dragon always knew, it seemed. Maybe it wouldn't be so frightening to be bonded. Or maybe he would lose himself somewhere along the way. Didn't slayers say that stronger minds shaped the weaker?

Saynan cocked his head. *"What mistake are you referring to? Surely not the Maker's?"*

Falier let out a sigh. *"Why on A'dem would the Maker choose to create a mind-kin pairing between Graydonn and a worthless slayer like me? I can barely speak without another telepath's assistance. What good does it do for us to have the potential to bond?"*

"Perhaps it's because he knew you would listen," Graydonn said gently. *"Few would, but you did."*

"Then why not give me more strength, knowing I would need it to help in this mission?"

Saynan spoke before Graydonn could answer. *"It is unwise to attempt to fathom the infinite. Even the strongest break under its weight. But—"*

The ice dragon looked Falier full in the eyes. The depths of his gaze seemed infinite itself, as if one who stared into them long enough might be lost forever.

Falier looked away.

"—your bond does give me an idea. What if Graydonn poured his psychic energy into Falier?"

Falier started at the use of his name, then shook his head as he realized what Saynan was proposing.

"It will work better if you two are truly bonded, but if you two are mind-kin, you should be able to do this without adverse side-effects. Then, in a battle situation, Graydonn can focus on physical attacks while Falier focuses on the psychic. The two of you would be brilliant."

Graydonn looked back at Falier, his eyes brightening. *"That could work."*

Excitement and anxiety fought for control of Falier's heart and stomach. It could work. It could work really well. But could he wield so much power without hurting himself, Graydonn, or any of the others?

"We won't know unless we try it," Graydonn answered the unspoken question. *"I want to. Do you?"*

Falier relaxed the tension in his shoulders. *"Why not?"*

Saynan thrummed. *"Both of you, focus on your communication tether. Falier, your job is to relax and open your mind to Graydonn's energy. Graydonn, your job is to channel your power through the bond without giving so much of yourself that you slip into unconsciousness."*

Falier jerked his head up. *"That's a possibility?"*

"Unlikely, but I will catch both of you."

"Calm down, my friend," Graydonn said. *"This is what you were made for."*

"Falling to my doom?" Falier tried to joke, but nerves churned in his stomach.

Graydonn thrummed. *"Are you ready?"*

Falier sighed and closed his eyes. He breathed deeply and felt the line connecting him to Graydonn. It felt green, pulsed with energy, and flowed in gentle curves between Graydonn's mind and his own. He could almost see it.

The pulsing grew deeper, like a goblet drum, as Graydonn's psychic energy flowed through their tether-line. It trickled into his mind at first, then grew steadily stronger. His body trembled with the power and his heartbeat quickened. It was wild and tickled over his mind like static. He breathed deeply again to try and steady himself, but the power pounded against his skull from the inside.

"Release it, Falier," Saynan's voice came from so far away. *"Send a psychic bolt into the clouds, now!"*

A yell of effort wrenched from Falier's throat as he imagined the power as a lightning bolt flying from his mind. Such power should have made giant thunderclap, but all that could be heard were the remnants of his own voice and the ringing in his ears. But at least the pounding had stopped.

"I'm sorry, Falier," Graydonn said. *"It was too much at once."*

"That worked brilliantly for a first attempt," Saynan said, his eyes brightening. *"The problem came when Graydonn gave more power than Falier could handle. The two of you need to find an equilibrium, where the power flows easily between the two of you rather than being held in only one mind. Let's try it again."*

Falier worked to steady his heartbeat and breathing, and Graydonn prodded his mind gently. *"We can wait. We don't have to do it again."*

"No." He had to do this. He wouldn't be dead-weight if he could help it.

"Let's try again."

They did. Once. Twice. Three times the power coursed from Graydonn to Falier and refused to be controlled in any way other than releasing in silent lightning. Falier's mind seemed only able to take in the power, not create a push and pull balance with Graydonn.

Falier breathed heavily and Graydonn's wing-strokes slowed. The rest of the group had nearly caught up to them now.

"Well done, you two," Saynan said. *"You've taken a huge step."*

Graydonn perked his head up and looked around. *"I sense dreki. Angry dreki."*

"Dreki?" Falier raised his head to look too.

"Great Maker!" With a fearful trumpet, Saynan speared for Aree.

Falier followed with his eyes, his jaw dropping. A flock of perhaps twenty dreki circled the rest of the group, each one barking and fully aglow.

41

A CHANCE

Alísa shut her eyes against the frantic visions from the strange dreki. "Stop! P—Please, I c-c-can't handle it!"

It did no good. Dark shapes against clouds, fire, and a mountain range dominated the images crowding her mind, but they flitted by so quickly that details escaped her. Agitation from the dreki shook her mind, while the dragons' frightened confusion made it cave in on itself. It seemed a miracle that neither clan had attacked the other yet. Her stomach churned like she had been spinning for far too long.

Sesína flew above Alísa now, growling. *"Shut up, will you! Can't you see you're hurting her?"*

For whatever reason, Sesína's outburst did the trick. The dreki's glow diminished as they separated their minds from each other, and two landed on Koriana's back—a blue and a ruby.

"Relay." Then a flash of lavender. *"Chrí."*

Alísa breathed, trying to calm herself enough to respond. *"What—what did Chrí say?"*

A mental affirmative, then another picture, one of many dragons—forty, at least—converging on a single mountain.

"Rorenth."

Alísa's heart stopped. So many dragons—more than she had thought. This picture stayed in her mind longer than most drek images, and as her mind's eye fluttered over the scene she recognized multiple columns of smoke rising from different points. She shivered and her stomach roiled.

"This is a warning of what is to come, not a report," Sesína said. *"There is only*

one column of smoke on the horizon." Before Alísa could ask after Me'ran, Sesína supplied the answer. *"West of the Nissen."*

"Soon," the dreki said.

Alísa nodded, relief flooding her veins, followed closely by guilt. How dare she feel happiness that her friends in Me'ran were safe at the expense of strangers?

The longer the image stayed, the more Alísa felt that something wasn't quite right. The mountain looked different. Then the image began to focus on a grove of trees at the base of the mountain. It pulled closer and closer, until she recognized the outlines of tents among them. As familiar patterns and faces drew nearer, dreadful realization filled Alísa—the image came from the western side of the mountain, not the eastern! There was Trísse standing with the horses. Farren carrying a ladle and bucket of water. Kallar sharpening his sword. Her mother holding fast to her father, his body language tender, but his eyes hard with vigilance.

Those eyes were the last thing she saw, looking to Rorenth's mountain as the image faded and the present came back into view.

"Papá." Tears ran down her cheeks, unnoticed until now.

"What is it, Alísa?" Koriana looked back at her. *"What do they want?"*

Alísa swallowed, staring at the dreki. *"Are you sure?"*

"Chrí."

There was finality in this answer as the lavender floated by again, as if that name said it all.

Alísa's mind spun with numbers and fear and little black dots.

"Take us down, Koriana."

The dragoness acted immediately, and the rest of the clan followed. The dreki stayed with them, their agitation only simmering now that their message had been delivered. Alísa barely noticed when they landed, her fingers glued to Koriana's spine.

No, no, no. This isn't right, it's too soon.

But they can't. Papá can't—there's too many. They fight clans of twenty, not forty!

"Alísa?" Koriana's concern wafted over her. *"What are you talking about?"*

Sesína's voice was so far away. *"Come down. You'll fall."* Only then did

Alísa realize Koriana was crouching for her. She could barely move her fingers, her arms like lead. She pulled them from the spine, then teetered. The ground seemed a long way down.

Falier was suddenly there, reaching for her. His arms were strong—a dancer's arms that wouldn't let his partner fall. He lowered her gently, and when her feet didn't accept her weight, he took them both down to their knees.

"What happened?"

I can't.

I have to. More will die.

No, there's too many.

Eight—no, Aree—seven. Against forty. Against thirty.

Too many.

Save them.

Save Sesína. Six.

Save me.

Fire meets fire.

"Líse?" Something shook her. "Líse, wake up."

Breath filled her lungs and escaped in trembling sighs. She opened her eyes to Falier's earthy-brown jerkin. It smelled like sweat and dirt and love.

"They're coming," she whispered.

Falier's arms pulled tighter around her, his shoulder pressing against her temple, his hands supporting her back.

"I know. Sesína told us."

She swallowed. Breathing was hard.

The Illumination bond opened wider, and Sesína's presence soothed over her like gently rippling waters, lifting away the dust and grime and tears.

"I'm sorry I didn't think of this before you fainted. I was so scared."

Alísa breathed, feeling stronger already as Sesína shared the mental exhaustion. *"It's all right, dear one."*

She squeezed Falier's arm. "I n—need t-to stand now. Help me?"

Falier hesitated, worry in his eyes. She gave him the most confident mask she could muster.

"Please."

He did as she asked, pulling her to her feet and offering his arm. He didn't take his eyes off her. It reminded her of Tenza. They would have to talk when all of this was over—assuming they made it through.

The dragons gathered around her, all displaying concern—dimmed eyes, drooping wings and tails, lying on their bellies. What a way to begin her leadership, fainting from anxiety and over-stimulation. Thankfully, only the two dreki she had talked to were in sight—she couldn't handle another round of their mental barrage right now.

"I sent the rest of them away." Sesína nosed under her hand. *"They'll return if you call on them."*

She was about to do more than that. As her mind cleared, her plan solidified. It was bold, awful, and would risk everything, but if she did it right, she would prevent many deaths and perhaps save her father's clan. The only alternative was to continue home to Me'ran and watch as the western villages burned. As much as she wanted the time to grow the clan to full strength, she couldn't live with those deaths on her hands. Especially her father's.

"Sesína, link me to them, please." The link formed, and Alísa stood taller, her arm still linked over Falier's in case the dizziness returned.

"Dear dragons, the dreki have sent terrible news. As we speak, Rorenth gathers his dragons for continued assaults on humankind, and my family marches to meet them."

She trembled, and Falier steadied her once more. This wasn't a dizzy spell, though—it was purely fear. She pulled at the emotion as it wafted from her. She had to keep it under control, or she would affect the others.

"I can take it," Sesína whispered, shivering as she opened the bond wide once more. *"Be brave, dragon-heart."*

Alísa breathed in and blew it out. *"They will not make it—there are too many dragons for them. They may thin Rorenth's clan, but in the end, my family will die. Without wayfarers in the area, Rorenth will continue to burn villages and grow his clan. I cannot let that happen."*

She looked each dragon in the eye. *"I know I said we would wait until we became stronger, but we have a chance to stop Rorenth's violence now and perhaps turn more dragons and slayers to our cause. My father marches on Rorenth's mountain. If he and his men are alone, they will be slaughtered. But if we attack as well, we will force Rorenth to fight on two fronts, halving his clan and calling any dragons to us who would repent and stand against him."*

"*Singer, if I may?*" Faern stepped closer, his head low. She nodded her assent, and he spoke to the group. "*I admire your courage and loyalty to your family, but it will take a full day's flight to reach Rorenth's mountain. You will have no time to address your family beforehand, and we will be killed by them alongside the enemy.*"

Alísa shook her head firmly. "*Not if we keep our part in the battle far from the mountain. The slayers will focus on the immediate threat—the dragons defending their caves. My song will draw Rorenth's attention even from far away, so long as he can hear it. We will keep far from the slayers until the battle is over.*"

"*And then what?*" Koriana growled. "*You will go to them, allow them to do to you what they did to Bria?*"

"*Papá would never—*"

Koriana's grief and rage slammed into Alísa. "*Those slayers were her family too, yet they destroyed her! We already know your former clan is willing to kill the innocent—shouldn't they die alongside Rorenth?*"

Alísa was silent. She had no argument to refute the dragoness, none besides her love for her family. But her family had killed hatchlings and slaughtered Koriana's mate. Graydonn's father. How could she treat them differently than she treated Rorenth?

Graydonn stepped in front of his mother. His eyes were dim with his own grief, yet he held his head high before her.

"*No, Mother. Not yet. Those slayers kill innocents, yes, but they do so out of ignorance. They need to hear the truth and have a chance to turn. Rorenth's clan will have that chance when she sings to them, but the slayers will need more.*"

Graydonn's voice remained calm and logical as he reasoned with her, but his talons digging into the earth showed his underlying tension.

"*You know there's a reason she is called a Dragon Singer—her songs are tuned to a dragon's heart and they know she cannot lie by them. Slayers will hear the songs and see the visions, but they, as humans, will only sense the power, not the truth behind it. They deserve the chance to turn.*"

Koriana snapped her jaws. "*They deserve nothing but death!*"

He shut his eyes. "*Father would have wanted to give them this chance.*"

Koriana's tail sliced through the air as she stared down her son.

Graydonn didn't back down, nor did he make any sounds or movements that communicated ire. The world seemed to still as it waited for them.

Then Koriana threw her head back and roared—a long, loud cry that shook the ground and made Alísa's heart race like the birds fleeing from their trees. Graydonn joined her, his tenor voice adding to the grief spilling from Alísa's eyes. It was so strong it threatened to sap all her strength, and she pushed back against it, leaning into Falier.

Deep respect and awe flowed from Falier, all fixated on Graydonn, as though he were seeing the dragon for the first time. In a way, they were all seeing Graydonn and Koriana for the first time. There were no masks here, only true, deep grief, like a thunderstorm that washed away the smoke and ash of yesterday, yet left its own mark upon the world.

Then, as suddenly as it came, their song of sorrow ended. Graydonn nuzzled Koriana's cheek, and the dragoness returned the gesture. Then her eyes locked on Alísa.

"My son bears the wisdom of his father. Maker knows he did not receive it from me. I will not move against the slayers until you have given the word." She dipped her head low and rumbled in her chest. *"I will follow my alpha."*

Graydonn copied the sound and gesture, followed by Saynan, then Faern and the others, until finally even Sesína bowed her head. Falier placed his fist over his heart, his face more solemn than Alísa had ever seen. So many good *anam*, ready to follow her into fire.

Maker, help me. Tomorrow is the day.

42

RORENTH'S MOUNTAIN

The dragons flew fast and hard through the rest of the day and settled for the night amidst a small grove of trees on the western side of the Nissen, an hour's flight south of Rorenth's mountain. A quick scouting venture by Faern confirmed the battle had yet to begin, and Alísa thanked the Maker for the provision of rest, light though it would be. The river pounded in her ears as she laid down to sleep, the fears and sorrows of the day sweeping her into fitful slumber.

She dreamed of fire and death—not for her, but for her dragons and her father's clan. Even Kallar burned in one, Alísa echoing his cry as she woke. Sesína and the few southern dreki who slept nearby tried to comfort her, Sesína even entering her dreams, but nothing stopped them from coming.

She woke with dread in her stomach and the acrid taste of sorrow on her tongue. With the rising of the sun, the true test of the Dragon Singer's clan was upon them. Their strength and resolve would be tested by the violent beast who had plagued her nightmares. His blood-red scales flashed in her mind's eye—his fangs snapping at her dragons' tails, his claws slashing at their wings, his fire threatening to burn the hills and the forests until the world turned to ash.

Alísa closed her eyes and breathed. Dread would not stop her, no matter how it gnawed.

She placed a hand on Sesína's cheek. *"It's time, dear one."*

Groggily, they stood. Alísa's legs trembled underneath her and she placed a hand on Sesína's shoulder to steady herself. Muscles rippled under Sesína's scales and a hint of pride peeked through Alísa's nerves. Her sister was strong and able, and she carried enough courage for them both.

But how could she send such a young one into battle? Sesína had only a little combat training and experience. Perhaps she shouldn't——

"No," Sesína declared with a swish of her tail. "*I am not staying behind. You're giving me a flight-partner, and your song will strengthen me beyond Rorenth's cronies. I'm fighting beside you today.*"

Alísa looked down at Sesína's serpent bite. It had only been a couple weeks. Her scales were still growing back, and she still limped when she thought Alísa wasn't looking. Worse could happen today.

"*You should stay with Aree and protect her, in case she's found. The effects of the ruby bark will put her at risk.*"

Sesína shook her head and growled. "*She won't be found. She's staying here, miles from the battle.*"

Alísa searched her mind and grasped for a reason, any reason. "*But there could be slayers out here. She needs——*"

"*Do you honestly think I'll be more able on my own against slayers than out there with the clan and your song?*" Sesína stood on her hind legs and placed heavy paws on Alísa's shoulders. "*I am not a hatchling anymore, and every great step in my development has been because you were at my side. If we separate now, we are fools. And if you think I'll listen when you tell me to stay, you are a fool. I am your wing-dragon, and that is final.*"

Alísa sighed. Sesína was right—she couldn't stop her from joining the battle.

She wrapped her arms around Sesína's ribs. "*I hate you.*"

Sesína shifted her forelegs into the closest she could get to a hug, then wrapped her wings over the top for good measure. "*I know.*"

Her sister pulled back her wings, allowing Alísa to survey her clan. Harenn, Koriana, Graydonn, and Falier stood in a semi-circle. Faern and Komi were missing, probably scouting. Saynan stood before Aree, nuzzling her as she lay with their opalescent egg between her forelegs.

Falier headed for them, an apple in one hand and his pack in the other. Alísa's own stomach tied in knots. *How can he eat at a time like this?*

Sesína nudged her shoulder. "*Because he's smart. And male.*"

Falier offered her the fruit and Alísa shook her head.

"You've got to eat something," he said unhelpfully.

"No. I'm afraid I'll lose it in today's" —she searched for a word— "excitement."

"If by 'it' you mean consciousness." He nodded at the apple. "At least try."

Alísa sighed, letting her shoulders sag, but she took it nonetheless. It tasted like dirt and settled heavily in her stomach.

She must have grimaced, because Falier shook his head. "Three more bites and I'll leave you alone."

"What are you, my mother?"

His eyebrows pushed up and together in a pained expression that sent a jolt to her heart.

"It was a j—joke. I'll eat it." She averted her eyes and took another bite. It wasn't worth it to make him worry about her.

He gave a half-smile. "Good."

A shadow crossed over the clearing as she took a third bite, and the group looked up to see Faern and Komi banking over them. Alísa inclined her head, and they headed to the brown dragons landing in the center of the small clearing.

"Any news?"

Faern dipped his head. *Dragons converge on the mountain. We saw two scouts coming from different directions. One was a strong telepath and felt our presence, but our flight-training exercises and Illumination bond quelled any suspicions.*

Alísa nodded. *And the slayers?*

Komi thumped her tail on the ground. *There is commotion on the mountain, and I heard shouting. They have likely engaged.*

Alísa's heart raced. They still faced an hour's flight. *Thank you. Do you require rest before our departure?*

We are ready when you are, Singer.

Alísa cast her eyes over her clan. Seven dragons ready to fight, a dragoness who stayed behind to protect the future, a slayer with limited training but a heart of gold, a group of dreki—possibly another if Chrí and her clan had stuck near the mountain—and one Dragon Singer, who must lead them all.

Nerves shot from her heart to her extremities. It was time, and she felt anything but ready. But as she looked from face to face, as she thought of the villagers whose deaths would be prevented, as she remembered the faces of her father's clan, it didn't matter. This was the moment she had been made for. *By Maker's wings.*

She rose up tall and called to her clan with the words they responded to in Tsamen's cave.

> Who will seek wisdom in an age of violence?
> Only the quiet, who stand by nothing else.
> Who will listen to the quiet in a time of chaos?
> Only the ones who tire of the noise.
> Who will stand with the weak through the storms?
> Only the ones who too are affected.

Power cascaded from her in waves of strength. In place of glazed eyes and bowed heads, were flexed wings and rumbling chests. Each dragon and drek exuded confidence, and their emotions fed her even as she strengthened them.

> None will listen. None will stand. None will seek the truth,
> Until fire meets fire, and sword meets sword,
> Until man gives life for dragon,
> And dragon gives life for man.

She raised her voice in a final call reminiscent of her chieftain father's.

"We will listen. We will stand. We will bring the truth. By Maker's wings, I bid you rise!"

The dragons trumpeted and roared in a mixture of elation and determination, and the dreki barked and trilled their own battle cries. A grin spread wide across Alísa's face. At the very least, these were *anam* she would be proud to walk beside as they entered the Maker's halls.

A hand found her shoulder and she turned to Falier. Strength flowed from him, but his eyes were soft with pride.

"Eldra Branni strengthen your hands."

She gave a single breathy chuckle—it was the first time he had ever given her the traditional words. She no longer needed to hide behind E'sall or any other Eldra. As she entered this fight to protect her slayer family, she finally felt assurance that Branni still watched over her as the Maker had always intended.

Truly, neither she nor Falier had to hide anymore. She reached out her arm with the warrior's response, but added a draconic twist. "Branni's courage, and Maker's wings."

Falier hesitated only a moment before clasping her arm, a wincing smile on his face.

"W—what's the matter?"

He shrugged. "I've never been called Branni's charge before. I hope I live up to it."

He looked to Graydonn and Koriana coming up alongside them, then gave Alísa a half-smile. "Work wonders out there, Líse. And don't do anything stupid."

She chuckled. "Like riding into battle on a d—d-dragon?"

"No. I'm pretty sure that's the wisest thing you could do at this point." He looked to Koriana. "Take care of her."

"Same to you and Graydonn. May the Maker grant you strength, young slayer."

Falier nodded firmly and moved to mount Graydonn. Koriana crouched in front of Alísa, and she leapt to the dragoness' back. Together they led the clan, rising into the air and shooting straight into Rorenth's territory.

The dragons linked telepathically and Alísa spoke through the connection. *"Faern, Komi, lead the way. Get us to that mountain!"*

"By Maker's wings," they spoke together, breaking past Koriana and taking positions at the front.

Alísa took psychic stock of her clanmates, memorizing each mental signature so that she could recognize them when she sang.

She smiled to herself. Mere months ago, she would never have dreamed she would be able to control her psychic abilities in this way. No empath could focus on an individual mind while connected to a large group. Now she did it with relative ease, and she would use that ability to fuel them through the battle, while leaving the enemy dry.

The only member of this troop she couldn't quite recognize psychically was the dreki clan. Right now, they flew with minds separate, sprinkled amidst the dragons. She couldn't connect to all of them. When they formed their collective mind, however, she should be able to recognize their psychic signature in the battle.

But would that strengthen them? They had reacted to her songs before, but they weren't dragons. Graydonn had said yesterday that humans weren't as affected by her songs as dragons. Did the same go for dreki? She had felt their pain as viscerally as she had dragons, but perhaps it was only because their collective mind was larger than any other she had sensed.

She reached her hand to the drek nearest her—a green—and waved for its attention.

"Singer?"

Fen. The name came to her with the image of a glossy green beetle's shell.

"Shiny!" Sesína squealed with delight as she caught the image.

Alísa pushed back a grin. *"Fen, I'm working to learn your clan's mental signature. Could you all connect so I can learn?"*

"No."

Alísa cocked her head. *"Why not?"*

"Taxing."

"Oh." So, it took a lot of effort to hold together. It seemed there were a lot of things she still didn't understand about dreki.

"It doesn't help that their communication-style leaves much to be desired."

The drek hissed at Sesína, and Alísa suppressed a grin.

"Fen, do you know if my songs will strengthen dreki?"

"Minimal." Fen sent an image of dreki surrounding a dragon as it fell from the sky. *"Able."*

Alísa nodded. She would focus her powers on the dragons today, not on the dreki.

The mountain loomed large now, powerful and unmoving against the backdrop of the sky. Twenty more minutes. After five, the roars of battle were faintly heard. Ten, and tiny specks of color were visible against the rocks, most gathered on the north side of the mountain.

Hoping to store up as much energy as she could within her clanmates, Alísa sang her strength song. She pushed it first through Sesína, then Koriana and Graydonn, then latched onto the mental signatures of the rest of her clan, each one locking into place like clasps on a chest.

When they were perhaps three minutes' flight from the battle, Alísa raised her fist. *"Stop! We make our stand here. Push no further, or the slayers will catch you too."*

Koriana swept left, followed by the others, all of them flying along the line Alísa had drawn. She switched to the song she had used to gain access to Tsamen's cave, changing the words as needed and pushing forward her desire that they join her.

"This song's for you—hear me! Follow me!"

A thunderous roar shook the air, reaching across the distance and rattling Alísa's heart and lungs. It halted the song in her throat, silencing the world around her. Then she saw it, the dull red scales and flashing white eyes that had haunted her all last night.

Rorenth.

The distance did nothing to mask his size as the alpha dragon spread his wings wide—easily twice Graydonn's span. His scales shone in the sunlight like freshly-spilt blood.

Rorenth launched himself forward with another bone-shaking roar. Dragons fell into formation behind him, more rounding the mountain and spearing in his wake. Twenty dragons at least.

Twenty, against her tiny clan.

Graydonn's voice entered her mind. *"I can sense conflict within some of his dragons, but there is mostly fear. It keeps them from moving—they cannot cross him."*

Courage. They needed it just as much as she did. She forced herself to sing again, the song's fire infusing her dragons with bravery to cover their mounting fear. Even if none turned to help them, they were ready. She focused on them, grasping for their courage as a drowning woman to an outstretched hand. The enemy closed the distance rapidly—the battle was about to begin.

Fire stirred in her veins. *Dragon-heart. I am dragon-heart!*

"Go!"

43

BATTLE OF MINDS

Faern and Komi twisted through the air, bolting for the mass of dragons. They dove under the enemy and pulled up fast to each catch a dragon from underneath. Their move scattered Rorenth's clan in an explosion of color, and the rest of Alísa's clan split up to attack.

Alísa's stomach dropped as Koriana soared up toward a group of four dragons, Sesína staying just behind her left wing. Alísa gripped Koriana's spine with white knuckles. She looked behind and saw the great red alpha pull up after them, his flashing eyes locked onto hers.

Rorenth's outrage and fury became a psychic arrow to her mind, and she cried out in pain. Saynan's words about multitasking had made her think it was impossible for a dragon in physical combat, but impractical was perhaps more accurate. It seemed a strong enough dragon could afford to split his attentions.

Rorenth was that strong.

Koriana pulled out of her pursuit of the four dragons, turning her flight into evasive action. Twisting and turning through the air, Koriana dodged dragons until Alísa couldn't keep her eyes open to watch anymore. Even with eyes closed, Rorenth's presence was palpable. He targeted her alone, his hatred coursing through her like molten rock.

Koriana's evasion took them to the outskirts of the battle. Somewhere along the flight they lost Sesína, leaving only her concern for Alísa's safety flowing through their bond.

"Darling, find—Graydonn and—Falier. Stick—with them."

She shook her head, trying to clear it, but Rorenth's rage rattled her so hard she could hardly speak psychically. His rumbling laugh filled her mind and expanded, barely leaving any room for Alísa's own thoughts.

"YOU DARE TRY TO STEAL MY DRAGONS?! YOU, WHO ARE NOTHING BUT A HATCHLING? THE TIME OF VERMIN IS ENDING—YOU WILL FALL LIKE ALL OF YOUR PEOPLE!"

He pressed images of his clan's violence into her mind, and she cried out, shutting her eyes against the visions.

Children bleeding out.

Husbands diving over their wives, both burning in an inferno.

Slayers trying to stop the madness and being trampled underfoot.

The screams. Oh, the screams! Enough to crush any human in pain and sorrow.

Alísa curled in on herself, her heart pounding in her chest as though it might explode. The visions swirled around her and pressed until it felt like her mind would cave in under the pressure. The monster's triumphant memories.

It was wrong.

Vile.

Everything she had come to fight.

Alísa forced herself upright once more, gritting her teeth against the onslaught. Each breath she drew filled her with fire.

I am no mere human to be crushed by him! I have a dragon inside me!

All at once, the very sorrow and pain seeking to destroy her became fuel for the flames. They burned against Rorenth's attack, and a battle cry ripped from Alísa's throat, the note shattering his hold.

"You. Won't. Win!"

With a surprised trumpet, Rorenth's energies snapped back from her. Pride poured from Koriana, and she added her own roar to the call. Alísa's cry infused her with power and Rorenth soon fell behind them.

"Hang on."

Koriana pulled up so quickly Alísa found herself upside-down, and she laughed as the dragoness twisted to right herself just above Rorenth. The murderous brute snapped at Koriana's tail but couldn't turn fast enough, and she raked her talons across his armored wing and slapped it with her tail as she passed. He turned to follow them, roaring in outrage.

"*Shall I continue attacking him?*"

Alísa looked at the fray before them. "*No. The others have been without my song too long—they need our strength.*"

Trumpeting shook the air around them as Koriana swept them back into the battle—her clan's already-tired bodies and minds once more infusing with strength. Pain rushed to Alísa through the psychic link. No mortal wounds, but they had taken beatings. Saynan and Harenn had been separated. Harenn now flew with Graydonn and Sesína with a bruised wing, while Saynan flew alone.

Alísa breathed, allowing the air to vitalize her once more. It stoked the fire and formed a new song on her lips—one not only of strength for her clan, but of justice against Rorenth's.

> We are two peoples unified—a clan the world has never known.
> Justice bids us rise and fight against the wanton violence sown.
>
> We are wind. We are sky. We are mountains, fire, sand.
> We will fight. We will fly. We hear our Maker's call to stand.
>
> All will hear the song we sing, and if we fall they'll rise instead.
> None will stop the wrath we bring, till peace brings life unto the dead.
>
> We are wind. We are sky. Mountains, fire, river, all.
> We will fight. We will fly. We are rising—join or fall!

If controlling Graydonn's psychic power had been hard before, Alísa's song made it near-impossible. Falier strained against the power as it coursed over him, trying to push it back before it overwhelmed him.

"*I need to stop,*" Graydonn said as he dodged another dragon's blow. "*You're going to harm yourself.*"

Falier gritted his teeth. "*No. I can do this!*"

The energy zapped and crackled over his mind, bringing pain greater than any headache. It wrestled with his own energies, small though they were, in a frenzied rhythm, like two drummers fighting for control of the tempo.

Nahne—Branni—help me. I can't do this.

An enemy dragon speared at them, locking its hate-filled eyes on him, and he released a psychic bolt. Like lightning, it struck the dragon, which seized under the blow and dropped. It tumbled through the air as it tried to recover, but Sesína dove after it. She seemed the most affected by Alísa's song, the playful and sassy dragon now one with a deadly mission.

She went for the wings, slicing through from mainstay to end, then pushed off its body to return to Graydonn, leaving their attacker to fall to its demise.

"This would work better if you could release those bolts more frequently, Falier," she said, fluttering right past another attacker with her heightened speed and agility and coming up beside them.

Already the static built up again, the power so wild, so unwilling to bend to his will. It couldn't be Graydonn's fault—he gave freely, he believed in him. The problem had to be on his own end. Sure, he had power now, but he was still too weak to control it. A failure, as he had always been.

Another dragon streamed toward them, large and red. *Rorenth?* Falier searched for its eyes—it was the only way he had found to control where the lightning struck. Once it made contact with his—

"Friendly!"

Falier flinched as Graydonn shouted in his mind. The red dragon speared past them and barreled into another behind them. Falier's hands shook with the power building inside of him and the weight of the mistake he had almost made.

"Who—who was that?"

"Q'rill. He and his mother have turned to our side, as have two others."

Falier grimaced. *"How do—you know?"*

"You don't look so good," Sesína said.

"I need to—release—"

"Let it flow back into me," Graydonn said, dodging another dragon. *"If you hold it all until it explodes out of you, you'll hurt yourself or a clanmate."*

Falier searched desperately for another dragon's eyes—one he didn't recognize.

"I'm trying!"

The power was too much. It tore at the edges of his mind, leaping and yanking back like wolves on tethers.

Too much. Too much!

"Down!" Sesína yelped.

Falier's heart flew into his throat as Graydonn pulled his wings in. Flames sprayed where they had been, mere feet above Falier's head.

Then the power released.

A dragon's scream of agony.

Trumpets of fright.

Graydonn's wings and tail flipping over limply as they fell.

"Graydonn!" Falier shouted, gripping the dragon with all his might as they tumbled in the sky.

What had he done?

A streak of black zoomed past them. The tumbling stopped with Sesína's grunts and cries of effort.

"Wake him up, Falier! I can't hold you for long."

"Graydonn!" He shouted with mind and voice. "Graydonn, come on!"

Another dragon shrieked above him, and he whirled to see a brown descending with talons fully extended. Its cold blue eyes spoke murder.

A flash of silver dove between them and the beast, accompanied by a human's battle cry. Koriana wrestled with the brute, and Alísa dodged claw and wing as she continued her song.

All he could make out was one word: Bind. She repeated it over and over until the dragon seized up and fell from Koriana's clutches. Alísa continued as the dragon fell, only stopping once it hit the ground.

"What happened?" Koriana's voice rang savagely. *"I can't feel our Illumination bond!"*

"I'm trying to wake him." He didn't dare go into the story of his own inability now. He still felt the connection to Graydonn, though faint. *"Wake up!"*

Sesína strained underneath them, but kept them aloft, while Koriana watched for any other dragons who might take advantage of Graydonn's unconsciousness.

"I feel nothing as I hold him," Sesína worried. *"No psychic energy—nothing but his breathing!"*

Falier shook his head. *"I feel him. He's still here, just unconscious."*

Koriana's eyes flashed. *"You feel him? Even I don't."* Then her eyes dimmed and softened. *"Mind-kin. It's time, Falier."*

His name echoed through his thoughts in Koriana's voice. What did it mean for her to use it now, for the first time? Didn't she understand he was the one who hurt Graydonn?

Alísa locked eyes with him, and her words poured into him, even as she continued her dragon song.

"Don't be afraid, Falier. I've never met anyone more trustworthy than Graydonn. Save him and join the fight together."

Falier shuddered with the weight of her words. She was right. Graydonn was good and kind. He fought for innocents and even for the chance for the corrupt to repent. For those who killed his beloved father to turn.

No one was more noble. No one more trustworthy.

Falier set his hand on Graydonn's neck, and breathed. He closed his eyes and reached out with his mind, feeling—no, seeing the connection between them, the pulsing green of their minds in the darkness of the astral plane.

"Graydonn. I'm sorry I hurt you. I don't know how to accept the bond, except to tell you I do. I trust you. Please, my friend, wake up."

A jolt zapped through their connection. It buzzed and crackled, like when Graydonn had shared his power before, but this time, Falier gave back. Their psychic energies synchronized, each with a different rhythm, but both to the same beat.

Graydonn started awake, flapping his wings to lift off of Sesína's back. He gave a loud trumpet, one that spoke victory and joy.

"Thank you, my friend."

Sesína released a sigh of relief and darted up to Alísa. *"Finally!"*

One of Rorenth's dragons rushed them and Falier felt the power focus inside him. This time, he didn't wait for eye-contact. The bolt flew from his mind into the dragon's like an arrow from a bow. The dragon screamed and fell.

Koriana thrummed, taking one last look at him before she rushed back into the fray.

"Welcome to the battle, Slayer-Falier."

44

FLAMES

It was all a mess. A great, bloody mess.

Pain surged through Alísa's bond to her clan as they took talons and teeth and ramming blows, but she couldn't allow herself to be affected. When it ached, she sang through it. When it pounded, she changed her tempo to its beat. When it speared, she turned her cries into weapons, binding dragons in mind-chokes.

Rorenth was nowhere to be found. Perhaps he had gone back to defend his mountain throne from her father.

Is Papá okay?

"*Focus, Alísa,*" Sesína said. "*The best thing you can do for him right now is focus.*"

Alísa pushed the worried thoughts from her mind and urged Koriana and Sesína toward Saynan as five dragons swarmed him. Her song made him faster and stronger, but five were far too many. Blood sprayed into the air from one of his hind legs, but he didn't slow. He spewed a volley of ice in the face of an attacker as he flipped backward over another dive-bomber.

Koriana growled and headed straight for a dragon as it tried to catch Saynan's tail. "*Hold on!*"

Alísa stopped singing, gritting her teeth as they plowed into the attacker—better to stop for a moment than risk biting her tongue clean off. She nearly flew from her seat as the dragons tumbled through the air in a mass of wings, legs, and tails. She held to Koriana's spine for all she was worth, until the dragoness dealt a death-blow and pulled out of the fall not fifty feet from the ground.

Koriana pressed back into the fray, leaving Sesína with Saynan. An emerald dragon now rushed to join her, one of those who had turned from Rorenth. As soon as they had turned, the four new dragons joined the telepathic link to Alísa's clan, making their mental signatures recognizable to her and each of the dragons. She didn't know what they looked like, but she knew them if they came close.

"*Hail, Rayna!*" Alísa called.

"*Hail, Singer,*" she answered. "*Your call is well-timed. My mate and I had been looking for the opportunity to escape Rorenth's hold. Now I get to take a few of his brutes down first!*"

Koriana rolled to avoid a dragon falling from the sky, his wings completely frozen with ice, while Rayna pulled up rapidly and caught another dragon, sinking teeth into its underbelly.

Alísa shivered and looked away. So much blood. So much death. They refused to turn from their violent ways—she shouldn't feel sad for their deaths—but at the same time, how could she not?

Harenn swooped and rolled nearby, alongside two other red dragons, both of whom were turned. They pursued two dragons and had four more on their tails. Koriana flew straight through the swarm, scattering them and allowing Harenn, Tora, and Q'rill a quick reprieve. Tora's wings were torn in places, and Q'rill seemed particularly upset until he set eyes on Alísa.

"*That's her, mother! The one with the pretty voice!*" He was larger than Harenn, almost as large as his mother, Tora, but his voice was soft and reminiscent of a hatchling's.

Tora's voice was deep and low as she ripped after a large green dragon, snapping at its tail. "*Yes, but focus. Do not waste the strength she lends.*"

Alísa spied a blue dragon charging Koriana. "*To your left!*"

The blue's shining emerald eyes met hers and the conflict inside of him flowed through their brief connection. She recognized him. Sareth—the scout who had let them pass through Rorenth's territory all those weeks ago.

He changed course, avoiding the collision, and Alísa followed him with her eyes as he spun around to fly after Tora instead. He would turn—all he needed was another push.

"*Koriana, get above Sareth!*"

Sesína's voice came through loud and clear as her presence drew near again. *"I'll catch you if he doesn't."*

Alísa smiled—her sister knew the plan. As soon as Koriana pushed above Sareth, Alísa began to sing.

I believe in you, dear Sareth;
Your heart calls for hope to mine.

Alísa lifted herself to stand and leapt down Koriana's back into the open air. Koriana trumpeted in alarm, but Alísa pushed the thoughts aside and sang to Sareth as she passed.

I believe in you, dear Sareth;
Believe in me and we will rise.

Sareth trumpeted and dove after Alísa, his talons grazing her stomach only slightly as he caught her in his paw.

"You have the heart of a foolhardy dragon, young Singer."

Alísa smiled brightly. *"And you a heart of nobility."*

Sareth lifted her to his shoulder and Alísa pulled herself up by his spines. Sesína trumpeted joyfully beneath them as she rose to become Sareth's wing-dragon. Sareth joined her trumpet, and Alísa lifted her voice with them.

As they passed, Koriana scolded her with pride. *"Don't ever do that again."*

Alísa spied a large swarm of dragons attacking Saynan, Rayna, and her mate, Korin. *"Sareth, to the left—let's break them up!"*

Sareth rolled into a bank, nearly flinging Alísa from his back. She gripped tighter—he had never carried a rider before. This could get messy.

"I've got you," Sesína said from behind. *"Fear nothing, dragon-heart!"*

Rayna screamed as a dragon dug its talons deep into her wing, ripping it through from mainstay to tip. Alísa cried out in tandem as pain crashed through her, zapping from her spine through her left arm. Rayna was so far away—the pain must be excruciating!

Rayna fell into an uncontrolled dive and the black Korin rushed to catch her.

"Sesína, help him! Don't let her hit the ground!"

Sesína pulled her wings in tight and dove after the falling dragon, while Sareth kept his course to help Saynan. Alísa sang a strength song once more, her tired voice protesting and cracking. Her dragon-borne confidence began to wane—she hadn't anticipated losing her voice.

What then?

Sareth collided talon-first with a dragon and tumbled, Alísa clinging to him. Her strength flowed into Sareth and he quickly delivered a death blow to the dragon in his talons. Sareth spread his wings wide to stop their fall, rising quickly to pursue the dragons attacking Saynan. He reveled in the power gained by her song—joy coursing through his veins, even as he moved to attack his former clanmates. Alísa reached out with her mind to grasp some of that joy, trying to overcome her dread.

"Look out!"

"Sesína? What—"

A collision from beneath threw Alísa from Sareth's back. Her heart stopped as red jaws snapped shut around Sareth's neck, viciously wrenching his mind from hers in death. Hot dragon blood spurted in all directions as Alísa tumbled backward through the sky.

She faced the ground, her heart pounding, her arms flailing as she tried to slow her fall. She twisted, trying to catch a glimpse of one of her dragons who might catch her. Instead, she caught the terrible red scales of the monster who had ripped Sareth from her, who still held her friend's neck in his massive jaws.

Rorenth!

The beast let Sareth's limp body fall. Then he turned his eye to Alísa and watched her, roaring in his might.

"SO SHALL YOU FALL, ALONG WITH ALL WHO DARE TURN ON ME!"

With burning eyes, he dove after her, his teeth bared, each gleaming fang as long as Alísa's arm. He would catch her—snap her in half as he had snapped Sareth's neck. No song would stop her fall, but perhaps she could end Rorenth before he ended her.

"Bind!"

Rorenth's mind pressed against her attack and speared through her, ending her song with a cry of pain.

Trumpets of alarm sounded all around her, but she couldn't tell who they belonged to. She couldn't focus on anything except the jaws opening above her. He could swallow her whole.

Panic rushed over her as she twisted and rolled in her uncontrolled decent, closing her throat against another song. She would never see her family again, never give them the chance to turn. Sesína would die of a broken heart.

Fire brewed in Rorenth's throat, and Alísa forced her fear aside—her last thoughts would be honorable.

"Destroy him, my clan. Do not let him escape justice!"

Alísa shut her eyes tight as flames leapt from Rorenth's mouth.

"Singer!"

"Chrí?"

Heat and psychic pain battered Alísa, but no flames touched her. The screams of death accompanying the blast didn't belong to her. She opened her eyes, seven tiny charred bodies falling with her, wing-lights out, eye lights either gone or fading. Horror seized her heart as she recognized an amethyst glow.

Chrí.

Falier's heart pounded in his throat as Alísa continued to fall, each beat accented by Graydonn's wing-strokes. They were nearly to her, but so was Rorenth—would the rest of the dreki save her if flames poured forth again?

The creatures encircled the beast as he roared with fury. Rorenth twisted to blast more of them with his flames, raising more tiny screams of death from the few too slow to escape.

Graydonn's voice broke into his thoughts. *"They're trying to mind-choke him, but he's killing and wounding them too quickly. We can help them."*

Falier shook his head. *"Alísa is our first pri—"*

"I've got her, boys," Sesína's voice echoed through the clan's mind-link, her ebony form racing up directly beneath Alísa. *"Help the dreki!"*

Graydonn pulled up, pointing his muzzle at the brutish alpha. Rorenth seized, then broke free, seized again, then blasted more with fire. The dreki were losing.

"*Watch the astral plane,*" Graydonn said, almost upon him. "*Seal the gap. I'll attend to the physical.*"

Falier closed his eyes and saw it—the dreki's multicolored patterns fading into and out of white, shimmering over Rorenth's bright yellow, then breaking apart as he speared through it. Falier shot a bolt of energy at the brute, only then realizing he didn't know how to perform a mind-choke. The bolt speared into Rorenth, and the beast turned his eyes on them.

"*It's a steady flow of power,*" Graydonn supplied, changing course. "*Spread it over him and seal the gaps!*"

Falier shot again as Rorenth drew closer, gritting his teeth against the power. He tried to keep it constant, pouring his energy over Rorenth like oil in a pan. The green power spread, then Rorenth speared through it. Falier cried out, but turned it to a shout of effort, pressing his power further, through the pain. Again, Rorenth speared through, but this time Falier didn't make a sound. He changed direction, his power slamming against the dreki's.

The dreki latched on, holding to his energy like desperate talons. Falier hissed as the pain echoed through his mind, then pushed further, drawing all the energy he could muster from Graydonn and himself. Rorenth's body seized up, but his mind still fought, punching through.

"*Get ready to seal, and hang on tight!*"

Graydonn slammed into Rorenth with a roar, digging his talons into the alpha's side and belly. Rorenth screamed and batted him away, sending Graydonn tumbling through the air, but Rorenth's concentration broke in the process. Clinging white-knuckled, Falier's power flowed together with the dreki's, sealed the gaps, and held. Rorenth's mind squirmed against them as they immobilized him—pricking, biting, wriggling—but he couldn't get free of the choke or spread his wings to cushion his fall.

With a bone-shattering crack, Rorenth hit the ground. The struggle ceased, and after a moment of caution, the dreki pulled their power back. No one, not even a dragon so great as he, could have survived that fall.

Falier slumped against Graydonn's spine as he ended the flow of psychic energy. Roars of victory sounded Rorenth's death and spurred trumpets of fear from the rest of his clanmates.

"*Sesína has the Singer, and their alpha is dead,*" Koriana's voice came through. "*Finish it now!*"

All around them, their clanmates rallied and Rorenth's retreated. Graydonn's breaths puffed beneath Falier, but like the others, he turned to pursue the next target. Just a little bit more.

45

EMPATHY

Alísa trembled in Sesína's grip, dangling over verdant grasses, clutching Chrí to her chest. She breathed rapidly, trying to make sense of a world turned upside down. Moments rushed through her mind over and over again.

Sareth's death.

Falling uncontrollably.

Rorenth's gleaming teeth and flames.

His power cutting through her mind-choke.

Chrí's tiny, labored breaths against her breast.

"Breathe, Alísa. It's over. I'm taking you down. You'll be okay."

Sesína's words flowed into her, but were quickly chased out by Alísa's own mind.

"I'm dying."

"No, you're not," Sesína insisted. *"You're safe."*

"I'm dying!"

Sesína's voice softened as understanding and grief entered her. *"No, Alísa. Chrí is dying."*

The words hit her like stones. A sob wracked her body as she rebelled against them. *"No. Chrí can't die. She's so small and kind. She can't!"*

Sesína landed on her hind legs, gently lowering Alísa to the ground. Alísa knelt and stroked Chrí's neck as the drek's breathing slowed. She opened her mouth to speak, but sorrow choked her from the inside.

"Sesína, please connect me to her."

"I don't know if that's a good id—"

"I won't let her die alone!" Alísa growled.

Sesína didn't react to Alísa's outburst, instead lowering to her belly and draping a wing over her shoulder. More pain entered Alísa as Sesína connected them, but she forced herself to remain upright. She had to be strong. For Chrí.

Soft images flowed from the little drek. The céilí where they first met. Dancing in the air at Alísa's calls. A drek with a red mane curled around two sparkling eggs.

Alísa tried to smile through her tears. *"Is that your family?"*

Chrí sent an image of her and the red drek nuzzling in a tree.

Alísa's heart became heavier. *"I'll find them. I'll tell them of your bravery."* She sobbed harder, her whole body quaking with the force. *"You weren't supposed to do that. Thank you."*

Their connection dimmed. *"Love."*

Alísa shut her eyes tightly as the link ended, her heart wrenching in two. "I—love—you—too," she whispered between sobs.

Sesína nuzzled her cheek with a low purr. No words, only sorrow and love.

A chirp brought Alísa's eyes up. Five other dreki hovered in the air around her. One was Laen, Selene's friend. Chrí's friend. The drek lowered herself in front of Alísa, her emerald eyes dimming with grief.

"Release," she ordered gently, her name and the feeling of rain dripping off leaves filling Alísa's mind.

Alísa shut her eyes and pressed Chrí's body close one last time before holding the heroic drek up to her kin. She pressed her lips together and closed her eyes, unable to bear the sight of the charred body.

Bright light brought her to open her eyes again. Each drek glowed as shimmering specks of light separated from them and floated to Chrí. They surrounded her, glowing brightly around the body until they obscured it. After a moment of silence, the weight of Chrí's body lifted from Alísa's hands and the specks scattered, leaving amethyst sparkles in their wake.

The new sparkles twisted in the air, dancing above Alísa's hands. They circled behind her neck and through her hair, tugging gently as Chrí's wings and tail had done so many times. Then, with a little trill, they rose into the sky.

Laen watched as Chrí disappeared into the clouds. *"Free."*

Alísa pressed her lips together. Chrí might be free, but that didn't make things better for those she left behind. For her mate and unhatched children. For her friends. Her freedom left an empty hole in Alísa's heart, one that felt like it might never be filled again. Chrí had been the first she ever told of her relationship with the dragons, a fierce protector, and the one who brought her here to save the lives of so many humans and dragons. And now, she was gone.

Sesína pulled Alísa close. *"I'm sorry."*

Alísa leaned against the warm scales and closed her eyes. She tried to focus solely on their connection, allowing Sesína's presence to comfort her. She had known many good men and women who had lost their lives in this war. Now she knew a dragon and multiple dreki too.

When would it end? How many more would she see snuffed out before her eyes?

Chrí.

"Alísa." Koriana's voice came through softly.

She looked up, blinking away tears to see the dreki gone and Koriana and others standing nearby. She couldn't bring herself to take roll—what if someone else was missing?

The dragoness bowed her head. *"I'm sorry, but you are needed. It's not over."*

Sesína growled. *"Let her be."*

But Koriana was right, and they both knew it. Alísa sat up straight, tears still falling.

"What is it?"

"All that are left of Rorenth's clan have fled, but Tora says there are still two eggs and a hatchling in the nurse's cave. Her son Q'rill is there now, trying to calm the hatchling, but the little one's in turmoil. She will need to be restrained. He cannot carry both her and the eggs."

Tora stepped up, urgency pulsing from her. *"The slayers are checking the caves now. It won't be long before they find this one—it may be too late to send more dragons to the cave to take all three."* Tora's eyes dimmed with the weight of her words. *"Should Q'rill save the hatchling, or the eggs?"*

The question was a fist to Alísa's gut, stealing her breath and stinging her eyes with renewed tears. Save a single hatchling who would suffer more than eggs would? Or save two eggs, rescuing more innocents?

How could anyone make such a choice?

She shook her head. *"Can you take us to them, Tora?"*

Tora's head pulled back and tilted. *"Yes, but the slayers——"*

"Q'rill is Illuminated to you?"

"Yes."

Alísa stood, resting a hand on Sesína's withers to steady herself. *"Good. Tell him to grab the eggs and go. You lead Koriana and me to the cave. We will not engage the slayers unless we have to."*

"I'm coming too," Sesína said.

"No! I am not losing you to my father." She looked Sesína in the eyes. *"This time, you will listen to me."*

Sesína huffed. *"I will not!"*

Graydonn padded to Koriana's side, Falier still on his back and looking exhausted. *"We will stay with her, Sesína. We will see her back safely. You have our word."*

Alísa fixed her eyes on Sesína. *"I'm trusting you to lead the rest of our clan far from here, somewhere the slayers won't be able to find them. We need rest, and I'll be able to find my way back to you through our bond."*

Sesína's tail slashed the air in agitation, but then her eyes dimmed. *"Fine."*

Koriana entered the conversation again. *"Rayna is still alive, but with her wing ripped through she will need assistance. Though you all tire, get above the clouds so the slayers cannot see where you go. And you must send someone to retrieve Aree. Lead well, little one."*

Sesína lifted her head, her eyes still dim, but her stance proud and purposeful.

"I will."

Alísa kissed Sesína's nose, then hurried to Koriana's side. The dragoness crouched and offered her muzzle as a step, as she had the first time they flew together. Alísa took the help gratefully.

"Just a little more, Alísa. Take heart."

Koriana's tenderness nearly broke her down into tears again. She was spent in every way, but she would not leave the hatchling to die by her father's hands.

Never again.

Alísa sang softly as they neared the cave, praying that the slayers further down the mountain wouldn't see where they entered. Her voice cracked and certain notes wouldn't come, but she kept it up as best she could.

They didn't pass Q'rill on their way, but Tora assured them he was still safe inside the cave, refusing to leave without Iila, the hatchling.

"He is tender and kind," Tora said, a mother's pride filling her voice. *"In Rorenth's clan, those qualities make a dragon a target, but he never allowed that to change him. He fought well today, as he was taught, but he prefers caring for young ones to anything else."*

Tiny trumpets and shrieks echoed from inside one of the larger caves in Rorenth's mountain, each one ripping through Alísa's heart and adding to her grief. She hadn't considered this possibility. A part of her was repulsed by the thought of hatchlings having to live under those who quite possibly killed their parents, but what else could she do? Certainly not abandon them to die. Even if their parents were unrepentant, these little ones hadn't had a choice in the matter.

The darkness of the cave enveloped her as Tora led them inside. The cave was wide with a relatively low ceiling, forcing each dragon to land quickly and shuffle out of the way for the others.

Alísa's eyes adjusted to the darkness quickly. Q'rill stood on the right, his wings opened as a barrier between the eggs and a little silver hatchling, perhaps no more than two weeks old. The hatchling's shriek echoed sharply through the cave, and with their sightline came her words:

"Traitor! Serpent! Betrayers, all of you!" Iila. She turned her eyes to Alísa and flared her wings out. *"You follow this vermin to our doom! I hate you! I hate you!"*

Her pain enveloped Alísa, sharpening the sword already stabbing her heart. *Chrí.*

No, she had to focus. Somehow, Iila needed her help.

"Koriana. Lower me, please."

Koriana crouched. *"Stay close. She might attack you."*

"Maybe I deserve it."

Graydonn nosed Alísa's arm. *"You did what you had to do."*

"Then why is everyone else suffering for it?"

Iila hissed. *"You carry a slayer on your back—how dare you call yourself a dragon?"*

Q'rill lowered his head. *"Iila, I know you're sad, but the Singer can help."*

Iila screamed again. *"Traitor! Murderer! Serpent!"*

Tora faced the cave entrance. *"Her shrieking will call the slayers. Hurry, Singer."*

Iila's pain and turmoil ripped through Alísa once more, and she cried out with her, falling to her knees on the stone floor. She shut her eyes tight as memories of ceremonies past poured over her—the emotions of hatchlings had always been more visceral than those of adults. The raw pain of a young one who had never known such sorrow before, with no filters to dull it, crushed her like an avalanche.

What was she supposed to do? Iila was traumatized, and rightly so, and now her pain called black spots to Alísa's vision. She pushed against it with her empathy, first with calm, then with anything and everything she could muster, but the pain and rage and sorrow only pounded harder in her skull.

"Alísa," Graydonn said, *"stop fighting it. You'll fall unconscious."*

Alísa choked on a sob. *"If I don't—fight it—I will."*

She opened her eyes as Iila screamed once more, her heart wrenching within her. The poor thing. She was alone. She had never been alone before, and the pain of complete solitude was breaking her heart. She masked it with rage, but it was there all the same.

Graydonn came beside her and lowered to his belly. *"You've been trained to fight feeling dragon emotions your whole life, but you don't have to. You breathe in human emotions, positive and negative, every day, and it makes you stronger. Now you've learned to accept positive dragon emotions, but you still fight the negative with all your might. You were made to feel it, Alísa-Dragon-Singer."*

Alísa trembled with the strain of pushing against the sorrow, and Graydonn nudged her arm with his muzzle.

"I once told you to own your power rather than fight it. Now is the time. You were made to help dragons with your song—you can help Iila now. Breathe it in—all

of it—and show her your heart."

Alísa looked up as Iila screamed again. Her empathy had almost always been a curse, a hindrance to her life as a slayer, a weakness rather than a strength.

But now, staring at this little dragon who had no one left in the world, she saw the truth in Graydonn's words. It was her empathy that set her on this path. It had pushed her to free Graydonn. To bond with Sesína. To refuse to turn her back on her people. It was a part of her, something the Maker had purposefully given her, just like the rest of her Dragon Singer abilities.

Maybe it was time to embrace this too.

She let go and allowed her empathy to flow through the space. She felt the distress of the others in the room, and then she felt the intensity of Iila's grief. She pushed herself off the ground and staggered forward. Koriana spoke a warning, but Alísa barely heard it, focused solely on the terrified, raging hatchling in front of her.

Pain and sorrow bubbled within her until it poured out in a wordless song, sung for Iila and the sorrow they now shared.

Iila stared at her, her eyes beginning to glaze. Her mouth fell open in a snarl, and though her wings stayed spread, they stilled. Slowly, their mental connection deepened until Alísa could speak telepathically, and she continued her lament, even as she spoke soothingly to the hatchling.

"I know you're afraid and in pain, Iila. I feel your sorrow as my own. I'm sorry for my part in it—I never would have wished this on you. We came to bring a chance for repentance, and then to bring justice for those who refused. We didn't come to harm the innocent. We will not hurt you."

Iila's sorrow didn't diminish, but as Alísa continued, the mask of rage melted away. The fire in her eyes dimmed, and she let her wings droop to her sides. At her heart, she was a child, like any of the hatchlings Alísa had been forced to watch be tortured and killed.

Not this hatchling. Not this time.

"We will take care of you and these eggs until the time comes that you can take care of yourself. Then you may decide whether to stay with us or go your own way. We will not keep you against your will, nor will we retaliate if you decide to leave. Until then, we will care for you. Don't fear, Iila. Rest, and don't fear."

Iila's eyes drooped. Her grief was still potent, and probably would be for a long time, but her resistance was gone. *"I see truth in you, Singer. I believe you."*

Alísa smiled softly. *"Good. We're going to take you and the eggs to our camp now. All will be well."*

She turned to the others, and it was like the whole world had faded away and was slowly coming back into focus. All the dragons watched her, their eyes dimmed with sorrow, entranced, though she hadn't tried to pull them into her song. Only Falier was still awake, looking back at the entrance and slapping Graydonn's neck frantically.

"W—What's wrong?"

Then she heard it. The crunch of boots on rock, the clatter of metal on metal.

Slayers.

"Everyone, we need t-t-t-t-to g-go, now!"

The dragons snapped out of their trances. Koriana and Tora faced the entrance and growled in their throats while reestablishing the clan mind-link. Human voices snaked into the space, their unintelligible words almost as frantic as Alísa's heart.

"Q'rill, take the eggs. Iila, get on Tora's back. Move!"

Alísa waited for the dragons to follow her orders, watching as Iila clambered onto Tora's back. Koriana crouched for her, still facing the entrance for a quick getaway.

"Get ready to sing, Alísa. I fear we are too late to avoid confrontation."

Alísa whirled to the other dragons, focusing on Tora and Q'rill, who didn't know the situation. *"Do not attack unless you are—"*

Her words were drowned out by a battle cry, fierce and raging. Metal scraped against metal as three slayers formed a barrier at the entrance of the cave, their shields overlapping each other like a dragon's scales. They dropped behind their shields, expecting fire.

Alísa ran forward, passing Koriana. *"Everyone, when I sing, fly. Koriana and I will go last."*

"STOP!" She shouted, flinging her hands up just as heads began peeking over shields. Her voice squeaked with overuse, her throat rasping, but still she spoke.

"W—we're on the s-same side!"

The shield on the end dropped with a clang that reverberated throughout the cave. Copper hair stuck to the man's sweaty face, clashing beautifully with a red streak of war-paint across his forehead. His eyes were so filled with shock and fear, it was a wonder he didn't drop his spear too. But there he crouched, his lips moving, though no sound passed through.

Then, as though his *anam* had left and then returned, Karn stood and grasped the spear in both hands.

"Get behind me, Alísa." He growled at the dragons. "I won't let them take you again!"

The other men stood with him, Kallar and L'non, both raising their shields and grasping their swords.

"*Alísa...*" Koriana warned.

"It's n—n—not—"

Karn charged, pulling his arm back to launch his spear. Alísa had no time to think, only to sing.

"Bind!"

His body seized, then collapsed. Only his eyes moved, wide with shock and betrayal. He didn't even fight as her telepathy held him down.

Kallar shouted, rage rumbling from his throat, and ran at her next. She pushed her powers, trying to engulf him in the mind-choke too, but he broke through as easily as Rorenth.

Graydonn roared and Falier threw his hand forward, their combined power constraining Kallar. He, too, fell to the ground, his war-cry strangling in his throat.

"*Fly!*" Alísa ordered. "*Fly now!*"

Q'rill pressed past the slayers and flew out the entrance with the eggs, L'non's sword just barely missing him. Tora followed, smacking L'non with her tail on the way past and flinging him back out of the cave. Alísa's heart stopped as he cried out.

Graydonn and Falier followed, and as soon as they passed, Koriana's giant paw wrapped around Alísa's middle and lifted her into the air. Stone gave way to sky, and the dragons pushed through it, leaving the slayers far behind. Alísa caught a glimpse of L'non scrambling to stand about ten feet down from the cave.

Alive. Praise the Maker.

Calm pressed into her, foreign and terrible as it collided with everything burning inside her. Koriana's voice soothed over Alísa, carrying the peace deeper into her frantic mind.

"You can end the mind-choke now, Alísa. He can't get to us anymore."

Alísa's voice squeaked to a stop, and as soon as it ended, the tears began. She had choked him. Papá. He hadn't waited, hadn't listened, and she had choked him to the ground.

"You saved your clan. You did what you had to do."

"But I didn't get the chance to tell him. To show him!" She sobbed. *"Why won't he listen to me?"*

"He was afraid, dear one. He had the same instinct of every parent when they think their child is in danger." Koriana huffed, almost to herself. *"It was far easier for me to hate him before now, but there is a good father within him. You will get your chance to tell him everything, but tonight, try to rest in the knowledge that even I could see his love for you."*

Alísa shivered in Koriana's paw as they rose toward the clouds, the chill of the wind ripping through clothing, skin, and bone. She shut her eyes against it and tried to relax in the dragoness' strong grip. She wanted nothing more than to fall into unconsciousness, where her father's wide eyes and Kallar's screams of rage could no longer haunt her. Where blood and flames and sorrows didn't exist and the world could be at peace for moments or years.

"Guide us to Sesína, Alísa. Then your work will be done."

"Sesína." Alísa reached for their bond and sent her words trembling through it. *"Are you safe?"*

Sesína's concern for her preceded her words, its warmth spreading over her like a blanket. *"We are. We're over the Nissen, looking for a good place to land. Come find us."*

Alísa focused until their bond appeared in the astral plane, stretching into the distance. *"We're on our way."*

"Stay strong, dragon-heart. You're almost home."

46

PURSUIT

It took perhaps thirty minutes to find the others, but it might as well have been hours. Everyone was silent on the flight, with random emotions fluttering on the wind, too indirect to affect Falier's own. They poked and prodded him, as though mocking his lack of understanding, until he finally raised his shield and blocked them out.

How did empaths do it, living their lives without the ability to create a shield against the emotions of others? The constant battle would be maddening.

He glanced at Alísa, still hanging limply in Koriana's paw. She looked unconscious, though he knew she guided Koriana toward Sesína and the others. His heart ached for her—if he was worn out, how much more she, who had fought for just as long, lost two friends in the space of five minutes, and then had to fight her own father?

Graydonn landed clumsily, and Falier rubbed a hand over his neck.

"I'm all right," the dragon said. *"Only weary, like everyone else."*

Falier slid down Graydonn's side and barely caught himself before he fell on his face. His legs wobbled beneath him as life prickled back in, and he hissed as pain entered alongside.

Sesína bolted past them, galloping across the small clearing to offer Alísa a steadying shoulder. Even from here, he could tell Alísa was shaking uncontrollably, her face contorted in pain. At Sesína's touch, however, the clouds over Alísa's face lifted, as though Sesína's shoulder bore more than just physical weight.

"She's taking on some of the pain Alísa bears," Graydonn said, once again

answering an unspoken question. It didn't feel nearly as intrusive as Falier had anticipated before the bond. What would the battle have been like if he hadn't been afraid, if they had entered the fray already bonded? Would lives, or even just time and energy, have been spared?

Graydonn didn't dignify that unspoken question with a response.

The dragons spread out in the small clearing, family groups sticking together. The hatchling, Iila, lay beside Saynan and Aree, perhaps having sensed the dragoness' motherly instinct. Harenn stayed with Faern and Komi, and Tora and Q'rill kept the orphaned eggs with them.

On the other side of Koriana, Alísa and Sesína stood beside Rayna, the dragoness with the ripped wing. Rayna's ebony mate, Korin, draped a wing over her back, the vulnerable underside of his wings resting lightly over her spines. What a dangerous place for him to be as his mate moaned and flinched in pain, yet there he stayed, watching over her with dimmed sapphire eyes full of care.

Alísa knelt at Rayna's head and placed a hand on her scaled cheek. The dragoness was big enough to kill her with a single swipe of a paw or snap of her mighty jaws, yet Alísa showed her all the tenderness she had given little Iila, rubbing a hand over Rayna's face and surely speaking mental words of comfort.

Rayna moaned with pain again, causing Alísa to flinch, and it took everything within Falier not to run over and separate them. Alísa was giving too much of herself. It was a wonder she hadn't fallen unconscious.

Sesína prodded Alísa from behind and Alísa backed away from Rayna, placing her hand on Sesína once more.

Praise the Maker for that dragon.

They returned to Koriana and Graydonn, and Alísa looked over the other dragons. Sesína established the full clan's connection for the first time since the battle ended, and Alísa's tired psychic voice came through.

"Thank you all, for what you did today. I know it was at great cost. Now rest. Tomorrow—" She stopped with a sniffle, and images of Chrí and Sareth slipped into Falier's mind. *"Tomorrow is a new day."*

Then she sang, her voice light and breathy with fatigue. It was a song Falier recognized, a memory from long ago, a lullaby sung by his mother in the midst of a thunderstorm. With it came a peaceful sleepiness, one Falier felt breaking down all the barriers around Graydonn's mind and settling deep within the dragon.

The song knocked at the doors to Falier's mind too, its call so wonderfully tempting. But as every dragon, including Sesína, settled into sleep, a terrible image entered his mind—one of Alísa left to bear the remnants of their pain alone, with only the darkening sky as her companion.

He raised the telepathic shield Kerrik had taught him all those years ago and let the song pound against it.

"*Hush,*" it called. "*Peace. Sleep.*"

No.

The song only lasted perhaps a minute before the dragons all slept soundly. Alísa cut off the song in the middle of a word, her voice squeaking to a halt, as though unable to go on. She had been singing all day, so perhaps that was true.

She collapsed to her hands and knees on the ground, her eyes tightly shut and her mouth open in a silent scream. Falier rushed over, sliding to his knees in front of her.

"Alísa?"

She trembled, her fingers gripping the blades of grass beneath her. He received no answer, only her quiet gasps of breath. He bent lower and placed a hand on her shoulder.

A jolt of pain zapped where his finger touched her skin, traveling up into his skull. Rorenth's gleaming teeth and brewing flames shot into his mind, and he instinctively jerked his hand away with a yelp.

Alísa gasped, louder this time. "D-d-d—don't t-touch me." She sounded more afraid than angry.

"Is that what you're feeling right now?" he whispered. "Your empathy?"

She didn't answer.

"Did I take some of it away?"

Another sob was her only reply, her body jerking from its weight. Swallowing back his fear, he reached to lift her chin.

"Don't t-t-touch me."

He pulled his hand back and placed it on his knee. "You really don't want me to? Or you're afraid of hurting me?"

She tensed at his question. "It—it's not your b-b-burden to bear."

His heart twisted as she shook again. *It could be. Can't you see it?* But he couldn't say it that way—not now, while she was so vulnerable. If she didn't return his feelings, she might not allow him to help her. Or worse, she might play along simply for the comfort.

But a friend could bear burdens just as easily as a lover. Perhaps more so.

He reached out his hand. "You've been carrying everyone else all day. Let me carry you, if only for a little while."

"I can't put this on you," she whispered, her eyes finally lifting to his. The last vestiges of daylight shone over the tears in her eyes and the trails falling down her cheeks.

He swallowed his fear and placed his hand over hers, curling his fingers around her palm.

"You aren't."

The pain shot through him, burning in his skull as images plagued him. In his mind's eye, Sareth's death flashed, Rorenth's teeth gleamed, and bloody remains of dead dragons and dreki littered the ground. Rayna's fear echoed through him, Q'rill's unrest from upheaval shuddered through, and Iila's rage and grief nearly broke his heart.

The worst of it came when her father's face appeared, then morphed into his own father's, wide-eyed and open-mouthed as if Falier had just stabbed him in the stomach. It took all his strength not to jerk his hand away again.

Then the visions cleared, and he saw her face, the crevices of pain and anxiety smoothing into relief. She breathed through her nose, still heavily, but without the gulping gasps. It filled him with the strength to hold on, to press through the pain and never let her go.

Her eyes met his and filled with worry. She tried to pull back, but he held her fast.

"No. It's okay."

Alísa stared at him, more tears filling her searching eyes. The sorrow they now shared diminished slightly, giving way to something else, an emotion that reached from mind to mind and pulled them together.

A tiny smile pressed at the corners of Alísa's lips, and she lunged forward, wrapping her free arm around his ribs and laying her head on his shoulder. Shocked by her sudden move, he returned the embrace gingerly.

"Thank you," she whispered.

The shift in emotions suddenly became clear—it was love. Not just his, but hers as well. Alísa loved him back with a love that helped her through the sorrows she now bore.

Reassured, Falier tightened his embrace and rested his head against hers. More than anything he wanted to tell her he loved her too, but she needed different words today. Hopefully, she would understand.

"I'll stay as long as you need."

As though his words had been permission, her breathing became ragged against him with fresh sobs. "I—I'm n—not f-fighting it. I'm d-d-d-doing what G—Graydonn s-said. It—It's just s-s-so much."

Falier nodded against her. "I know."

Chrí flashed through his mind, and Alísa's sorrow came again like tiny talons in his heart. Then Sareth, the strange blue dragon who had only been part of their clan for a few minutes. Her grief for him was different than that for Chrí, but still potent.

"He—He let me g-go. When K-K-K—" A sob stopped her progress. She pulled her hand from his and placed a finger to his throbbing temple. Though the pain didn't increase, he winced at the change of entry point.

She pulled her hand away. "S-S-Sorry."

"It's okay."

Falier took her hand again and shifted, his legs starting to go numb from kneeling. She pulled back to look at him, questions in her pain-filled eyes. He looked back at Sesína, sleeping only a few feet away. Leaning against her would offer rest and warmth, and perhaps more comfort for Alísa.

"Come with me."

They rose to their knees and sat back against Sesína's side. Falier kept an arm around Alísa, pulling her head onto his shoulder again, keeping their hands firmly clasped at their stomachs.

Is this okay? Are you comfortable?

She nodded against his shoulder and breathed deeply. Sesína's stomach expanded and deflated behind them in an easy rhythm, each inhale stretching her scales apart and releasing more warmth into the chill of the evening. The dragoness hadn't even flinched when they leaned against her, still happily asleep from Alísa's lullaby.

"She tried to stay awake," Alísa said, her own fatigue creeping into her mind-voice. *"But I wouldn't let her. She had already given so much of herself today. They all have."* Her hand shifted in his. *"You have. You don't have to stay."*

He shook his head. *"You were telling me about Sareth?"*

Maybe that wasn't the best thing to remind her of, as her heart became heavy again. But she had wanted to tell him before, even without him asking. Perhaps talking through her grief would help in some way.

"He guarded Rorenth's territory at the place where Koriana, Graydonn, and I entered on our way east. He was a skeptic when Koriana told him I was a Dragon Singer. He called me a scared hatchling, and I was—I feel so much older now."

She shook her head, as through clearing her thoughts. *"It was his job to either kill me or bring me to Rorenth, but he let us pass, saying he trusted Koriana with me more than he trusted his alpha."*

Alísa shivered as images rose in their minds. *"And look where that got him. Brutally murdered by that monster!"*

Falier gritted his teeth against the bloody memory. *"That isn't your fault, you know."*

"Yes, it is." She pulled back to look him in the eyes. *"I am the alpha, and my clan follows me to both victory and defeat. I don't get to take the credit and not the blame."*

Falier studied her stony expression. Even in moments where she had spoken with authority, Alísa had always retained a certain timidity. Now, he looked back at the chief's daughter—the part that had watched and learned, despite being told she would never be able to rise up and claim that role.

"I could have taken us home to safety, but I chose to send my clan into battle. All of the deaths and injuries that inflict my clan while they follow my orders are on me."

Alísa laid her head back down. *"I once thought I wanted this—to lead, like my father. I was upset when I realized I couldn't, but now..."* She buried her face in his shoulder. *"I don't want this. To be thrust into the fray, to lose those I'm responsible for, to make orphans. Why did the Maker pick me? Why did he pick a scared little girl who can't stomach the violence?"*

Falier blinked back the tears her fear and sorrow brought to his eyes. What could he say to ease her doubts? What would Selene say?

He swallowed. *"I can't speak for the Maker, but I can tell you what I see. I see a woman who cares even when everyone else tells her it isn't worth her time. I see a woman who is sick of the violence and wishes to see it gone from the world, even if it means having to wade through it herself in order to see it happen."*

He turned his head to look at her. Her face was still buried in his shoulder, but her sobs had eased. If only she would look up and allow him to see those beautiful eyes.

"I see a woman who has pushed through fear time and time again. Leaving behind all you've known, living among what our people call beasts, going into battle to save the very people who won't listen to you."

He tightened his embrace, hoping it might convey his sincerity.

"You're one of the strongest women I've ever met, Líse, and I love you."

Time froze.

His mind had slipped—he had thought it, knew it was true, but he wasn't supposed to say it! What a time to confess his love, while she was torn apart from the inside out. Even if she could sense it already, she had just lost friends and fought her family. Betrayed her father.

How could he have been so careless with his thoughts?

"I—I'm sorry." Idiot. He shouldn't apologize for it. *"I mean, you don't have to respond. I shouldn't have said that just now. This is about you, not me, and—"*

"I love you too, Falier."

Her voice was soft, a rasping whisper through trembling lips. She pulled her hand from his and wiped her face on her sleeve with a whispered apology, then looked up at him. Her eyes still glimmered with tears and drooped with fatigue, but the smile on her lips was warm and true.

"I've felt this way for a while now, but tonight…" Her fingertips whispered over his, and he grasped her hand again, allowing the pain and emotions back in, though they seemed only echoes of what he had felt before.

"In all my years of feeling dragon emotions, no one ever tried to help me by taking it on themselves. My father wanted to shield me with a mind-choke, but was afraid that

by doing so I would never get better. Kallar ignored it all until he learned about the pain, then also spoke of shielding me. Neither ever offered to simply take my hand and carry the burden with me."

She pressed her lips together, then allowed the corners of her mouth to lift. *"That's what I've always liked about you. You've reached out to protect me before, and I admire and appreciate that, but far more often you've just stood beside me. So, thank you."*

He gave her a soft smile and squeezed her hand. He had already started them down this road, and she had followed willingly, even run out ahead of him.

What was his next step?

"Alísa, I meant every word I said about you, and though I'm perhaps not yet worthy, I want to pursue you."

He savored the way her blink of surprise gave way to a smile. Though the words weren't a proposal, they were a promise, one of time and words, emotions and deeds. A declaration of his intent to continue exploring their relationship to see where it might one day lead.

But he couldn't walk that path alone.

"Is there a chance that one day you'll let me catch you?"

She looked down, and he couldn't tell if her shoulders shook with sobs or laughter. Either way, her smile was genuine when she met his eyes once more.

"Yes."

47

DRAGON'S EYES

Alísa awoke to Falier stirring beside her, their backs against Sesína and his arm around her. His hand still clasped hers, Falier having refused to leave her to her pain the night before. She blinked her swollen eyes, all the emotions of the night before buzzing in the background of her mind.

Loss, guilt, hope, fear, love.

Love. That one wasn't an echo. That one actively reached from Falier's heart into hers and prodded it, begging it to open. It didn't need to beg, not after weeks of falling into it and hoping against hope that he felt the same way.

She pressed against Falier and he tightened his arm around her, bringing a light smile to her lips.

"How are you feeling?" he whispered drowsily.

"M—M—" She stopped as scratchy pain filled her throat and larynx. Yesterday's songs and shouts had taken their toll.

A psychic connection buzzed to life between them. *"You probably shouldn't talk verbally today, huh?"*

She nodded once. *"Otherwise, I'm feeling much better. I'm going to try letting go now."*

Alísa opened her fingers, and Falier lingered only a moment before releasing her. As soon as they separated, the constant buzz turned to ringing. She breathed low and let it out before standing.

"I can manage. When Sesína wakes, she'll be able to help too. Thank you."

He stood as well, watching her, as though he expected her to collapse any moment.

"I'm fine. Really."

Her stomach growled—it had been a full day since she last ate, two days since her last full meal.

Falier's eyes lit up. *"I think we still have some bread and dried meat. I'll be right back."*

She laughed to herself as he jogged away. *Typical holder boy.*

Dragons stirred around them, some blinking groggily while others stretched sore muscles. Faern, Komi, and Harenn were missing, likely for a morning scouting venture. There could be wayfarers in the area.

Her father flashed in her mind's eye, standing beside Kallar and L'non. His sad eyes weighed down her heart, but she pushed the image away. She had grieved long and hard yesterday, and though her sadness and guilt over that encounter might never truly leave her, she had to press on. She had done what she had to do, and perhaps one day she could share with him the truth about the dragons.

Until then, she couldn't let it drag her back anymore.

Falier came back with both of their packs, courtesy of Aree, who had kept them during the battle.

"Do we need to ration still, or will we make it back to Me'ran today?"

"Come on, Falier," a sleepy female voice sassed. *"You don't know how to find home?"*

Alísa whirled and wrapped her arms around Sesína's neck. She kissed the scaly face, then pulled back to examine her.

"How are you feeling?"

Sesína rose to stretch her back and legs. *"That was the best sleep I've had in a long time. I blame your song, Alísa. It even got Rayna to sleep through her pain."*

Sesína pointed with her muzzle, and Alísa looked at the deep green dragoness. She still lay under Korin's wing, but her head was high and alert. Gingerly, she flexed her wing, then moaned as pain shot through her.

Alísa sucked in a breath at the stab of pain, then breathed it out slowly as it settled back into the constant ringing. She would make it, as would Rayna. Graydonn had made a full recovery after his wing had been torn two months ago. Granted, he hadn't been injured nearly as badly, but there was hope. Maybe someone in Me'ran could help her stitch it and apply healing salves, or maybe dragons had their own healing methods for these injuries.

Time would tell.

"*Did you sleep at all?*" Sesína whispered.

"*I did, actually. Falier helped me through the pain.*"

Sesína cocked her head. "*You didn't put him to sleep too?*"

"*I tried…*"

Falier waved a hand. "So, yes or no? Rationing?"

Alísa looked up at the sun. It was high—late morning.

"*We'll be back this evening. Assuming there are no issues along the way.*"

"Good," he said, drawing the last of the sweetbread from the pack. "I'm starved, and ready to sleep in a bed again. I don't know how you do it, sleeping on the cave floor all of the time."

He broke the bread and gave her half—a fist-sized chunk just beginning to go stale. "You know, now that you don't have to hide who you are anymore, you could stay at the Hold."

Alísa shook her head. "*I'm the alpha, it wouldn't do for me to sleep apart from the clan.*" She glanced at him sideways. "*Or to make it too easy for you catch me.*"

Sesína's eyes darted between the two of them, then brightened with mirth. She whispered knowingly. "*Ah. So this is why you told me to go to sleep. And why you didn't put him to sleep.*"

Heat trickled to Alísa's face. "I assure you this wasn't planned. I tried to—"

"*Sure it wasn't.*" Sesína winked at her before swinging her head and baring a playful fang at Falier. "*Just what do you think you're doing, young slayer? Making moves on my sister without talking to me first?*"

Falier's eyes widened and his body went rigid. "I…"

Alísa pressed her lips together to hold back a grin. Only a second later, Falier relaxed, a smile on his lips. He bowed exaggeratedly to Sesína.

"*My apologies, great dragon, but I felt it best that Alísa herself make the decision, rather than another for her.*"

Sesína chuckle-coughed before turning serious. "*Well spoken. I approve, but know that I'm keeping my eye on you.*" Her tail sliced through the air behind her, the draconic statement of authority.

"*I wouldn't have it any other way.*"

Alísa smiled softly. Both man and dragon had her best interests at heart, and it filled her to overflowing, drowning out the pain and sorrows of the day before.

Today was a new day.

"*Now, I would like to talk to Alísa alone,*" Sesína said. "*She'll be with you for the rest of her breakfast shortly.*"

Falier nodded and picked his way across the grass to Graydonn.

"*I have decided,*" Sesína declared, pulling Alísa's attention to her. Excitement blazed in the young dragoness' eyes. "*Today, I will fly you.*"

Alísa raised an eyebrow. "*After a day like yesterday? You should take more time to recover.*"

"*It's time,*" Sesína hummed, swishing her tail through the air. "*I'm rested and ready. There are eleven other dragons who can catch you if you're so worried about me dropping you.*"

"*You know that's not what worries me. I don't want you to hurt yourself straining to fly.*" She looked past Sesína to Rayna. "*Maker knows we don't need any other injuries.*"

Sesína's voice softened. "*I won't be able to hide my pain from you. We'll stop if it's too much.*" She pressed the bridge of her nose to Alísa's cheek. "*You think you have to carry everyone and that the only reason there are injuries is you weren't strong enough to stop them. This is false. We all gave of our own free will.*"

"*But I'm your alpha. It's my responsibility to take care of you.*"

"*And sometimes the alpha must rest and let the betas step in.*"

Alísa smirked. "*Promoting ourselves, are we?*"

Sesína hummed and pushed her over, and Alísa landed on her backside with a yelp. A twinge of mirth pushed through the dragoness' annoyance.

"*I'm the beta.*"

Alísa chuckled. "*No, you're not.*"

Sesína prodded Alísa's stomach with her muzzle, eliciting a laugh. "*Say it.*"

Alísa pushed back against the dragon's head, but it was no use. Even holding herself back to avoid hurting Alísa, Sesína was far too strong. Sesína shoved her to the ground and placed a paw over her torso, pushing just enough to hold her down. Her emerald eyes brightened with mischievous mirth and she blew hot air in Alísa's face.

"*Say it.*"

"Okay, okay! You're the beta!" Alísa laughed.

"And?"

"And you can fly me home, you big bully!"

Sesína gave a toothy grin and let Alísa up. *"We're going to dominate Graydonn and Falier in the skies!"*

Alísa shifted at the base of Sesína's neck as the dragoness took her first laden strides, muscles rippling under the shining ebony scales. Confidence clashed with apprehension, accented by the aches and pains of the other dragons around them.

"Your nervousness isn't very encouraging," Sesína grumbled. *"To me or the others. I have enough confidence for both of us, but you still need to lead the clan."*

Alísa forced herself to sit a little taller. She surveyed her dragons, almost all of them laden with some burden. Rayna's hurt wing was firmly strapped to her side with strips of Sesína's rock-straps. Korin and Q'rill, the two least-injured dragons besides Aree, stood at her front and hindquarters, ready to bear Rayna for the first leg of the journey. Komi stood at Rayna's side, prepared to fly underneath her in case of problems.

Aree held her egg in her claws, while Saynan carried Iila on his back. The hatchling had refused to speak or eat all morning, even at Alísa's urgings. Understandable, but worrisome.

Tora and Faern each clutched one of the orphaned eggs; they would switch out with the dragons carrying Rayna as the day pressed on. Harenn and Graydonn stood on either side of Sesína, Falier already in position on Graydonn's back.

Sesína began the clan's mind-link unbidden, and Alísa looked to the sky. *"Let's go! Rayna first, to make sure we've got her covered."*

Humiliation wafted from Rayna as Korin and Q'rill lifted her into the air, yet the dragoness held her head high, seemingly fighting to keep hope alive. The inspiration of her hope clashed with the sobering sight of her bound wing, neither cancelling out the other.

Sesína stretched and flexed her wings as the other dragons began taking off. She shifted her weight from foot to foot, and Alísa gripped her spine tighter, leaning with the movement.

Falier gave them a teasing smile. "You two nervous?"

Sesína huffed and smacked Graydonn's wing. *"I'll show you nervous."*

Graydonn blew hot air at Sesína's face. *"I didn't say anything."*

"Whatever," Sesína looked to the sky. *"We're flying!"*

Graydonn and Harenn each broke into a trot before launching into the air. Alísa jolted against the spine behind her as Sesína followed them. Her heart beat heavily against her ribs, fueled by excitement and apprehension. One mighty flap, and Sesína vaulted into the air.

Alísa gripped hard as they climbed together, Sesína banking into an upward spiral. Her wings beat furiously until they rose above the trees into the open sky. The jolting, uneven ride smoothed as Sesína caught an air-current under her wings. The dragoness trumpeted in elation and Alísa began laughing.

"You did it!"

Sesína lifted her head to follow the young males and put on a burst of speed. The wind flowing over and around them invigorated Alísa and she drank deeply of the rapidly-cooling air. Her joy mingled with Sesína's as they rose higher and higher. Though their flight today had purpose—getting home to Me'ran—no mission pushed them to their destination. Today could be about the journey.

"Sing for me, Alísa, just a tiny song. I want to take you to the clouds!"

Sesína's excitement spread a grin wide across Alísa's face. She sang barely above a whisper, keeping most of the pain at bay, yet strength still flowed into Sesína. As they rose faster and higher, a laugh interrupted her song, all the pain and sorrow she had felt earlier melting away in their flight. Guilt prickled—she could not forget those they'd lost—but she latched onto Sesína's elation even more tightly.

"The dreki didn't save you for guilt, Alísa. Mourn them, yes, but don't forget to live the life they ensured you would have."

Alísa pressed her lips together and nodded firmly. It was the same with fallen slayers—though they died in battle the day before, even their loved ones would attend and partake in the celebrations of victory. To do anything less would dishonor the deceased's sacrifice as they watched from the Maker's halls. It was time to focus on the present.

"Sesína, I want to know what it's really like to fly. Can you share your vision with me?"

"Of course."

Alísa closed her eyes and allowed Sesína's view to flood her mind. Everything grew into sharp focus. The leaves and needles on the trees beneath them were visible as individuals, the birds in the distant skies recognizable by species, the scales on Graydonn's back and curls on Falier's head distinct as they flew past.

The extra details pulled Alísa further into the experience, but it wasn't enough. She opened her link to Sesína wider, allowing Sesína's emotions to flood her own mind. The dragoness followed suit and their thoughts flowed unhindered.

Flight brought a lightness to Sesína, even beyond Alísa's own delight. It was pure freedom to her, as if she were a gust of wind in a dance with the others, air currents at once clashing and complimenting, flowing and colliding.

Alísa let go of herself. Though she acutely felt her body holding onto Sesína, gripping the spine with her hands and the scaled neck and shoulders with her thighs, she wasn't simply Alísa anymore. And though she felt the effort that went into each wing-stroke, the tired muscles both protesting and reveling in the exercise, she wasn't Sesína either. She and Sesína simply were.

Clouds rushed at them as they rose, cold air clearing away any remaining drowsiness. Droplets pummeled them, wetting scales and skin in the bright fog, and then, sunlight! Graydonn and Harenn chased each other in and out of the clouds, and Alísa and Sesína joined them, jumping between blurry, wet half-light and the clearest daylight they had ever seen.

Harenn came at them from behind, and they turned sharply to slap his neck with the blunt underside of their tail. They laughed with delight and dove into the clouds again. The feeling of diving into gravity's hold was pure adrenaline and they let it take them back beneath the clouds.

Sesína and Alísa passed the adult dragons and sped toward the treetops, stomachs pressing upward, rapture filling their hearts. They dared gravity to hold them down, then pulled up just before crashing into the treetops.

They banked to the left. To the right. Faster and faster until they were sure they would disintegrate and become the wind itself. They lifted their voice in a final songful trumpet as they climbed once more, spiraling in an upward current toward their clan. They breathed heavily, spent from the physical and mental exertion.

Alísa opened her eyes, pulling her mind back to herself. Her mind relaxed like shoulders just rid of their burden, though the joy that had accompanied the exercise more than made up for the strain. With training, perhaps they would be able to join for longer periods without tiring.

"Thank you for sharing that with me," Sesína thrummed beneath her. *"I told you we could fly together."*

"As if that was what you meant." Alísa laughed as she flexed arms and feet, trying to feel at home again in her own body.

Harenn and Graydonn trumpeted above them, still dipping into and out of the clouds in play. Sesína's desires lay with them, though she tried to hide it.

"Why don't you take me back to Koriana for a bit and go play unhindered? You can take me flying again afterward."

Sesína hesitated. *"I can keep going with you for a while. I don't need to do anything fancy."*

"And miss your chance to trounce Harenn?" Alísa chuckled. *"You've proven you can carry me, and you'll do so again. Go have fun!"*

Sesína sighed and slowed her pace. *"Fine. But if anyone asks, I let you off because you wanted to talk to our new clanmates, not because I wanted to maneuver better."*

They fell back, Sesína lowering until she was just above Koriana, so close that Sesína could touch the gray dragoness if she stretched out her forelegs. Both dragons spread their wings in a glide, and, gulping back apprehension, Alísa grabbed two of Sesína's spines and swung over her side. Her feet could almost touch Koriana's outstretched wing, and she let go, landing wobbly and bending forward to catch herself with her hands.

She quickly and carefully made her way to her seat at the base of Koriana's neck. Once she was settled, Sesína took off toward her playmates.

"You've done well, Alísa," Koriana said softly, using a private mind-link.

"Between your strength in leadership and your growing bond with Sesína, you're coming into your own as a Dragon Singer. I couldn't be more proud of you."

Memories of nearly being killed by Rorenth rose in Alísa's mind. *"You are kind. I have far to go."*

Koriana arched her neck to fix a single eye on Alísa. *"Have you known me to lie to you?"*

Alísa looked away. *"You don't know what went on inside of me. I felt like a warrior dragoness for part of the battle, but when Sareth was killed—No. Before that. Maybe it's my fault he..."* She shook her head. She couldn't let herself think like that. *"I lost my confidence. Fear overtook me and I nearly lost."*

Koriana's eyes softened, turning back to face front. *"It is not in your nature to be a warrior, yet you became one all the same. That is the mark of a leader—being whatever your clan needs you to be. Your fierceness in battle brought us strength, and even if you faltered toward the end, it propelled us to victory. And everything you did afterward, while you yourself felt fragile, showed you deserve the position of alpha."*

Alísa bowed her head and smiled. Though her own mind spoke of failure, Koriana's opinion was worth as much as her own. Perhaps more.

Two mountain peaks stretched into the sunlight straight ahead of them, perhaps six or seven hours away at their current speed. She would be home soon, and she would return victorious. She had gained enough dragons to be a true clan, defeated a dragon who would destroy any weaker than him, and secured peace for Me'ran.

But now what challenges lay ahead?

She looked to Rayna and her wounds, to Iila as she grasped onto one of the dragons who had wiped out her clan, to three eggs clutched in taloned paws, two of which needed to gain an attachment before they hatched, or they would die.

A trumpet sounded above her, and she squinted at the clouds. Sesína dove in and out, chasing after Harenn, Graydonn, and Falier in joyful play. Sunlight bounced off their jewel-like scales and painted the clouds with dancing lights.

Her heart swelled. No matter the challenges ahead, she wouldn't want to face them with anyone else.

Her clan.

EPILOGUE

The world was silent but for the snapping of twigs beneath Kallar's boots and the ringing in his ears, left over from the mind-choke and his own anger. It had been hours since they had started their trek back down the mountain, hours since their victory had been ripped out from under them.

Hours since Alísa had betrayed them.

Alísa was alive. It would have been enough to move even him to praise the Maker, if it weren't for the fact that her fate was almost certainly worse than death.

'I won't let you end up like Bria!'

But he had. He had broken that promise.

He had failed her.

Why had he listened to Karn, when he knew better? He should have taken matters into his own hands, told her what she was and helped her process it. He could have made her strong, like Allara. In the process, she might have even come to love him, or at the very least respect him. Instead, he had listened to the pleas of a frightened father. The chief was wise in the ways of leading the clan and slaying dragons, but Alísa had always been his blind spot. Now it had cost him, cost her, perhaps even cost the war, if they couldn't do what needed to be done.

A shock of anxiety ran over his arms and into his stomach, and he laughed wryly to himself. *And she thought I didn't care.*

But he did. More than anything, he had wanted to destroy the dragons in that cave and purge their hold on her. She would have cried as the pain and relief washed through her mind, and he would have held her close, stroking her hair and telling her she was safe and that he would never let them have her again.

That desire had blinded him today, made him rush into the cave like a fool instead of breaking Alísa's hold on Karn and working together with him to bring the dragons down.

Stupid mistake! Rookie mistake! Because of him, the dragons now had more time to dig their talons into Alísa's mind. What if she got to the same point as Bria, where there was no more hope of freeing her? Would Karn have the guts to hold the knife?

The answer hit Kallar in the stomach like an avalanche of stone. No, the job would fall to him. It would be a mercy-killing, one that would save her soul and save the world from what the dragons would twist her to become. That fact wouldn't make it any easier, but if it came to that, he would do it.

But it hadn't come to that yet. He saw the guilt in her eyes, the fear. She was still lurking somewhere within her own mind, just waiting for him to set her free. His Lísa.

Sounds of camp muffled around him, the women and children running to embrace their loved ones, or else find them gone. He pushed past the laughter and the tears, avoiding Trísse's eyes as she searched the crowd. He had barely been able to look at her brother as two of the other men tore him away from their father's charred bones, unable to witness the grief he himself had when his own mother was taken from this life.

Hanah met his eyes for the first time in weeks, her own questioning. He jerked his head back toward Karn. He couldn't say a word to her, knowing what he knew now. Better for Karn to tell and comfort her than for him to get mixed up in the middle. With Hanah blaming him for Alísa's departure, and Karn as witness to today's blunder, he wanted to keep as far away as possible.

But he couldn't just run to his tent and sulk. He had to figure out what to do next. No one saw where the dragons had taken Alísa, except that they flew east and up into the clouds. They probably changed direction from there—there wasn't much for dragons in the forests. Could they do nothing more than wait for some random messenger to bring word of a Dragon Singer? Barely anyone but chiefs and their seconds and apprentices even knew what a

Dragon Singer was.

Bria's story belonged to the silent stories, guarded carefully by the chiefs so that the knowledge didn't spread and cause panic. It was meant to protect people like Alísa, those who felt dragon emotions uncontrollably, from being killed simply because they showed similar symptoms to Bria.

Though she had fought for the slayers, Allara's story belonged there too—hers so recent that many chiefs didn't even know it, in order to protect her children.

But.

What if they weren't secrets anymore? What if they were known and told in such a way that protected those who had that strange connection to the enemy? What if the tale spread through messenger, bard, holder, and chief, all with the call to watch for and help those who felt it? If all of Arran knew the tale, surely word of Alísa would make it back. There was a risk that another wayfaring clan would find her first, one with perhaps less compassion for her than her own, but even then, at least Alísa would finally be at rest. Hopefully it wouldn't come to that, but it would still be a better alternative to leaving her to the dragons forever.

He certainly didn't have the finesse to do it, but he knew someone who did. Someone who cared for Alísa just as much as he did and would want her found and safe.

He waded back into the crowd, his telepathy pulled in to block out the raging emotions. It didn't take him long to find Farren amidst them, tall even with his head bowed in prayer. The songweaver lifted his head and gave a final look of sorrow to those he comforted.

"Farren. I need your help."

The old man's brow creased, and he lifted a hand to his temple. This was probably the first time anyone had spoken with him mind-to-mind.

"I will volunteer for watch-duty tonight, and I want you to meet me then." Kallar lifted his chin and gave the look that called his men to follow him into the darkest of caves. *"I have a song for you to weave."*

ACKNOWLEDGMENTS

The book-writing process is long, hard, and involved. There is no way I would be where I am today—an author with a debut novel going out into the hands of readers—without the love and support of many people.

Victor and Kelly Bruhn—parents, readers, and encouragers. You've always told me I could do anything and never once told me that the arts weren't valid. I know you expected a music album before a novel, but though you questioned, you never wavered. You two are the best!

Bethea Gliebe—alpha-reader, sounding-board, and best friend. Ten years and you still aren't sick of my geeky fangirling, sudden self-revelations, or cat voices? You be crazy. Thank you for sharing in my laughter, tears, freak-outs, and various strange author ways.

Claire Banschbach—awesome author-friend and beta-reader. You were the first writer to read *Songflight*, and your enthusiasm meant the world! Thank you for your support, insight, and friendship.

Katie Phillips—editor, coach, encourager, and friend. Thank you for taking me from a blushing girl who hid her fanfiction to a still-shy-but-willing-to-speak author who can be proud of her original work.

Gina Woolbright, Ericka Heether, Kayla Rogers, Celeste Walberg, Jessica Joiner, and Serianna Rosberg—my wonderful beta team. Thank you all for your help in making this story be great and make sense!

Everyone who has encouraged me and waited with bated breath to see what would come of all of this—thank you!

Finally, El Roi—the God Who Sees. Thank You for seeing me when no one else did. Thank You for giving me a heart for the unseen and for continuously shaping it into Your likeness. May the truth shine amidst the fiction and bring glory to You.

ABOUT THE AUTHOR

Michelle M. Bruhn is a YA fantasy author whose stories focus on outcasts, hard questions, and hope. She is passionate about seeing through others' eyes and helping others to do the same, especially through characters with diverse life experiences. She finds joy in understanding others, knows far too much about personality theories, and binge-watches TED Talks on a regular basis. She spends the rest of her free time making and listening to music, walking, reading, and snuggling with her cats.

www.MichelleMBruhn.com
News & Musings: www.MichelleMBruhn.com/follow

Discover where Alísa's connection to the dragons all started in *Mindsong*, available for free in ebook & audio formats at www.michellembruhn.com/mindsong

Alísa has finally started developing her psychic power of empathy, growing in her psychic strength as every slayer must. But when the excitement of the clan's ceremonies is drowned out by foreign sorrow, rage, and fear, Alísa and her father discover there is more to her developing empathy than they'd initially thought—a mystery that may one day condemn her in the eyes of the clan.